DREAM TOWN

Los Angeles, 1952. It is New Year's Eve, and PI Aloysius Archer is dining with his friend and rising Hollywood actress Liberty Callahan when they're approached by Eleanor Lamb, a screenwriter looking to hire him, as she suspects someone is trying to kill her.

A visit to her Malibu residence leaves Archer knocked unconscious after he stumbles over a dead body in the hallway. Meanwhile, Lamb seems to have vanished. With the police now involved in the case, a close friend and colleague of hers employs Archer to find out what's happened.

Archer's investigation takes him from the rich, glamorous and glitzy LA to the seedy, dark side of the city, and onward to the gambling mecca of Las Vegas. In a place where cops and crooks work hand in hand, Archer will cross paths with Hollywood stars, politicians, criminals — and Death . . .

DAVID BALDACCI

DREAM TOWN

Complete and Unabridged

CHARNWOOD
Leicester

First published in Great Britain in 2022 by
Macmillan
an imprint of Pan Macmillan
London

First Charnwood Edition
published 2022
by arrangement with Macmillan
an imprint of Pan Macmillan
London

A catalogue record for this book is available
from the British Library.

ISBN 978–1–4448–4931–8

Published by
Ulverscroft Limited
Anstey, Leicestershire

Printed and bound in Great Britain by
TJ Books Ltd., Padstow, Cornwall

This book is printed on acid-free paper

*To Tiffany and Bruno Silva
and the Landing Love Project,
for helping so many in need*

1

It was New Year's Eve, 1952.

Aloysius Archer was thirty years old, once a decorated soldier, and next a humbled inmate. He was currently a private detective with several years of intense experience trolling the darker side of life.

He was riding in a 1939 bloodred Delahaye convertible with the red top in the down position because that was how he liked it. He had bought the car a little over three years before with lucky gambling winnings in Reno. It had also very nearly cost Archer his life. He still loved the car. Any man with a pulse would. And so would any woman who liked a man with a nice car.

He was currently heaving over the roller-coaster humps of Los Angeles. The city was decked out in its finest livery for the coming of the new year. That meant the bums of Skid Row had been goose-stepped off the streets by junior coppers who did what they were told, the hookers had been ordered not to solicit on the main thoroughfares, and most everyone had put the lids on their trash cans and brushed their teeth.

The town had brought in about four million strings of lights, an equal number of balloons, and enough confetti to choke the Pacific. And every actor and actress with a studio contract, and even some without, would be showing their toothy mugs in all the right, and wrong, places. While the town definitely had its seamy side, the City of Angels had all the tools and incentive to do showy and shallow better than

1

any other place on earth.

It could be a wonderful place to live, if you had money, were famous, or both, which Archer didn't and wasn't. Over the years, he'd worked a slew of tough cases, and had come to know the town and its denizens maybe better than he would have liked.

It was a town that took every single dream you had and then merrily ran it right through the world's biggest meat grinder. And when the famous were famous no more, the meat grinder treatment was even worse, because those people had tasted what life could be like if enough ink was spilled on you and sufficient butts sat in seats to watch you emote. When that ride was over, it was like being dropped from the top of the Empire State Building to land in a squatter's shack in Alabama.

Los Angeles had two million souls sprawled over nearly five hundred square miles. Some people were crammed into slums, tract housing, and shadily built tenement death traps, like staples in a stapler, while the wealthy and famous had room to both flex and hide. All this in a city founded on the remnants of a village settled by the Tongva, an indigenous Indian tribe, who called it Yaanga, which translated to 'poison oak place.'

Well, they got that right, thought Archer. But for a private eye, LA could be a fascinating study of human beings, and all their many foibles.

He turned left and then right as he moved from dirty LA to rich LA and then to dirty-and-rich LA. He passed a prowler car and saw two of the LAPD's 'finest' sitting inside and sipping on coffee in vending machine cups. They stared at Archer as he passed, probably wondering whether he'd stolen the car or was delivering it to some Hollywood mogul or a desert sheik who'd bought a piece of the city's myth, along with a fancy ride.

Archer eyed the prowler in his mirror, hoping it would stay right where it was. To his mind, the LAPD was one of the largest criminal enterprises in the world. And they did it with a smile, and a gun, where appropriate. Or with beatings that didn't show.

Archer had had a police baton or two land on his head, and he'd also spent time in the tank on bogus charges merely for asking questions deemed impertinent, meaning ones directed at finding the truth, because the truth often found LAPD badges mixed in with the other crooks.

These coppers were probably taking a coffee break before heading to a string of ghetto street corners with their dozen-block-deep slums in the rear, to make their quota of busted heads for the week like the good little foot soldiers they were. They were just one crew in a pitched battle for the soul of the city. And there was no doubt in Archer's mind which faction was winning. If LA were a human body, the criminal elements were the capillaries: small, everywhere, not often seen, but absolutely vital to overall life.

His destination was Universal Studios. He only knew one person there, but it was an important person, at least to him. Liberty Callahan had left Bay Town more than two years ago. That was where Archer lived and worked with Willie Dash's 'very private' detective agency. Callahan had gone to Hollywood to make her dream come true in the land of make-believe. As far as he knew, she was still working on making the town believe in her.

He'd met Callahan in Reno, where she was a dancer

and hoofer at a dinner club. They'd traveled to Bay Town together and nearly gotten killed several times along the way. There was nothing like confronting death to cement a friendship.

There was a great deal of private detecting to do in LA. People here seemed to keep killing and robbing and cheating and blackmailing one another to an astounding degree. But when you had a lot of money in one place, some folks were always tempted to take it from both their lawful and unlawful owners.

He passed buildings that were intricately cut into the city's steep grade and looked lopsided and unrooted as a result. The roots here were always shallow, never deep. Deep required commitment, and there was none to be had here, at least that Archer could see.

Tall, double-stemmed streetlights in the shape of goalposts, which made them look like they were being held up at gunpoint, illuminated the LA night. The NBC sign blinked back at him from Sunset and Vine, while a few blocks south stood the swaggering arch of Paramount Studios. A block over the other way on Holly.wood Boulevard, tourists from all over were lined up in front of Grauman's Chinese Theater to stare at handprints set forever in cold, unforgiving concrete.

He kept steering his ride east and glanced at the Hollywood sign ablaze in the hills. A disconsolate actress had climbed up on the sign's letter *H* back in 1932, when it still spelled out HOLLYWOODLAND. When she got to the top, she jumped to her death. Archer imagined the meat grinder had gotten to her. She'd probably chosen *H* because that was the first letter in *hell*.

He pulled up to the main gate at the studio and

presented his driver's license to the guard there, a beefy type who looked hot and bothered, although the temps were in the chilly fifties at this time of night. The man's hair was thin and grizzled, his face was fat and wide, and his body matched the face and not the hair. He looked like he'd end up with a coronary if he actually had to hoof it after a gate runner. His holstered .45 slapped against his meaty thigh as he walked around the car, eyeing it like a pretty girl in a swimsuit contest.

'Steering wheel's on the wrong side, bub,' was his final judgment.

Delahaye was a French company, but this particular Delahaye, a Model 165 cabriolet, had been built for an Englishman, and the wheel had, of necessity, been shifted to the right.

'Not from where I'm sitting,' Archer replied.

Beefy looked at his clipboard. 'Who you visiting again?'

'Liberty Callahan. She's a friend.'

The man grinned. 'Lucky man.'

'I take it you know her?'

'Gal's got what you call *personality*.'

'Among other things.'

'She's on Stage Three, just follow the signs. You can park right down there,' he added, pointing the way after handing Archer back his license. 'She's shooting a Roman gladiator picture.' He gave Archer a look that guys give each other when they're thinking about what women could do for them that nothing else can. 'She wears one of them *to-gas*.'

'I'm sure she wears it better than anyone else.'

The man gazed at Archer, his brown button eyes greedy and hopeful in their lust. 'When the sun

5

catches it just right, you can see right through the damn thing.'

'As I'm sure she can you,' Archer said, driving off.

2

Archer parked the car and followed the signs to Stage 3. Along the way he passed the casting office, where hopefuls would spend their lives sitting in intentionally uncomfortable chairs waiting for something that would never happen. The red light was on outside the soundstage, so he leaned against the weathered parchment-colored stucco walls and waited. He spent the time looking down at his brown wingtips and wondering whether he should have chosen the midnight-blue serge suit over this brown pinstriped woolen one. He commenced to twirl his fedora between his fingers, an indication of nerves. He hadn't seen Callahan in months. Every time he came to visit the lady, he expected her to have changed somehow. She clearly had the Hollywood bug, which was a virus no medicine could cure. But she had always been the same woman, at least to him. Even so, there was always tomorrow.

Or tonight.

A buzzer rang and the light went off, and soon the foot-thick door popped open, and the Roman legionnaires started trooping out.

Callahan was among the stragglers, and Archer's face lit up when he saw her. Sometimes it seemed that the only redeeming quality in this whole city came down to this woman, at least for him.

She was tall, in her bare feet only four inches under Archer's six-one. Curves in all the right places, naturally blond hair that danced liberally over her bare

7

shoulders and made his blood race with each bounce. Her face had all the finishing touches that could make men leer for years at a time. Her smile was immediate when she saw Archer, her hug tight and sincere. The kiss she planted on his lips alone made the trip worth it.

They were not a couple. They had slept together exactly once; this was back in Bay Town more than three years ago. But then, mostly by silent agreement and a few mumbled words over too much alcohol that had, surprisingly, given them sufficient clarity, they had decided that their friendship was worth more than occasional sack time with no clear runway ahead. She was the most beautiful woman of his acquaintance, and she often intimidated the hell out of him, which only heightened the attraction. Shrinking wallflowers had never rocked Archer's boat or heart.

He had begun to feel things for her that every man hoped to feel about a woman one day. But maybe those feelings had been there for a long time, only their weight had compressed him into silence. He was thinking of maybe one day soon breaking that silence.

'You made it,' she said, as though he had braved mighty seas to reach her instead of driving eighty miles due south on smooth roads.

'I can't say no to a pretty girl. It's a weakness.'

He offered her a Lucky Strike and lit her and himself up, and they walked down the concrete alley toward the dressing rooms. Cowboys and Indians, and two Martians reading the next day's call sheets, passed by them.

'How's Willie?' she asked.

'He's Willie. And Connie is Connie. And Bay Town hasn't fallen into the Pacific yet, though it may be only a matter of time.'

Connie Morrison was Willie Dash's ex-wife and current secretary. They needed each other far more now than when they were married. Willie was a first-rate investigator and had taught Archer more in three years than a man had any right to expect.

'How's the movie career coming?' he asked because she would want him to.

'The production I'm on now is strictly B-movie stuff. I mean, the budget is so low we only have twelve legionnaires; they have to shoot them at really tight angles, and then over and over again to make them look like twelve hundred. And we don't even have any real lions on set. They just use stock footage of them pawing the air and roaring to edit in, and then shoot the gladiators reacting. The MGM lion is scarier. I mean, it's pathetic.'

'Gotten any good parts lately?' he asked, again because he felt he had to.

'Well, you know that last year I *did* have a decent role in *High Noon* with Coop. But you don't know I did a screen test for *The Quiet Man* last year but didn't make the cut. I would've loved to meet Duke Wayne, but they filmed it in Ireland. And if you're gone from this town too long they forget about you.'

'Anything cooking right now, other than gladiators?'

'Hitchcock is going to be filming *Dial M for Murder* in the summer. It's based on a play. My agent is arranging an audition. But if that doesn't work out, word is that after Hitchcock finishes *Dial M* he might direct another picture called *Rear Window*. It's supposed to start shooting in November.' She looked at him inquisitively. 'You heard of it?'

9

Archer puffed on his Lucky and shook his head. 'I don't read the trades. I have a hard enough time reading my mail and my own mind.'

'It's sort of a voyeuristic mystery story. Anyway, there's a nifty female lead character, described as tall, blond, and assertive — you know, professional with her own career, but still looking for the right man to give her a ring and babies.'

'Sounds like the part was written for you, except for the ring and the babies.'

He gave her a look that perhaps hoped to compel a deeper answer to his statement than was warranted under the circumstances, only the lady didn't bite.

She did a little twirl in her toga and almost collided with a Viking coming the other way. Archer pulled her safely out of the range of both his ax and lecherous glare.

'Anyway, when the time is right my agent will try and get me an audition for that one, too, and then maybe a screen test if the role they want me for is big enough. And if I land that part and one in *Dial M*, it could really be a springboard. I mean, being in not one but two Hitchcock films in the same year!' The next moment her hopeful look faded.

'What's the matter?' he asked, noticing this.

She glanced at him, and in that look he saw something in the woman Archer had thought he'd never see: resignation.

'Nothing,' she said. 'It's just . . . hard sometimes. You work your guts out and get rejected a hundred times to land one lousy part. It . . . gets to you after a while. But I guess there's always tomorrow.'

He nipped a piece of tobacco off his tongue as he felt the Hollywood bug inserting itself between them like a border wall. 'Fingers crossed,' he said encouragingly. He didn't think Hollywood was a good place for her, but he also knew how much she wanted to be a star here.

'But I've been working steadily. I'm not a star under contract, so I got three pictures going at two different studios, including this gladiator pic for Universal. I'm at Warner Brothers next in a spy flick involving *atomic* secrets. Then I go on location in Arizona in a romantic comedy, again for Warners. And my name is getting around and the money is really good, and I'm not even a midlevel actress yet. They can pull in three grand a week. I only make half that.' She paused and glanced at him, excitement once more dancing in her eyes. 'And Archer, I just bought a nice two-bedroom bungalow off Melrose near the country club, *and* I have my own car.'

Archer perked up at this. 'What kind of car?'

'A *Volkswagen*. It's green with a split-screen rear window. You ever seen one?'

'Not since I was fighting my way through to Berlin.'

Her features turned somber and he didn't think it was his comment about battling Nazis.

'But I turned thirty last month and the clock is ticking. I'm not Kate Hepburn. My face won't look good playing spinster aunts or being a mom with grown kids. I'll just look old. And I don't want to end up a small-lot dust-off with a baby spotlight on me for my one line in a lousy picture that'll probably never make it out of the editing room. Or spend my remaining pennies on studio coaches and no-class agents to get me back in the door, while people talk crap about me right in front of my face.' She looked at him. 'If you see that happening, shoot me, Archer.'

He took all this in and said, 'Well, if it makes you feel better, I pull in a fraction of what you make when crime is really good, but I do get most Sundays and Christmas off.'

'I know I should appreciate what I have, but I worked my rear end off for it. And the story of the casting couch is no myth, let me tell you.'

He looked at her sharply. 'You didn't —'

'What I did, Archer, is between me, myself, and I.' She looked wistful, which she almost never did. 'But I hear TV is really taking off,' she said. 'Maybe I should think about trying that.'

'I saw an episode of *Dragnet* the other night at Willie's place. It wasn't bad.'

'I heard they work with the police department to make it authentic.' She glanced sharply at him. 'Hey, Archer, you're a *real* gumshoe. You could be Joe Friday's new sidekick. You'd make a lot more money. And we'd both be actors.'

The way she said it was a bit sad, thought Archer. It was as though she just wanted a friend to be out there fighting for a career right alongside her.

'But I wouldn't have nearly as much fun. So, what's the plan for tonight?'

'Dinner at Chasen's, then drinks at the Cocoanut Grove, then we head upstairs to the penthouse suite and ring in 1953 with the bubbly and some VIPs.'

'How'd you score the penthouse at the Ambassador Hotel?'

'The director on this garbage movie, Danny Mars, that's how, Archer. It's his wife, Gloria's, pad. His *third* wife's. Gloria has her own money, inherited from back east. And, in case you're wondering, no, I am *not* going to be wife number four.'

12

'Glad to hear it because four is definitely not your lucky number.'

The thought of her marrying another man had made Archer's heart skip a beat.

They walked along arm in arm. They passed what Archer thought looked like Rin Tin Tin taking a piss on a poor bum trapped in a cheap suit of studio armor.

He and Callahan kept right on marching to 1953.

3

Archer drove them over to West Hollywood and valeted the Delahaye. The slender uniformed man who took the key and gave him a ticket in return scratched his head when he saw the positioning of the steering wheel.

'I can park it myself,' Archer said off this look. 'Only questions are, how much do *I* charge, and are you a good tipper?'

'Ain't a problem, sir. Mr. Cary Grant's got him a right-hand-drive Rolls. Jimmy over there knows how to handle the thing.'

'Good for 'Over There Jimmy.' Now, except for the bullet hole on the windscreen post, there's not a scratch on her now, and you'll make sure there won't be another scratch when I get her back, right?'

'Bullet hole?' the man said, his jaw going slack.

'Just a misunderstanding. But not another scratch. Capiche?'

'You're the boss.'

Archer passed him a buck to seal the deal.

They walked in under the long awning to find the place in full swing. A lot of the big stars had their own booths here, and many of them had turned out in the tuxedoed-and-gowned flesh to welcome in 1953 with steak and asparagus dripping with hollandaise sauce, coconut cream pie, and the best cocktails on Beverly Boulevard.

When they got inside he watched as Callahan looked around at all the legendary stars partying there. Her

14

manner at first became subdued, as though she was as overwhelmed by this as any out-of-towner would have been. But then her expression changed to one of sheer excitement to be in their company.

'Don't look now, but omigosh there's Frank Sinatra, and Groucho Marx,' whispered Callahan.

Archer eyed those two gents and their substantial entourages along with Bob Hope, Milton Berle, and James Cagney, all in various states of sobriety. In a back booth surrounded by male admirers was the woman who was just beginning to take the town by storm. Archer thought if there was a lady to give Callahan a run for her money in the come-hither department it was Marilyn Monroe. An old-looking Clark Gable outfitted in a tailored sharkskin suit and loosened burgundy tie was downing shots at the bar like a man who had been thirsty his whole life. Word was he'd never recovered from his wife Carole Lombard's going down in that plane a decade before.

They were escorted to a table by a guy in a striped linen suit that was far nicer than Archer's, with a fresh gardenia in his buttonhole, expensive shoes on his wide feet, and a quarter-size rock on his finger. Archer had always heard the tips at Chasen's were the best in town. He was very happy that Callahan had insisted on paying.

They sat and had their menus delivered by a gal in a tight blue skirt, with a yellow rose pinned to her white blouse. They ordered drinks from her, a whiskey highball for Archer and a sidecar for Callahan.

While they waited for their cocktails, Callahan looked around. 'I still can't believe I'm part of this world, Archer.'

'Don't you come here for dinner all the time?' he

15

said, smiling.

'I'm just a working girl. In fact, I've only been to Chasen's with you, mister!'

A few moments after their drinks came and they tapped glasses, a voice called out, 'LC? Is that you? Is that *really* you?'

Archer looked up to see a slip of a woman around forty, all sharp angles and energetic intensity and with straight black hair, approach their table. Through tortoise-shell specs, her green eyes looked like round frog's eggs. Her skin seemed like it had never finished forming, leaving bare the bony emotional edges underneath. Archer figured if she was an actress, that would be one nifty element for the camera to capture.

'Ellie?' said Callahan, looking as surprised as the other woman. 'Is that *you*?'

She fingered her dark, slack hair. 'Got tired of being a bottle blonde who slept on curler rolls. Too many blondes in this town. I don't mean you, LC.'

'Sure, I know. It's a swell look on you. Pull up a seat and have a drink. This is my friend, Archer. Archer, Ellie, well, *Eleanor* Lamb.'

They shook hands. As she gave the waitress her drink order he ran his eye over her again. She was barely five-two, and the scales would never get to three figures with her. Everything about her, from the cheekbones to the chin to the elbows to the knees, was knifelike. It appeared you could cut yourself in innumerable ways on this lady.

Her dress was a fluffy crimson number with a line of ruffles at odd places; the sleeves ended before the elbows and the hemline before the bony knees. The stockings were black silk that made her skinny legs look more robust. It somehow all sort of worked.

16

For her part, Callahan was housed in a simple, form-fitting red dress that plugged every curve she had like a four-inch headline in the *LA Times*. Around her shoulders was a fringy black wrap, and down below long, stockinged legs that constantly drew men's attention.

'LC?' Archer said.

'Some people refer to me by my initials,' explained Callahan. 'Ellie is a screenwriter. The first movie I worked on here was one of her scripts. It was a United Artists film. Where are you now?'

'Same independent production company as before. We were hired to do the UA screenplay.' She took a moment to light up a Chesterfield from a silver cigarette case she slid from her handbag. Archer noticed her hand shook a bit as she took a drag on the Chesterfield, propelling out the smoke from both barrels of her nose. She shot him a glance before looking away. 'I'm working on a script for Columbia as a comeback vehicle for Bette Davis.' She tapped her smoke into the glass ashtray at their table.

Archer gave her a puzzled look. 'Wait, Bette Davis needs a *comeback* film?'

Callahan said, 'You stay in this town long enough, *everybody* needs a comeback film.'

'And *All About Eve* was two years ago,' interjected Lamb. 'Which is twenty years in Hollywood time, at least for women.'

Archer glanced at Callahan, who appeared to take this comment hard. The rest of her sidecar disappeared down her throat.

'I'm actually working on the project with Danny Mars.'

Callahan looked startled. 'The director of the

17

B-movie I'm on is doing Bette Davis's comeback film?'

'Well, he's attached, for *now*. Davis will have final approval on the director, of course.'

'Who are you here with, Ellie?'

'Some guy who failed to show up. I don't think you have that problem.'

The waitress presented Lamb with her glass of sherry and bitters with a curlicue orange peel apparently for window dressing. Archer didn't know anyone who really drank sherry unless they had to, but he thought he might just be hanging out with the wrong crowd.

'Archer is an old friend from Bay Town, just up the coast. He put his detective work aside for one night to ring in the new year with me.'

Lamb swiveled around and laid a look on Archer that he had seen plenty of times before, just not in that particular shade of jarring green wrapped with framed portholes.

'You're a detective? A real one?' This almost came out as one word.

'A *private* one.'

'*Private* is what I need.'

Callahan said, 'Ellie, why in the world do you need a private eye?'

The frog eyes turned on her with steadfast urgency. 'Because I think someone might be trying to kill me.'

4

Over the years Archer had learned that when someone said they thought another human being was trying to off them, they were either: hating their life and vying for attention; paranoid and beyond the help of someone like a private detective; or someone, indeed, was trying to kill them. With Eleanor Lamb he didn't know yet if it was one of the three or whether he would learn a new reason.

'What makes you say that?' Archer asked as he nibbled on a handful of peanuts that Chasen's put on every table. 'Have you received any direct threats? And if so, from whom? And why haven't you gone to the cops with them?'

'Geez, Archer, why don't you give the lady the third degree or something?' exclaimed Callahan.

'It's okay,' said Lamb. 'Those are all pertinent questions. To answer them, no, I have received no direct threats. So I don't know who might be behind it. And I don't want to go to the cops, because it might cost me my job.'

'Why would your boss get mad about that?' asked Archer.

'If someone is trying to kill me, it might put the people I work with in danger.'

'And who do you work for?'

'Green and Ransome Productions.'

'Is there a Green and a Ransome?'

'Bart Green is a prominent producer who's worked with everybody in town. The firm provides an array

19

of services to the studios. Talent, writers, whatever is needed.'

'But I thought the studios did all that in-house.'

'Mr. Green was a big-time producer with Warners and then at MGM, so he has major connections. He's got film projects going with pretty much every studio in town.'

'How did Danny Mars get in the loop to direct Davis?' interjected Callahan.

'He and Mr. Green are longtime friends. The old boys' network, you know.'

'Yeah? Well, I'm waiting for the old *girls'* network to kick in,' quipped Callahan.

'And Mr. Ransome?' asked Archer.

'*Miss* Cecily Ransome is an up-and-coming writer and director.'

'A *woman* director?' said Archer, glancing at Callahan.

'Girls *do* direct films, Archer,' said Callahan in a brusque tone.

Archer tacked back to Lamb. 'Why exactly do you think someone is after you?'

Lamb took a nervous sip of her sherry and Archer watched an errant drop of it spoil Chasen's fine table linen. 'The first was a weird phone call I got about a week ago, at home. It was someone breathing heavy — a man, I think. It said that I was in danger.'

Archer hiked his eyebrows and lowered his expectations. 'You didn't recognize the voice?' She shook her head. 'What else has happened that was weird?' he continued.

'I've gotten two hang-ups in the middle of the night. The phone rings and scares the hell out of me, but when I answer it, all I hear is breathing and then . . . click.'

Archer sat back, his interest waning. 'Come on, that just sounds like some drunk or doped-up kids playing around. Next, they'll be tee-peeing your house.'

'Really? Well, I woke up one morning to find my front door wide open.'

'Any signs that anyone had been in your house?' asked Archer. 'Was anything taken, or moved around, or was anything left behind?'

She shuddered. 'There was a bloody knife in the kitchen sink.' She paused. 'Does that sound like drunk or doped-up *boys*?'

Archer leaned forward, engaged once more. 'Was it one of your knives?'

She nodded. 'A paring knife.'

'Where did the blood come from?'

'I have no idea. How could I?' She blinked her green eyes at Archer. 'Wait a minute, are you implying that I put the knife there, covered in, what, my own blood! How dare you?'

Her voice had risen as she spoke and people at several tables looked over.

Archer leaned across the table and said in a muted voice, 'I'm not implying anything, Miss Lamb. I just wanted to know if you had any ideas. And we don't have to share your private business with the rest of the town, do we?'

She glanced around and lowered her gaze, and when she next spoke, her voice was barely a whisper. 'Well, I don't have any ideas. And there was a strange car on my street the past few nights. I think there was a man sitting in it.'

'You recognize him or the car?'

She shook her head. 'It was a four-door Ford, dark blue I think. It's hard to tell at night.'

'Okay, look, I think you should go to the cops. It might be nothing, some stupid guy just messing around with you. But it could also be more than that, especially with the knife and the blood. And the police know how to deal with that sort of thing. They can send a radio patrol car around. But tell me, have you broken up with anyone lately? Got any ex-boyfriends with a beef against you? How about the guy who was supposed to show up tonight?'

She shook her head dismissively. 'We haven't known each other long enough for him to get all creepy.'

Callahan added, 'Most guys take a little while to work up to pure nasty. It's Mother Nature's built-in escape hatch for women. Darn nice of her.'

Archer had to smile at that one. 'Anyone else with a problem?' he asked Lamb.

She shook her head but wouldn't meet his gaze.

Archer studied her closely and came away certain that she was holding something back. 'So are you going to go to the cops?'

'Can't *you* help me?' she said in a pleading tone.

'I'm fifty a day plus expenses.'

'That's not cheap.'

'Well, I don't get all of it. I work for another guy. And it's not like I work and get paid that much every day. I probably make less in a year than you spend on clothes. And most jobs don't come with the possibility of getting shot or your neck broken.'

'Okay, I guess I can see that.'

'And I don't live in LA. I usually rent a room at the Y to keep costs down. And there'll be a contract for you to sign. I have some in my car.'

'Heck, Archer, you can stay with me for free,' said Callahan. 'I have a spare bedroom now.' She gave him a friendly look that did not raise any possibilities other than sleep.

'I do like to get a $200 retainer up front. If I don't work through it all, you'll get the balance back.'

'I don't have my checkbook with me. We'd have to go to my house.'

'Where do you live?'

'In a canyon in Malibu. Las Flores.'

Archer said, 'That's where the Sea Lion Restaurant is. Used to be the Las Flores Inn.'

She eyed him with what Archer regarded as unease. 'You know Malibu?'

'Bad things happen in Malibu, too, you know.'

She looked at them nervously. 'But Las Flores is a hike from here and you two are out on the town tonight. How about you come by my office tomorrow?'

'Where's your office?'

'Off Wilshire near San Vicente.'

'Okay. Just write your home and office address down. I can get the check and have you sign the contract. And then we can head out to your house. Whoever is doing this obviously knows where you live.'

Lamb took out a piece of paper and pen from her clutch purse and wrote down the address of her office and also that of her house and passed it to Archer.

He glanced at it. 'How do you like living in Malibu?'

'It was fine until all of this started up.'

'You're near the Malibu Movie Colony. See a lot of stars out?'

'None that I can't see *in* town,' she answered with pursed lips that puzzled Archer. He could understand

23

her being gassed out on the celebrities of the day, but in his limited experience the movie business was built on relationships.

'Okay, what about your neighbors?'

'There's one on either side of me. The Bonhams are currently in France. The other neighbor is Sylvia Danforth. She's eighty, widowed, and lives with her cats.'

'So it's doubtful the threats are coming from them?'

'Yes, very doubtful.'

'But what about the Bonhams? Anyone staying at their place while they're away?'

Lamb glanced guiltily at Callahan. 'Look, it's New Year's Eve, and you're here to have a nice dinner. Come to the office around ten.'

'Not taking the day off then?' said Archer.

'For me, tomorrow is just another day. It'll be quiet. I can get some actual work done.' She gave Callahan a peck on the cheek and disappeared into the crowd.

Callahan watched her go and then glanced at Archer. 'So?'

'So what?'

'What do you think?'

He shrugged and lit up a cigarette. 'I don't think anything. Not yet. What do you know about her?'

'She's from back east. Went to college there. Boston. She's smart, well-read.'

'I thought I caught a bit of Yankee Doodle Dandy underneath the LA grease coating.'

'It does bother me that I didn't know about her working with Mars on the Davis film.'

'Why *would* you know? And why would that bother you?'

'If you don't know what's going on in this town,

24

you can't take advantage of opportunities. I'd love to work with Davis. She'd eat me alive in every scene, but I could still make a splash, and the movie will be big news because she's in it. And I could learn a lot.'

'How about Lamb personally? She seems a little high-strung to me. Is she prone to hysterics? She's a writer, so her imagination must be good. Could she be making all this up?'

'No. She does her job and minds her own business.'

'Well, from what the lady said, she stopped curling and dyeing her hair blond and went back to her natural brunette with hair straighter than my spine. I wonder why.'

'She told you why. And she's right, this town has too many damn blondes. The next time you see me, I might have pulled a Maureen O'Hara and all you'll see is *red*.'

'Do you know Green or Ransome?'

'I've certainly heard of Bart Green. He's done a lot, knows everybody, like Ellie said. I don't know Cecily Ransome, though I'd like to.'

'Why?'

'She's the change this town needs, Archer. Ransome is making pictures that are gritty, honest, and bone deep. I'd love to work with her.'

'If I meet her I'll put in a good word. You ever been to Lamb's house?'

'She had a one-bedroom in West Hollywood when I first met her.'

'So the move to Malibu was fairly recent, then?'

'I guess within the last two years or so. Is that important?'

'Malibu isn't cheap, and most working writers like to be nearer the action. She's not an heiress or anything, is she?'

'Not that she mentioned. And she never acted like she was in the money.'

Archer finished his smoke and killed it off in the ashtray. 'Let's eat.'

But his mind was now clearly elsewhere.

5

Archer next drove them to Wilshire Boulevard and through the gates of the Ambassador Hotel, a twelve-hundred-room extravaganza set on over twenty acres with pools, tennis courts, columns of private bunga-lows, and enough pretentiousness to satisfy the most inflated of egos.

A spiffy valet in a mauve-colored uniform took the car key with a grin.

'That's a Delahaye 165 cabriolet,' he said.

'Yes it is,' said a surprised Archer. 'How do you know that?'

'My granddad's French,' he said. 'He worked at the company before World War I.'

'Great, but this has the steering wheel on the other side of the English Channel.'

They entered the main dining room. It had once been the grand ballroom for the hotel; a thousand diners were eating and drinking, all while sitting next to fake, full-sized palm trees with mechanical mon-keys swinging overhead.

Archer knew the Academy Awards had been held here numerous times, and he had a feeling that Callahan would love nothing more than to walk down the red carpet with that little statuette. Now he looked at Callahan, and she eyed him back.

'I won't be long,' she said in an apologetic tone.

'Sure you won't,' he said dully.

They had talked about this on the way over.

Callahan was not really here for a drink. She was

27

here to work.

While Callahan went to mingle and see who she needed to see, Archer reversed course and went directly to the hotel bar, which looked like the world's biggest palm tree had sprouted right behind the smiling countermen. Archer didn't want a frond in his face, just a drink in his hand. And a minute later, in return for two bucks, he was saddled with a whiskey and water, where the whiskey appeared as a nominal oil slick on the water's surface.

One fresh-faced girl, presumably from out of state and there with her equally goggle-eyed parents, came up to him and, giggling excitedly, asked if he was famous and could she have her picture taken with him.

'I'm famous, but only in my own mind,' he had dutifully replied.

And she still had her picture taken with him and would go back to wherever to tell everyone about her once-in-a-lifetime encounter with someone who was so famous he denied being so.

He downed his weakened whiskey and thought, *Only in this town.*

He got up once and peered into the Grove and watched as self-important tuxedoed men sat around in their wicker chairs ignoring their meals and their powdered and primped wives and girlfriends while looking for fresh, if wildly impossible, female prospects. For their part, the wives and girlfriends smiled regally and tried to rise above it all, while really wanting to strangle their gents.

Despite the flow from an air-conditioning system, sweaty waiters carried trays piled with steaks rare, oceans of mushrooms, and mountains of fried onion rings. A live orchestra played away, while lithe and limber dancing girls helped to boogie-woogie and tango in the new year. Ingots of golden light illuminated the show to such a bright degree that Archer eyed several patrons who had donned sunglasses.

When Callahan circled back to him later, he said, none too happily, 'See who you needed to see, or do I have to sit here hydrating with more water than whiskey, while you make another pass through the chow line?'

She stroked his cheek in apology. 'I know, Archer, it gets me down, too.'

He got her a drink because she looked like she needed it. 'Is it really worth it?'

'I don't know. Yet. And look at you.'

'Look at me what?'

'You're right here in the thick of it in wild and woolly LA. Must be a reason.'

'Maybe I just like to be close to you,' he said, eyeing her over his tumbler of whiskey.

'Right. When you work down here the only ones you're close to are your clients and whoever ends up dead. And you're thinking about Ellie Lamb. I know that look.'

'I admit she interests me.'

'Why?'

'She's holding back. Clients who lie to you are always interesting.'

'What makes you think she's lying?'

'Just call it a professional hunch. She may not know who's doing these things to her, but I think she has an idea *why* they are.'

'If she does, why won't she tell you?'

'And therein lies the interesting part.'

29

6

They entered the hotel's lobby and took the automatic elevator up to the top floor. Callahan presented her engraved invitation to the petite young woman with a Dutch boy haircut who was checking the guests in. She obviously knew Callahan and was a little star-struck.

'Oh, Miss Callahan,' she squeaked. 'Everyone here wants to meet you.'

Callahan said, 'Donna, you're cute. Go get a drink and enjoy yourself.'

'But I have to make sure nobody crashes the party,' she squeaked again.

'Trust me, honey, they *want* people to crash it. That's how you know you're really having a party worth going to in this town.'

While Callahan went to powder her nose, Archer walked around. There was an odd mixture of black oak paneling in one room, cloister-vaulted ceilings in another space, and bleached-wood floors in the library. And then there was a waxed ceramic tile floor arrayed in a complex geometric pattern in the living room. Anyone drunk looking down at that was going to toss their cookies and leave their *own* pattern, Archer concluded.

Positioned everywhere were mammoth bright blue chesterfields paired with painfully straight-back Spanish-style wooden chairs. Bowls of cigarettes and mints and nuts were on every low table. On every high table was booze. Archer spotted what he thought was an original Rembrandt on the wall. It was something to consider that the painting was worth far more than he would make in his entire life.

There was a circular mirror on the ceiling in the large dining room, which was filled with massive Baroque pieces that would have looked dated in the twenties. He did wonder if the ceiling-mirror theme was repeated in the master bedroom.

A platoon of waiters with slicked-back hair and white dinner jackets was handing out trays of champagne and canapes. The more serious male drinkers were lined up at the portable bars looking like a stiff one or four was exactly what was needed to propel them to 1953.

A lavish blond wood radio, phonograph, and television console with curved lines was set against one wall, partnered with a tall glass-doored record cabinet. When Archer took a look at the record collection he found far more jazz and R&B than crooners and classical music. He picked out one record and looked at the label.

'That's Ray Charles, he's blind,' said a voice behind him.

He turned to see an auburn-haired woman with a Veronica Lake peekaboo standing there with a drink in one hand and a long-barreled cigarette in the other. She was around forty and flavored with an exotic perfume; the woman's high-slitted Saks dress fit her figure like a hot wax mold. High-heeled gilt slippers graced her small feet. The pale, freckled skin of her upper thigh arrayed against the emerald-green dress looked marvelous to Archer. Her small, red-lipsticked mouth looked like trouble, though, and her amber eyes matched the mouth. She looked expensive and

31

no doubt was. These were the times when Archer was thrilled he was poor.

'Is that right?'

She bit down on her porcelain cigarette holder. 'I think he's going to be really big.'

'Good for him. I can't carry a tune with a shovel.'

She put out a hand. 'I'm Gloria Mars.'

He shook it. 'Archer.'

Mars was the Roman god of war, and she struck him as gladiator-like. Her features were hard-edged, her manner was swaggering and confident, and her lean frame portended strength. In his mind he dubbed her *Warrior*.

'I saw you come in with Liberty Callahan. She's in my husband's next picture. It's a piece of crap, but I'm sure Liberty's already told you that. Danny just likes swords and shields, fight scenes, and busty women in see-through garments. She's wasting her talents with this one.'

'She'd be glad to hear that.'

'Oh, I already told her. You look like you need a drink. What's your poison?'

'Can you do a White Russian, or will that get me up before Joe McCarthy's committee?'

'You hang around long enough, Archer, you'll find I can do *anything*. And screw McCarthy. You mark my words on him, too, that son of a bitch's on the way out.'

She left him and went in search of a mixer man to orchestrate his drink. When she came back with it in an old-fashioned tumbler, they clinked glasses and he took a sip.

'You like?' she asked, her eyes glistening like they had been splashed with tonic.

32

'Yes I do. I hear you come from back east. You like LA?'

'Some days. Most days I want to shoot everyone in it, and I don't mean with a camera.'

I get that, Warrior, thought Archer. 'Nice place you have here.'

'Danny tells everybody that it's his. It's not. We have a prenuptial agreement. This isn't my first rodeo. When we go our separate ways he can find someplace else to live.'

'Not betting on going the distance with him?'

'I play the odds, just like I do with the ponies.'

'So why'd you marry him, if you don't mind my asking?'

'I *do* mind, but I'll tell you anyway. He used to be really great in bed.' The eyes ran down him like an X-ray machine. 'It's not like Danny is going to thrill me with his culture. He grew up on a farm in Oregon. Came here in the twenties to get away from cow shit.'

He sipped his drink and said, 'Ran into Eleanor Lamb earlier tonight. Understand she's working on a script for your husband to direct Bette Davis?'

She eyed him coolly. 'Bart Green is just throwing him a bone. Only Danny doesn't know it or doesn't want to admit to knowing it. No way in hell Bette Davis is letting Danny direct her. It would be like Lassie directing Brando, and that's an insult, actually, to the *dog*.'

'So, Green and your husband go way back, I understand?'

'Farther back than me and Danny, but we've only been married three years. That's the number wife I am by the way, three.'

'You know Lamb well?'

33

She looked over Archer's shoulder and didn't answer right away. 'We've spent some time together. We're certainly not best friends or anything. Why?'

'She might be in need of my services.'

The X-ray look came out again. She moved closer and the bare skin of her thigh smacked the flesh of Archer's free hand. He didn't move it, because he wanted information. Besides, her smooth skin felt nice.

'And what services *do* you perform for women, Archer?'

'I'm a private investigator. Oh, and I take on male clients, too.'

She moved away from him. He saw a tiny red patch on her leg where his hand had maybe stroked it. She took a drag on her smoke. 'Why does she need a PI?'

'Why does anyone need a PI? They have a problem they want solved.'

'And what is her problem?' Mars asked, a line of worry suddenly creasing her brow, which intrigued Archer.

'Can't get into it. Professional ethics. But what can you tell me about her?'

'You sound like you're investigating your own client.'

'Archer just likes to be thorough, don't you, Archer?'

Callahan had a glass of champagne in one hand and her clutch purse in the other. Her nose and the rest of her face looked superbly powdered.

'That's right. And getting to know the client often helps solve the problem.'

'Liberty, you never told me you had such a tall, dark, handsome, and *curious* friend.'

'I like to keep him under wraps. The competition

here is murder.'

Mars plucked out her smoke from the holder, dumped it on a passing tray, and loaded in a fresh cigarette she took from a crystal glass stuffed with them on a highly polished refectory table. Archer lit her up and she blew smoke out of her nostrils.

'To answer your question, Ellie always struck me as a straight-laced, nose-to-the-typewriter type. Very focused. Once she knows what she wants, she goes out and gets it. She's not a party girl. She was invited to *this* party, but I don't think she's going to show.'

'You know anything of her personal life?'

'I've been out to her place in Malibu.'

'Why was that?'

'A few times Danny needed some script notes delivered to her and I was going that way. Another time she had us over for dinner with Bart and his wife.'

'Why does she live in Malibu?'

'Why does anyone live in Malibu? For the sand? For the privacy?'

'A little pricey for a typewriter type.'

Mars gave him an unreadable look. 'Maybe Lamb has another source of funds. People do, you know. My grandfather worked with J. P. Morgan. And my mother's side comes from U.S. Trust money. I freely admit I did nothing to earn it. But I haven't squandered it, either. I'm a girl who lives on the interest and doesn't touch the principal. And I don't let Danny touch it, either.'

'Any other thoughts?' asked Archer.

'Danny spends more time with her. You might want to talk to him.'

'Thanks. Can you point me in the right direction?'

'It's easy. Find the cheapest-looking dame here with

35

the biggest boobs, and he'll be the really tall, bald guy right beside her looking down her dress for the sheer thrill of it.'

Callahan hooked him by the arm. 'Come on, I'll introduce you.'

7

'What the hell are you doing, Archer?' scolded Callahan after they walked away from Gloria Mars. 'Ellie didn't want anyone she works with to know she hired a PI. I bet Gloria is going to phone Bart Green right now and tell him.'

'Why isn't Bart Green here for the party if he and Mars are best buddies?'

'He likes Danny, sure, but he's going to be boozing and celebrating with folks a few steps above this crowd. The only reason Danny got this kind of turnout is because it's in the penthouse at the Ambassador. But my point is, now Green is sure to find out.'

'It's a calculated risk, Liberty. And if someone *is* trying to kill Lamb and succeeds, everyone's going to know about it anyway. But if the threat is coming from close by, having them on notice that a PI is digging around might give them pause.'

'I hope you're right.'

'Gloria Mars doesn't like her husband very much.'

'And that surprised you? I thought you handled divorce cases.'

'Maybe I was just hoping there was one happily married couple in this damn town.'

'Not in this price range. But you keep right on hoping.'

'Do you see Danny Mars?' asked Archer.

'I do. He's about six-six and bald as a cue ball, so he's hard to miss. And Gloria was spot-on. There he is next to Miss D-cup of 1952.'

37

'Is that her official name or did her mother give her another?'

'I just call 'em like I see 'em, and I see two really big ones right now.'

'You want to see if you can pry him away from her?'

She bumped him with her hip. 'You think there's any doubt I can?'

Archer held up both hands in surrender. 'You could seduce the collar off a bishop.'

'You should've heard me in confession. The priests enjoyed it way more than I did.'

She sauntered away, and in about thirty seconds Danny Mars was shaking Archer's hand while leering at Callahan. Mars was at least fifteen years older than his wife, had the neck of a water buffalo and the face to match. His brow furrows were so deep Archer could have hidden paper clips in between them. He had on a suit of creamy white gabardine with a yellow-and-blue-checked ascot at his throat, and his shirt was a bright orange silk. His pocket square matched the ascot. His white shirt cuffs had gold-plated links. His shoes were brown calfskin. A man who took care with his appearance, Archer concluded. He ordinarily didn't trust such men. They were too calculating and usually had a lot to hide.

She explained Archer's interest in Ellie Lamb.

'You know, she *has* been acting a little strange lately,' said Mars.

'How so?'

'She's been writing from her house, not the office.'

'Why'd she move to Malibu?'

'Maybe it was for the sea air and lying on the beach.'

'She's in one of the canyons,' said Archer.

'Well, you'd have to ask her,' said Mars as his gaze

38

worked the room.

'When did she move out there?' asked Archer.

'Couple years ago or so, something like that. Hold on there, boy.' Mars stopped one of the waiters and nabbed a glass of champagne off his tray, and at the same time neatly slipped an arm around Callahan's waist. 'Now, this gal is going places. After my new film comes out everybody's going to be talking about her.'

When his hand dipped to her buttocks and stayed there, Callahan said, 'Time to powder my nose again. Archer, I'll leave you boys to it.'

Archer knew young actresses had to powder their noses all the time.

Mars quickly turned to Archer. 'How is she in the sack? Amazing, right?'

'I wouldn't know,' lied Archer. 'We're just friends.'

Mars eyed him closely. 'You're not one of them pansy boys, are you?'

'Not that I know of. Lamb ever mention any problems? You ever meet any guy she was dating?'

'I wasn't aware she was dating anyone. For all I know she likes women.'

He finished his champagne and grabbed another one off a passing tray. He eyed the waiter carrying it as he walked off.

'I don't know why they don't just stick with the colored waiters. They're reliable, and they don't look at you all funny, like the Japs do. These Mexies I just don't trust. They put too much grease in their hair. Sticky fingers. I'll have to get Gloria to count the silverware.'

'I really don't trust anybody, regardless of skin color.'

Mars gave him a puzzled look. 'Whose side are you on, anyway?'

'Tell me why we're fighting and I'll pick a side.'

Mars seemed to think he was joking. 'You always this funny?'

'It's the booze. So no idea on anybody Lamb might be seeing?'

'No. And why does she need a PI?' he added with a growl.

'She never talked to you about it?'

'*I'm* the director. A king doesn't get personal with the chambermaid.'

'You really need to read more history. I understand you and Bart Green are good friends,' Archer said, deftly moving the conversation where he wanted it to go next.

Mars set his champagne flute down and lit up a Pall Mall. 'I've been in Hollywood for thirty years and I've known Bart for twenty-nine of them. He's not all that much older than me, but he was well up the food chain by the time I hit town. But he's been great to me, always throwing stuff my way. It's why I'm working with Ellie Lamb.' He paused and looked at his cigarette. 'We're kind of like brothers. Although he rose a lot higher than I have. C'est la vie.'

'But it beats Oregon and cow shit?'

Mars grinned at him, but the motion didn't light up his features because there was nothing genuine behind it. 'Gloria likes to throw that in my face. Yeah, I grew up in the middle of nowhere, and worked my ass off to get out. She grew up on Fifth Avenue with truckloads of money, none of which she earned, went to an elite women's college, and has never had to work a day in her life. So who has the right to talk cow shit?'

'I'm a workingman just like you.'

Mars genuinely smiled this time and raised his glass. 'To workingmen everywhere.'

'I understand you're in line to direct the Bette Davis picture that Lamb is scripting?'

Mars's genial look faded a few watts. 'Well, Miss Davis has the final say on that. But we had a good first meeting, and Ellie's script is coming along.'

'What's the story line?'

'Officially under wraps.'

'When is Lamb supposed to have it finished?'

'Soon. I hope whatever she has going on won't mess that up,' he added with a glare aimed at Archer. 'I've got a lot riding on this. It could lead to bigger and better things.'

'I understand you've been to her place in Malibu.'

'Nice house, high up in the canyon, like you said.' He tapped his chest. 'Almost had trouble breathing at that altitude. I'm more of a sea-level guy.'

'So she never told you why she chose Malibu to dig in?'

Mars started to shake his head, but then said, 'Wait a minute. Okay, yeah, I recall it was because of a friend who lived there. Ellie wanted to be closer to that person.'

'That person have a name?'

Mars shook his head. 'I meet so many people and I'm lousy with names.' He glanced at Miss D-cup, who had a line of men just waiting to tell the lady how they could make her a star.

'Now, I *do* remember faces really well.'

'Just faces?' said Archer, who had followed his gaze to the woman.

The man barely tried, and thus failed, to look shocked. 'I'm a married man, Archer.'

Archer drained his White Russian dry. 'To married men everywhere.'

41

8

Archer sat on the bed in Callahan's spare room staring at his shoes. The house was decorated with a Bohemian flair that he knew was all Callahan. This was not the land of tea cozies, patchwork quilts, and dusty knickknacks. The woman had hit the 1950s in full stride with colorful walls, minimalist chrome and wood furnishings, and large ceramic dishes like the kind they made in Laguna Beach hanging on the walls. The kitchen had every convenience GE and others could offer, like a dishwasher, a garbage disposal in the sink, an electric range, and even a deep freezer that was large enough to hold an elk. The coffee table was topped by recent copies of *Daily Variety* and *The Hollywood Reporter*. He had brought along a map of the stars and pretended to have found her new house on it. Her laugh had been worth the fifty cents.

There were also paintings that would never have seen the light of day in any grandma's house. On the wall of his room was a painting of a naked woman. She was grotesquely large, with bloated breasts and swollen thighs and belly, and was holding what Archer would delicately describe as a cucumber broken in half. Callahan said it was done in the avant-garde style. He'd asked her what she saw in it, and got, at first, a coy look in return. 'Life, Archer, only from a woman's perspective.'

He and Callahan had kissed on the stroke of midnight in the Ambassador's penthouse. Then they, and apparently everyone else, had gotten the hell out of

Dodge, including at least one of the hosts. As Archer was waiting in the valet line, he had seen Danny Mars driving off with Miss D-cup in a silver Rolls. He didn't know where Gloria had gotten to. Maybe she was still in the penthouse with one of the Mexican waiters, shorn of slitted gown and gilt slippers, and white jacket and pants, respectively. They could be lying on their backs on the dining room table looking up at the ceiling mirror and contemplating the prospects of a heady 1953.

He continued to sit there until he saw Callahan's light go out in her bedroom. He waited ten minutes more and then went into the next room, found the phone book, and looked at his watch. It was five past two. He looked up Eleanor Lamb's number in Malibu and made the call. If she was there, he'd hang up. She might be more than just the worker-bee writer with nothing more complicated in her life than reams of heavy bond paper and a mountain of Corona ribbon and dreams of crafting comeback stories for aging stars. If so, he wanted to understand her and maybe help the woman.

The phone rang three times and then a voice said, 'Hello?'

It was a man. Okay, this was not starting off like he wanted it to.

Archer made his voice high-pitched and echoey. 'Can I speak to Eleanor Lamb?'

'Do you have any idea what time it is?'

'Yeah, I do. What are *you* doing up?'

The man didn't answer.

'Can I speak to her?'

'Who the hell are you?'

'Her brother. I wanted to wish her Happy New Year.'

'She doesn't have a brother.' The line went dead.

Archer slowly put down the phone. He could call in the LA County cops. But when the dispatcher asked him what was wrong, what was he supposed to say? That a guy had answered an unmarried woman's phone at two a.m. and hung up on him? They would just tell him that Eleanor Lamb had gotten lucky on New Year's Eve. If Archer pushed it, that would get *him* a quick trip to the can for wasting police time.

He left a note for Callahan just in case he didn't get back before she woke up. She had told him she wasn't due on set today. That meant the lady would be sleeping until well past noon.

He pulled his street map from the Delahaye's glove box, found Las Flores Canyon Road on it, and set off.

9

The weather was chilly and it looked like it was going to rain again, so he had put up the top. He had also pulled his Smith & Wesson .38 from the glove box and inserted it in his shoulder holster. He didn't like carrying a gun after WWII, but he liked dying even less.

He passed through neighborhoods where the old palm trees were losing their luster and the older homes their integrity. Many of these places were now renting out as tourist traps. If the water wouldn't turn on or the heat didn't work, you'd get a sob story about stolen pensions and unpaid hospital bills from the owners who lived in the basement or over the garage. He next passed various renditions of Skid Row, which backstopped the industrial hide of LA, like a long-ignored malady now out of control.

As he left LA proper and headed west, the Pacific was etched in the darkness as a long black stripe until the breakers ruptured white and sharp onto the golden sand. He drove through monied Santa Monica and then past Pacific Palisades, where folks who didn't have the bank account to get into Malibu could put down semi-gilded roots. Far out in the water he saw a single light. Probably a cargo ship heading in or out. He watched the light until it vanished in a marine fog that sprouted up around here like mushrooms after rain.

Soon, Archer got within a pistol shot of the ocean, and the drum of the waves seemed to unspool like a movie in his head. The breakers were moodily

45

fascinating to watch, though the ending was always the same. He turned off the road near the Sea Lion Restaurant. Back in the day the place had been built as a destination for travelers, because it was at the end of the public road in Malibu. It was only fairly recently that the beaches of Malibu had been opened for public consumption.

Across from there the single bright light of the Albatross Hotel blazed away. Archer thought he could hear some late-night New Year's Eve partygoers splashing around in the pool. That place was a cash cow for any PI with even a modicum of talent. He had personally handled a half dozen divorce cases where the photos and recordings and other details he'd amassed at the Albatross had given his female clients the wherewithal to take their adulterous husbands to the proverbial cleaners. He had always been amazed by the fact that many of these men hadn't realized that the distance between LA and Malibu wasn't enough to overcome their wives' ingenuity and anger.

'It's thirty miles, pal,' one dazed husband had told Archer, as they sat out in the hall of the LA County Superior Court. His Albatross honey was sitting outside in his Bentley, waiting for her newly freed man. But maybe not as eager as before since the little wife had taken him for half. 'Thirty damn miles!'

'Ever heard the phrase 'a woman scorned'?' Archer had told him.

The man wiped the sweat off his brow. 'I don't have to hear it, buddy. I *lived* it.'

'If you're going to walk the aisle with the pretty gal out in your car, and then pull the same on her, do it in another country. Tijuana's not *that* far. But it's more than thirty miles.'

46

'Don't worry. There won't be a next time.'

'Then you're finally growing up, *pal*,' Archer had replied before walking off.

He turned right and made his way up Las Flores Canyon Road. A house light in the canyon above the fog line winked down on him. One of seventeen canyons in Malibu, Las Flores grew very steep very fast. The darkness, which was pretty complete already, was thrown into pitch blackness by the canyon walls.

He drove slowly, both so he wouldn't hit anything, but also because he was afraid of missing Lamb's house. He actually did miss it and had to backtrack, finally pointing his headlight at a drab brown mailbox with the right numbers on it. There was also a four-door dark blue Ford parked across the street from her house. So she had been telling the truth about that.

Archer drove around a bend in the road, killed his lights, and then his engine. He got out and made his way back up the canyon road with a turned-off flashlight in hand.

He squatted on his haunches and eyed the Ford. He saw no movement inside, not even a shadow trying not to move and pretend it wasn't there. He pulled his gun and crept up to the back of the vehicle, doing his best to keep out of the sight lines of the car's mirrors.

He reached the car and edged over to the rear window. The back seat was empty. So was the front. He tried the trunk hatch and found it unlocked. Nothing. He checked the car's registration. In the beam of his light he saw it was owned by one Cedric Bender with an address in Anaheim. He pulled out a pencil and his notebook and wrote this down along with the license plate number.

He closed the car door and headed up the path to

Lamb's house. He shone his light down to see the flag-stones with grass growing between as they zigzagged up to a large Spanish-style home. The place had white stucco walls, a red tile roof, and small, Moorish-style windows with honeycombed windowpanes set in silver trim and window surrounds painted green. He could smell wood smoke coming from somewhere, even as the breakers down below hurled their sound tentacles up here. Fire and water all tied up in a neat sensory bow.

He saw the sleek two-door silver coupe in a carport next to the house. He touched the engine. It was cold. He tried the doors, but they were locked. He took a moment to write down the coupe's plate number. If this was Lamb's ride, he could confirm that later. He'd rather the lady confirmed it right now, even if she got mad at him for waking up her and her sleep-mate.

He decided to bypass the front door and headed to the rear. A set of colorful Mexican tile steps led him up to the rear yard. The smell of eucalyptus was so prominent it was like someone had injected a liter of it directly into his nostrils. The sharp, dry chaparral grabbed at his trousers. The clay that made up the canyons was geologically unstable, resulting in the area's being acutely susceptible to mudslides when the hard rains came, which they always did. On top of that, the thick brush and Santa Ana dry winds made for frequent wildfires, with the chaparral being one of the prime ignitors. In spite of all the flooding and burning, the folks just kept coming. Maybe a swarm of locusts might do the trick and get the builders and home buyers to knock it off. But he doubted it.

In the distance Archer heard a fox scream and then

another one answered right back. Maybe they were celebrating the new year, too. Then a coyote chimed in. Now they just needed a bear and they'd have a quartet.

He came around to a concrete patio, on which sat a couple of thick-boned teak chairs around a table with a decorative tile top in blues and gold, and a beige umbrella with a frilly edge set in the down position. A small corner fountain in the shape of an urn and raised up on some rough stone slabs gurgled away like a dying man with a slit throat. A hedge of cypress shielded the rear yard from the scrub oaks clinging precariously to the canyon's edifice. Trailing lobelia rising out of the dirt had tacked itself to the home's stucco, adding a dash of color. And there was a pool, oval in shape. He could smell the chlorine as it rose off the surface. He put his hand in the water and was surprised. It was heated. That wasn't cheap.

The back door was locked. There was an enclosed deck on the upper level that one reached by a set of metal circular stairs. So Archer reached them and went up. The beige French door leading into the house was not locked. He opened it and went inside.

His light showed him this was a bedroom. The bed was made, and there were no discarded clothes any-where that he could see. He stood in the middle of the room, listening. The house was as still as any morgue he'd ever been in. Yet there was nothing scary about a morgue. Other than the coroner, everyone else was dead. A pitch-dark house maybe full of lethal sur-prises was a different ball game altogether.

He looked into the en suite bathroom. Blue and white tiles, blue tub, and towels monogrammed with an *L* were neatly arranged on a built-in shelf; no dead bodies were behind the shower curtain or stuffed in the linen closet. He grabbed a washcloth and used it to open the medicine cabinet, where he found the typical items like face powders, a box of Tampax, creamy moisturizers, tonics, and other patent medicines. He also found a bottle of black hair dye, and a hair straightener. So the lady was *not* a natural brunette with straight locks. Why had she lied about that?

He next searched the other rooms up here. One was no doubt a guest bedroom outfitted in Spartan fashion, with a bathroom that was half the size of hers. But maybe Lamb didn't want to encourage guests, so she made the accommodations uninviting on purpose. He could easily see her being that sort of introvert.

Another room was obviously Lamb's office or writer's den, or literary sweat shop, whatever one wanted to deem it. There was a portable Smith-Corona typewriter in its open carrying case on a desk with a chair in the kneehole. Next to it were stacks of yellow legal pads and loose white pages with notes and doodles littered over them. They all seemed to pertain to various scripts she was working on.

On the other side of the typewriter was a script marked 'Bette Davis film.' He didn't bother to open it. If he ended up seeing the movie, he wanted to be surprised.

There were other scripts marked 'DRAFT' stacked next to it from a number of other projects, with several other studios. Lamb was one busy scribe. Next to the telephone was a Wheeldex. He fingered through the cards there and saw some famous names and others that were obscure. His first inclination was to take the whole thing; his second inclination won out,

50

and the Wheeldex stayed where it was.

He looked through the drawers and found a check register. There was no bank balance listed, but her checks seemed to be made out to the sort of folks you made checks out to. He made a note that she banked with the Second National Bank of Malibu. He wondered if the First National Bank of Malibu was still in business and, if so, why a town this small needed a spare.

Against one wall was a small leather couch with fluffy pillows embroidered with cats and puppies, and a coffee table with stacks of books. There were bookshelves filled with more books and scripts. The sole window held a view of the canyon. Archer noted that Lamb's back would be to it. Focus, focus, apparently.

A large world globe sat next to the couch. When he hinged it open, revealed was a bar with bottles and glasses arrayed in round cut holes.

He glided down the stairs, reached the ground level, and turned to his right.

He stumbled hard and hit the floor with a grunt; his light fell from his left hand and his gun was knocked out of his right with the sudden impact. The next moment he was smacked on the back of the head with something hard enough to qualify as a blunt instrument. He briefly saw fireworks and then the flames went out and the coal-black around him became complete.

When he slowly came to, he rubbed his neck and stretched out his jaw, which had seized up with the blow to his skull. Vague stars knitted against a black background floated through his mind. He slowly checked his watch. It was now after four in the morning. He reached up and massaged the back of his

51

head where a lump had risen like a volcano from the ocean of his scalp. His fingers came away sticky with his blood. He groped around for his light and his gun. He found both and turned the light on to see what he had stumbled over.

The person was dead, that was certain. The pupils were fixed, and neither one bit even a little on Archer's light. Only it wasn't Eleanor Lamb. It was a man.

Someone had ushered him into 1953 with one right between the eyes.

10

The first thing Archer did was find a bathroom on the main floor off the foyer, where he threw up everything he'd eaten and drunk on New Year's Eve. The White Russian felt particularly egregious coming back up his throat, like his own painfully private Cold War. After that he snagged a washcloth, filled it with some cubes from the refrigerator, and laid it over the bloody bump on his head. He'd had concussions before, and he knew he was suffering from one now.

He sat on the bottom step and stared dully at the dead man. The guy was in his fifties, with thinning, gray hair and a florid face that was turning paler by the minute. He was around five-ten and about two hundred pounds. The bullet wound on his face was blackened, with the skin crusted up like furrows of dirt in a tilled field.

That told Archer that whoever had shot him had been close to the guy. He was dressed in a gray two-piece that looked off the rack and was baggy and off-kilter in all the places a cheap suit always was. His tie was red and too short. It barely reached the top of his now-slack belly.

Archer looked at his face more closely. There were bruises on his cheeks and jaw and one on his neck. His nose looked puffy and swollen. He checked the dead man's pockets. The suit was courtesy of Sears, Roebuck and Company, the label said. If this was the Ford man, Archer could match the name from the car. Only the fellow had no ID and no wallet. And no car keys. And there was no business card or other clue that would solve the whole thing in short order. So someone had rolled him and taken everything that could tell who he was.

Except the damn car. *So is this Cedric Bender?*

That would make sense. The car was outside and the dead guy was inside. But Archer needed to be sure. He glanced down at the corpse again. Archer had no idea how the man had lived his life, but that life was now over. It was a callous and sad send-off, however you looked at it.

Archer put the ice back on his head and took another minute to think what to do. He decided to search the rest of the house to make sure that Lamb wasn't lying somewhere with a hole added to her head as well.

He didn't find Lamb's or any other body. He saw walls and beamed ceilings that were all painted white. The fireplace surround in the front room was etched with musical notes, and film awards were aligned on the mantel. Hanging on one wall was a cuckoo clock. There was a white china cabinet and a built-in buffet.

The kitchen had all the latest appliances and gadgets, marble countertops, an island with bar stools around it, a large refrigerator with practically nothing in it, and an electric stovetop. There was a library filled with books that actually looked read, and a door that led to an outdoor shower enclosed by a wooden wall. A small dining room had a rectangular Craftsman-style table with six chairs. This was no doubt where the Marses and Greens had eaten during their visit. Aside from that there were comfortable couches, chairs, rugs, a portable bar outfitted in chrome, some paintings, interesting light fixtures, and lots of windows both large and small.

Other than that, the only things in the house were a dead body, and a very much alive PI nursing a cracked head and a bruised ego for letting someone so easily sandbag him.

He went back up to Lamb's office and looked through the Wheeldex again. His fingers plucked out two cards that seemed promising because, unlike all the others, they each had a large *X* written in under the name.

When in doubt, X marks the spot. That must be in some PI mail order course somewhere.

He wrote the information down and put the cards back. He liked to play fair with the cops, even if they didn't always play fair with him.

He went out the way he had come, wiping his prints off along the way. His sense of fair play had its limits, thus Archer wasn't about to leave behind any evidence that might earn him a trip to San Quentin to sniff a bunch of cyanide gas as the concluding frame of his personal horror flick.

He got back to his car and drove off, winding his way down after winding his way up. He stopped at a call box on the highway and reported a dead body at Eleanor Lamb's house, giving the address. He didn't provide his name, rank, or PI license number despite the dispatcher's demanding all personal info from him except his ring size. It might come back to bite him, but so would willingly sticking his neck out.

He didn't want to meet the deputy sheriffs on the drive east. At this hour of the morning, in a car that stood out, that would only get him pulled over with difficult questions to follow. So he drove past the Sea Lion and the Albatross and headed west. When he was far enough away from Las Flores and reached a part of Malibu that was far less developed, he pulled over to the beach side and parked behind some scrub bushes, just in case the cops decided to look for who-ever had called them, or killed the guy in the house.

He got out, took off his shoes and socks, and put them on the car seat, then rolled up his pants and walked along the beach. It was low tide, and the coolness of the sand worked its way up to his injured head. He found a dry place to sit down and watched the ocean recede south toward San Diego and Tijuana. During the summers a surfing crowd had started invading the beaches here. He'd watched the surfers serenade the bathing suit ladies with their tales of derring-do, often strumming a ukulele while doing so. He'd seen more than one fresh-faced, wide-eyed young woman taken in by this glib crap, which usually ended with a face slap and/or a paternity suit.

He looked out to the water and saw a white light. It might be from the cargo ship he had seen earlier, but then again probably not. Enough time had passed for it to be well out of sight by now. And this light was far closer. The ship was probably making for port along the coast.

Malibu was a slender appendage sticking out from the torso of California. He was on a part of Malibu sand that also had sharp, vertical bluffs as a backstop. At high tide some of the old caves would fill up with water. People would occasionally find gold doubloons from Spanish vessels that had gone down in the noto-rious storms that made this section of the coast a mariner's nightmare back in the day.

In the distance a few minutes later, he heard the LA County Sheriff's radio patrol cars come flying along the coast road, the pitch of their sirens wound so high

56

they could probably be heard high up in the canyons. He was too far away to see them from here, but he could imagine their flashing lights being like stark embers in the darkness. He listened to their cacophony until the canyon swallowed them all whole, just like the whale had Jonah. Only then did he rise on shaky legs and start to walk to his car.

The next moment he dropped to the sand. He had happened to glance back out toward the water and his gaze had held on that same light out there. It had changed course and was coming closer by the second. He could hear its motor revved high over the crash of the waves. He knelt there, his heart hammering, as the now-revealed boat swept over the line of breakers. It quickly beached and the men swarmed off. Archer lay flat on the sand and continued to watch as one of the men splayed a flashlight beam around the area. The light passed just over the sharp brim of Archer's hat and then swung back.

Under the moonlight he saw the other men begin to unload large crates from the boat. It had to be illegal what they were doing. Honest businesses did not do their work well before dawn on a deserted beach on the first day of the new year.

He edged back on the beach as the men carrying the boxes headed to the dry sand.

Some words came to him over the sounds of the breakers. Spanish, then English.

Archer began to inch backward in a crabwalk because the men's path was taking them dangerously close to where he was. He managed to reach a spot that seemed far enough away to commence a hastier retreat. He turned, half rose, and hoofed it, his bare feet struggling in the loose sand and his injured head

57

pounding beyond all reckoning.

He had looked back to make sure no one had seen him when he suddenly slammed into something hard. He and the other man went down in a tangle of arms and legs. Archer couldn't see the fellow's face because of the darkness and the extreme thrashing the two were engaged in, with their bodies rolling around violently. He had to keep shutting his eyes because their movements were causing the sand to fly all over them. Archer felt a hand reach for his throat and grip there. He pushed the palm of his hand into the man's face, levering the neck back enough to where the man gasped and let go his grip.

The next instant Archer saw the glint of a knife and the blade came at his throat. Before it plunged into him he grabbed the man's wrist and luckily found his strength superior to his opponent's, so he could keep the knife at bay. He smelled the garlic and tobacco breath and felt the foul spit on his face as they writhed and tussled in the sand, each trying to gain control of the weapon.

Then, needing to end this before the other men on the beach saw what was happening, Archer closed his eyes, gritted his teeth, and rammed the crown of his head into the left side of the man's jaw. The man cried out and he dropped the knife. Archer next clocked him with a stunner of a right cross, and the man fell limp to the sand, with his face turned away. Archer got to his feet, fought the blinding pain in his head, and ran for it.

The sand got more densely packed the farther he went. Archer picked up speed, but his strides were still wobbly and clumsy. He heard the report of a gun and felt a round crack past him and embed itself in

58

the wood of a fence set up to stop erosion. It couldn't have been the guy he'd fought, it had to be the men from the boat, which meant they had spotted him.

He redoubled his efforts, running flat-out, his breaths coming in bursts and his heart beating so fast he wasn't sure what would give out first, his lungs or his ticker.

More shots came, and with them he heard feet running hard behind him and the cries of the men to whom those feet and gunfire belonged. As he approached the road, from the corner of his eye he thought he saw what looked like a truck parked about a hundred yards away on the edge of the sand. He reached his car where it was hidden behind the scrub bushes, slid into the front seat, turned the key, and slammed down the starter button. The French beast roared to life. He wheeled the Delahaye around, pointed it to the coast road, and pushed his bare foot down hard on the accelerator.

He hit the asphalt, and in the straightaway he wound the car up to a hundred. He zipped around the first curve as the car banked around the wall of a canyon and he was out of the sight line and range of the guns. He drove fast for another mile and then, conscious that more cops might be on the way to the murder scene, he slowed down and drove the rest of the way back to Callahan's place at a sedate pace. He reached it just about the time the milkman dropped off three fresh bottles on her front porch. Archer pressed his face against the steering wheel and thanked God and everyone else he could think of for sparing him tonight.

11

Callahan had given him a spare key earlier that night, just in case he needed to crash at her place in the future. He staggered inside and put the milk in the white Frigidaire refrigerator, then walked to his bathroom and cleaned up his head with a bottle of peroxide he found under the sink. It stung so badly he almost threw up again. He got some ice and put it on the growing bruise on his head where he'd slammed it into the man's face. At least his hair hid much of the damage.

He stared in the mirror and saw someone looking older now than three decades. Nineteen fifty-three was not doing wonders for him so far.

In one night he had fallen over a dead body, gotten sapped, run into smugglers on the beach, and been nearly killed. Maybe he needed to run out and buy a box of rabbits' feet to change his fortunes. But then again, he had survived it all.

So, you are one lucky son of a bitch after all.

And then he turned his mind to the murdered man at Lamb's place. *That* was his case. The smugglers were somebody else's problem.

While a small gal like Lamb might not have been able to sap him that hard, she sure could employ a couple foot-pounds of force to pull a trigger. That meant the woman was not off the hook for the killing. Was the dead guy the same one who answered the phone? It wasn't like Archer could check his voice against the one he'd heard on the call. If not, who was he? The betting was pretty good that the Ford belonged to him since the dead could not drive off into the sunset. If so, the loved ones of Cedric Bender were in for a rude shock.

So who had sapped Archer? Whoever killed the guy? The shooter had cleaned out the man's pockets, presumably to prevent an ID, but he'd left the man's car across the street. How did that make sense? But if Bender *was* the shooter, why was his car still out there? You kill someone, you usually wanted to get away, fast.

And the big question: Where was Eleanor Lamb? Guilty or innocent? Dead or alive?

He stripped down to his skivvies, and then flapped his clothes through an open window to get out most of the sand. He hung them up in the closet and dropped into bed, closing his eyes at twenty minutes past six. He reopened them sometime later when Callahan knocked on his door.

'Archer, you in there? What's this note about? Did you go somewhere last night?'

He sat up and groaned. He'd forgotten to toss the note.

'Don't pay any attention to it. It's a moot point.'

'Can I come in?'

'Sure.'

'You decent?'

'When the hell did that ever matter to you?'

She walked in wearing a white nylon chiffon robe over a pale blue nightgown with some frill around the bodice and fluffy heelless slippers, looking as fresh and ready to go as if the late night and drinks had never happened. Sunlight was streaming in through the gaps in the venetian blinds. That only made Archer's head throb worse.

61

He sat up and blinked at her.

'The best I can say is, you look like shit, Archer.'

'Well, that's exactly how I feel, so there's that.'

Callahan sat on the bed next to him and gaped when she saw his assortment of injuries. 'What in the hell happened to your head?' she gasped.

'Will you make me some coffee if I tell you?' he said groggily.

'I'll *buy* you coffee *and* some breakfast.'

He looked at his watch. It was after twelve. 'Damn, when did that happen?'

'Yeah, Archer, the little hand on the clock just keeps going round and round even when you're getting your head busted. But I know a joint around the corner. They serve breakfast until I say so because the owner likes me. Now spill, what happened?'

'I went out to Lamb's place in Malibu last night.'

'What! Is that where you got your head bashed?'

He told her about everything, including the phone call he made and his finding the dead man and getting sapped for his troubles, and the battle on the beach and his nearly dying there.

Callahan's expression became more and more distraught and her hands trembled. 'Oh my God, Archer, it's a miracle you're still breathing.'

He sat back against the pillows and didn't reply.

'You know one day your luck is going to run out,' she warned, her expression now one of weary resignation.

'It wasn't all luck.'

She looked at his head. 'You didn't do such a good job there. I can clean it up better and bandage it. I got some aspirin in my bathroom.'

'A half bottle should do fine.'

'And you don't know if anything happened to Ellie?'

'Does she drive a two-door silver Chevrolet coupe?'

'Yes.'

'It was locked and I couldn't check, so her body could be inside.'

'Oh, Jesus! You said the cops went there after you called them?'

He nodded. 'I'll shower and shave, shake the rest of the sand off my clothes, and then we can get something to eat. After that I'm going to call the LA County Sheriff's Department. I got a friend there. I'll see what I can find out.'

'Don't mention that you were there. They could arrest you, Archer.'

'Wouldn't be the first time. The cops really like busting PIs.' He gave her a lopsided grin, which made his head hurt even worse. 'I think they're jealous we make the big bucks.'

She smacked him lightly on the cheek. 'In that case, Rockefeller, you can buy *me* breakfast.'

12

After a filling meal, and with his face shaved and his clothes reasonably cleaned and his head bandaged, and aspirin taken, Archer called Connie Morrison at Willie Dash's office in Bay Town. He told her what had happened and asked her to find out whatever she could on Cedric Bender. He also told her about what he had seen on the beach and his struggle with the man there.

'Should I tell Willie?' Morrison asked.

'Even if I say no, you're going to.'

'These last three years haven't been wasted on you at all, Archer.'

After that he phoned the offices of Green and Ransome. It rang and rang.

Next, he called the LA County Sheriff's Department. His contact there, Barry Drews, knew all about the dead man in Las Flores Canyon. Archer said nothing about the boat and the men on the beach, because he didn't want to get pulled into an unrelated case. That was, thankfully, someone else's headache.

'How'd you find out so fast about the dead guy?' Drews wanted to know.

'Friend of a friend. Who's running the investigation?'

'Phil Oldham.'

'I know Phil. Would it be a problem if I went up there?'

'Why? What's your interest in all this?'

'The lady who owns that house is a client of mine.'

Drews said, 'Any idea where she is? Because Phil

and his boys can't find her.'

'I might be able to help. Can you call them about me coming up?'

'I'm not too sure about this, Archer.'

'Come on, Barry. We're both on the same team here.'

'But you keep things close to the vest.'

'If I didn't I wouldn't be in business. My clients expect confidentiality. So will you make the call?'

He heard the man sigh. 'Just share whatever you find.'

'I'll do all I can on that score.'

'You going out soon?'

'Soon as I hang up with you.'

He put the phone down and looked at Callahan, who was sitting across from him.

'Do you know what you're doing?' she asked in a worried tone.

'I'll find out.'

'But Ellie never even wrote you a check. So she's not really your client.'

'A guy's dead and it looks like Lamb has vanished. And someone tried to push my brain into the rest of me. I'll figure the business end out later.'

'You're more of a Boy Scout than you'll admit.'

He gingerly put on his hat. 'That's just what this town needs, more damn Boy Scouts.'

'Will you please be careful?' she asked.

'More careful than I was last night.'

She kissed him, not on the cheek, but on the lips.

'What was that for?' he said, giving her a questioning look.

'Luck. Doesn't take a genius to see that you're going to need it.' Her words were joking; the rest of the lady was not.

13

The traffic on New Year's Day was light, and Archer made good time on the drive back to Malibu. The place was named after a Chumash village, Humaliwo, where the 'Hu' part was silent. In Chumash it meant 'where the surf sounds loudly,' and there was no denying that.

Las Flores Canyon Road looked far different in the daylight. What was dark and foreboding then was now interesting and aesthetically pleasing. He parked in front of Lamb's house and observed right away that the dark blue Ford was no longer there.

Okay, there could be two reasons for that. Either the cops impounded it, or someone else came during the night to take it. Maybe the owner, Cedric Bender.

Archer chastised himself because he couldn't remember if the Ford was still there when he had left the house. His head had been hurting so badly he hadn't bothered to notice.

He got out of the Delahaye after looking at the coroner's black meat wagon standing by in the driveway behind the coupe. A sedan was behind it with the CORONER plaque hung in the window. There was an old Plymouth parked at the curb, with a radio squad car nearly touching its back bumper.

Archer was surprised they hadn't taken the body away by now. He gave his name to the uniform on duty and was quickly admitted into the house.

Now, start to tap-dance really fast, Archer.

66

Phil Oldham was a big, blunt-faced homicide detective reluctantly housed in a Harris Tweed jacket and wrinkled gray slacks that nearly matched their owner's skin. He had the reputation of being a decent cop with a sense of fair play on his good days. That made him about as rare as a politician who *wasn't* on the take.

Oldham and two other plainclothes were standing near the body, over which someone had placed a dirty white sheet. The edge of an unlit, beaten-down stogie stuck out from the right corner of Oldham's mouth.

'Hello, Archer,' he said with a nod. 'I got buzzed on the two-way from Barry. Said you'd be heading over. You missed most of the show. We already took our pictures and drew our chalk line, case is practically solved.'

'Glad to hear it.'

'Tell me something.' He took the stogie out and looked at it like he was wondering how it had gotten in his mouth. 'Willie Dash has a good business going up north. And I hear you're a worthy pavement pounder for him. So why play down here in the sand?'

'This one rolled right across my eye line,' said Archer.

'Understand she was a client, meaning the lady of the house.'

'That's right. She said she thought someone was trying to kill her.'

'Well, unfortunately for this fellow, someone *was* looking to kill somebody and he got tagged to be the corpse. But maybe the wires got crossed, who knows?'

He lifted the sheet off and Archer pretended to be surprised. But in the light of day he was seeing things

67

he hadn't seen last night, which was the reason he'd wanted to come here.

'Got an ID yet?'

'Nope. No wallet on him. Not sure how he got here. No car, either.'

'Is that right?' said Archer. He looked around the body. 'No blood.'

'Nope. Just a little on the stiff. Slug's still in him.'

Archer bent low. 'You shoot somebody that close, you're gonna have blood all over. The floor, the banisters, the risers.' Archer eyed Oldham. 'He was shot somewhere else.'

Oldham didn't concede or deny this, but Archer knew the man had already concluded the very same thing.

He caught Oldham staring at a spot on his head. Archer notched his hat down to cover the edge of the bruise on his forehead. Oldham made no comment and Archer volunteered nothing. Cops took any words you said and used them to put you in a cage.

'Somebody worked him over good. I wonder why.'

Oldham shrugged. 'To find out what he was doing and what he knew, why else? And where'd you get that bruise on your noggin?'

Okay, tap, tap, tap, Archer.

'It's called dancing while drunk.' Archer stood. 'Doesn't look like they were satisfied with his answers.'

'If he gave any. So, where's your client?'

'I called her office this morning. Nobody answered.'

'New Year's Day. LA takes every opportunity not to work. But not us county stiffs.'

'With that new guy, Bill Parker, in charge at LAPD, you county boys feeling the pressure? Sounds like they turned over a new leaf in the City of Angels.'

Oldham snorted. 'Yeah, all the rotten chumps Parker fired tried to get on with the county. We told them to go jump in the Pacific with lead feet.'

'Is that right?' said Archer. He was not going to point out that a number of county cops had been paid off to form a protective shield around the Clover Club, the nicest gambling joint in southern California and just outside of LA's city limits. The gangster Mickey Cohen had been rousted by this squad to leave the Clover alone. He had retaliated by using a recording showing a high-ranking detective on the take. The ensuing scandal had brought down some top county and city cops.

Oldham was just getting worked up. 'Yeah, that's right. I don't like dirty cops, never have. Sure, I could have looked the other way and got slipped extra dough in my pocket easy enough, and buy a nicer car with it or take the wife out to a nice place to eat. But I like my Plymouth and I like my wife's cooking.' He turned to stare directly at Archer, his eyes hard, mean flint chips. 'And LA is LA, Archer. No matter who they got in there to clean house, whether it's this Parker guy or anybody else, at the end of the day the stink will come back, like flies on shit. It always does. City of Angels? Now, that's a good one. Name me one vice you can't buy in that town.'

'Well, LAPD did take down Mickey Cohen.'

Oldham barked, 'No, the Feds did. That Senator Kefauver got him. On *tax evasion*. Hell, that don't count.'

Archer was done with the professional chit-chat. 'Got a time of death yet?'

Oldham looked at him funny. 'Why do you need to know that?'

'Just professional curiosity.'

'Damn, the coroner told me, but I plum forgot.'

Archer eyed the other plainclothes who were staring at him with unfriendly eyes. Maybe Oldham wasn't such a good egg after all, he thought. Or maybe Archer had finally worn out his welcome with the county's thin blue line.

'You find a weapon?'

'Nope. From the hole it made in his head, I'm thinking a .38 or bigger.' He side-eyed Archer. 'Maybe your client mistook him for a burglar, shot first, saw what she did, got spooked, and hightailed it. Dames do that, you know.'

'And the lack of blood?'

'She shot him outside and dragged him in here.'

'If she thought he was a burglar, why go to all that trouble? She was within her rights. She'd call the cops, end of story.'

'But maybe she knew the guy? Maybe she *wanted* to kill him.'

'That's a lot of maybes, Phil. Let me throw one back at you. *Maybe* somebody killed *Lamb* and took her body and left this stiff behind to confuse things. And, as to *your* theory? I've met Lamb. She's less than half this guy's size. She wasn't dragging his butt anywhere.'

'She could've had help.'

'You find blood outside?'

'Still looking.'

'And you're saying she went on the lam. And yet there's a Chevy coupe in the carport. It belongs to Lamb. Hopefully her body's not inside.'

'We're going to pop the lock and see.'

'Well, if she *did* run, I guess she wouldn't want to

do so in her own car,' noted Archer. 'You talk to the cab companies yet? Maybe she took one to the train or bus station or the airport.'

'Working on it. But first things first, we need to identify the stiff, and the sooner the better. So, where'd you meet her?'

'At Chasen's last night. I was having dinner with a friend of hers and she showed up and dropped her story on me when she found out what I did for a living.'

'Chasen's, huh?' He slipped out the stogie and looked at his colleagues. 'You two ever been to Chasen's?' They shook their heads. 'Me neither. Out of the range of my salary. Didn't know you moved in such uppity circles, Archer. You on the take or what?'

'What do PIs have to offer?' Archer countered.

'You still drive that fancy car? The one with the steering wheel on the wrong side?'

'Yeah. But I basically won that playing roulette in Reno.'

'You that lucky?'

'I was that night.'

Oldham lazily scratched his chin. 'And she thought someone was trying to kill her?'

'Yeah. I was going to go by her office this morning to talk to her.'

'And why didn't you?' said Oldham sharply, going in for the kill now. 'And how the hell did you know to call Barry in the first place about this? Come on, gumshoe, spill it. I don't have time to kick the shit around with you or anybody else.'

'Heard the call out about a body being found at Lamb's address on the police radio.'

That merely inflamed Oldham's inferno. He chest

71

bumped Archer. 'That call came in well before dawn. You called Barry this *afternoon* and said you heard from a friend of a friend. You sure it wasn't you who called in the body?'

Archer was ready for this. 'I was nowhere near. What I meant was a local *associate* of mine heard the call out and didn't think anything of it because he didn't know Lamb had retained me. I was actually supposed to meet Lamb at her office this morning. I called there, like I said, just to make sure we were still on. When no one answered, I started to get worried. I talked to my associate and that's when I found out. Then I called Barry.'

'What's the name of this *local* associate?'

'I start answering those sorts of questions, I might as well turn in my license, Phil.'

Oldham didn't seem convinced by this, but he also didn't seem inclined to pursue it. He put the stogie back in his mouth and clamped down on it.

'Any of the neighbors hear anything?' asked Archer.

'Old lady named Danforth didn't. Said she was sound asleep. She looks to be a hundred, so I tend to believe her. The neighbors on the other side are out of the country. Danforth says they're in France.' Oldham put the stogie in his jacket pocket, unwrapped a stick of chewing gum and stuck it in his mouth. 'I was in France once. Only there was a war going on.'

'Yeah, me too. It was a real kick.'

At that moment a short, white-haired, flabby man in a three-piece dark suit with a soiled shirt collar and a straight black tie appeared from somewhere looking tired and uninterested. 'All right, Phil, we can get the body outta here now.'

A stretcher had been leaned against the wall and

72

the two plainclothes were about to lift the body onto it when Archer bent down to help. 'I got this side, fellas.'

They heaved and the body went on the stretcher and was carried out by the two men.

The coroner turned to Oldham. 'I'll do the post-mortem this afternoon. I'll take a leap and say a bullet to the head killed him.'

As Archer watched the coroner leave he flexed his fingers. Rigor mortis had completely passed on the body. Archer calculated that the man had been dead no later than around two or three in the afternoon yesterday, or around five hours before Lamb had approached them at Chasen's.

He looked up to see Oldham staring dead at him. The homicide man made a show of glancing in the direction of where the stretcher had disappeared and then looked at Archer's hands.

'Guess you got your answer on when he bought it, Archer.'

'You going to file a missing person's report on Lamb?'

'Not up to me.'

Archer turned to leave.

'Oh, and Archer?'

'Yeah?'

'Happy fucking New Year, you prick.'

73

14

Outside, Archer lit a Lucky and walked over to the coroner, who was standing next to the meat wagon, while Oldham's boys loaded the corpse in, loudly cursing its corpulence. To them he wasn't a dead man, just dead weight.

'Damn shame,' said Archer.

'What is?' said the coroner.

'The guy getting *murdered*,' said Archer, snatching a look at the man.

'Hell, if they didn't there goes my job. Homicide is a thriving business in these parts.'

This guy reminded Archer why he didn't like hanging out with coroners. 'Understand it was maybe a .38 or larger caliber.'

The man lighted a stubby cigar pulled from his side jacket pocket and took a few puffs before hacking up maybe some leftover tobacco from his lungs and spitting it into the graveled driveway. 'Looks to be. I'll dig it out. Hey, you working the case with Phil?'

'My client owns this place. Me and Phil are trying to find her.'

'Private dick, then?'

'Who works with the cops pretty regularly, yeah,' said Archer vaguely because he needed to be vague but he also needed information. 'Think we're looking at least twenty-four hours on the time of death?'

'Sounds about right, little more, little less. Always tricky. Usually the stomach tells me a lot. We are what we eat, in life and in death.'

'Did you guys impound a car on this one?' Archer asked this because, despite what Oldham had said about there not being a car, he didn't believe anyone without corroboration.

'Car? Nah, nothing like that. Just the body.' He flicked his ash into the grass. His fingers were so thick Archer wondered how he could hold a scalpel, much less use it to slice precisely through human tissue. But maybe he wasn't that precise.

'They got coyote and even bears up here, you know.' The coroner cleared his throat and waggled his wide head, taking his two chins along with the gesture. 'Would not have been pretty if the body had been outside, no siree.'

'It wasn't pretty *inside*,' replied Archer curtly.

A minute later the meat wagon pulled away with one of Oldham's men driving while the other one went back inside. The coroner's somber car trailed the wagon, with him idly flicking cigar ash out the window.

Archer ground out his smoke, glanced back at the house, and then walked across the street. He stretched and took out his pack of Luckys, but then dropped it. This was intentional because he knew Oldham's junior-grade man might be watching. He knelt down to pick the pack up and got a good look at the oil slick on the asphalt. It was relatively fresh, which made sense being there from at least the night before. On either side of Lamb's house, but separated by about a couple hundred feet both ways, were her neighbors, Danforth and Bonham. He didn't know which was which, so he took the one on the right first.

The place was large and done in what Archer had come to learn was the Colonial Revival style because there was a lot of that around here. It had a main block and two wings with a brick chimney stack sprouting from one of them; another chimney stack soared into the sky from the rear. The porch was covered and had a wooden railing atop it, and there was a line of dormer windows fronting the roof. The yard was mostly rock and desert ground cover with a few gnarled scrub trees taking up space. He knocked and then knocked again. He heard nothing from inside.

He walked over to the single-car garage. It was detached from the house with a short, roofed breezeway connecting the two structures. It had a copper roof that was being patinaed by the elements. Flowery vines wove through the lattice that covered the breezeway's sides. The overhead garage door was solid wood with no windows, and it was locked. He went over to the side door of the garage that was under the breezeway. It was also locked. He peered through the upper glass partition. He couldn't make out much, but there didn't seem to be a car in there.

He gazed around, took out his pocketknife, inserted it between the lock and doorjamb, and drew the locking bolt back. He pushed against the door and went inside. Archer flipped on the wall light switch and the illumination of one bare lightbulb cast the small space into murky shadows. The place smelled of oil, grease, gas, mothballs, and mildew, but held no car. Yet there was something of interest.

He bent down and looked at the oil slick on the floor. He couldn't tell if it had come from the blue Ford, but it might have. He also supposed most garage floors had oil slicks on them. However, this one looked quite fresh. And if the Bonhams had been in France for a while, their car couldn't have made it.

76

Had the Ford been driven in here *after* Archer had been attacked? Then it could have been driven away later. Or, again, maybe this slick had nothing to do with the one back on the road. Cedric Bender might be safely in Anaheim, unless he was headed for a slab at the LA County morgue.

There were tools and long-spouted oil cans and the things one normally finds in a garage. He rifled through some old *Life* and *Look* magazines in a box. He checked the address labels. They were in the names of Peter and Bernadette Bonham of this address, Malibu.

Archer returned the magazines to the box and went back outside.

He passed through a waist-high wooden gate and entered the backyard. It was flatter and larger than Lamb's was, with a patch of lawn and perimeter flower and shrubbery beds that looked well tended and watered, though with the canyon walls, it probably got only limited sunlight. There was no pool, like Lamb had. But maybe the Bonhams weren't that sort.

However, there was a span of lawn that was lumpy and uneven.

Moles, thought Archer. They could do a number on the surface, all without seeing the light of day. *Just like the bad guys.*

He went to the back door and knocked. He decided against picking the lock. A garage was one thing, a home was something else. And if Oldham caught him, Archer could see a charge of breaking and entering in his future and maybe sticking.

Archer made an executive decision and moved on to something else that he hoped might hold promise but probably wouldn't.

And such was the life of a pavement-pounding PI on a slow dance to maybe nowhere.

15

He walked to the other house, which he now knew was Mrs. Danforth's. It was smaller than the Bonhams' but larger than Lamb's, and older. There was a good-sized bay window to the left of the front door, which had a small Judas window set at eye level. He knocked, and a few moments later he saw a head appear in the glass. The door opened to the extent of the latched brass chain.

Two wide eyes peered anxiously through the gap. 'Yes?'

'Name's Archer.' He flashed his license and asked if he could come in.

'Is this about next door?' said the thin mouth below the pair of deep-set watery eyes.

'Yes it is. I'm working with the police.' *Forgive me, Lord, for I have lied.* 'You're Mrs. Danforth?'

'Yes, Sylvia Danforth.'

'I'd like to ask you some questions, if that's all right.'

She undid the chain and revealed herself as small and shriveled with a silver curlicue wig, fake eyelashes, an easily discernible girdle to hold her figure the way it used to be, and enough makeup for pretty much any stage play. He thought she batted her eyes at him, but Archer couldn't be sure; the light was tricky, and so might she be.

The woman led him into a small front room piled with two things: furniture and cats. He had no objection to the first, and none really to the second. Even when three of them wrapped themselves around his ankles and one plopped on his lap when he sat down. However, when a fifth musketeer climbed on his shoulders he did file an objection with the court and picked it off, placing it on a couch. Set across the breadth of the room on a variety of surfaces were pink seashells burned brittle by the sun, frilly hassocks, an abundance of pincushions, and framed photos with dainty, dust-catching doilies underneath. Against one wall was a prewar phonograph on a table with a stack of records beside it. A large cabinet TV was next to it.

She sat across from him, her features somber. Her thin, fragile lips trembled. 'A policeman came by to ask questions. He said a man had been found dead. In dear Ellie Lamb's home. I can't believe it. Is she all right? He didn't say.'

'We don't know. We can't find her. When's the last time you saw her?'

'Yesterday.'

'You remember the time?' Archer asked as he plucked the lap cat off because it was starting to claw his crotch.

She tapped her thumb against her mouth. 'Time, time . . . it's so difficult, you know.'

Archer took out his notebook and pencil and chewed on the eraser end. 'Well, let me help you out. Was it daytime or nighttime? Let's start with that and work our way along.'

'Oh, the daytime, certainly the sun was still up.'

'How long does the sun stay up in the canyon this time of year?'

'Oh, not that long. Three or four p.m. at the most.'

'Okay, was the sun starting to go down when you saw her?'

'Oh, I see what you're doing. How clever.'

'Yes, ma'am, I certainly try.'

'I think the sun was going down. Yes, it was definitely growing dark.'

'Was she walking? Driving? Did she come by to see you?'

'She drove by in her car, that little silver one.'

'You didn't see her after that?'

'No.'

'Did you see anyone else around yesterday?'

'No, the Bonhams are in France. I told the nice policeman that, too.'

'But other people live on this road.'

'Yes, but these three are the only houses around here. The others are farther down, or farther up, and they're around long bends.'

'Okay, you ever see a dark blue four-door Ford parked across the street from Lamb's house?'

She looked uncertain. 'No, I don't believe so.'

'Do the Bonhams have a car?'

'They do, but they drove it to the airport before they flew to France.'

'When was that?'

'They left about a month ago. They like to spend time there. She's French.'

'They fly out of LA International?'

'That's right.' Her expression grew animated. 'I went to Europe back in 1921. My husband, Oliver, and I went by ocean liner. We sailed out of New York and over to Southampton. We got dressed up and danced every night. It was very romantic.'

'I'm sure.'

'Oh, where are my manners? Would you like something to drink? I have coffee, orange juice, or scotch.'

Archer was a bit taken aback by this wide selection.

'Um, I don't know. What do you usually have?'

'Don't let me influence you, young man. But I don't like coffee or orange juice. On the other hand, I am partial to scotch.'

Archer glanced at a grandfather clock in the corner to check the time. 'I guess a finger of scotch would be fine.'

She clapped her small hands together. 'Oh good, I was hoping for a visitor today so I could open the bottle. I don't like to drink alone, and the cats don't count. And the nice policeman was on duty and couldn't imbibe.'

She left and came back with two large scotches. Archer noted that his finger of liquor had transformed into a hand.

He took a sip while she seemed to prefer a long swallow.

'So, do the Bonhams just leave their place unoccupied?'

'Oh, no. They have a gardener who comes. He makes sure everything is all right. And I keep my eyes open, too. We've never had a bit of trouble.' She took another taste of her scotch and wiped her small mouth with a hanky plucked from her sleeve. 'Until now, of course. Do you think it's the work of gangs?'

He hiked his eyebrows at that one. 'Do you have gangs up here?'

'I don't know.' She glanced at the TV. 'I do watch *Dragnet*. They seem to have violent criminals all over.'

'Do the Bonhams have kids?'

'Oh, no. That's why they can pick up and travel to France for months at a time.'

'What can you tell me about Eleanor Lamb?'

'She helps me with my cats and goes to the store

82

for me. I don't drive anymore.'

'And your husband?'

'Oliver died in 1943. He went out to water the plants and dropped dead in the flower bed.'

'I'm sorry. Do you have any family left?'

'Yes, my daughter, and my grandchildren, but they never visit. They live in Hartford. Her husband is an insurance executive. Apparently being an insurance executive requires one to live in Connecticut.'

'So, anything else on Lamb?'

'She was a writer.'

'Past tense?' said Archer.

She caught a breath and looked embarrassed. 'I didn't mean that. But there's so much evil out there. You hear of a young woman missing and you assume the worst. They never did solve the Black Dahlia murder, you know. Someone cut the poor woman in half and drained all her blood.' She looked both sick and intrigued. 'How demented do you have to be?'

'Pretty demented. So, did she have any visitors? Boyfriends? Lady friends? Not the Black Dahlia, Eleanor Lamb.'

'I never saw any. She lived a very quiet life.'

'She ever talk to you about any problems?'

'Like what?'

'Anything, really. I heard she stopped going into the office and was writing at home.'

'I didn't know that.'

'I also heard that she moved out here to be closer to a friend.'

Danforth looked genuinely puzzled by this. 'I didn't meet her until she moved here, and that was about two years or so ago. I don't believe she knew the Bonhams before. She never mentioned anyone else.'

'Did she make many changes to her house?'

'Oh, yes. I went over there once while they were working. I knew the Hendersons, who lived there before. Ellie had the pool put in and the kitchen and bathrooms updated and, well, everything lightened up.'

'What can you tell me about the Bonhams?'

'Oh, Bernadette and Peter are delightful. They have another home in Paris.'

'Paris, huh? They must have some serious dough.'

'Oh, they do. Peter is very successful in business.'

'What kind of business?'

'Well, I heard that he worked overseas, sort of hush-hush. Maybe he was a spy. How thrilling that would be. Then he came back and then, oh, I guess he made money the way men usually make money.'

'And their ages?'

'Peter is over fifty. But Bernadette is only forty.'

'Second wife?'

'Oh no, it's his first.'

'You say you don't drive, but do you have a car?'

'Yes, it's in the garage. It belonged to my husband. It's a Buick Roadmaster. Oliver only had it two years before he passed. I'm old enough to remember when there were no cars. Just horses and buggies. I was originally from Oklahoma. I moved out here when I was a young girl because my mother thought the sea air would be good for her.'

'And your father?'

'That was the other reason my mother moved out here. To get away from him.'

'You mind if I have a look at the car?'

'Help yourself.'

'So, you didn't see Lamb after around three or so?

But did you see a cab or another car come up here after she got back home?'

'Oh, that's right. I *did* see a taxi yesterday evening around six, one of those yellow ones. I was eating dinner on a TV tray and looking out the bay window. I went to the door to see where it was going and it turned into her driveway. She must have called for it. I assume she was going out to celebrate the New Year. I just stayed home with my cats and drank a glass of champagne at eight thirty. I can't stay up until midnight anymore. I'm too ancient. And I've celebrated over eighty new years. It sort of loses its luster after that.'

Archer knew that the cab was probably taking Lamb to Chasen's. The only question was: Had she ever come back? She hadn't been at the Marses' party as far as Archer knew, but he would have to confirm that. So where had she gone between Chasen's and when he was getting his head pummeled at her house?

'And you wouldn't have seen the cab bring her back because you were asleep?'

'If it was after eight thirty, no.'

'What time did you get up this morning?'

'Oh, around seven thirty. Slept like a baby.'

Archer rubbed the back of his head. 'Yeah, me too.' He rose and handed her one of his cards. 'If you remember anything else you can ring me on this number. You can reverse the charges. It's in Bay Town.'

She took the card with fingers that were trembling. 'Do . . . do you think anything has happened to dear, sweet Ellie?'

'I wish I could answer that for you, Mrs. Danforth. I'm certainly going to try.'

16

Archer gazed in wonder at the four-door convertible Buick Roadmaster. It was thousands of pounds of metal and chrome with a grille and bumper that looked like the mouth of a saber-toothed tiger hunting for its dinner. Its interior was large enough to seat an Army platoon. Detroit knew how to make them back then.

He peered under the car to see if there was an oil slick. There wasn't. The tires looked dry rotted, and the interior smelled like no one had been inside since Mr. Danforth had fallen dead into the flowers. He was pretty certain the thing wouldn't even start. And since he saw a pair of car keys hanging on a hook, he took the opportunity to test his theory.

Deader than a doornail. Wouldn't even turn over.

He left Danforth's, got back to his car, and headed down the canyon road.

He stopped at a 76 service station, looked up the phone number, and made another call to Green and Ransome.

'Yes?' said the voice.

For one frozen moment, Archer thought it might be Eleanor Lamb.

'Who is this?'

'Who is *this*?' the woman countered.

Now Archer knew it wasn't Lamb.

He explained who he was and why he was calling.

'Oh my God,' said the woman. 'I can't believe this.'

'And you are?'

'What? Oh, I'm Cecily Ransome.'

'I tried earlier but no one answered. Don't you have a service?'

'We're in the process of changing who we use. There's been a gap, unfortunately, but we didn't think it would matter over the holidays.'

'Look, will you be there for a while? I'd like to come by and ask some questions.'

'Yes, certainly. I'll be here.'

'Have the police contacted you yet?'

'No, do you think they will?'

'The county boys are very thorough. I can be there in about an hour because I'd like to speak to you before they do.'

'All right, Mr. Archer. I'll see you then. I'll be in the lobby to let you in. The building is technically closed today, of course.'

The Delahaye soared like an eagle, and he made it to Beverly Hills in fifty-five minutes. The production company's offices were in a sleek, modern five-story glass-and-chrome building that trumpeted both money and prestige. He parked at the curb and strode to the bank of metal-wrapped glass front doors. One opened and there, presumably, was Cecily Ransome.

She was about Archer's age, and the same height as Callahan, but there all resemblance stopped. Her hair was inky black and hung limply to her shoulders. She possessed the lean hips of a teenage boy and the broad shoulders of a man. She was dressed in dark slacks and a white jacket with canvas tennis shoes that showed off bare ankles. Her blouse was made of silk chiffon, and she didn't appear to be wearing a bra under it.

Whether these were her ordinary working duds

or her New Year's Day casual getup, or whether she hadn't been home since the clock had struck midnight, he didn't know. Her features were attractive if eclectic; she wore no makeup, not even eyeliner or rouge. Her eyes were big enough without any such aid, and their mossy shade of green exercised some emotional pull on him; he wasn't sure exactly what.

'Mr. Archer?'

'That's me,' he said, showing her his license.

'I'm Cecily Ransome. Please come in.'

They went up to the top floor in an automatic elevator. Archer had noted that the lobby was as sleek and minimalist in decoration as the exterior, but he still could tell everything here had cost a pretty penny. The lobby marquee had been full of companies with successful-sounding names. And with the rents that Archer knew they charged here, it couldn't be all hot air; these companies were successful.

She led the way down a plushly carpeted hall and unlocked a massive wooden door with nice moldings, then ushered him into the cinematic kingdom of Green and Ransome Productions.

'Nice,' said Archer as he glanced around at the trimly outfitted interior. It reminded him of a ship's cabin: lots of stainless steel, marble, wood, and no clutter. Potted plants danced in the late-afternoon sunlight coming through floor-to-ceiling windows. There was a receptionist's desk, walls of bookshelves with scripts bound in leather, and an abundance of film awards. On the walls were photos of a number of celebrities of the day — all of them signed, he noted.

'It's a wonderfully quiet place to create, because the film business is so frenetic otherwise. And we're right in the thick of things here. Unless we have to go

88

out to the Valley or away on location, everything else is right here.'

'Got a lot of film projects going?'

'Maybe too many. Ever since the war ended, people want entertainment and lots of it.'

'I hear TV is really taking off.'

'It is. We're involved in that, too. Have you heard of *situation comedies*?'

'No, but I've always been more of a radio man myself.'

'They seem rather trite to me, but people like to laugh.'

'I tend to work in the land of frowns and tears.'

'We can meet in my office.'

She led him down another hall and opened the door. She clicked on the light and he entered and glanced around. The space was a good size, about twenty by twenty. There was a bleached mahogany desk with a deluxe Smith-Corona typewriter, lots of pens and pencils in a round holder, a few legal pads with notes in neat cursive, a Dictaphone, and a regular phone next to a metal-shrouded Wheeldex that Archer was certain was filled with the current movers and shakers of Hollywood. A wooden chair with back and seat cushions was in the kneehole; a small couch and two chairs were clustered around a low wooden coffee table.

On the walls were framed movie posters. Archer noted the credit lines showed Ransome to be both writer and director on all of them. He recognized a few but had seen none of them. After his experiences in the war, no celluloid images could come close to rousing his emotional interest. The windows were covered with dark rollerblinds.

89

On the built-in shelves dotting the walls were stacks of movie scripts and books.

'Would you like some coffee? We have a pot in the kitchen.'

'Thanks. Just black for me.'

'I drink a lot of coffee. I think most writers do.'

She left and came back in with two cups of coffee in white mugs. Archer had spent the time walking around her office and taking a closer look at things. He had settled on the couch by the time she returned.

They sipped their coffees and Archer said, 'If you don't mind my saying, you're sort of young to be partners with a guy like Bart Green. He's been described to me as kind of a big cheese in this town and has been for a long time.'

'He is, and I *am* fortunate. But I bring a different generational perspective to the business. What entertained people even ten years ago no longer does. We have to keep up.'

'Okay, so when was the last time you heard from Lamb?'

'She worked at home yesterday. She phoned here yesterday morning with some questions on a project.'

So before the man was dead.

'I understand she's been working at home lately instead of coming to the office.'

'She has. But there's nothing unusual about that. I do too, sometimes. As long as the work gets done, we don't care where people write. Writers often need to cocoon.'

'She sound okay?'

'Yes, totally fine. Look, did they really find a dead body at her house?'

Archer was a bit surprised by this clumsy segue. 'Yes, they *really* did. That's why I'm here.'

She sat back and coolly appraised him now. Archer could feel her friendly veneer start to slide off her back like a skin-shedding snake. He actually preferred things that way. It saved time. He needed to understand the real Ransome, not a caricature presented for someone's agenda.

She shook out a cigarette from a pack of Camels and lit up. 'I write and direct films about the dark side of life, Mr. Archer, but I've never *personally* experienced it. You must forgive my naivete.'

'I can forgive a lot and have.'

'You might be a good source of material for me.'

'I might. On her call with you did she mention that she was going out anywhere yesterday afternoon?'

'No.'

'I saw her last night. She knows the actress I was having dinner with. When she found out I was a detective, she said she wanted to retain me. I was supposed to meet her here today to finalize things, and then we were going to drive out to Malibu. Then the body shows up on her doorstep and she's vanished.'

'Who was the actress?'

'Why?'

'Just professional curiosity.'

'Liberty Callahan.'

'Okay, I think I've heard her name.' But the way the woman said it, Archer thought she was just being polite. 'Why would Ellie need a detective?'

'She said she thought someone was trying to kill her. She ever mention any concerns like that to you?'

Ransome looked genuinely surprised by this revelation. 'No, never.'

'She was invited to Danny Mars's party, but I don't think she made an appearance. I understand that you and Bart Green were at another party.'

'Actually, we were at several. You have to make the rounds. I was bored beyond belief, but at least most places had good liquor. It made up for the lack of interesting conversation.'

'And what conversation do you find interesting?'

Her gaze roamed over him. 'Did you know that we detonated a hydrogen bomb in November over an atoll in the Pacific? And that the Soviets are rushing to do the very same thing? It's insane. And human beings are imperfect.'

'Meaning they make mistakes,' said Archer.

'You make a mistake with a hydrogen bomb, you could kill a million people. And worse, it might not be a mistake, it might be intentional. Because in addition to being imperfect some human beings are cruel and like to hurt people.'

'I can see how you would be very popular at New Year's Eve parties.'

Archer did not mean that as an insult and Ransome did not seem to take it as such.

'I make my movies with a certain viewpoint, with a message that I hope transfers in some way to the people watching. But sometimes I really wonder if I have any impact at all.'

'I certainly don't want a hydrogen bomb dropped on my head. But right now, I'm just concerned with the safety of one person — Eleanor Lamb.'

'I'm sorry, Mr. Archer. I carry my soapbox with me everywhere. It's an existential threat to my continued relevancy in this industry.'

'I'm sure. And you got back home when last night?'

92

She puffed on her cigarette. 'Why is that of any concern?'

'We detectives ask a lot of questions, some may seem nonsensical.'

'Yes, they do. I got in around two.'

'Do you live around here?'

'My house is near the Beverly Hills Hotel, or the 'Pink Palace,' as some now call it.'

'Nice, easy commute for you, though.'

'Nice enough.'

'Can I see her office?'

'Why?'

'We detectives also look for *clues*. There might be some in there.' Archer hunched forward. 'And let's not lose sight of the fact that a dead man was in Lamb's house, her car is still in her carport, her clothes are still in her closet, she's nowhere to be found, and no one's heard from her since around seven thirty last night. As someone who does this for a living, I can tell you this is about as serious as it gets if you care about finding her.'

'Which I very much do,' Ransome fired back.

He rose. 'Her office?'

17

Lamb's office was two doors down from Ransome's and about half the size. Unlike Ransome's, it was cluttered and claustrophobic.

'Shall I leave you to it?' said Ransome. 'I know the timing is lousy, but I do have some things I need to get done. It's why I came in today.'

'I'll poke my head in when I'm finished here.'

She left him there, and Archer started going through things. Lamb certainly had a lot of film projects going. However, he didn't find much at all to help him, until he jimmied the locked bottom drawer of her desk. He took out the book of matches, one of a half dozen located there and all from the same place: the Jade Lion Bar in Chinatown.

He looked at his notebook, where he'd written down the two names from Lamb's Wheeldex cards marked with the *X*. One had the name Jonathan Brewster, and written under that had been the Jade Lion Bar, Chinatown. The other card had the name Alice Jacoby written on it along with a phone number. He picked up the phone on Lamb's desk and dialed the number.

Someone answered on the second ring.

'Is this Alice Jacoby?'

'Yes, who is this?'

Archer told her who he was and why he was calling.

'Oh my goodness. I . . . I haven't seen Ellie in over a week. I hope she's okay.'

'Can I come by and see you later?' asked Archer. 'The sooner we find her the better.'

94

'Yes, yes of course. My home is in Bel Air, near the country club.'

Bel Air? thought Archer. *And near the country club.* 'Say in about forty minutes? I'm just finishing up another line of investigation.'

She gave him her address. Archer wrote it down and hung up.

He looked through the office once more and then left and walked to Ransome's door. He didn't knock right away because he heard Ransome speaking. Apparently to someone on the phone because he only heard her voice. And then he heard his name spoken twice, with some urgency. As he bent closer to the door he heard Ransome say clearly, 'I can meet you tonight, around seven, at Boleros.'

Archer knew the place. It was a dive bar in West Hollywood.

When she put down the phone he stepped back down the hall, then walked loudly forward and knocked on her office door.

'Miss Ransome?'

'Come in.' She looked up at him from her desk. 'Did you find anything helpful?'

'We'll see. Tell me, were you close with Lamb? Or was she just an employee here?'

She said slowly, 'We worked together. I appreciate her talents. We got along fine.'

He looked over her appearance. 'I think she appreciated you, too.'

'Did she say that?' Ransome asked with a level of anxiousness that seemed off to him.

But then again, maybe not, Archer thought. 'She didn't have to.' He handed her a card. 'If you think of anything else,' he said.

95

'What are you going to do now?' she asked.

'Keep digging.' He started to leave. 'That's how investigations work.'

'Wait a minute, Mr. Archer. You said you were going to meet Ellie here today and she was going to give you a check?'

'For my retainer, yes.'

'How much?'

'Two hundred up front. I charge fifty a day plus expenses. I've officially been on the clock since around noon.' He was not going to charge for last night's fiasco as a matter of personal pride, and also for his being an idiot.

Ransome opened a drawer and pulled out a checkbook. 'How about I write you a check for $500?'

'That's too much, and you're not the client.'

'If you don't use it all, you can pay me back. And as far as the client, I just want you to find her, okay? And I'm sure she'd want that, too.'

'Okay. You can make it out to the Willie Dash Private Detective Agency.' Archer took out a sheaf of papers from his jacket pocket. 'And here's a contract for you to sign. My boss is a stickler for the rules. I was going to have Lamb sign it, but . . .'

'Of course.'

She made the check out and passed it across to him. Then he filled in the contract using her pen and had her sign it. He gave her a copy and put his and the check in his pocket. 'You really care about her, I take it.'

'Just find her, Mr. Archer.'

He tipped his hat, shielding his bandaged head from her sight line, and let himself out.

It appeared that Archer had a new client. Now he just needed to find the old one.

18

Bel Air had been founded in the twenties by an oil millionaire who apparently wanted separation from those without barges of money, and this place certainly fit the part. It was off Sunset within a rock's throw of the UCLA campus. Archer passed through massive Spanish gates and headed up to the land of the wealthy and high-minded. The LAPD's bunco squad was kept busy in Bel Air, he knew, because the con artists swarmed here to relieve old widows of what their hubbies had left them. And these same very dead men had left many a disappointed mistress in the lurch, with nothing but broken promises and memories of late-night hotel visits. And, if they were lucky, the occasional private plane trip to Acapulco when the wives were away visiting family.

The driveway to Alice Jacoby's house was nearly as long as a runway. When he rounded the last curve and saw the house ahead, he just had to whistle. In his work he had seen a lot of wealth and a good deal of poverty; he had never seen much in between.

The mansion conveyed the impression of quiet, refined elegance. It was the best of classic European and American architecture melded together with functionality. Archer thought these folks might be an anomaly: rich people with good taste. In his experience too much money often tended to deliver crass instead of class.

He parked in front of the round-columned colonnade and got out. Before he could even knock, one

97

of the ten-foot-tall rounded double doors with knobs the size of coconuts opened, and an old man with a creaky back and dressed in a butler's uniform stood there like a statue.

Archer stared back at him, waiting for the statue to speak. The way the man was peering up at him, he seemed to think that Archer had missed the service porch entrance.

Archer introduced himself and added, 'The lady of the house is expecting me.'

The statue hinged painfully at the waist. 'Yes, Mr. Archer. She is. This way.'

And so Archer went that way. They passed rooms where two uniformed maids were dusting and vacuuming and apparently getting things just so for the evening.

He was deposited into a room nearly as large as a pope's cathedral, but a bit more welcoming. A fire was lit in a fireplace cavernous enough for him to stand in. The furniture was costly, elegant, not too much, not too little. He felt like he could breathe in here, unlike back at Mrs. Danforth's place, and not just because of the cats. He saw a stainless steel cocktail bar set up against the wall with jiggers and tumblers and shakers and a soda dispenser bottle and an ice bucket with a fresh layer of condensation on the sides like downy dew on grass. His lips started moving as he read over the assortment of whiskeys, gins, and bourbons. Detecting was thirsty work.

'Mr. Archer?'

He turned to look at the woman who had appeared in the arched doorway.

She was around forty, five-eight with a blocky build that was well nourished, a wide face, a long, smooth brow, and a pair of friendly, intelligent blue eyes. Her brown hair was wrapped in an elaborate French braid, and draped over one shoulder.

Her day dress accentuated her formidable hips. She had on sheer stockings that highlighted her muscled calves and slender ankles. She was an attractive woman who held herself with poise and confidence, though in those blue eyes Archer could detect some nervousness. That could just be because of his line of work. He was rarely around happy people, because happy people were never in need of his services.

'Yes. Mrs. Jacoby?'

They shook hands and she said the magic words. 'Would you like a drink?'

'If you're having something, whiskey and water would be great, no ice. I can mix it.'

She brought over the two glasses and a stirrer and Archer did the alchemy, leaving out most of the water. He noted that she opted for a bourbon and soda on the rocks with a wedge of lime. He had watched her make it with a practiced hand. He thought that bar must get a lot of use. Some people just loved alcohol and also had a happy marriage. They were in the minority, he'd found.

They sat in high-backed chairs by the fire.

'So, please tell me what's happened to Ellie.'

Archer gave her a more detailed account, only leaving out the fact of his falling face-first over the body. He was going to take that one to the grave, unless the county cops beat it out of him first.

'And how do you know her?'

'We went to college together back in Boston, then I moved out here and she came later. She went into writing. I went into set design. I work at Warner Brothers.'

99

Archer looked around. 'Which explains this place. It's got an artist's eye.'

'I could never afford a home like this on my own, of course. My husband is in finance, and he also comes from money. In fact, this was his parents' home. Simon's firm underwrites a great many film productions. He got into the field because of his father, who was a very successful producer. There were lots of connections available for him, you see.'

'I absolutely *see*. Business is good, I take it?'

'Hollywood is hitting on all cylinders, as my husband likes to say.'

'Any kids?'

'Three. The oldest just turned twelve.'

'Nice. You mentioned you and Lamb went to college together back east?'

'Yes, at Wellesley. I was an art major and Ellie was an Agora.'

Archer set his drink down. 'Art I get, but what's an Agora? It sounds like one of those islands in the Caribbean.'

Jacoby smiled weakly. 'She was a history and political science major, and belonged to the *Agora* Society. They don't have sororities at Wellesley, Mr. Archer, so these college societies became sort of like a sorority would be for us. Before she moved here, Ellie worked in Washington, D.C., as an intern or aide. She's very smart, very . . . worldly, I guess you can say, unlike me. Her father was in the diplomatic corps. Consequently, she's traveled all over. She can speak two or three foreign languages. I think that's why she's in such high demand as a writer. The studios like her renaissance quality, her je ne sais quoi, if you will.'

'Now, that's a term you don't hear every day. I

100

spoke to Cecily Ransome, earlier. She is very concerned about Lamb and even hired me to find her.'

Jacoby looked into the fire for a moment, her features distant and opaque. 'Cecily's taken Hollywood by storm. She came at a good time — the war was over and sensibilities and expectations were changing. We came out of that dreadful time a more hopeful, but also a more sober, country,' she said, her wide shoulders slumping.

'After I came back from the fighting I wasn't *sober* for about a year.'

She smiled briefly. 'But I think people want something new, something different.'

'And Ransome can deliver that?'

'She's done over a dozen pictures already, most of them with the major studios. Each one more daring and provocative than the last. They sometimes blanch at how far she goes and won't write the check or allow their stars to appear, and then she just turns to one of the minor outfits, and enlists fine actors and gets her films done. They all make money because she has a devoted and growing following, and they get a lot of attention from the press. The studios *love* free publicity. She directs, too. That is very rare.'

'Have you done any of her set designs?'

Jacoby chortled over her bourbon, though he saw there was no corresponding levity in her features. 'Our tastes and sensibilities are *not* simpatico, Mr. Archer. The reality is my schtick is fairly simple: I do the grand ballrooms, libraries, pools, and lavish bedroom sets. Early on in my career, I cut my teeth on screwball comedies with Ginger Rogers and Fred Astaire, and Carole Lombard and William Powell.' She smiled. 'I referred to them as 'gowns and good golly' pictures.

The cinematic effect was wealth beyond all reckoning, but in the form of a comedy. I mean, no one really lives like that.'

Archer made a show of looking around and said, 'Could've fooled me.'

She flushed at his words, but then smiled and said, 'Touché.'

'Hey, live and let live. And if you work for Warners, I know you work hard.'

'The sets are wonderful to create. I could live out every fantasy I had.' She glanced at him before continuing. 'I guess you would be surprised to know that I grew up in a small town in West Virginia where my father was a coal miner, and we lived in a shack in the *hollers*.'

Archer lifted his eyebrows. 'You've come a long way from a valley in West Virginia. And I don't hear any accent.'

'I spent a lot of money getting rid of it. People do that here, you know.'

'Do what?'

'Reimagine themselves. When I was a little girl, I would go to the one little store in town and leaf through the fashion and movie magazines and dream about . . . something better.' Her voice trailed off and she looked down into her bourbon like maybe other dreams were hiding in there for her to find.

Archer let her hang out there for a moment. He appreciated the background information she had just given him, without his having to ask a single question. He had learned that silence was sometimes a PI's best tool. And the more he learned about Lamb's friends, the more, ultimately, he would learn about her.

But he felt he had figured out something about

102

Jacoby already. An image appeared in his mind, prompted by her name: Alice in Wonderland.

She's going down every rabbit hole looking for something that she doesn't have. And she'll keep doing it until her last breath.

'And Cecily Ransome's work?' prompted Archer finally.

'Her stories are gritty and, to put it bluntly, shorn of all decoration. She's an actor's director, meaning the story is absolutely centered on their performances and the dialogue, not the accoutrements that I typically provide.' She looked off for a moment, as though she was seeing things she didn't want to necessarily confront. 'She represents a new age, at least for women. I think she has a shot at being one of the great ones when all is said and done.'

'And her partner, Bart Green?'

Archer noted that the woman changed color and took a quick sip of her bourbon before answering. 'I've worked in this town for nearly twenty years, Mr. Archer, and they are one of the oddest business couples I've ever seen. Don't get me wrong, Bart Green has been immensely successful. But let's just say his bread and butter is what Hollywood has been churning out for decades. Nothing daring, nothing that would shock a grandmother's sensibilities. And he has made a fabulous living doing so.'

'But he doesn't quite have the je ne sais quoi of Cecily Ransome?'

'No, he doesn't, hence my description of them as an odd couple.'

'So why do you think they ended up as business partners?'

'Bart Green may have a meat-and-potatoes idea

103

of what films can and should be, but he is also very canny, and quick to spot talent. I think he knows that in the very near future the sorts of films he has the wherewithal to make will no longer be popular. And he also knows that Cecily's films will not only appeal to the new audiences coming to the theaters, but will also be award winners and stand the test of time. In this town little Oscar is solid gold in more ways than you can count. Did you know they're going to televise the Academy Awards for the first time ever this year?'

'No, I didn't, but I'm not in the business.'

She said wistfully, 'Bart has all the money he needs. Now he just wants a fitting legacy, at least that's my take. So he brought Cecily in and she has a free hand to do what she wants.'

'And you got all this from her or Lamb?' asked Archer.

'Mostly from Ellie and a few others, but Cecily and I are acquaintances as well. At least I hope she regards me as such,' she added.

Archer cocked his head. He wasn't in the business, per se, but he had been around the film world long enough to have figured some things out. And he could read people better than most. 'Do I see a desire to build bare-bones — deeply in the background so actors can emote — set designs on a Cecily Ransome *bohemian* production one day?'

She smiled coyly and raised her glass to him. 'My, my. I've been married for over thirteen years, and my dear husband would have no idea what you're even talking about.'

'You said you hadn't *seen* Lamb for a week. But had you *spoken* to her after that?'

'Yes, a few times. We were actually supposed to have

104

lunch tomorrow, at the Warners commissary.'

'She sound okay?'

'Yes, nothing out of the ordinary. Nothing that would explain what has happened.'

Archer took the matchbook out. 'You ever been to the Jade Lion Bar with her?'

She blinked rapidly. 'The Jade Lion Bar? Where is it?'

'Chinatown.'

'I don't go to Chinatown, Mr. Archer, and I don't know anyone who does. I don't believe it's safe for people like me.'

'Well, speaking on behalf of people like *me*, I've been there, it's not that bad. And your friend had a half dozen of these in her desk drawer.'

'I don't know why she would have them.'

'Okay, do you know a Jonathan Brewster?' he asked.

'Jonathan Brewster? No, I've never heard of him.'

'Do you have a recent snapshot of Lamb?'

'Why?' she said sharply.

'Well, when a person is missing it's helpful to have a picture of her I can show around to see if someone has seen her.' He'd meant to ask Ransome for one but had forgotten, and he'd found none at Lamb's house, which was curious in itself.

'Oh, of course. Give me a moment.'

While she was gone, Archer walked over to the wall next to the fireplace and eyed the long, framed photo there.

The caption read, WELLESLEY CLASS OF 1934.

He scanned the rows of smiling women. There was a younger and thinner Alice Jacoby beaming away and looking like the sun would never set on her dreams. And to her left and one down from her was

105

the diminutive Eleanor Lamb. She was blond, with what looked to Archer to be natural curls. And she wasn't smiling.

Jacoby walked back in and handed him the snapshot. It was her and Lamb arm in arm. The background was the Pacific and there was sand under their feet. They were dressed in jeans and matching white cable-knit sweaters.

'That was taken last January.'

'Malibu?' said Archer.

She gave him a surprised look. 'Yes, that's right. How did you know?'

'Just a lucky guess. Thanks. I may be back for some more questions if that's okay.'

'Oh, yes, anything to help.' She took out a business card from her dress pocket. 'Here's my number at Warners. I'm usually there during the week.'

He left without need of the hinged butler leading him.

He climbed into the Delahaye and looked at the photo once more.

Jacoby was again beaming. She did it quite well, he had to admit.

Eleanor Lamb, on the other hand, looked like she wanted to murder someone.

Which made Archer wonder if the worldly writer with a Wellesley degree had.

19

Archer drove back to Callahan's and found a note inside saying that she had slipped out to run some errands and would be back around six thirty, and what did he want to do for dinner.

He called Willie Dash's office, and this time the man himself picked up.

'Willie, it's Archer.'

'I was hoping it would be you. Now, I want to hear everything you told Connie, plus everything else you've found out since you talked to her. I doubt you've been dragging your feet. If anything, you sometimes move *too* fast.'

Archer complied, ending on his conversation with Alice Jacoby.

'Malibu, Bel Air, and Beverly Hills, huh? You're running in some high circles, Archer, and some dangerous ones.'

'It's not by choice.'

'It *was* your choice to hustle work in LA, *and* to take this case.'

'True.'

'I know Phil Oldham. He'll seem like a nice guy right before he rips your heart out and drops you in a cell for nothing much. You watch yourself around him and his boys.'

'I will.'

'Connie told me about the guys you ran into on the beach.'

'Yeah. I was just wrong place, wrong time. Has to

107

be smugglers, don't you think?'

'There used to be gun and rum runners in Malibu years ago, especially during Prohibition. Hell, Ramirez Canyon used to be called Whiskey Gulch. I'll let you figure that one out. The whole coast down there was a smuggler's paradise. Portuguese Bend, Rancho Palos Verdes. The mother boat stays out to sea and they run the small fast boats to shore with the stuff and a lot of manpower. Quick in and out.'

'Sounds exactly like what I saw last night.'

'You were lucky, Archer. You might not be so lucky next time.'

'I'm not going after smugglers. Just a missing writer.'

'So, the Jade Lion Bar.'

'You know it?' said Archer.

'I don't have to. I got nothing against the Chinese, but you can't go in there thinking normal rules apply because they don't. Thirty-forty years ago you had opium dens and gambling houses and whorehouses and Tong warfare all over. That's been cleaned up since they knocked down old Chinatown to build Union Station and they all got moved to what used to be Little Italy a mile away. Now the place has nice shops and restaurants and nice people living and working there, just like they do in other communities. But just like in other communities, you got good and you got not so good and you got really bad. And the really bad places all have the same MO.'

'Namely?'

'Their side business is selling one thing — booze, food, medicine. Their main act is always selling something else and it's the something else that breaks a book's worth of statutes.'

'Well, Lamb might have been a frequent visitor to it.'

'I understand your interest.'

'Did you find out anything on Cedric Bender?'

'He's in our line of work, Archer.'

'You mean he's a PI?'

'And apparently a respected one. I got a physical description for you.' Archer heard paper rustling. Dash said, 'Five-ten, heavy set, thinning gray hair, in his fifties.'

'That matches the dead guy. And his car is missing, too.'

'So the questions are who killed him, where, and why? And what did they do with his ride?'

'He had to have a connection to Lamb.'

'Why?'

'I found him in her house!'

'You can't jump to that conclusion. Someone could have dumped his body there to incriminate her.'

'I actually fed that line to Oldham. He didn't bite on it.'

'And the guy who answered the phone couldn't be Bender. He was already dead.'

'Maybe it was the guy who killed him.'

'Killers don't normally answer phones. And since it looks like he was killed elsewhere, chances are they dumped him there for some reason. And that reason isn't good for Lamb, since it's put the county cops right on her doorstep. She may have gone on the run. And she might not be running just from the likes of Phil Oldham.'

'Or else she's dead. And then there's the matter of who knocked me out.'

'Could've been the guy who answered the phone. Or it might have been Lamb. Big enough sap and enough motivation, even a lady could lay your butt out, Archer.'

'Makes me wonder why they didn't finish the job with me.'

'Could be simple. They had one body to deal with and didn't want another one.'

'So you think whoever killed Bender is trying to frame Lamb?'

'Considering they had the world's biggest ocean right next door to dump him in but used her home sweet home instead, it's a plausible theory. What's your next move?'

'I've got one lead to follow up with and then I'm going to hit this Jade Lion Bar tonight and see what shakes out.'

'You want me to come down?'

'I can handle it, for now. When I can't you'll be the first to know.'

'How's Liberty?'

'If anything, even more beautiful.'

'Oh, Archer, you got it so bad, son.'

20

Archer put the phone down and looked at his watch. It was almost six. He scribbled a note to Callahan and went back out to the Delahaye. He drove to Boleros and parked on a side street to hide it from sight, since Ransome had already seen the car. He passed by competing billboards for the Roy Rogers TV show and Gene Autry's program. Both men were in full frontier regalia. Rogers held a pearl-handled six-shooter, while Autry brandished a fancy guitar. There wasn't a speck of dust or dirt on their colorful cowboy duds. Their smiles were sparkling white even in the growing gloom. This made him think of Jacoby's comments on maybe a more sobering and substantive dawn coming for the country. Well, Archer, for one, thought it was long overdue.

He walked into Boleros and looked around. It was pretty much like every other dive bar he'd been in. Wooden stools worn down by drunken butts, a slick, scarred bar with a string of names either carved by knife or via the long fingernails of the inebriated, a few rickety tables, a scattering of more private booths, three tiered rows of bottles behind the bar, and cigarette smoke grazing the ceiling like trapped clouds. The only things that looked out of place were a battered and dusty black baby grand piano with fake gold trim by the window, and a cadaverous old man dressed in a tux from the early forties with a tacky white carnation pinned to his lapel sitting at the piano. He had a toothpick dangling from bloodless

111

lips and an old bowler hat pushed back on his mostly bald head. He was pecking out an Andrews Sisters tune that was impressing truly nobody, not even him. When someone dropped a dime into the neon juke-box and Eddie Fisher came on to sing 'Tell Me Why,' the cadaver got up to hit the men's room.

The bar wasn't crowded yet but Archer knew that would change, particularly on a holiday. LA liked its booze and a place to sit and drink that was not home, particularly if you were married and your wife didn't understand you.

He picked the booth that would allow his back to be to the door, but also have him facing the mirror over the bar, enabling him to see anyone coming in. The woman who escorted him to that booth asked for his drink order. She was petite, in her early twenties, brown-haired, slim-hipped, and full of spunky attitude.

'Make it a cup of coffee black to start and we'll go from there. And make sure it's fresh.'

'Oh, what a dream customer you are.'

He slipped the woman a five and she clammed up and went away to fetch the coffee.

Archer kept his hat on to hide the bandage. He got his coffee, which was good and hot, and watched as it started to rain, the chilly drops pitter-pattering the glass like liquid bullets.

Archer suddenly remembered he hadn't had any food since his noontime breakfast. 'What do you have to eat in this place?' he asked the waitress.

She leaned down with a pouty look and said, 'Sand-wiches, potato chips on the side. And a fat pickle.'

'Any good?'

She put her elbows on the table. 'Tell you what,

112

dreamy, for another five I'll grill the rye and make it myself with love and kisses. A Reuben do it for you? We got *real* Russian dressing.'

'Sold, but go light on the Russian dressing.'

'Why?'

'Haven't you heard? We're in a Cold War.'

He ate while the rain drizzled down. The Reuben was warm and excellent, and Archer ate fast. He was finishing his last potato chip when, at seven on the dot, he saw her glide in. Cecily Ransome hadn't changed clothes since he'd seen her before, only now she was wearing a man's black fedora and a dark peacoat with a white scarf, because the rain had dropped the temperature. With the coat and her hair hidden inside the hat, she could have easily been mistaken for a man. She lowered her umbrella, looked around, and walked over to a corner booth on the other side of the room.

The jukebox had gone quiet for the moment, but the cadaver had come back from an extended performance in the john and was doing an Irving Berlin tune, badly. The growing number of people around the bar, both young and old, took turns glancing his way and probably wondering what the hell he was even doing here.

Then the cadaver stopped plunking keys. To Archer's surprise, he walked over and sat down across from Ransome. They immediately started talking in low voices.

When his waitress came by Archer said, 'What's with the piano player?'

She followed his gaze. 'We don't have a piano player. Least not anymore. Guy we had quit months ago. They don't pay nothing and the tips are lousy. And we got the jukebox now. They just don't want to

113

pay to have the piano moved out of here is all.'

'So what's with that guy?'

'He just walked in tonight and started playing.'

'And nobody thought to ask him why?'

'Hey, it's not my problem. If the guy wants to play, what's the big deal?'

'He a regular?'

'What's it to you?'

'Just to remind you, angel, I paid you ten dollars for a buck-fifty meal and thirty cents' worth of coffee. Can I at least get a passable return on my investment?'

'Okay, okay, I've never seen him before.'

'That's better. You know the lady?'

'She's been in a couple of times.'

'Alone or with someone?'

'Alone. Hey, how was the sandwich?'

'Much better than the pickle.'

She blew him a kiss. 'That's what they all say, dreamy. See, I don't make the pickles.'

A while later, Ransome leaned across the table and gave Cadaver a hug and a peck on the cheek before she left.

When the old man exited a minute later, Archer followed him out into the rain.

21

Ransome must've either driven to Boleros or gotten into a cab, because Archer didn't see her in any direction. Archer tugged up the collar on his jacket and angled his hat down farther over his face as the LA rain splattered over him.

Cadaver was up ahead and walking slowly. He didn't seem in a hurry to get out of the inclemency, and Archer wondered why. And he also wondered what he and Ransome had been talking about. He was obviously the man she had arranged to meet during the call he'd overheard from her office. A call in which Archer's name had been prominently mentioned. So that led him to suspect he wasn't uselessly chasing a shadow down a one-way street. But the kiss and hug at the end *had* surprised him. He didn't quite know what to make of that.

Cadaver surprised him again when he suddenly turned and walked directly up to Archer.

'You must be Mr. Archer. Name's Sam Malloy.' He put out a pale, veined hand, which Archer shook.

'Little café around the corner. Know you already had coffee back at Boleros, but I could use one. At my age, this chill gets right in your bones. I don't like LA this way. I only like the weather they have on the brochures. Sunny all day every day.'

Archer followed him around the corner and they got seated at a table near the back. Malloy took off his hat and set it on the chair next to him while Archer studied the man. He had tiny lines stamped all over his face.

They were of such fine detail that any cartographer would have been proud to claim ownership. His face was hairless and he had no eyebrows. The eyes were a translucent blue that made his skin seem paler still. There was a discernible edge of spirited life in his manner, and intelligence in the man's alert eyes. But Archer also saw in them pain, a bit of dread, and, finally, resignation. It was a lot to ask from a pair of eyes, he knew, but the man's pupils somehow managed to deliver.

They ordered coffees and waited in silence for them to arrive. The rain picked up outside, and they could see people scurrying along to get out of it.

'What's with the tux?' asked Archer when the waitress had departed after delivering their drinks.

'I like to dress up when I go out, though I don't go out much anymore.'

'And the piano pecking?'

'Gave me a chance to watch you without you thinking I was a threat, or that I was waiting for someone like Cecily to show up. Plus, I used to be a good key plunker, although the arthritis has pretty much done me in on that score.'

'Then you played your part well, because you had me snookered.'

'You smoke?' Malloy asked Archer.

Archer nodded and drew out his pack. He offered one to Malloy, who shook his head.

'My health, what's left of it, no longer permits. But I do enjoy seeing a man smoke. And drink, because I can no longer do that, either. What's left in life after that, I'm not sure.'

'You got health problems?'

'Any man my age who does not have health problems is *dead*, Mr. Archer.'

Archer lit up and said, 'Just make it Archer, Sam. Can you tell me how you knew who I was? Ransome never spotted me, I know that for sure.'

'I like to get to places early. Cecily has an eye for detail and she had told me of your distinctive car. I spotted it passing by, saw you drive around the corner and then walk to the bar.'

'Did you tell her I was there?'

'No. Cecily has enough on her mind.'

'And how do you know her?'

'She's my grandniece.'

'Okay.'

'And I am, or rather was, with the LAPD. Started on the force longer ago than I care to remember, and worked my way up to detective before retiring. I say this with the utmost candor and pride: I was one of the honest ones. Back then we were few and far between. I could have spent my entire career arresting people who carried the same badge I did.'

Archer tapped his ash into the glass bowl on the table. 'I believe that. So she called you to meet after I spoke with her.'

'And you must have overheard her conversation.'

'Something like that, yes.'

'I made some calls about you, Archer. You work with Willie Dash up in Bay Town, correct?'

'Why ask, if you already know?'

'Just the old cop in me. He and you have excellent reputations.'

'Willie is as good as they come and he taught me the same. But why did Ransome phone you?'

'Isn't it obvious? She is concerned about Eleanor Lamb. I'm the only person connected to law enforcement whom she knows. She wanted my advice.'

117

'And what did you tell her?'

Malloy sipped his coffee. 'How long have you been around Los Angeles?'

'About three years but some days it feels like thirty.'

Malloy nodded and put his cup down. 'I've been here my whole life, and I have yet to even begin to understand what really makes this town tick. On a superficial level, of course, the analysis is easy. Money, power, fame. In that regard it's much like any other city. But it also has the added element of Hollywood, which makes it totally unique, with a criminal element that is dead set on exploiting those in the movie business to the utmost degree and for myriad reasons. Thus, while the disease is easy to diagnose, its mutating variations are not so easily discerned, because they change so rapidly. And that makes a cure nearly impossible.'

Archer looked bemused. 'I feel like I'm back in college listening to professors pontificating. But I usually came away from those lectures wondering what the hell they actually meant, so if you'd care to simplify? It's just a request — I can't make you.'

Malloy rested his bony elbows on the table. 'Then let's get down to it. I spoke with some folks I know at the county sheriff's office. And what they tell me is that the man found dead in Eleanor Lamb's house was a private investigator named Cedric Bender, from Anaheim.'

Archer didn't bother to feign surprise, because Malloy didn't look like he would have believed it.

'How did they track him down?'

'They didn't have to. Someone at the county recognized him when his body was brought into the morgue.'

'Okay, where does that take us?'

'Bender had a good reputation. He was a careful man. The fact that this happened to him means we are *not* dealing with the usual sort of snot-nosed riff-raff running around playing tough guy.'

Archer rubbed the back of his head. 'Yeah, I figured that out, too, not that I ever really thought that was the case.'

'PIs, as I'm sure you know, do not usually snoop around the house of their employer, so it is doubtful that Bender was working for Lamb.'

'Well, considering she wanted to hire me, I tend to agree with that. Most people only need a single gumshoe, and they grouse about paying one bill, much less two. But what if he was killed elsewhere and dumped there as a warning to her?'

Malloy looked intrigued. 'Do you think that's what happened?'

'I know you told me who you are, but you got some ID that shows you used to be a cop?'

Malloy took a wallet from his pocket and removed from it a card. 'I kept this when I retired. My badge, of course, I had to turn in.'

Archer examined the card and then handed it back. 'Okay. Lamb told me about a blue Ford that was parked on her street. She was concerned someone was watching her. I saw the car and checked the registration. It was Bender's ride.'

'And if she had hired Bender she would have known it was his car?'

'That's what I'm thinking,' said Archer.

'So placing his body at her home was a warning to her, you were suggesting?'

'A stiff in your house will scare anyone.'

'But what was Lamb involved with that required her to be warned in such an extreme manner?' mused Malloy.

'If I knew that, this thing would practically solve itself. You said Ransome is your grandniece and you've been in LA all your life. But she's a recent arrival?'

'Her mother is my brother's daughter. They live back east. Cecily graduated from college there and came here to make films. She's doing very well.'

'So I heard.' He hunched forward. 'Can I ask a candid question?'

'What other types of questions should a detective ask?'

'In hair and dress Lamb is, albeit on a smaller frame, a carbon copy of Ransome, eccentric, so to speak. Two dark, moody straight-hairs in a wavy blond cutie-pie Hollywood pond. Anything else there I should know about?'

'In what way?'

'In *any* way.'

Malloy pressed his pale lips together tightly for a moment. 'While I am of a generation that does not condone those who are attracted to the same gender, this town is full of them. Thus, I can neither confirm nor deny what you are so obviously thinking, Archer.'

'And would you have a problem if Cecily falls outside of the conventional?'

'Cecily has *always* fallen outside of the conventional. That's why she has become as successful as she has. In case you're wondering where my loyalties lie, I am immensely proud of her. And while I admit that I would prefer that she adopt a more traditional approach when it comes to matters of the heart, I have seen enough of life to know full well that my fellow human beings come in all sorts of packages and desires. My dear wife would be horrified to hear what I am saying, which is why I never say it to her.'

'What else did you tell your grandniece?'

'She told me that she had retained you to find Lamb, and after I checked into it I informed her that she was in good hands.'

'You two could have done all that over the phone.'

'Yes, but I wanted to see her. She is very busy, as young people so often are, while I have nothing to do except sit and wait for my time on earth to end. I can't see her face over the phone. And I wanted to see her face.'

Archer nodded. 'And thanks for the vote of confidence.'

'What's your next move?'

'The Jade Lion Bar in Chinatown. Lamb seemed to have been a frequent visitor there.'

'I almost died twice in raids we made on some Tong gangs in Old Chinatown back in the twenties. Kill you as soon as look at you.'

'And new Chinatown has some wild parts to it, under the Hollywood facade.'

'People are people, so whether it's old or new some of them like things on the wrong side of the law and always will.' He tapped a bony finger against the table. 'So, you have no idea what Lamb is mixed up in that could cause her to believe that her life was in danger?'

'Not yet. Did you ever meet her?' asked Archer.

'Twice. Once at a party Cecily invited my wife and me to, and another time at a movie premiere, where I loved her film without really understanding a bit of it.'

'So what was your take on Eleanor Lamb?'

The pale blues suddenly took on a fiery spark, like living, pulsating Bunsen burners.

'For what it's worth, I didn't like her, Archer. I would never trust her. And I don't think you should, either.'

22

It was ten o'clock and the chilly rain was persisting when Archer walked through the West Gate on Hill Street and entered Chinatown.

A dull crack of lightning speared toward the earth nearby and was followed by a hollow sound of thunder. The new year seemed to be looking for trouble as it stumbled out of the starting gate.

As Willie Dash had alluded to, the current Chinatown had sprouted up after the original Chinatown had been bulldozed to make way for Union Station. Filmmakers and set designers had helped create the look of the new Chinatown, and thus Archer passed by a veneer of architecture that one might have seen in Hollywood pictures about China. To him, it deprived the place of any real, granular identity.

He passed dragons on walls, Chinese characters graffitied all over, and locked roll-up gates in front of shops because thefts and burglaries happened here just like everywhere else. The streets were mostly empty, a few bikes splashed down the street; he saw a car turning left, its brake lights burning the rain the color of fire. He saw only Chinese people, who gave his white face wondering looks before hurrying onward in the rain.

The Jade Lion was a four-story brick building that sat robustly on a corner lot at an intersection that was neither major nor insignificant. The eponymous lion in the form of a greenish marble statue stood guard outside the bar's garishly red-lighted exterior.

It looked angry and patient all at the same time, as though just waiting for a passerby to make a mistake before pouncing.

A white man in a gray suit was standing in profile under the bar's narrow covered entrance smoking a cigarette, so Archer couldn't get a good look at him. But he noted the Chinese man standing next to him was wearing colorful garb, including a close-fitted, fur-lined cap. On the man's belt was an empty knife holder made of what looked to be bronze. Archer wondered where the knife was.

As Archer headed up the sidewalk, the man in the suit turned and quickly went back inside.

The Chinese man stepped forward to block Archer's path. He was heavyset with no neck and a long, stringy mustache that bracketed his mouth.

'Yes?'

'I'm here for a drink.'

'Name?'

'Why? Is that required to get a whiskey and soda in this place?'

'Name?'

'John Smith,' replied Archer.

'Many men who come here have that name.'

'I bet.' He took out the book of matches. 'I have this. I'd like to return it to a friend. They might be inside.'

The man glanced down at the matches and his expression changed to one of interest. 'Who is your friend?'

'I'd like to keep that to myself.'

'You police?'

'No.'

'You do not carry a gun, do you, mister?'

'I do not,' said Archer.

The man searched him expertly, from his chest to his hips, then moved aside and held the door open for him.

Archer said, 'If I didn't have the matches and the name, and I *had* a gun, would you have let me in?'

The man smiled without showing his teeth. 'Enjoy your time here, Mr. *Smith*.'

Archer pulled out the photo of Lamb and showed it to him. 'You ever seen her here?'

'My memory is no good. I will forget *you* when you step inside the door.'

Archer said, 'Is that for when the police come looking and you deny having seen me?'

The man let the door go, turned back to the street, and watched the rain fall.

Archer moved through the door and his nostrils immediately ran into the aroma of heavy incense, and his ears bumped into a sea of intriguing noises coming from every direction. He entered a small foyer and looked around. There were multiple beaded doorways leading down other corridors. He had an inkling the Jade Lion would resemble a rabbit's warren inside a maze, encased in a labyrinth, all outlined in indecipherable Chinese.

Archer had worked cases in Chinatown before. He had found that the people here didn't relinquish their secrets easily and usually not at all. It wasn't that they were naturally unfriendlier than anyone else; they had just been burned a few times too many by people who looked just like Archer. And when people didn't treat you like you were human, there was no possibility of trust or engagement. But still, he was a PI working a case, so he had to try.

From another beaded doorway appeared a woman. She was in her early twenties with black hair cut close to her small, oval, and painted face. She wore a tight-fitting yellow dress with red embroidery across its front in the shape of a dragon. She had on red heels and no stockings. 'Drink, mister?'

He looked around. 'Yeah, *is* there a bar? Or did I read the sign outside wrong?'

She pointed at the beaded doorway to his left. 'That way, honey.'

'They have good drinks here?'

'That way, honey.'

Archer took out the photo and showed it to the woman. Indicating Lamb he said, 'You ever seen her here before?'

'That way, honey.'

Archer put the photo away and smiled down into her petite face framed with large dark eyes topped by fake lashes so long it looked like someone had glued spiders to the lids.

He pointed to the beaded doorway. 'Let me get this straight: that way, honey?'

She smiled and walked through another set of beads, swishing her full hips just so as she did. She had a tattoo on her muscular left calf. It was a long-bladed knife with drops of blood on it.

Well, that was charming, he thought, as he pushed through his own set of beads in search of the bar.

And Eleanor Lamb, alive or dead.

23

Down a short hall was the bar. It was not like any bar of Archer's acquaintance, certainly not like the over-the-top Cocoanut Grove. It was not even like the decrepit Boleros. While it was small, dark, and dingy with a gummy plank floor, it also held splashes of color in the form of wall sconce lampshades and puffy balls tied to the ceiling, and framed Chinese-inspired masks behind the bar. Elaborately clothed and face-painted barmaids carried drinks on round trays to thirsty customers. There were no mirrors, no rows of bottles, no jukebox, no grand piano. No tables or bar stools, either. Folks were either standing at the small wooden counter or else in the middle of the room in groups of two or three chatting quietly. A quick sweep of the area told Archer that he was the only white man in the place. The customers here were of various ages and sizes and dressed in everything from three-piece pinstriped suits to long, embroidered robes. The drink glasses they held weren't big; in fact they were all thimble-sized.

To a person they all turned and looked at him as he invaded their little domain.

He walked up to the bar, found a slot in between a tall, lean man wearing a scarlet embroidered robe and a chubby man in a two-piece seersucker suit and a dark-colored shirt. Chubby's face was growing jowls, and the space over his mouth was trying and failing to birth a mustache. The man smiled, revealing enough gold fillings and caps to allow Archer to retire if he could find a way to extract them. The robed man sipped his drink and did not look Archer's way. He bent over his glass as though he were saying a prayer.

If so, Archer hoped it wasn't for him.

The bartender, a giant dressed in a long cloth robe the color of grain, and who would have looked perfectly at home in an arena wrestling a rhino, walked slowly over, cleaning a glass with a rag. He eyed Archer but said nothing.

'Can I get three fingers of whiskey with a splash of soda, pal?' Archer said.

The man looked him up and down, then walked away to discuss something with another gentleman who was, apparently, more to his liking.

The suit next to Archer said, 'They don't serve whiskey here, fella.'

'How about gin?'

The man shook his head and showed his gold again.

'Rum? Bourbon? Vodka?'

The man just kept shaking his head. 'No, nothing like that.'

'I thought this was a bar. Do they serve *any* alcohol or should I ask for milk?'

'Tell him you want this.' He held up his thimble glass.

'And what is that?'

'*Baijiu*. It's what we all drink.'

Archer looked at the robed man, who was staring at his empty thimble glass like he was wondering where his *baijiu* had gone.

The suit waved to the bartender, who came back over. He didn't look at Archer. The suit said, 'He wants the usual.'

The giant walked away, picked up a bottle from

below the counter, and poured some liquid into a thimble glass. He brought it back over to Archer and said something in Chinese.

Archer looked at the suit.

'He wants payment, fella. Two American dollars.'

'For that?' said Archer, staring at the tiny glass.

'It is what you Yanks like to call quality, not quantity.'

Archer passed two bucks across and the giant drifted away.

Suit raised his own glass and said, 'To your health.'

'How do you drink this thing, fast or slow?'

The gold smiled at him. 'We do it as a *shot*, as you Yanks say. But I think you might want to take it slow, fella.'

The suit drank his in one tipped-back swallow.

Archer sniffed the liquid and was surprised that it held no odor familiar to him, though the smell was very distinct. It was also clearer than any water he'd ever seen.

'It is an ancient process in China to make *baijiu*,' explained the suit, wiping his mouth. 'Very labor intensive. Americans cannot make it. The fermentation is the tricky part. It comes in different varieties, you can tell which by smell: light, medicinal, spicy, sesame, extra strong. We are lucky Jade gets some. That is why we come here.'

Archer took a sip and it immediately felt like he had swallowed liquid fire. As it went down his throat and landed like an inferno in his belly, the fire turned to something else and he thought he might be sick. He put one hand against the bar and closed his eyes, steeling himself to not vomit or pass out.

In about ten seconds, the twin sensations passed.

He turned to the suit and croaked, 'Impressive that you can slam this back, buddy.' It wasn't just impressive, he thought, it was a damn miracle. As he looked around at the others, young and old, tossing their thimbles back and going on with their conversations as though they hadn't just sucked down a flaming sword, the idea of Americans being the hardiest people on earth simply faded from Archer's mind.

'It is an acquired taste. This version is forty-five percent alcohol.'

'Please tell me that's the extra-strong one, because another sip and I'd be squiffed.'

The suit shook his head. 'Pretty mild, actually. We Chinese do business around drinking, usually with *baijiu*. We feel it makes the true self come out. And we like to *truly* know who we do business with. Ha-ha!'

Archer coughed and cleared his throat. 'Speaking of business.' He took out the photo. 'You ever see this woman in here before?' He pointed to Lamb.

The suit glanced at the photo and grinned in gold once more. 'No, mister. Who is she?'

'A friend I'm looking for.'

'I cannot help you.'

'Okay.' Archer showed the picture to everyone else there and got no replies in return, only blank stares. He didn't know if it was the *baijiu* or just him. He turned to leave.

The suit said, 'You won't finish your *baijiu*? It is bad form.'

'Better form for me if I don't.'

'You are leaving the Jade?'

'I am leaving the Jade,' Archer lied.

He exited the bar area and made his way back to the front room. The woman who had been there earlier

130

had not returned. He looked out the front to see the Chinese gent open the rear door of a sleek silver Rolls-Royce. Out from it stepped a platinum blonde whom Archer recognized as a famous actress, although he couldn't remember her name. She wore dark glasses and had a hat and fur stole that partially obscured her features. But she had lowered the glasses for a moment and that was when he recognized her.

She headed up the steps and Archer quickly looked around. There was a three-panel leather room divider set in one corner he had noticed before. He slipped behind that and almost stumbled over some boxes stacked there. He positioned himself so that he could see through one of the narrow openings between the panels.

The actress came in and was immediately greeted by the same woman in the yellow dress. She had appeared so quickly Archer assumed she had been watching from a window somewhere and had seen the woman's arrival, too.

She didn't point out the beaded doorway to the bar. She instead took the woman's coat, hat, and glasses and escorted her through another beaded opening. The actress kept her gaze on the floor. She looked like she didn't want to be there, and so Archer wondered why she was.

He waited for a few moments to see if the yellow dress appeared. She did and then vanished through another beaded gateway. This place really was a maze, he thought. If there was ever a fire here, everyone was going to die.

Archer had started to step out when his foot slipped on something on the floor. He bent down to see what it was.

The particles were small and gritty. *Sand.*

He took another look at the boxes. They seemed familiar to him, but crates like these were all over town. He felt along the sides of them. They had gritty sand stuck in some of the crevices, and bits of it had fallen to the floor. He lifted the top off one. It was empty. He put the top back in place, and checked to make sure the room was clear before stepping out. He passed through the same doorway the actress had. After a right turn he came to a long hall that had doors set on both sides. They had little slips of paper with numbers on them set in brass holders. He gently tried the door marked Number One. It was locked. And someone from inside the room called out, 'It's taken. Scram!'

He did that four more times until he came to one that wasn't locked.

As soon as he eased it open, he heard someone coming. He ducked inside and closed the door behind him. A few moments later footsteps hurried down the hall.

They're looking for someone and I think it's me.

He hadn't brought his flashlight and he didn't want to risk turning on a light. There were no windows in the room, so the only illumination came from the small gap under the door.

He let his eyes adjust to the absence of light and looked around.

There was a bed, a nightstand, and a large armoire with Chinese symbols carved on it. And there were mirrors on all the walls, and when he looked up, he was staring at a dim reflection of himself and the room because there were mirrors up there, too. The only part that wasn't glassed in was where a heavy chandelier was located.

Narcissus would have loved this place.

He opened the armoire, and inside was some of the gaudiest women's lingerie he had ever seen, and his experience with that, especially in his younger and stupid years, was extensive. There were also handcuffs, belts, ropes, and other bindings. And a long, black whip. Now, that was something he had no personal experience with, but he also knew this town was full of those who couldn't get enough of it.

As if on cue, from somewhere down the hall Archer heard what sounded like the crack of a whip and then a scream.

He closed the doors of the armoire and kept looking around. The bed was springy and fitted with quality linens and a bedspread with intricate embroidery on it. He looked closer, but couldn't make it out. He risked turning on the lamp on the nightstand.

He saw that the embroidery had created an impression of flames so colorful and real-looking that the cloth almost seemed to be on fire. With the light on he made a closer examination of the room and even looked under the bed.

There he found a small glass vial that was empty. But that wasn't entirely correct. There was a bit of residue inside, a few white grains. He sniffed it, and then pocketed it.

The parts of the walls not covered with mirrors were wallpapered in a pattern that looked like purple lotus plants. He kept looking around before his gaze went back to the ceiling.

The chandelier had six light fixtures, all pointing down. But only five had bulbs in them. He stood on the bed and looked at it more closely.

Damn.

Unless he was much mistaken, there was a camera lens in the one light post missing a bulb. He hoped to hell no one was looking at him right now.

He climbed down, turned off the light, and went over to the door. Footsteps were coming. He also heard voices. A man was saying something loudly, but Archer couldn't quite make out what it was. He slipped across the room and slid under the bed. A few seconds later the door was thrown open. He waited for them to look under the bed. But the door closed and the footsteps moved on.

Archer waited a few more minutes before he eased out into the hall. He made his way in the opposite direction of where he had come. Passing one door he heard what sounded like Beethoven, along with soft moaning, and then a woman cried out in pain. His hand slipped to the knob. It was locked. From his wallet Archer pulled out a lockpick. He inserted it as quietly as he could. After a few seconds of manipulations, the sounds of which were covered by Beethoven, the lock clicked free and Archer slowly eased the door open a couple inches.

The actress he had seen earlier was dressed in black lingerie. Her hands were cuffed to the bedpost. A phonograph was on a table, the classical music coming from the record rotating on it. A man with gray hair and dressed in a long robe held a belt and struck her on the buttocks, making her yelp and stand up on her stockinged toes. Archer looked at her unfocused eyes and her sluggish features. She was clearly high on something.

'You have been bad,' said the man. 'You must be punished.'

'Yes,' she said breathily. 'I *am* bad.'

134

Archer looked up at the chandelier and wasn't surprised to see one lightbulb missing from it, too. He was sure every room had the same setup. Part of him wanted to walk in and knock the man through the wall. But the woman *was* there of her own free will. Still, he was about to intervene when that decision was taken away from him.

He eased the door closed and hurried down the hall as the sounds of footsteps and voices suddenly came back.

24

Archer ducked down another corridor as the footsteps behind him picked up momentum. He had a strong feeling now that if he were discovered he would not be around to see the sun rise. LA had an abundance of lonely roads, shallow rivers, and empty concrete aqueducts in which to dump bodies. It was actually a thriving industry and created lots of jobs, but he didn't want to contribute to that particular economy. He stopped and listened, imagining himself to be a scout once more with the Army in Europe. The only trouble was that was a long time ago, and a slender corridor didn't provide nearly as much room to hide as a continent. In any event, after nearly eight years away from the Army, Archer wasn't sure he was up to the task any longer.

He looked quickly around and saw a door with a porthole window at eye level. He raced to it and was through the opening and closed the door behind him before the men appeared in the hall. Archer found a storage room down here, and he hid behind some boxes for a good half hour, desperately wishing he had his gun.

After that he peered out into the hall and spied another door that might be a way out. He reached it, found it opened to a stairwell, and was about to head down when he heard someone coming up. He went the other way on the stairs, reached the top floor, opened the door, and gazed quickly around. This part of the building looked unused, with crates, old draperies

136

and beds, furniture, and discarded metal equipment of various sizes and functions. Their disuse was represented by the smells of mildew, mold, and rot. He couldn't hide here, but he did spot a way out: a window. He went over to it and finally saw something in his favor. The window was difficult to raise, but he managed it.

He stepped out onto the wrought iron fire escape and looked down. He figured he was gazing onto the alley at the rear of the building. He made his way down each set of fire escape steps and platforms until he reached the last one. As he slid the ladder down and dropped to the ground he looked up in time to see a man peering down at him from the top window. A moment later a gun was pointing at him. A second after that it was firing at him, but Archer had already fled around the corner toward the front of the building.

He could hear shouts from all over now and knew his odds of escaping were slim to zero, and his final resting place might be in a hole in Chinatown, or the silty bottom of the Pacific. Neither one appealed to him.

The next second Archer ran headlong into someone and he felt the man's fingers close around his throat. It was the struggle on the beach all over again. Although this time his opponent was the doorman. And his empty knife holder apparently hadn't really been empty, because the curved blade was in his hand.

Archer didn't waste a second because he didn't have one to waste. He grabbed the knife hand and held it away from him. Next, he planted an elbow in the man's face, breaking his nose. Then he kicked his foot out and bent the man's knee the wrong way. The

137

man went down screaming in pain, and then Archer laid him out with a crushing hook to the jaw. He had to keep thanking the Army for teaching him so thoroughly how to fight, win, and stay alive to fight again. As he kept running he looked down at his hand: It was wet.

The guy's knife hadn't entirely missed. Archer had a two-inch-long gash in his left palm. He took out his handkerchief, wound it around his hand, and kept running.

Just as he got to the front entrance the silver Rolls pulled up, and the same actress staggered down the steps and into it. Archer followed right behind the lady, pushing her into the far seat and closing the door after him. The Rolls sped off, the driver apparently not even aware that he had a spare passenger.

Archer looked out the window in time to see the man in the gray suit hustle out of the front entrance and look around. He had obviously not seen Archer slide into the Rolls. But Archer did get a good look at him. He was in his forties, trim and hard, standing about five-ten. There was nothing particularly memorable about him, except for the sets of ugly intersecting scars across his face. Archer had been unable to see these marks when he had first arrived here, because the man had ducked away too quickly.

As the Rolls turned the corner and sped up, Archer looked at the woman next to him. He wasn't sure *she* was aware he was there until she turned to him and said, 'Who the hell are you?'

The words were not uttered in anger or fear. She just seemed curious.

'Just hitching a ride to where I parked my car, if you don't mind. You like the Jade?'

'I go there for kicks.'

'I'm sure you do. You're in pictures, right?'

Her lovely face now showed alarm. She sat up and said, 'You're not some dirty reporter, are you? So help me God if you're with —' She tried to hit him but he caught her wrist an inch from his face.

Archer looked toward the driver, but he was old and maybe a little hard of hearing, or he was used to arguments in the back seat of this car. Whatever the reason, he just kept looking out the windscreen and driving while the car's radio played Nat King Cole.

'Relax, lady, I don't work for any rag. I was at the Jade on my own business.'

'What sort of business?' she snapped.

Archer could see why she was a star. The camera would love the angles of her face, the way her eyes widened and then brightened like precious stones before they tapered back to a dull glow that was even more interesting and perhaps telling of what she was thinking, and of a possible vulnerability. And the way her full lips quivered just so.

'I'm a detective.'

'What were you doing in there, then?'

'Detecting.'

'Says you. I don't believe a word of it.'

'Yeah, I probably wouldn't either if I were you.' He looked out the window to see where they were. 'Hey, Pops, right at the next street and then two blocks down, you can drop me.'

The old man eyed him in the mirror, suddenly aware that he was there. 'Miss —'

'It's all right, Alan, just do as he says.' She looked at Archer and then her gaze dropped to his hand. 'My God, you're bleeding.'

139

'It's nothing. Fell on a knife back there that a guy was holding.'

'What happened to him?'

'When he wakes up, I'm sure he'll try to figure it out.'

'Did *you* figure out anything back there, Mister Detective?' she said.

'Yeah, but the Jade's not a good place if you ask questions, or want a drink that doesn't incinerate your throat. How long you been going there for kicks?'

'Ever since I got famous, hell, didn't you know?'

'No, I didn't. Which begs the question of why you need that kind of place now.'

Archer didn't need an answer to his question. She had to go back because she couldn't not go back. But she could get her fix from anywhere, including her own studio, so what was the draw of the Jade?

She seemed to know what he was thinking. She turned away from him and curled up in her furry fox stole. 'Just leave me alone.' Her voice was no longer breathless; it sounded normal, and upset.

'You got a good thing going, why mess it up?'

She looked back at him. 'If I had a choice, maybe.'

'And you don't?'

'Who in this town really does, Mister Detective?'

Archer was about to reply with something pithy and mildly scolding, but then he thought about Callahan and the casting couch. If a person like Liberty . . .

'I see what you mean.'

She looked back at him, her full lips parted in pleasant surprise. 'Do you really?'

'I got friends in the business. It's got this public side with the pictures of good-looking people doing wonderful things, all the glam, the money, the homes, the

140

yachts. Then you got the other side, which is about ninety percent of the pie, like the part of the iceberg no one sees until it's too late. That part isn't pretty at all. But you know that better than I ever will. It's a high price to pay, but people pay it. Lots of them.'

She was nodding before he stopped. 'You're cute. And smarter than you look.'

'Cute men often are.'

'Did you happen to see me back there?'

His grin faded. 'Back where?'

'You know where. And why else would you be advising me to quit that joint unless you saw something?'

'I saw more than maybe I needed to see. But it goes no farther. I promise.'

'Hell, people make promises in this town every minute of every day with no intention of ever keeping them.' She turned away. 'I came here from a little place in Minnesota. I don't want anyone to know about . . . the Jade.'

'I'm not telling anybody. And what studio owns you, by the way?'

'MGM. Why?'

'They have a pretty decent fixer group. I know one of them. You shouldn't have to go this alone. Where are they on all this?'

'Nowhere, because they don't know.'

'And you think that's smart?'

'I'm actually happy about it. If they knew, the studio would make me sign a new deal, *and* I'd have to go to bed with the asshole who runs it, *again*. I don't want to. I'm sick and tired of it. And he's old *and* married.'

'Who is the clown?'

'Never mind. There're a million just like him, so

what does it matter?'

'You want me to talk to him for you? Lay down the law?'

She laughed. 'What are you, a Boy Scout or a choirboy, or both?'

'I have my moments. But while I have you here . . .' He pulled out the photo of Lamb. 'You ever seen her at the Jade?'

The woman looked at the photo. 'Sure, a few times.'

Archer looked surprised, because he was. He tapped Lamb's image. 'You're sure? Take a closer look.'

'No, not her, the other one.'

Archer gazed down at the beaming Alice Jacoby. 'Her? You're certain?'

'Didn't I just say I was?'

The car slowed and Alan said, 'Right here, sir?'

Archer looked out the window and saw the Delahaye parked across the street. 'That'll do, thanks, pal.' He opened the door, but then looked back at her. 'For what it's worth, if you never go back to that place, it'll be the best thing you could ever do.'

'For my career?' she said with lovely, hiked dark eyebrows. The feeble illumination in the car seemed to make her platinum hair shimmer like descending sunlight on rippling water.

'No, for your *life*.'

She leaned over, nuzzled his neck, and then kissed him on the lips, running her soft hand down his jaw. 'I've never had a man jump into my car before. I kind of like it.'

'I have to do it more often then.'

'Maybe our paths will cross again.'

She sounded like she was delivering a line from a bad script, but was believing every word. Not wanting to pop her drugged-up bubble, Archer finished the lousy scene by kissing her cheek and saying, 'You can cross my path anytime, lady.'

He got out, and the Rolls drove on.

Archer knew if the woman were lucky her career would last until this time next year. If she were unlucky, she'd be dead by the end of the month. And they'd find a hundred just as lovely and breathless to take her place, no problem. The Midwest alone was turning them out like GM did cars.

Archer left Chinatown behind with a lot to think about and make sense of. He needed some more peroxide and a bandage and, most critically, a drink, a real one. And Archer knew exactly the lady he wanted to have that drink with.

25

'I'll have to play a nurse in one of my next pictures, Archer. I mean, look at all the practice I'm getting with you.'

Callahan had washed the slash on his hand, dabbed enough peroxide on it to make the hairs on Archer's neck stand up and salute, and then applied ointment and a bandage, winding it around his wrist and tying it off.

He had told her some of his adventures from the night, and she kept shaking her head and warning him that the next time might not be so easy for him. Yet her look was far more worried than her words.

'I didn't think *this* one was easy,' he said.

'Who was the actress? I'm just wondering if that's her lipstick on your collar.'

'She *was* a little loose with her affections. Comes with the drugs. I don't remember her name. She was platinum blond and curvy and appropriately breathless.'

'Well, *that* narrows it down to just about everybody. You sure you can't remember a picture she was in or something?'

'I don't go to the movies all that often. Sort of a waste of time for me.'

'Thanks, Archer, a lot.'

'I didn't mean it that way. Anyway, she said she was with MGM. The fixer there doesn't know about the Jade, at least that's what she said. She also said if they did know, they'd use it to blackmail her into a new deal, and she'd have to sleep with the studio head again.'

'And what, you're surprised by that?'

'But if she keeps going back there, her career is going to be over because she's going to croak.'

'Maybe she wants that.'

'She had a fur coat and a Rolls with a chauffeur and she was maybe our age.'

'At first it's the money and fame and it's great. But then all that takes a back seat, because they've *all* got the damn furs and a Rolls with a driver. It's a lot of pressure, Archer. Some folks get to the top and suddenly realize they don't want to be there. They don't want to have to keep doing what it takes to stay there. She just might be looking for a way out. I just hope she's breathing when she finds it.'

He flexed his injured hand and then mixed himself a whiskey and soda, and a gin and tonic for Callahan. He handed hers over and said, 'But her only way out might be a grave.'

Callahan sat in a chair with one long leg elegantly crossed over the other, and sipped her drink. 'She wouldn't be the first and she won't be the last.'

'That's pretty tough,' he finally said.

'I know it. But I'm not a star, Archer. No one's trying to hook me on drugs and that bondage stuff. I'm not valuable enough.'

'And if you ever *get* that valuable?'

'Then I'll have to deal with it. But that's a long road, at least for me.'

'And somebody's taking pictures of her. I saw the camera.'

Callahan thought for a moment and said, 'Maybe that's why she keeps going back.'

'So the *Jade* is blackmailing her?'

'This is LA, Archer. Somebody is always blackmailing someone else.'

He looked at his drink and shook his head. 'This place stinks right down to the core.'

'And still *you* keep coming back. And it's not just to see me.'

'There is a certain intoxication with the place, I'll admit that. Plus, the cases here are . . . more original.'

'Can't get that same high in Bay Town? Because in a way, *you're* an addict too.'

'Keep going, Liberty, I'm not nearly depressed enough yet.'

'So, Alice Jacoby goes to the Jade? But she told you she'd never heard of it.'

'The lady tonight was on drugs. Maybe she was mistaken. But she seemed pretty sure. And if so, Jacoby lied to me.'

'What would Jacoby be doing at the Jade?'

'She struck me as being pretty straight-laced, but sometimes it's those very same ones who end up being the wild spirits.' He took out the vial he'd found in one of the rooms. 'I got a pretty good idea what's in here.'

Callahan looked at it. 'What?'

'Heroin. They bring it in from Mexico mostly.'

'So, what are you going to do now?'

'Sleep. I haven't done a lot of that in the last couple days. Hey, can you do one thing for me? The gal checking people in at the Marses' party?'

'Donna, what about her?'

'Can you talk to her and see if Lamb ever showed? I have to be really certain about it.'

'Sure, I can do that.'

She rose and sat on the arm of his chair, running a hand gently over his head, avoiding the bandaged part. 'Is it really worth it, Archer? I mean, like you said, you make just a fraction of what I do standing up in front of a camera and regurgitating someone else's words. And no one's trying to kill me while I'm doing it. Hardly seems fair.'

'I'm reasonably good at being a PI, I enjoy the work, and I hope I'm doing a little bit of good.'

As he heard himself say these words, Archer wondered if any of them were really true.

She stopped rubbing his hair. 'And if you end up getting killed?'

'Then you can miss me.'

She frowned. 'That's not funny. You're the only real friend I've got.'

'Then you need to get out more.' He rose. 'Go to sleep. You're on set tomorrow. And I need my shut-eye. Things will look better in the morning.'

She stood and faced him. 'How was her kiss?'

'I've had better.'

'Oh really? From who?'

He said, 'You've already forgotten?'

'I didn't forget, Archer. I plan on taking that memory with me for the long haul.' She kissed him on the cheek and left, shutting the bedroom door behind her.

Archer went over to the window and looked out.

Was it worth it?

He didn't have a ready answer, which might have been an answer in itself.

Archer did not sleep much. Every dream he had did not end well for him.

26

Archer heard a knock on his door at six thirty a.m.

Callahan called through the wood, 'I'm heading to the studio for my early call, Archer. There're eggs and sausages in the fridge and bread in the box, and I've got plenty of coffee. I'll check with Donna about Ellie. And I'll leave a note with the guard if you want to drop by the set later.'

'I'm sure he'll be thrilled,' he called back. 'So long as you're in your *toga*.'

An hour later Archer rolled out of bed, showered, shaved, and dressed, and had two fried eggs, a sausage link, two pieces of buttered toast, and half a pot of coffee. And he was still feeling lethargic. It might have been the almost dying two nights in a row.

He had sponged his clothes off the best he could, but at some point he would have to drive to Bay Town and pick up clean stuff. And he could report in to Willie.

He phoned Green and Ransome at nine on the dot, and an efficient-sounding female voice answered. He asked for Cecily Ransome. She was not in, he was told. After he told her he had been hired by Ransome to locate Lamb, the woman told him to wait. When she came back on the line she said, 'Mrs. Green would like to talk to you.'

'You mean Bart Green's wife?' asked Archer.

'Is there another?'

The call was transferred and another woman's voice came on. It was cultured with a bit of flame attached

148

at specific intervals, noted Archer.

'I'm Mallory Green, Mr. Archer. Cecily spoke with me early this morning from her home and told me about her meeting with you and what you're investigating. She is very concerned. And I'm very interested in this matter as well. Very interested. Ellie has become a good friend of mine.'

'Okay.'

'I'd like to meet with you. And I think you should speak with my husband as well.'

'All right. Is he in town?'

'No, he's in Vegas, but I can have our pilot fly you there today in our plane, if you wish.'

Our pilot, our plane, thought Archer. It made one's little mind go round and round about what some people called normal.

'Let's talk and then we can go from there. Where would you like to meet?'

'At my home. I was just in the office this morning to check on a few things. I'm leaving now.'

'Let me have the address.'

He wrote it down. It was in Beverly Hills off Santa Monica Boulevard. The address sounded expensive and no doubt was.

He gave her time to get there and then got into his car and drove to her home. The rain was gone, and 1953 had its first day of sparkling California sunshine, at least through the dense smog, which was provided courtesy of all the smokestack and car exhausts huddled over them. He had taken off his head bandage, combing his hair straight over the wound, but redressed the one on his hand. At this rate, he might start looking like a mummy.

The Green estate was gated with a large *G* on the

wrought iron just so no one would be confused. High prison walls encircled the place. There was a phone at the gate to call the house.

Archer duly called and the gates duly creaked open. It was a typical Beverly Hills mansion: impressive in both large and small detail, with lots of terraced lawns, formal flower beds, and greenery sculpted by strong, experienced hands, and none of them belonging to the owners. He wasn't speculating about this. About a half dozen muscled Mexicans were hauling dirt in wheelbarrows, spading the earth, putting large bushes in holes, and making this particular Beverly Hills palace all hunky-dory.

There was a Greek revival thing going on with the home's facade, and the round columns looked substantial enough to hold up the Treasury Department. The number and size of the windows was all LA, though, and impressive, allowing the potent sun to filter through and ignite whatever the interior looked like to new levels of grandiosity for the visitor. It had the standard large central block and two wings set at obtuse angles to the main. It looked like the imposing place was trying to reach out and hug him, an impression that was a bit off-putting.

He pulled in front of the house on a cobbled motor court with grass growing perfectly between the pavers, and stopped next to a gray-and-white Bentley. He got out and felt the other car's engine. It was warm. Mrs. Green had arrived, in style. He wondered if she had driven herself. He doubted it, but maybe the lady would surprise him.

He knocked on the door and then stood there, his hat twirling between his hands. He was led inside not by a butler, but by a young woman in a dark blue pencil skirt, long-sleeved white blouse, and white pumps, with a thin strand of fake pearls around her slender, freckled neck. She had introduced herself as Sally Dennison, Mrs. Green's personal assistant.

Well, that was progress over the aged, liveried statue at Alice Jacoby's place, thought Archer. Maybe the fifties really were ushering in a whole new dawn of bright, personal minions in cheap heels and faux pearls.

Mallory Green was waiting in a large room that could have been anything, really, thought Archer, so long as it looked expensive.

She was in her late fifties, around five-five, and thin in a way that perhaps spoke of skipped meals. Her gaunt, sibylline face reminded him of an ax blade, but the eyes promised greater subtlety than that. Her features, despite the gauntness, were both attractive and interesting in equal measure. Her lips were set firm and level, like a pair of two-by-fours. The blue eyes were alert, and seemed to flash whenever a bit of light from a lamp or the windows struck them, like exposed wires nestled together. The woman's hair was piled on top of her head, except for a few curlicue strands that trickled down over her small, lovely ears. Green had allowed her hair to go white, a confident woman gracefully aging.

She was encased in a dress of electric blue that served to emphasize the color of her eyes, not that they needed it. The dress flared out, providing the appearance of width to her narrow, boyish hips. The hem ended just above the bony knees, which were imprisoned in sheer stockings. The Cartier diamond-encrusted watch sat on her wrist looking like the world's fattest ring.

For nine thirty in the morning the lady was solidly put together and already in full battle gear.

Archer took a breath and waited.

27

Mallory Green introduced herself and offered him coffee, which he accepted, because the effect of the half pot already consumed had worn off. Eager-beaver Sally went off to relay the order.

A maid in full servant regalia brought it back in a cup and saucer with a fine filigree design. Archer sipped his coffee without slurping, just to show that he, too, had a bit of culture at nine thirty in the morning while wearing a still sandy, hastily sponged suit.

'So, you've had no word from Lamb?' he said after the maid had departed.

'None, neither has Cecily. We're all terribly worried.'

'You might want to file a report with the county's Missing Persons Bureau.'

'My God, aren't they already looking for her?'

'Not necessarily. She's an adult woman who can come and go as she pleases. I suggested to the cops that they consider her missing. But you filing a report can't hurt.'

'Yes, of course. I will do so.'

'So they haven't been by to talk to anyone about her?'

'Not that I'm aware of.'

Archer didn't know what to make of that. 'Does she have any family locally that needs to be notified?'

'No, but I believe she has family back east.'

'So Lamb has worked at your husband's company for how long now?'

The ax blade took a swipe at Archer and cleaved off a layer of his skin. 'It's *our* company, Mr. Archer. I'm a producer in my own right, though I create documentaries on subjects of importance. I've won two Academy Awards for my work, meaning Bart has *two* fewer than I do,' she added, in a matter-of-fact manner.

'Excuse me, I didn't know that.'

'It's all right. No one ever assumes the wives in this town have anything to do other than dress nicely, stay skinny, not dribble what little food we do eat down our fronts, and never, ever drink as much as our husbands, at least in public. To answer your question, Ellie has been with us for a number of years.'

'I would imagine you can do what you want, Mrs. Green, being as accomplished as you are.' He wanted to add, *Like eat a proper meal every now and again.*

'Documentaries, Academy Award–winning or not, do not make much money, Mr. Archer. But they cost quite a bit to make. Bart's simple fare, on the other hand, practically mints the stuff. Thus, certain compromises must be reached.'

Archer was now done with discussing the Greens' business arrangement, otherwise known as a festering marriage. 'So, you wanted to talk to me?'

'Yes.'

'What about?'

'A status update on your investigation, of course.'

'Those are usually reserved for the *client*. Right now, that's Cecily Ransome.'

She looked put out. 'But Ellie's my employee. And I care about what happens to her.'

'I understand. So while I'm here, do you know any reason why someone would want to harm Lamb?'

154

'No, none at all.'

'A man was found dead at her house. Someone had shot him in the head.'

'Yes, Cecily mentioned that. Do the police know who he is?'

'He's a PI from Anaheim named Cedric Bender.'

If Archer had pulled a rattlesnake out of his pocket and thrown it at the woman, it would not have had a greater effect on Mallory Green.

Her eyelids fluttered, and then her pupils rolled like slot machine plates right into her head. He thought she was going to pass out, and she did slump to the side. She sat there breathing hard and looking distressed, holding her chest.

'Are you okay?' he asked quickly.

She nodded, but still looked weak and distraught.

He rushed over to the bar, poured some brandy into a cut crystal glass, and brought it to her. 'Drink this. You'll feel better.'

Green sipped the brandy and looked over at him, finally managing an embarrassed smile. 'You must think I'm mad or something.'

'No, I just think you were shocked to hear a PI named Cedric Bender is dead. Would you like to tell me why?'

She grimaced and put the glass down. 'I'm not sure what came over me. It's not like I know him. I have been feeling unwell lately. Maybe the flu. It's going around.'

'It's not the flu.'

She glanced sharply at him. 'I tell you that it is. I've been feeling poorly all week in fact.'

'And you're sticking to that story?'

'It's the truth!'

155

Archer put on his hat. 'Okay, I'll be heading out now.'

She looked up at him, her blue eyes crackling with energy. 'What! Why? You just got here.'

'I've been retained to find Eleanor Lamb, preferably alive. I don't have time to waste with people who are lying to me. Even *I* charge too much for that.'

She looked at the floor. 'How dare you accuse me of lying —'

Archer broke in. 'It wasn't that hard in your case. Most people don't nearly faint and then lie so badly afterwards they have to stare at the floor because they're too embarrassed to look at the poor slob they're trying to blow smoke at. So either Bender is your maiden name and Cedric is your beloved brother or other close relative, and you're understandably upset at his being murdered. *Or* you hired PI Bender to do a job for you. In the course of doing that job, someone killed him. I told you he was dead. You clearly didn't know that, and it shocked you. If I'm off, just tell me so, but tell me so while looking *directly* at me, lady.'

Archer wasn't sure whether she was going to cry, attack him, or have him thrown out by the brawny Mexican grounds crew.

She surprised him. 'You're obviously very good at your job, Mr. Archer.'

'And I also have something called pride in my work and a couple of morals resting in my pocket, one of which includes telling the truth. I know that's out of style in this town, but I keep trying. So why'd you hire Bender?'

She looked up at him, those two-by-four lips now twisted in anger. 'To investigate my husband. I'm *certain* that crummy bastard is cheating on me. Again.'

156

28

Green had a second brandy and Archer watched her drink it dry. When she was done, she put the glass down, cocked her two-by-four lips just so, and looked at him like she was itching for a fight with someone about something, and he was the only one within pummeling distance.

'I suppose you have many questions for me,' she said icily.

'If Bender was sniffing around your husband's infidelities, why was he in Las Flores Canyon? Do you think he was having an affair with Lamb?'

'Of course not. Bart only goes in for young and gorgeous. Ellie is neither.'

'Well, then that leaves out her neighbor, Mrs. Danforth, since she's around eighty.' When Green didn't respond, Archer did for her. 'So that brings us to the Frenchwoman, Bernadette Bonham. But she's around the same age as Lamb and she's in France with her husband.'

'Is she?'

'Well, I was told that, but I haven't verified it.'

'Then maybe you should.'

'I'm not working on your divorce case, Mrs. Green. That was Bender's job.'

'I'm not seeking a divorce.'

'What then?'

'That's *my* business. As you said, it's not *your* job.'

Archer shook out a cigarette and held it up. 'You mind?'

'No, the lighter's over there.'

Archer picked up the lighter, as bulky and nearly as heavy as a cannonball, and lit his Lucky. He blew rings to the frescoed ceiling that held babies swirling amid clouds.

'When did you hire Bender? And why him?'

'I've used Mr. Bender before, when Bart was out carousing with other nubile women.'

'How'd you hear about him? He's way down in Anaheim.'

'Other women in Los Angeles that I know had used him when their husbands . . .'

'Yeah, I understand. Go on.'

'One of them recommended him highly. And I didn't want anyone from this lousy city. They all talk to each other. I did not want to be a laughingstock. Any more than I already am,' she added testily.

'Okay, I get that. And I'm not laughing at you. I just want to understand the situation.'

She set her glass down and looked at him expectantly.

'Did you suspect your husband was seeing Bernadette Bonham?'

'The fact is, I don't know if it is her. Bender, I believe, was following up some other leads, too.'

'His car was seen outside of Eleanor Lamb's house.'

'Who by?'

'Eleanor Lamb. And me. It's now missing. But I guess Bender was watching the Bonhams' place, not Lamb's. He provide you with any reports?'

'Why?'

'If he has, I'd like to read them.'

'Why?' she said more sharply.

'Because he was found dead in Lamb's house. The

158

connection sort of speaks for itself.'

'I . . . yes, he did. The reports. I have them in my study.'

'I can have copies made and get you the originals back.'

Green flipped a hand carelessly in his general direction. 'Oh, all right.' She rose and left him, coming back a minute later with a yellow manila folder; she handed it to him.

'Was this the only communications you had with Bender? Did you speak to him? Over the phone, or here? Or another place?'

'We had discussions on the phone.'

'Okay, so what did Bender tell you?'

'That Bart covers his tracks well. He has places arranged that he goes into and then out of from different doors. That Bart is always very careful never to be seen in public in the company of other women. This was all done with the purpose of allowing him to consort with other ladies who are not *me*.'

'You mentioned he had done this before?'

She rose and poured herself another drink. This time it was whiskey with no qualifiers. At this rate she'd be snookered by lunch, thought Archer.

She took a swallow and sat back down. 'Twice before. Once with a 'starlet' in one of his movies, who was young enough to be his daughter. She is no longer in acting. She went back to Wisconsin or wherever the hell she came from.'

'So she couldn't act?'

Green gazed at him in stern amusement. 'You don't have to be able to act, Mr. Archer, to become a star in Hollywood. But you do have to have a ruthless fire in the belly, because the competition is like nothing else on earth. And you have to be willing to sell a significant portion of your soul, or perhaps all of it.'

Archer momentarily thought of Callahan. 'And the second time?'

'A secretary at his office. Bart surprised me on that one.'

'How so?'

'He likes women with big chests, like the best race-horses. She was as flat as a pancake, but I guess she had other appealing attributes.'

Archer couldn't help but glance at the woman's slender frame. She caught this look and smiled. 'Bart and I have been married for over thirty years and have four children together. We met when Bart was different, and I was different.'

'There's always divorce.'

'Marriage, for some, is a competition, and divorce signals winners and losers. And in this day and age, the *men* are the winners if they can get to that finish line. If I let Bart go now, he could *publicly* go out and get whoever he wanted. I, on the other hand, could not. And I would be blackballed in this town, because all the studio heads are lecherous men just like him. So if he wants to engage in adulterous liaisons, I just want him to have to work harder. That is really my only recourse.'

'Getting back to Bender. When was the last time you spoke to him?'

'The morning of New Year's Eve. We were going to meet for lunch tomorrow and he was going to fill me in on things.'

'Did he give you a teaser over the phone?'

'No, he said he wanted to do it in person.'

'Well, that won't be happening now.'

160

'You can't possibly think that Ellie Lamb killed him? Why would she?'

'I don't know. Did Bender ever mention that he thought someone was on to him?'

'No, nothing like that,' she said quickly, maybe a beat *too* quickly to Archer's thinking. 'I take it you don't want to fly to Las Vegas and interrogate my husband?'

'Not today, no. When is he coming back?'

'He spoke of tomorrow or the next day. He was rather vague.'

'You have a photo of your husband?'

She rose again, rifled through a drawer, and pulled out a framed photo. She undid the backing and handed him the picture. She answered his puzzled expression with a terse 'Why would I want to look at him?'

Archer gazed down at the photo. Green was standing next to his wife. He was shorter than her, and far wider with a blunt face, bald head, deep-set eyes, and a thin mustache over thick lips. The chin was weak, the cheeks inflamed, and still the overall look of the gent screamed a superior arrogance.

'Looks like a peach,' noted Archer.

'With cyanide inside.'

He rose. 'I'll get you Bender's original reports back as soon as I can.'

'Don't rush. What the hell am I going to do with them?'

Archer took his leave while Green poured another drink.

He had met a number of remarkable and distinct women in a very short period of time. Archer had a fairly firm understanding of Gloria Mars, the warrior. And of Alice Jacoby, the dreamer always looking for the greener grass.

The other three were less firm in his mind, but he was beginning to form a few impressions.

Cecily Ransome seemed to be everyone's idea of the next generation's great filmmaker. A breath of fresh, honest air in a town full of fuggy smog and dreary, worn-out ideas. He had found her interesting and confident, but perhaps not fully grasping the dark world in which she wanted to spend her days as a writer and director.

Mallory Green, the two-time Oscar winner, was old-school, but also hard and bitter about her unfair plight in life. He could appreciate it; he well knew the double standards employed between men and women in this town — hell, in this world. But she also seemed ruthlessly transactional in her approach to life and marriage. She would make her husband suffer for his infidelity, but she would not sever that bond because her own career would take a clear, if unfair, hit.

And then there was Eleanor Lamb. Missing person, afraid for her life, screenwriter extraordinaire, and a woman, at least according to Ransome's granduncle, Sam Malloy, who should not be trusted.

And I'm going to have to make my own decision on that at some point. If I ever find the lady.

29

Archer sat in the Delahaye out in front of the Green mansion and read through the few pages of Bender's typewritten reports. The dead PI had not articulated a clear theory of the case yet, nor had he identified, conclusively, the woman Bart Green was allegedly *consorting* with, to use Mallory Green's term.

But to Archer's thinking, it had to be Bernadette Bonham. Who else was there? But Bonham was supposed to be in France.

Then Archer thought about something Sylvia Danforth had told him.

He put the car in gear and headed back out to Malibu.

The cops had gone from Las Flores Canyon. He parked across the street, squinting against the sun, and walked over to Lamb's house and into her backyard. He made his way up the same set of outside steps to the second-floor deck and entered through the same door, which, obviously, the coppers had not bothered to secure, even if they had noticed it was unlocked.

The body, he knew, was gone. However, the chalk line was still there, a poor facsimile for a departed life, he thought. But that was all you ever got from the homicide boys. The coroner would have already hacked up Bender. He wondered if the bullet in the man's brain had held together enough to be identified, and then matched against the gun that had done the deed, if they ever found it. And he wondered if the autopsy had shown anything else. And he could keep right on wondering, because Phil Oldham would probably blow out his own brains before sharing any case notes with the likes of Archer.

Happy 1953 to you too, asshole.

He looked in Lamb's desk drawer and pulled out her checkbook. He sat down at the desk and examined the woman's handwriting and signature on the carbons. He took out a piece of paper from a drawer, grabbed a pen off the desktop, and slipped one carbon under the thin paper where he could make out the lines of her handwriting and signature through it. He traced these over and over until he felt comfortable enough to try it for real.

He made out a check to the Willie Dash Detective Agency for $200 and signed it 'Eleanor Lamb' in the lady's small, precise hand. He worked the check free and slipped it into his pocket.

He left the way he had come and walked over to the Bonhams'. He jiggered the garage door the way he had before and walked in, securing the door behind him. Danforth had told him that the Bonhams had driven their car to the airport before heading to France. He slipped out his notebook and checked what she had specifically said.

They left about a month ago.

Archer knelt down and again looked at the oil slick on the garage floor. As Archer had thought before, that might be because Bender's blue Ford could have been driven in here to hide it. But really what would have been the point in that? Would you take the chance that the cops might look in your garage and see a dead man's car? Lot of uncomfortable questions would follow. Yet that meant these marks could have come from the *Bonhams'* car, and, as he had thought before, they sure as hell weren't a month old.

He left and got back into the Delahaye. Archer looked over at Lamb's house as the rising sun started to wield its full heat and light on the canyon. Bender had met his end somewhere around here, unless he had been transported by car. But Archer didn't see it that way. The man's car had been parked on the street. Sometime before three in the afternoon or so on New Year's Eve, somebody grabbed him, beat him up, and when they were done, they put a bullet in his brain just to be sure he wouldn't be telling anyone what had happened. Then, at some point, they dumped the body at Lamb's place.

The problem with that was: How could they be sure Lamb wouldn't be at home then? Had they been watching the place, or known for a fact she'd be out on New Year's Eve? But if she had been home, they would have had another person to silence and thus another body to deal with. Why make trouble for yourself? Unless Lamb were in on it. But what would be the angle? Was Bender simply investigating an adulterous husband and got caught in the crossfire of something far more serious?

Wrong place, wrong time, just like I was on that sand. Only I got lucky and Bender didn't.

As he was driving away he saw Mrs. Danforth in her front yard plucking, presumably, at some weeds. She had on a mauve house coat and a pair of white slippers. Her real hair, mottled gray, was down around her shoulders. From this distance she didn't look a day over seventy-five. Two cats were watching her every move like a pair of prison guards in the exercise yard.

Archer didn't wait for her to spot him. He had other things to do today. The first being a trip to the Second National Bank of Malibu.

30

Archer didn't know what the *First* National Bank of Malibu looked like, but the *second* resembled an In-N-Out Burger restaurant, including the red-and-white-striped awnings on three sides. But the bank was far bigger than the In-N-Out Archer had visited in Baldwin Park, California, while he was there on a case. The food wasn't bad and it was cheap, and Archer thought the place might make a go of it.

He parked in front and could see through the plate glass four women at desks working away like dutiful bees. There was a drive-through teller on the left side and two more tellers inside. There were three cars in the drive-through, four cars in the parking lot, and five people standing in line at the inside tellers, waiting to do their banking business.

Commerce was just flowing in this place like a high tide coming in.

Behind a glass wall in one corner sat a big desk with a walrus of a man in a burgundy rayon suit that managed to somehow look faded. He was in his forties and certainly well-fed. He was well-groomed, too, although Archer wasn't sure whether the man's hair was actually his or was simply on loan from the bank at a competitive interest rate. Next to the desk was a brass spittoon that did not look ornamental. Here it was 1953 and people were still spitting their tobacco instead of driving it into their lungs.

Archer wasn't certain where they kept the safe, but every bank had one, which was why they kept

167

getting robbed.

Archer opened the door, causing a little bell to tinkle.

The women all looked up and smiled uniformly, apparently in accordance with strict bank protocols, while the walrus glanced his way once and then returned to scrutinizing the pages of the *Wall Street Journal*, as though his personal fortune was all wrapped up in there.

Archer approached one of the women and took out the check. 'I had a question about something having to do with this.'

He showed it to the woman. She was in her late twenties, brown-haired, doe eyes the same color, and with a serious, attentive look, as though one day she wanted to be seated where the walrus was. The woman next to her was a cool, clear-eyed blond gal with ambitions of her own, though her glimpse of cleavage where her sweater zipper had *slipped* down showed she was coming at the path to a better life from another angle than her coworker.

Doe-eye looked at it and said, 'What seems to be the problem? Were there insufficient funds to cover it?'

'No, I actually haven't tried to cash it. You see, Miss Lamb already paid me, but then this check came in my mail and I wanted to return it to her.'

The woman looked at the address on the check, and her confused look deepened. 'Well, she just lives right up in Las Flores Canyon.'

'Yes, I know. I've been there. But she's not there and the police won't let me in.'

'The police!'

'Yes, apparently they found a dead body in her house.'

Having obviously overheard this, the walrus put down his paper, rose from his desk, adjusted his cuffs, massaged the knot on his tie, and headed ponderously over.

'Can I help you?' he said in a smooth voice that Archer took an instant dislike to. As a teenager he'd bought a car from a guy who sounded just like that. And the car's transmission had failed as soon as the thicker oil the guy had poured into the gearbox to mask the failing gears clogged everything. When Archer had gone back to get his money, the gent disavowed all knowledge of the vehicle, Archer, or the existence of any known connection between them.

'I hope so,' said Archer, smiling because he felt he had to at the moment. He explained things again.

'A body?' said the man, who had introduced himself as Horace Mincer, the bank branch manager. 'I've seen nothing in the papers.'

'It just happened recently, and they're probably putting the kibosh on the reporters doing their snooping. Do you know Miss Lamb?'

'Well, yes, I mean, as a customer of the bank, I do.' He looked at the check. 'What did Miss Lamb need with a detective agency anyway?'

'I'm afraid that's confidential.'

Mincer shot him a glance. 'Well, what do you want us to do about it, fella?'

'I was wondering if you had another address for her where I could drop it off or mail it?'

'She has an office somewhere in LA, I believe. She's a secretary or something for a big film schmuck.'

'I tried there. They haven't heard from her and they're getting quite worried. And she's not a secretary. She's a very talented writer for the movies.'

The man looked at Archer like he was trying to feed him a line that could not possibly be true. 'Is that right?'

'Goodness,' said Doe-eye. 'She's gone missing?'

Mincer glanced sharply at her, as though trying to determine from which planet the woman might have fallen into his bank. 'Right, this way, Mr . . . ?'

'Archer.'

'Right. Better to discuss this in private.'

'It always is.'

The man gave him another stupid look that made Archer wonder if he could even add numbers much less provide cogent information.

They settled behind the glass wall and the man took out a cigar from his desk drawer, sheared off the end with a pinky knife, lit up, and puffed on it, his cheeks performing like fireplace bellows to get the ignited end going.

Archer watched him do this and looked him over once more. In the fellow's forty-plus years of living, Archer came away with the conclusion that the gent had possibly stopped maturing around the age of twelve.

Mincer put his wingtips up on the desk, blew out smoke, and then tacked on a stupid grin. 'Now that we're away from the little girls, give me the straight dope on this, buddy.'

'Come again?'

He held up the check and then dropped it on his desk. 'Who in their right mind turns down free money? You say the lady paid you twice? Okay, you keep both payments and she can ask for the overpayment back. What kind of nut *volunteers* to do it?'

Archer pretended to be offended as he picked up

the check and put it away in his pocket. '*This* kind of nut. Plus, I get the rep of cheating my clients, how long do you think I'd *be* in business?'

'Okay, okay, don't get all sore. It's no skin off me.'

'What can you tell me about Lamb?'

'Why?' Mincer asked.

'She's missing, as I said. I'd like to find her.'

'What do you want to know?'

'Is she a good customer?' asked Archer.

'No problems that I know of.'

'She bought a nice house up in the canyon, then did a big remodel. Put in a pool and everything. You people hold the mortgage on all that?'

Mincer put his feet on the floor and swiveled to face Archer with the expression of a man about to do some *business* of his own. '*Technically*, we're not supposed to talk about this stuff with third parties.' He hiked his eyebrows in a crude show of silent communication.

'Well, speaking for interested third parties, how much does it take to get around *technicalities* in this place?' asked Archer, reaching into his jacket pocket for his wallet.

Mincer glanced at the quartet of ladies, several of whom kept shooting darting glances their way. 'Not here. Let's go for a walk.'

'I'm all for fresh air.'

31

They crossed the road and walked along the beach where the sand was hard packed. The sun was high overhead, making it warm for January, and the tide was hovering in roughly neutral right now. However, even the distant breakers would cover any conversation they would have, Archer knew, which was probably why Mincer had headed over here, which meant the man wasn't all stupid.

'The mortgage?' asked Archer.

'There isn't one.'

Archer's jaw went slack. 'I know she makes good money with her job, but that house must have cost ten times what she pulls in during the course of a year.'

'Maybe more than that with all the improvements she made.'

'You sound like you know more about it than you let on back there.'

'Let me see your cash.'

'Okay, but keep in mind, pal, I'm a gumshoe, not a Rockefeller.'

'Would you go a grand?'

Archer's jaw went even slacker. 'Oh, sure, if Lamb walks safely out of the ocean over there the second the green hits your palm.'

'How about a C-note then? I'm taking a big risk here, buddy.'

'There's risk in getting out of bed every day. I tell you what, let me hear it first. Then I'll judge if it's worth the C or not.'

Mincer stopped walking and puffed feverishly on his cigar. 'Do I look like a monkey's uncle, pal? I'm a branch manager, for crying out loud.' He held up a foot. 'I'm wearing goddamn Florsheims.'

'Okay, let's say fifty. I pay you half on your promise of having the goods, and the other half when you're done. That work for you?'

'I guess.'

'That is not what I wanted to hear.'

'Okay, okay, yeah, it works.'

Archer passed him the money.

They started walking again.

'Lamb moved out here, oh, about two years ago. That's when she opened her account with us. She said she was buying the old Henderson place. We *did* have a mortgage on that. So I asked her if she wanted us to loan her the necessary funds to buy the property and fix it up, because she told me what she wanted to do with it. We had the survey and title on file and all, we'd just have to update it. All she needed was a male cosigner.'

'Come again?' said Archer sharply.

'An unmarried woman can't get a mortgage without a suitable man signing with her,' said Mincer. 'Didn't you know that, pal?'

'No I didn't. Why won't banks make loans to single women?'

'Don't be stupid. Banks need a guy on board to feel secure. And it's for the ladies' protection, too. Dames are clueless about money and such. They won't get taken for a ride with a sharp guy around. Turns out it didn't matter with Lamb. She told me she was paying cash for the property, *and* the renovations she planned.

So she didn't need a mortgage. And I guess there's no law against a dame buying a house with her own cash, though there probably should be. Like I said, women have no head when it comes to money and business. My dumb wife doesn't know the difference between a passbook account and Passover.'

'How much cash are we actually talking about here?'

Mincer gave him a meaningful look. 'A total of seventy-two thousand, five hundred clams.'

Archer whistled because how could a man not when hearing that sum. 'And how do you know that exactly?'

'I know the Realtor who did the sale. He sold me my house. And the contractor who did all the work is my brother-in-law. They told me.'

'It's nice to be talking to a guy so in the know. And she had that all in cash. Did she say where it came from?'

'No, and I had no legitimate right to ask. But I was damn curious.'

'Is there any way you can tell me what her balance is at your bank?'

Archer had seen from the woman's check register that her checking account had about fifteen hundred dollars in it.

'She has savings and checking accounts. Without getting specific, I can tell you that it was nothing close to what she put into that house.'

'So maybe she keeps it under her mattress?'

Mincer took a puff of his cigar. 'Hell, I figured maybe she was an heiress or something, or had a rich guy on the side, but she didn't seem the type. I mean, she was no looker, for Chrissake. For a guy to pony

174

up that kind of dough, you'd have to look like that Swede, Anita Ekberg. I mean, sweet Jesus. You seen the rack on that gal?'

'Not today I haven't. Did Lamb ever mention moving out here because she had a friend who already lived here?'

Mincer tapped ash into the sand, while Archer studied the ocean as it began to creep closer to them, like a predator in the high grass.

'I remember during our first meeting I asked her how come she was moving to Malibu. I mean, sure, a lot of people are buying out this way, but they're either famous or rich or both. Anyway, she said someone had recommended the place to her and *then* she'd found out that someone she knew from way back had a place out here. She wanted to rekindle the relationship.'

'Did she mention a name?'

Mincer dropped the cigar onto the beach, using his shoe to cover it with sand. 'No.'

'Man, woman?'

'Don't know. I mean, I could have asked, but I didn't really care. She was just opening an account. And I wouldn't be selling her a mortgage, so there goes that commission. And it wasn't like I was going to date her or anything.'

'And you *are* married,' said Archer, eyeing his wedding band.

Mincer grinned and gave Archer a wink. 'When did that ever stop a guy in heat? And my missus is actually old enough to *be* my wife. So, a body up there, you said. Know who it is?'

'Not yet,' Archer lied. 'It's a guy.'

'And you said Lamb is missing?'

Archer nodded. 'Whether by her choice or not, I don't know.'

'Damn. So anyway, where's the rest of my money?'

Archer reluctantly placed the bills in the man's palm along with his card. 'Anything else occurs to you, ring that number and you can leave a message.'

'Okay, but just so you know, mac, it'll cost you more.'

Archer tipped his hat before turning away. 'Boy, I didn't see *that* coming.'

32

Archer next drove to LA International, which was west of Inglewood and expanding at a rapid clip. What had once been a bean field was now one of the busiest airports in the country, operating twenty-four hours a day with planes regularly rising aloft from a flat basin and into the embrace of the prevailing trade winds.

As he was parking he watched a four-prop Continental plane land on the runway and come to a stop a bit farther down the tarmac. He wondered if the Greens flew their plane out of here or maybe out of Lockheed Air Terminal. Or maybe they had their own strip behind their mansion in Beverly Hills. The rich apparently did everything differently.

After questioning a couple of people he found the man he wanted to talk to, who oversaw parking at the airport.

He was of medium height and wearing a gutter-dented gray Stetson fedora covering curly silver hair. His vein-flecked nose and overly ruddy cheeks spoke of the man's fondness for the bottle. He stood at the doorway of a little building that was hardly big enough for him to stand inside. He looked Archer over as he asked his question.

'The Bonhams, you say?'

'Yeah, they live in Malibu. They flew to France about a month ago and left their car here.'

'So what do you want to know then?'

'Is it still here?'

'What's it to you?'

Archer produced his PI license and a fin. The man ignored the license and focused on the $5 bill, which Archer knew was good for at least two quarts of his favorite.

'I'm a curious guy.'

'You say they've been gone a month?'

'That's right,' replied Archer.

'Well, they didn't drive here then.'

'Why not?'

'Because the airport don't let folks leave their cars here that long. They don't have the space and they don't want the trouble if something happens to somebody's car. You got thieves in this town, you know.'

'Yeah, I heard that. But I was told they drove here.'

'They might very well have, only I'm saying they didn't leave their car here that long.' He suddenly grinned, showing all of his teeth, both real and false. 'But there are lots of places around here you can leave your car for that long. Feel free to check them out and ask your questions.'

'Come on, was that really worth five bucks?' asked Archer, frowning.

The man made a show of folding the bill and putting it in his pocket. 'It was to me.'

'Where can I find out if the Bonhams actually went to France?'

'Information desk in the terminal, they can help you.'

'Thanks. And if I come back with more questions, does the five still hold?'

'We'll have to see, won't we?'

Archer grinned and looked around at the shower stall digs the man called home. 'I can *see* why you got the big title and snazzy office.'

'One's born every minute, sonny.'

'Yeah, they are. Pardon me while I go suck my thumb.'

Archer found out that the Bonhams had indeed flown from LA to Idlewild Airport in New York with stops in between. And from there they had flown on an Air France Super Constellation to Paris, via Canada and Ireland. The transatlantic portion of the trip had taken a total of eighteen hours. They had arrived in Paris on December 2.

And then Archer got the whizbang follow-up that almost made him bite his tongue.

'And then returned here on December thirtieth,' said the pert, efficient woman behind the counter.

'Returned?' said Archer. 'Peter and Bernadette Bonham came back on the thirtieth?'

The woman looked at her records. 'No. According to this, *Peter* Bonham came back alone on a Pan American Airways flight from Paris to New York, and then he took a United flight here.' She looked farther down the page. 'Oh, that's a coincidence.'

'What is?' asked Archer, who was still trying to process what she'd already told him.

'You're here asking questions and *Mrs*. Bonham is flying in today. Her plane from New York lands in about an hour.'

Archer asked for and received the flight number. He tipped his hat and slipped the woman a Lincoln, which she'd deserved far more than the parking lot man had. After that, he headed to the airport bar to have a drink and wait for the Stratocruiser airliner to touch down in the land of glitter and dung.

33

While he was having his bourbon neat, Archer called
Universal Studios from a pay phone and left a message for Callahan, leaving the pay phone number for
her to call back on. She did so about ten minutes later,
during a break in shooting, she told him.

'Well, it's swell to hear that you're alive, Archer.'

'Keep your toga on. I plan to be around and kicking
at least until tomorrow. Look, did you get a chance to
talk to that gal, Donna?'

'Yeah, I did. Lamb never showed at the Marses'
party.'

'Okay, I figured that, but it's good to know for sure.'

'Where are you?'

'Waiting for a lady to arrive by plane after a trip to
gay Paree.'

'Well, aren't you the swanky one?' Her words were
joking, but her tone was not.

'It's all work. How about dinner tonight? I'm buying, so pick some place cheap.'

'Do you treat all the ladies this good, Archer?'

'None of them get it as nice as you, babe.'

'We knock off at eight. You can pick me up then. I'll
book the best burger joint on Skid Row.'

He hung up the phone, finished his drink, and
checked his watch. A moment later an announcement
came over the loudspeaker that the flight from New
York would be landing shortly.

Two minutes later he watched the Boeing dou-
ble-decker Stratocruiser descend into view out of the

thickening clouds, touch down smoothly on the runway, and veer toward the terminal. The ground crew brought out the mobile stairs, and a minute later the passengers began deplaning.

And that was when Archer realized he had no idea what Bernadette Bonham even looked like. Danforth had described her as forty and lovely and French. Well, there were about a dozen of those getting off the plane that he could see, so that was no good.

Archer watched them head toward the terminal building and then come inside. He followed the group to the baggage counter where, about twenty minutes later, a skycap appeared with a mountain of luggage and people started to call out and point to their pieces. They each paid him a tip for the privilege of getting their own property back.

As the passengers started to trickle out, Archer darted over to a courtesy phone and asked the woman who answered to page someone.

A few seconds later, over the PA came, 'Mrs. Bernadette Bonham, please call the courtesy desk. Mrs. Bernadette Bonham, please call the courtesy desk for a message. Thank you.'

Archer watched as one woman, a slim, medium-height brunette wrapped in a blue mink stole over a black skirt and jacket with a light green blouse and an Army-green veiled hat, gazed around, surprised, and then hurried over to a courtesy phone, her suitcase in hand.

Archer came up behind her. 'Mrs. Bonham?'

She turned quickly around and looked him up and down while he did the same to her.

Her features were pretty much flawless, Archer noted. Sharp, straight nose, large, luminous green eyes, firm chin, square jaw, stellar cheekbones, and a look of intensity that was actually a bit intimidating. But maybe that was just the French in her.

'Yes? And who are you?' A discernible accent underlay these few words.

Archer held out his PI license, and explained who he was and what he had been engaged to do.

Her very fine cheekbones sagged under the weight of all this. 'Eleanor Lamb is missing and a dead man was found in her house? You mean, right next door to us?'

'That's right. Can we go somewhere and talk for a few minutes?'

'I really need to get home,' she said, glancing around.

'Is someone picking you up from here?'

'No, I . . . I will take a taxi.'

'Long taxi ride to Malibu. Is your husband waiting for you there?'

She looked at him with what Archer thought was a fearful expression. 'What? Peter?'

'Yes, I understand he flew back here on December thirtieth.'

'No, I mean, yes, that is correct. It was then that he came back. And then I followed.'

'I just have a few questions. Maybe we can sit in the lounge and have a cup of coffee? I know it was a long flight from the East Coast.'

'Yes. It is very tiring.'

'I hope you stayed over in New York for a bit after flying back from France.'

Her green eyes fluttered so erratically Archer thought she might be on some drug. 'One night, yes. At the Waldorf.'

182

'Nice.'

He carried her leather suitcase with gold-trimmed straps, and she allowed him to lead her to the lounge, where he ordered two black coffees. She placed her stole on a chair and took out a pack of cigarettes that made Archer smile.

She noted this and said, 'Yes? You know these?'

'Unfiltered Gaulois Bleu. I had some French buddies smoke them during the war. Tried one. Strongest tobacco I ever put in my mouth.'

She seemed pleased by this acknowledgment. 'Yes, it is very strong. That is how we French like it, just like our café. Would you like one?'

He drew out his Luckys and shook his head. 'These helped get me through the war. And I recently tried drinking a Chinese liquor that nearly killed me, so I think I'll stick to what I know. I might live longer.'

He lighted her smoke and did the same for his own.

Their coffees came and were hot and bitter and strong.

'So, you met Eleanor when she moved out to Malibu?'

Surprisingly, Bonham shook her head. 'No, our families knew each other when we were much younger. Her father, Charles Lamb, was in the diplomatic corps for this country. My father, Matthieu, was the same for France. He was attached to the French Embassy in Washington. Eleanor and I went to school together there. Then, she went away to university, as did I, only in Paris. But we both came back to Washington afterward, and lived with our families for some time. Then my family moved back to France and I went with them.'

Archer thought about what the banker had told

183

him about Lamb moving out to Malibu to be close to someone from her past. And Danny Mars had said pretty much the same thing. Well, Bernadette Bonham had just moved to the top of the list for that trophy.

'And then all those years later, she moved to Malibu where you and your husband were living. I guess you were excited to see your old friend.'

Bonham puffed on her Gaulois and didn't answer. She looked out the window at a DC-6 taxiing for take-off. 'France has not changed much after the war. We go now for the last three years. There is still so much that is destroyed. Gone, never to return. It is very sad. So much beauty . . . poof. I did not like it. It is not the same.'

This statement didn't sit too well with the Army veteran Archer. 'Well, at least you're not speaking German. There *is* that.'

She settled her luminous eyes on him in a disarming manner. 'This is true what you say.' She took off her hat and set it on the table. Bonham tapped her ash into the ashtray and said in a contemplative tone, as though she were testing its veracity, 'Eleanor and I were not what you would call . . . very good friends, though our fathers got along splendidly. We . . . we were very different.'

'Having met her and now you, I can see that. But sometimes different is good.'

She glanced up at him. 'And sometimes it is not. She was always very intense. There was no, how do you say, *relaxing time* with her.'

'So her moving next to you wasn't a good thing, then?'

Bonham shrugged and said in a casual tone, 'I did not care one way or another.' She pointed her

184

Gaulois at him like a miniature sword. 'But I can tell you this — my husband did not like her.'

'Why not?'

She threw up a hand. 'I do not know. They just did not 'hit it off,' as you Americans say.'

'You have an example you can share with me?'

Her brows furrowed. Archer could see her translating his request in her head and deciding on an appropriate reply.

'We had a party at our house, this was about a year ago, you see. We invited people from Malibu, LA, you know. A nice, interesting group.'

'And did you invite Lamb?'

'Of course. I mean, she lived right next to us, and I knew her from before, as I said. It would have been rude not to. We even invited the old woman, though she did not come.'

'Mrs. Danforth?'

'Yes. But Eleanor *did* come. I welcomed her. We spoke of old times in Washington. She seemed, oh, I don't know, far more *casual* than usual. She actually seemed to be having a good time. But later I saw her and Peter having, what you would call, *words.*'

'Did you hear any of what they were saying?'

'No. Only that Peter was very angry and Eleanor was very cool and calm. Just like her father was. He was a very good diplomat, my papa used to say. When they saw me watching they smiled and went their separate ways.'

'Did you ask him later what had happened?'

'Yes. He said it was a difference of opinion over some property line disagreement.'

'Did you believe him?'

She stubbed out her cigarette. 'Do I look like an

185

imbecile, Mr. Archer?'

'Quite the contrary. But do you think there was any hanky-panky between them?'

'Are *you* an imbecile?' she exclaimed. 'You have seen me. And I presume you have seen Eleanor. As a man, do you think there is difficulty in choosing between us?'

'I guess not.'

'*Précisément*,' she said, giving him an incredulous look.

'What happened at the party after that?' asked Archer.

'Eleanor left shortly afterward. She even thanked me for a lovely time. She always managed to land on her feet. And I think that she got the better of Peter in whatever they were discussing.' She added, 'I understand that she is a very good writer of films.'

'Who'd you hear that from, Bart Green?' asked Archer.

'Why do you mention him?'

'Because Lamb works for his production company.' Archer left unspoken, *And Bart's wife thinks you're bed-hopping with her hubby.*

'Yes, I think I knew that.'

'So you know the Greens?'

'Yes. Peter introduced me to them some time ago. Bart Green is very successful in making movies, yes?'

'Yes. How did your husband and Bart Green meet?'

'In some business dealings. My husband has many interests.'

'Where'd you meet your husband?'

She looked more animated now. 'As I said, my family had moved back to France before the war began. Then, afterward, we were forced to flee to Canada.

186

We knew it was only a matter of time before the disgusting Nazis conquered our homeland. My papa was very outspoken about Hitler. We had to flee or we would have been killed! But after the war was over, we moved back to France and were living in Paris. Shortly afterward, I met Peter there and we were married in Nice. Then we came here. Peter had the house in Malibu already, you see. He bought it when he was no longer married . . . He was a . . . ?'

'Bachelor?'

'*Précisément.*'

'Wait a minute. So he was married before?' This didn't jibe with what Danforth had told him.

'Yes. But he does not speak of that time in his life. His first wife died. I know nothing more. And I do not care to know more.'

'He's from California, then?'

'I . . . I'm not sure. But he has business here.'

'You mentioned that. What sort of business? With Bart Green?'

'Oh, a great many things. But you see he is much older than me. He is over fifty now. But still very handsome. And he is very cultured and knows how to treat a Frenchwoman just so, and it is not an easy thing to do, n'est-ce pas?'

'Yeah. I tried and failed at that a few times during the war.'

Her big green eyes managed to widen even more. She looked intrigued and even graced him with an amused smile. 'Yes? You did this?'

'Oh, yes. Very poorly, and the ladies let me know it. So a great many businesses. Like what?'

'This and that. I have no head for it, and no interest. It provides a wonderful living for us. *That* is what

187

interests me,' she said candidly.

He looked over her expensive clothes. 'I'm sure.'

'So, thank you for the coffee but I have to —'

He cut in, deciding to go on the offensive now. 'Look, I can drive you out to your house and then I could talk to your husband. He might have some idea where Lamb is.'

She looked alarmed by this proposal. 'I do not think that is likely. As I said, he did not care for her.'

'But still, he might have seen something. I mean, he would have been there right when it all happened with the dead man and Lamb going missing.' He looked across at her as she sat there in her fine clothes with her intriguing French accent, and he wondered if she had been enjoying trying to play him for a sucker before he landed this counterpunch.

She seemed to think quickly, perhaps a bit too quickly. 'I . . . I don't believe he was there that night.'

She had made it all too easy to land the knockout blow.

'I don't believe I mentioned the *night* it happened.'

She took a few moments to light up a fresh Gaulois *and* give herself time to think of a response, Archer knew.

'I . . . I actually will not be going straight home, so I will have no need of your assistance. But thank you.'

'Just trying to be friendly.'

'Yes, you are too kind, Mr. Archer,' she said curtly.

'Just so you know, the county cops will probably be by to talk to you and your husband, now that you're home.'

She looked alarmed once more. 'But why would they do that?'

'A murder happened right next door. They've

188

already talked to Danforth. They tried your place but you weren't home. I guess your husband stayed somewhere else on New Year's Eve, because he didn't answer their knock the next day.'

'Yes, yes, he must have,' she said quickly.

'Do you know where that might be?'

'No, I suppose a hotel.'

'But you have such a swell place in Malibu.'

'He might have had business.'

'Is business the reason he came back here and didn't celebrate the New Year with you in Paris? It's probably a lot more romantic than Malibu.'

She looked up at him, all manner of friendliness struck clean from her. 'You ask a great many questions, Mr. Archer.'

'I know. It goes with the job, and I like to do my job well.'

'I think I will be leaving now.'

'I thought you might.'

'I need to powder my nose.'

'I'll watch your bag.'

When she got back there was no fresh powder on her nose. That had just been an excuse, and the woman was sloppy with details, it seemed. He wondered who Bonham had called while she'd been gone.

He carried her suitcase and walked her to the cab-stand. He left her there after giving her his card and asking her to tell her husband to leave a message at that number.

'I will tell him about our conversation as soon as I see him,' she promised.

I'm sure you will, thought Archer.

By the time she got into her cab he was in the Delahaye and took up the chase.

The taxi did not go to Malibu. It went, instead, to Chinatown.

And, more specifically, to the Jade Lion, which didn't surprise Archer one little bit. When Chinatown got involved in things, it tended to stay involved.

34

Bonham paid off the cab and walked up the steps to the front door. Archer eased to the curb a little down the street. It was too early for the Jade to be officially open for business, he knew. The doorman he'd fought before was nowhere in sight. If Archer was really lucky, he might be in a hospital.

But another man was there. Archer saw him as he came out to greet Bonham. It was the gray-suited gent with the scars, though he was now attired in a dark blue pinstripe with a pale blue pocket square. Now he knew who Bonham had called from the airport.

Archer popped open his glove box, snagged his Kodak camera, took aim, and fired off a few photos. The pair spoke for about a minute and then went inside. Even with his window down, Archer couldn't hear a word of their conversation from this distance, but he knew that he and his questions were probably the number one topic.

He drove off and headed to Green and Ransome. It was time he reported in with his client. Along the way he dropped off the film for development and paid for a fast turnaround.

When he walked into the office he was met by Audrey, the receptionist. She was in her fifties, with a pencil stuck in her hair bun. Archer wanted to snatch it out, as though it were King Arthur's sword in the stone, and freeing it would grant him all the answers he needed. But it was just a pencil stuck in hair, and the answers would have to come the hard way.

191

'While Miss Ransome is at Warners filming today, she said if you came by to tell you that she put your name on the visitor's sheet at the gate, Mr. Archer.'

'Thanks. I'll head over there now. I understand Bart Green is in Vegas?'

Efficient now looked suspicious. 'I have no idea where he is.'

'His wife told me that's where he was.'

Now Audrey just blinked at him.

'Have the cops been by to ask questions about Eleanor Lamb?'

She shook her head but said nothing.

'I hear Green flies up to Vegas on his own plane with his own pilot. Must be nice.'

That got him four blinks in staccato.

'Does he go to Vegas a lot? He likes to gamble, I take it?'

That got him five blinks and then Audrey picked up the phone before saying, 'Will there be anything else?'

'No, but can I compliment you on your answers? They're some of the best I've never heard.'

That got him a smile with no words or blinks tacked on.

He headed north to Warner Brothers, which was located in the southeastern tip of the San Fernando Valley in Burbank. The skies were still sunny, but with the chance of severe thunderstorms once he got there, depending on how things went with his client.

Archer passed through the suburbs of Burbank, where the partly built middle-income neighborhoods looked like they had been stamped out by tool-and-die concerns with the goal of a dull sameness that not even the Soviets could approach. But maybe that was okay. A house was to live in, not live your life through like maybe those monied folks did in Bel Air and Beverly Hills.

He found a parking spot down the street from the studio, which was a miracle unto itself. The guard at the gate found his name on the list and directed him to one of the soundstages. He waited until the red light went off and then rang the bell on the door. He gave his name to the woman who answered and asked to see Ransome when she had a moment.

Ten minutes passed and Ransome opened the door and stepped out.

'Follow me, Archer,' she said in a tone that made Archer think the woman was still in director mode.

She strode off and he had to step quickly to keep up.

Ransome was dressed in a man's suit, but tailored for her shape. Instead of a tie she had a colorful scarf around her neck. Her hair danced over her shoulders and was capped by a lavender beret. She would have looked *très chic* on the streets of Paris, he thought.

She led him to a series of small Spanish-style bungalows and unlocked the door of one.

They stepped inside, where Archer found a comfortable office space and casual seating, with a full bar set up against one wall. Movie posters from old Warner Brothers flicks were in frames on every wall.

She poured herself a club soda and lemon and asked him what he wanted.

'Same but the lime over the lemon. I'm working,' he added, smiling.

They sat across from each other in leather club chairs. 'Nice place,' he said. 'Yours?'

'So long as you make them money, the studios give

you *almost* whatever you want.'

Archer wondered what all that might encompass. 'What's the picture you're directing?'

'Let's just call it *Moby Dick*, only from the whale's perspective.'

'Should be a big hit.'

She made a show of looking at her watch. 'What have you found out?'

'You like Boleros?'

He had asked the question to see if Sam Malloy had filled his grandniece in on their conversation. By the look on her face, the old cop had decided to let Archer play it out for himself.

'I like it fine. Why do you ask?'

He explained what had happened after she'd left Boleros.

'Sam Malloy is a swell guy. He's very proud of you.'

'And I think the world of him.'

'He filled me in. You went to get his advice. It was a good move.'

'And he said I was in good hands with you.' She glanced down at his bandaged hand.

'What happened?'

'I just ran into a knife a guy was holding over in Chinatown.'

She sat back in her chair, crossing one leg over the other in the most unfeminine manner Archer had ever seen a woman manage. He was actually quite impressed.

'Why Chinatown?'

He decided to pull out the same matchbook he had shown Alice Jacoby.

'The Jade Lion?' Ransome said, reading the name off the cover.

194

'I found a bunch of them in Lamb's desk.'

'And what did you find there, besides the man with the knife?'

'I found a shot of pure fire in a glass, and then I went snooping.'

'And did you find anything connecting Ellie to this place?'

'Nothing directly, but I found out lots of other things.'

'Like what?'

'I'll keep them to myself for now. It might be safer for you if I do.'

'That bad, huh?'

'People will go to disgusting lengths to make a buck, let's leave it at that. You know a gal named Alice Jacoby?'

'I do, slightly. She works at Warners as a set designer. Good reputation.'

'Your tastes aren't simpatico, at least she said.'

'Aren't we getting rather far afield? Have you made *any* progress?'

'Have the county cops been by to talk to you?'

'No, they haven't.'

Archer sat back, puzzled. 'Okay, have they questioned anyone else at the company?'

'Not that anyone has told me.'

'All right, do you know Peter and/or Bernadette Bonham?'

'No. Who are they?'

'Next-door neighbors of Lamb's. I met Mrs. Bonham at the airport today. She was in France and now she's not. Same for her hubby.'

Ransome lazily rubbed her cheek, but her look was focused. 'Why is that important?'

'I told her about Lamb being missing and the dead body. She seemed surprised. I say *seemed* because I'm not sure. After she left the airport, guess where she went?'

'I don't like games, Mr. Archer.'

'The Jade Lion. And she met up with a guy that works there and —' On this Archer stopped because he had caught sight of a man on a movie poster who looked familiar. He was staring so hard that Ransome finally turned to look. 'What?'

'That poster. The craggy guy with the scars on his face.'

'That's Raymond Massey. That's the movie poster for *Arsenic and Old Lace* with Cary Grant. Why?'

'He just reminded me of the guy Bonham met today.'

She turned to face him with a pair of peaked eyebrows. 'I seriously doubt that Raymond Massey works at a bar in Chinatown.'

Archer had a thought. 'What was Massey's character's name in that movie?'

She thought for a moment. 'Mortimer, no, that was Cary Grant's character. Jonathan, Jonathan Brewster was Massey's character.'

'Yeah, I thought you might say that.'

'What does that have to do with anything?'

'What was Massey's role in the film?'

'A maniacal killer on the run from the cops. Even though the movie was a screwball comedy. Of sorts. Grant was really ham-handed in it, overacting and such, which he freely admits. But it made a lot of money. The movie was based on a Broadway play of the same title. In the play Boris Karloff was Jonathan Brewster, and Massey patterned his character and his face after Karloff.'

196

'And the scars?'

'The doctor he traveled with — Peter Lorre played him in the movie — had performed surgery on Massey's character to change his appearance. Lorre's character was a drunk. The result was a monstrous face full of scars.'

'My, my, how art imitates life.'

'What's the name of the scarred man who met this Bonham woman?'

'I'm going to have to find that out. But the thing is, Lamb had the name 'Jonathan Brewster' in her Wheeldex at her house in Malibu with 'the Jade Lion' written under it.'

Ransome immediately saw his point. 'So Jonathan Brewster was her *code* name for this scarred gentleman at the Jade? That way if anyone saw her Wheeldex . . . ?'

'They wouldn't know who she was referring to unless they were well up on their movies. And from what I've seen, you're being kind calling him a gentleman.'

'So you really think Ellie's been to this place?'

'Oh, I think so. And I think she knows Scarface, too, at least in some way. And if her neighbors the Bonhams know him as well?'

'Do you believe this could be connected to her disappearance?'

'Right now, I wouldn't bet against it. I just have to figure out *how* it's connected.' He took a swallow of his club soda and lime. 'I met Mallory Green earlier today. She said Bart is in Vegas. On business?'

She shrugged. 'I don't know. He doesn't really communicate his schedule or plans.'

'Does he like to gamble?'

197

'What makes you ask that?' she said.

'Why else does anyone go to Vegas?'

'I don't know if he gambles or not. Our relationship is pretty much restricted to filmmaking.'

'He has his own plane and pilot?' said Archer.

'Yes.'

'You ever been up in it?'

'No, I'm not keen on flying, actually. Well, Archer, I can't say I'm overwhelmed with what you've found out so far.'

'*I'm* not overwhelmed by it, either. But try this one on. Lamb paid nearly seventy-three grand for her place in Malibu, including the renovations.'

'That's a lot of money.'

'And she didn't take out a mortgage. She paid for it all in cash. Any idea where it might have come from?' asked Archer.

Ransome looked genuinely surprised. 'No. We pay well. But not *that* well.'

'If you did, I was going to try and get a job at Green and Ransome. Thanks for the time and nonalcoholic drink. I could almost get used to them. Almost.'

He rose. She didn't.

'What's your next move?' she asked.

'As soon as I figure it out, you'll be the second to know.'

35

Archer picked up his developed prints and the negatives and made a phone call from a pay phone in a Rexall drugstore. The man he was calling was named Jake Nichols. And what the man didn't know about Chinatown would barely fill a *baijiu* tumbler.

He was a former PI turned barkeep. Five years ago he'd been shot by police — accidentally, they'd said — while he was looking into a mob-backed gambling ring operating out of Chinatown. Turned out the coppers who pulled the trigger, *and* their immediate superiors, were actually all in with the mob boys. And when this was conclusively shown, Nichols had gotten a large payout from the city, large enough to buy his own bar. But not large enough to make up for the fact that the rest of his life would be spent without the ability to take a walk whenever he wanted.

The place was called, what else, Jake's. It was west of Central Avenue near Little Tokyo. On the ground floor of a three-story building, the bar wasn't too big or too small; Archer considered it just right. On the top of the building was a large billboard for the RCA Company. He'd been introduced to Nichols by Willie Dash. Both men had formerly served as agents with the Bureau of Investigation, now known as the FBI, before going over to the private investigation side.

Archer parked out front and walked in and was immediately greeted by a familiar voice.

'Archer, don't tell me. Willie can't snag a fifth of his favorite bourbon in that cow pasture you call home, and he sent you all the way down here to get one from yours truly.'

Archer smiled as Nichols came wheeling around the bar. He was a tightly packed man around sixty with white hair cut military style and mostly black sideburns, creating an interesting, bifurcated look. His face was tanned and leathery even in January, and his forearms — heavily muscled from propelling himself for the last half decade — were revealed by rolled-up sleeves.

His dead legs were covered with a dark blanket. A stogie was settled in one corner of his thin mouth. Despite his grin and good-natured barb, he seemed to be in pain and was. One bullet was still tethered near Nichols's spine. He would take it to the grave.

The bar wasn't your typical bottle joint. It looked like one you might find in Morocco or certain out-of-the-way places in Italy, both of which Archer had been to while in the Army. Jake's was always packed at serious drinking time, which would be in about an hour, Archer calculated, and the clientele was as diverse as the city, which was not the norm. And there was no pub crawling going on. When you came to Jake's you stayed at Jake's for all your drinking.

'He says he can never find liquor like you have here.'

'And he never will, because I'm not revealing my sources to that old son of a bitch.' He propelled his chair up to an empty table. 'What can I do you for?' asked Nichols as Archer sat down across from him.

Archer answered by pulling the photos out of his pocket and sliding them across. 'Guy's at the Jade Lion. You know who he is?'

Nichols immediately turned serious and studied the photos before looking up at Archer. 'Who's the dish?'

'Bernadette Bonham. Lives out in the canyons of Malibu with her husband, Peter. She just flew in from Paris. Told me she was going home. She went to the Jade instead after we had an interesting conversation about a case I'm working.'

Nichols slid the photos back to Archer. 'What do you know about the Jade?'

Pocketing the photos, Archer replied, 'They only serve one kind of drink and it'll nearly kill you unless you're Chinese. And they have cameras in the bedrooms taking pictures of famous people doing not-so-nice things. And they have sandy crates hidden around the place that once might have held heroin. And it was by the grace of God that I didn't take my last breath there the other night.'

Nichols took all this in and then relit his stogie. When he spoke his voice was low. 'There're lots of bars and dives in and around Chinatown, Archer. Not as many as there were in Old Chinatown, but they're getting there. Hell, my place isn't that far away from it. But the Jade is in a class of its own. And I don't mean that as a compliment.'

Archer nodded. 'I saw that for myself.'

'To answer your question, the man in the photo is named Darren Paley, and he is bad news all around. Dangerous as hell. Done time for some really bad stuff and came out way too soon, probably because of money changing hands, and he's now doing even worse stuff. They said he's killed more people than he has fingers on both hands.'

'And the cops just look the other way? I thought the LAPD was cleaning up its act.'

'They are. But they have to pick their battles, and low-hanging fruit brings faster headlines. Paley is a

201

cobra sheathed in armor. The cops go after him, they need to be ready for war. And he's got mob ties. That complicates things. It always does.'

Archer told Nichols about the actress and what he had seen going on there.

He nodded before Archer was finished. 'Blackmail to a tee. Unless she gets other 'famous friends' to take the bait, she gets outed. It's been done before and it works great.'

'And if all of these people get outed?'

'Film business takes a hit, city takes a hit, LAPD takes a hit. Why the hands-off on the Jade makes sense. Plus, they figure if you're stupid enough to get yourself in that kind of jam, you take your own medicine and don't look for rescue from the official machinery.'

'You seem to know a lot about this,' said Archer.

'Oh, didn't I mention? The mob-backed gambling ring guy I was nosing around on that got me stuck in this contraption for life?'

'Darren Paley?' said a slack-jawed Archer.

'I couldn't prove anything back then and he skated free. And the dirty cops were all over it providing him cover. But it was Paley all right.'

'Where'd he get all the scars?'

'Paley grew up rough and tumble back in Chicago; it's made him hard as steel. Among other prison stints, he got sent to the pen at Joliet on a murder charge, but it got overturned and he walked free after a year. He was only eighteen. He's got no heart and ice in his veins. He'll kill someone one minute and forget it the next. He was a hero in the war. Shot down twenty-some Luftwaffe planes when he was with the Army Air Corps. When that wasn't a thrill enough for the guy, he got his orders shifted and took his battle to the dirt with the regular Army. Word was they'd have to pull him off Krauts after he'd already killed them because he kept beating and shooting and knifing them. He got thrown out of the army in 1944 for stealing guns and ammo and selling it. The brass didn't court-martial him because he was such a 'hero' in combat and they didn't want the bad press. Then he jumped right into bed with the mob. This was up in Vegas. He was doing the gambling ring operation on behalf of the Vegas mob, who didn't want to leave all the illegal dollars to the local boys. Later, he moved here full-time, and now he's running the Jade. Never turn your back on the man, because he'll stick a very large knife in it.'

'What'd he do for the mob in Vegas other than run a gambling ring down here?'

'Knee and back breaker for Lansky, Siegel, Cohen, and boys like that. And he was really good at his job. He moved up quickly. They were probably sorry to see him go. But my thinking is they're still connected at the hip. That's my spiel on Paley, now talk to me about your case.'

Archer went on to explain about Lamb's disappearance and the dead Cedric Bender being found at her home.

'I actually met Bender a couple times,' said Nichols. 'I didn't know about his death. He was a good egg. Square and straight.'

'County cops seem to be keeping it under wraps. And they haven't been to Lamb's place of business yet, either.'

'Sounds like they got orders to slow-walk this. You got other angles to work, Archer?'

'A few. Hopefully, one will pan out. Anything else

you can tell me about Paley?'

'He's got plenty of smarts. Enough to get some of the solid action.'

'So he might have partners in all the stuff at the Jade?'

'My guess would be yes,' replied Nichols.

'Well, he was talking to the lady from Malibu. They obviously know each other. She said her husband has lots of businesses.'

'And maybe one of them is the Jade,' said Nichols.

'Well, they're not paying the electric bill and the hired help off one kind of booze.'

'Blackmail, selling dope, and making stag films bring in a nice living. What's next on your to-do list?'

Archer looked at his watch. 'Having dinner with the prettiest girl in town, and I can't be late.'

36

Archer picked Callahan up at eight on the dot outside the Universal gate. She was wearing black slacks, a white blouse with a collared neck, a black trench coat, and three-inch red heels. She looked like a million bucks, while Archer was still walking around with sand in his pants. Still, *he* felt like a Rockefeller with her sitting next to him.

She gave him directions to West Sunset Boulevard, where he pulled into a drive-in called Tiny Naylor's. Hollywood High School was right across the street. They slid into the only open slot because the place was packed.

'You weren't kidding about the burger joint,' he said.

'Calling Tiny Naylor's a burger joint is like calling the *Mona Lisa* a sketch. This place has class, Archer. And you don't have to get burgers and shakes. You can have a rib eye, baked potato, corn on the damn cob, and lots more, and it's delivered right to your car. *And* it's got a famous clientele because they don't have to get out of their car and show their faces.'

Archer looked at an ancient Packard next to them. 'Those folks having milkshakes look familiar.'

Callahan followed Archer's gaze, and gasped when she saw who it was. 'Gee, Archer, I wonder why? It's *only* Kate Hepburn and Spencer Tracy.'

Archer began leaning out the window to get a better look but Callahan said, 'Oh, for crying out loud, leave them alone. Guys like you are the reason they come to places like this, so people won't go gaga.'

He gave her a funny look. 'But don't movie stars want that? Isn't that why they work so hard to get famous?'

'It's complicated,' said Callahan slowly. 'Yes, they want to become stars because that's what movies do for you. And no, they don't want to be gawked at like zoo animals.'

'Well, I don't see how you straddle that fence.'

'You don't, Archer, which is why two big stars are here in an old Packard wearing sunglasses when it's nighttime. And of course the other reason is that Tracy's married. *And* he's Catholic.'

'Sounds like a match *not* made in heaven.'

As they ordered from the waitress, a giant man lumbered across the parking lot.

'Who's that?' asked Archer. 'The front four for the LA Rams rolled up into one guy?'

The waitress looked where he pointed. 'Oh, no, that's *Tiny* Naylor. He owns this joint.'

Callahan laughed dismissively and said, 'And you call yourself a detective.'

As they ate in the car, Archer laid out for Callahan all that he had learned. She shivered when he told her what he had discovered about Darren Paley.

'Omigod, Archer, he sounds like everybody's worst nightmare.'

'Yeah, he does,' said Archer quietly as he cut into his steak.

'Don't you get scared sometimes?'

He glanced at her to find the woman gazing worriedly at him. 'Everybody gets scared, Liberty. I'm no exception and I'm no hero coming in to save the day, either. They make those up in your business, not mine. I'm just one guy hitting the bricks and trying to grab the end of a firecracker fuse and see where it'll lead me before it blows up in my hand.'

'That's a pretty good line, Archer. Maybe you should write for the movies.'

'All I want to do right now is find Eleanor Lamb and Bender's killer. That's plenty.'

Callahan slid a forkful of mashed potatoes into her mouth. 'Do you think anybody else might end up dead?'

'I wouldn't bet against it.'

'Including Ellie?'

'I won't sugarcoat it. It's been long enough that I'm more likely to find her body instead of her breathing.'

Callahan slowly put her fork down and turned to him, taking his hand. 'Archer, what would you say if I got you a screen test with Jack Webb for *Dragnet*? Would you go?'

He looked at her with a bemused expression. 'And how exactly would you do that?'

'A guy I know knows a guy who knows Webb. That's how this town works. With your looks and experience and how you carry yourself, Archer, you could be a star in no time.'

'You mean by being a fake cop solving phony crimes and reading off lines somebody else wrote for me to say?'

'Well, you'd make a lot more money and nobody would be trying to kill you for real.'

'Is that where all this is coming from? You're worried I might get hurt?'

'You've already *been* hurt, Archer,' she snapped. 'And almost killed, twice, or three times just in the last few days. I lost count.'

Archer sat back and drank his coffee. 'There's a price to be paid for everything we do in life, Liberty.'

'But in your line of work the price you pay is pretty damn high for what you get back.'

'I'm not knocking what you do for a living. I'm proud of you. You're good at what you do and you work hard. Now, don't take this the wrong way, but you wearing a toga in some Roman flick with a bunch of fake lions, how does that help anybody? John Wayne pretending to be a soldier taking out Nazis doesn't get rid of the *real* bad guys.'

'But it *does* give people hope. I mean, that's why they shot all those wartime pictures showing us winning.'

Archer's face darkened. 'That's true. But the *real* soldiers won the war. And it's not about hope. This whole town is based on a fantasy and the fuel for the whole damn thing is money. But when someone dies in my line of work the blood isn't fake, and they don't get back up when the director calls 'cut.' They stay dead. So if I can keep that from happening to one person then *my* payoff is pretty good from where I'm sitting. I'll pack my lunch and my gun and go back the next day and try to do it all over again. And if that means I have to take on the likes of Darren Paley, I will. I don't want to be John Wayne looking tough and being anything but. And besides, I never learned how to ride a damn horse.'

He lit up a Lucky and blew smoke out the open window.

'You've been saving that up for a while, haven't you?' she asked, side-eyeing him.

'Maybe I have.' He looked over and saw that his words had had a crushing effect on the woman. 'And now, I'm going to walk some of it back.'

'What?'

'Remember when we were driving through the mountains to Bay Town?'

Her eyes widened at this. 'How can I ever forget, seeing as what happened.'

'You said you needed something else besides talent to make it in Hollywood. You said you needed —'

'— the It factor, yeah. The camera has to find something in you, something maybe you don't even know you have.'

'Well, you have *it*, whatever *it* is. Plus the talent and everything else a star needs. Every room you go into, you light it up like a bonfire. Everybody turns to look. You can talk a cop out of a felony arrest, because I've seen you do it. You walked into Midnight Moods and took it over. I know Monroe is coming on like nobody's business, but you can be bigger than she'll ever be.' He nodded at the Packard. 'More legendary than Hepburn even.'

'Oh come on, Archer. I'm —'

'I'm being serious here, Liberty! So just listen up.'

And Callahan closed her mouth.

'You can have this town in the palm of your hand. *If* you want to.' He suddenly gripped her hand. 'But I saw that woman at the Jade made to feel like she was worth nothing. And she *was* a star, Liberty. Right at the very top. And they were chewing her up and spitting her out.'

Her big eyes opened wider and seemed to peek into Archer's soul. 'So you're wondering why I'm working so hard to get *there*?'

He stared at her for so long, he almost forgot to answer. 'Yeah. I am.'

She glanced over at the old Packard where two Hollywood legends sat coiled around one another. 'Everybody has to get to where they have to look in the mirror and say, 'Is it really worth it?''

'And do you know what your answer will be?' asked Archer.

'I think it's one of those things where you won't know the answer until you absolutely have to ask yourself the question, for real.' She looked at him. 'But what you just said now makes any answer I have to give . . . a little easier.'

They kept holding hands and staring out the window at the darkened sky.

37

Archer dropped Callahan off at her place and hit the road. He arrived in Bay Town before eleven o'clock. He had a one-bedroom apartment near his office, which was located in a dilapidated building but the rent was next to nothing. He slept a full eight hours, showered and shaved, and dressed in clean clothes. Then he packed what he needed, had breakfast at a diner around the corner, and walked out feeling a lot better about things.

He walked into the offices of Willie Dash's Very Private Investigations at nine sharp.

Connie Morrison hadn't changed in the three years he had known her. Professional, efficient, blond hair parted with precision, she greeted Archer with a smile and said, 'He's waiting for you.'

Archer hung his fedora on the wall hook and headed to see Willie Dash.

The man was sitting on a Murphy bed that was in the down position from the wall. He had on a pair of reading glasses and was studying a newspaper.

An unopened bottle of scotch was on the table next to him.

Dash was in his midsixties, about five-seven, burly, and barrel-chested with a face of flint but a charming manner lurking right below. He had a brain with more in it than any man Archer had ever met, and fine-honed, crime-busting instincts to match. When Archer had first met him, Dash had worn a black toupee that was about as fake-looking as one could

211

purchase or make. He had now become resigned to wearing his baldness publicly. His jowls were lengthening with each passing year, but the mind was still sharp and so was the tongue.

'Sit, Archer,' he said without glancing up. 'Just been reading some stories about crime in LA.' He took off his glasses and looked over at Archer as he settled onto the edge of a faux-leather davenport. 'And you seem to be right in the middle of it. And I got a call from Jake Nichols late last night. Said you went to see him.'

'I did. He was very helpful.'

'What he mainly did was fill you in on the Jade and that lowlife Darren Paley.'

'Who Jake was investigating when he got shot by a couple of corrupt coppers.'

Dash laid the paper aside, straightened his plastic suspenders, and finished knotting his bowtie. 'Which makes what you're doing personal to Jake. And also to me. How does the case stand right now?'

Archer pulled out the contract Ransome had signed plus the check for $500 and handed them to Dash, who glanced at the signature and amount and then handed them back. 'Leave those with Connie on your way out. Now, spill everything to me that you got on this.'

Archer went through the case point by point, ending with his conversation with Nichols, but he did add that he'd had dinner with Callahan after that.

'This Bernadette Bonham knows the Jade?' asked Dash. 'And Paley?'

'Sure seemed like it. She went right there after getting back from France.'

'No, I think she went right there after meeting *you*, Archer. Paley's a killer all right, but he's no dummy. He can add two and two as well as any man. He knows of your involvement. He will have talked to the Chinese girl directing traffic at the Jade, and the doorman you tussled with, and the barman and everyone else you ran into that night, and they will have described you to a tee. That description will fit the one that Bonham would have given him. So he knows you were snooping around the place and probably saw stuff you shouldn't have. Bonham will add your name to the pile, because you told her who you were, and from that Paley will get more info on you, which he's no doubt already done. And more information on *me*, because you work at this firm. Now, where have you been staying in LA?'

'With Liberty.'

'Not good, Archer. You want to stay as far away from her as you can right now.'

'Yeah, I can see that.'

'Think real hard on this. Any sign of someone following you when you picked Liberty up from the studio, drove her to dinner, and then back to her place last night?'

'No. I always check on that. There was no tail.'

'Okay, second question, did you tell anyone about Liberty? That you were friends? That you hung out with her? Aside from Lamb knowing, of course.'

Archer thought back. 'I don't think so.'

'That's not quite good enough. Think some more.'

'I did tell Cecily Ransome when she asked what actress I was having dinner with when Lamb approached us.'

'Okay. And you were at a party with her, right? On New Year's Eve. People saw you two together.'

'Yes, but I don't think any of those people are involved.'

213

'Again, not good enough because you can't possibly know that to be true.'

'You're right. What should I do about it?'

'Have you called Liberty this morning?'

'No.'

'Do it now.'

'Shit!' exclaimed Archer as he picked up the phone on Dash's desk and dialed the number. As it was ringing Dash said, 'Could she be at the studio?'

'No, she told me she had the morning off. I — Hello? Liberty, it's Archer,' he said, his features full of relief. 'Yeah, I'm in Bay Town with Willie. Look, um, until I can get this thing figured out, I won't be able to see you again. What? No, it's for *your* protection. That's right. It's gotten to a funny point, Liberty. And . . . and can you find another place to lie low for a while? Just until all this gets sorted out? Right, someplace no one will know you're there. Yeah, like a hotel. But not under your real name. Right, look, I'm sorry about this. I . . . sure. Yeah, call Connie with where you'll be staying. Me? No, I'll find another place. Okay, thanks, thanks a lot. And please be careful and make sure no one is watching your place or follows you, and that includes at the studios . . . Okay, I will, thanks.'

He hung up and looked at Dash. 'She took that well, considering what I was asking.'

'How long you known her?'

'You know how long. Over three years.'

'And you still haven't figured the lady out yet?'

'What's that supposed to mean?'

'It means she'll do pretty much whatever you ask her to do, Archer. She cares about you, just like you care about her.'

'She wants me to audition for *Dragnet* so I can play a fake cop and not get hurt.'

'And you're surprised by that?'

'When you two were married Connie never asked you to quit being a PI.'

'Because if I did we would have starved, since she also worked here. And besides, she knows it's the only thing I'm good at. What am I supposed to do, go sell insurance? I'd eat a round from my gun before I'd do that.'

'Okay, with Liberty safe, I'll hole up at some dive in LA under an alias.'

'But leave the Delahaye here. Even in LA it sticks out. Do a rental. With $500 as a retainer, you got the dough.'

'Right.'

Dash picked up the contract and glanced at the signature. 'And what's the Ransome lady's story?'

'She works with Lamb and is concerned.'

'And? There's got to be more than that to shell out five hundred bucks.'

Archer had been thinking about this for a while and decided to test his theory on Dash. 'Lamb is a natural curly blonde. She told Liberty she wasn't, though, that she was actually a brunette. But I saw her college picture with her blond hair. And I found stuff in her medicine cabinet that confirms she has to color it black *and* straighten it.'

'So the reverse of what most women in that town do. But she's a writer, not an actress, so what does her hair matter?'

'Right, why go to the trouble?'

It only took Dash seconds to read between those wide lines. 'Let me guess. Ransome has black, straight hair, too. But that's probably her real deal. That means Lamb changed hers to match Ransome's. You think there's something romantic between them?'

'I don't know for sure, but I clearly get that feeling. And Ransome's granduncle seems to think Ransome isn't interested in men. And he strikes me as having really good instincts.'

'Right, the former cop you mentioned. Well, they wouldn't be the first gals to hit from the other side of the plate. But you still don't have a clear, developed lead on Lamb.'

'No, I don't. I keep getting sidetracked on other stuff.'

'Well, let me help you on that. Don't go back to LA just yet. I want you to go to Anaheim.'

'Anaheim?'

'Cedric Bender? I talked to his wife, Anne. I told her we were on the case. She's going to let you search Bender's office. He worked out of his house. The funeral's today. Connie will give you the address. Bring some flowers.'

'Okay, but what am I looking for?'

'Any notes on the Green case or items related thereto. I know Mallory Green showed you the reports, but any PI worth his salt doesn't put everything in the reports. And he might have found out stuff *after* filing his last report with her.'

'You figure he was digging into Bart Green's infidelity and ran into something totally unconnected? And bought it for his troubles? If so, I doubt his report will shed much light on Lamb's whereabouts.'

'We can't say for sure, because we don't know enough. Your job is to know more than you do now. So get going to Anaheim. Call me from there with what you find.'

'And what will you do in the meantime?'

'I'm going to be thinking and checking on a few things, Archer.'

'You've got other cases, Willie. I'm good to go it alone on this one.'

Dash shook his head, his features those of a man who has made up his mind and cannot be dissuaded. 'I've been waiting a long time to take down Darren Paley, Archer. And I don't plan on missing my shot.'

'I know you and Nichols are tight.'

'It's not just that. Jake saved my life, twice. The *second* time was after he was stuck in that damn wheelchair. Any man who thinks that debt will ever be repaid in this life isn't much of a man, at least in my book. So now Paley has two problems — you and *me*.'

38

Archer had been to Anaheim once before. Back then he had viewed the place as vast orange and walnut groves with a small town hiding therein. His opinion hadn't altered. He had changed into a dark suit, white shirt, and black tie, rented a green, two-door Buick Riviera in Bay Town, and driven to the address Connie had given him. As Dash had instructed, he'd stopped at a roadside venue to buy a small bundle of flowers.

Anne Bender lived in a modest tract house on the edge of an orange grove about a half mile outside the town limits. He could smell the oranges, and the pesticides clinging to their skin, from about a mile away, sort of like sugar and cyanide.

He pulled into the dirt driveway and got out. The screen door squeaked open and Anne Bender appeared there. She looked like a female version of her husband: gray, corpulent, and haggard, dressed all in somber black.

Archer introduced himself and she nodded slowly, her features full of sadness, grief, pain, anxiety, and fear, all the emotional elements rolled up into losing someone important. Her thin, gray hair was done up in a tight bun that pulled her brow wrinkles skyward. She had on a black sack dress with no ornamentation and low-heeled shoes that looked comfortable if not fancy.

With all the women Archer had recently met, in their mansions and penthouses and wearing the very best and costly garments, the comparison could not have been starker. But it seemed to Archer that Anne Bender, perhaps unlike all those other women, was living the very life that she had chosen for herself in the very way that she wanted to.

'Please, come in, Mr. Archer,' she said after firmly shaking his hand and taking the flowers from him, thanking him. 'Mr. Dash told me you would be coming.'

'I'm sorry to be here at such a bad time,' he said.

'Cedric always told me there was a chance of something like this happening in his line of work. But he fought in the First World War, right after we were married. And he could've been killed then, too.' She looked up at Archer. 'You like being a detective, don't you?'

'Yes, I do. There's not much money in it, but there're other things.'

'Oh, Lord, I know about the not-much-money thing, but we raised three children and had a good life together. Just not as long as I would have hoped.'

'Will your children be coming to the funeral?'

'My two sons are in the Army and can't get leave to come. My daughter lives in Michigan and is about due to deliver her third child, so she can't travel. I plan to get on a bus and go see her after the baby is born.' She looked around at a place that probably looked as foreign to her right now as another country would. 'Nothing to keep me here now.'

'Again, I'm sorry. I didn't know your husband, but I've spoken to people who did, and they all thought very highly of him.' He couldn't bring himself to reveal that he had stumbled over her husband's body at Lamb's home.

'Mr. Dash said you'd drive me to the church and the gravesite. I don't have a car.'

This momentarily jolted Archer, but then he thought, *Of course you don't have a car. You only had the Ford and no one knows where it is.*

'I'll take you wherever you need to go, ma'am.'

'Would you like some coffee or lemonade?' She wrinkled her nose and looked out the window at the nearby groves. 'I don't offer orange juice.'

'I'm fine. I'd just like to look through your husband's office before we leave for the service.'

'All right. We don't have to get going for about an hour or so. It's not far.'

She led him down a short hallway. As Archer looked around, it occurred to him that the entire house could have fit inside the room where he had met Mallory Green. With all that, she was no happier than the woman walking slowly in front of him. And Green hadn't lost her husband. At least not in the same way Anne Bender had lost hers.

'Here it is, Mr. Archer.' She handed him a key. 'Cedric always kept it locked. He was a real stickler on that, confidentiality and such.'

Archer took the key. 'I'm sure.'

He unlocked the door and went inside as he heard her shuffle back down the hall to do whatever it was a person did before going to their spouse's funeral: wait, cry, aimlessly wander through old memories, cry some more.

He closed the door behind him and surveyed the small space. Desk, chair, row of pens and legal pads, a ream of typewriter paper, telephone, four metal file cabinets, and a small, squat iron safe. No window, so there wasn't an orange or walnut grove in sight.

He searched the desk first and found little in the way of helpful information. There was no calendar, and he wondered why because every PI kept one. That could mean a little or a lot. He next methodically went through the file cabinets. They were alphabetized, which helped quite a lot since he simply jumped to the letter *G* for *Green.*

And that was when he ran into a big problem. There was no file for Mallory Green. It went from *Harold Gompers* right to *Josephine Gustavo.* He checked the entire cabinet just in case Bender had misfiled it. No *Mallory Green.* He went through the other cabinets. They all seemed to be in order but held no file for Green. And she had told him that she had used Bender before, after he'd been recommended by other wives with cheating hubbies. Yet not even that old file was here.

Archer sat down at the desk and checked the Wheeldex. All the entries were in neat block lettering, just like all the copies of client reports Archer had glanced at in the file cabinets. Mallory Green's address and phone number weren't in there, either. He looked at the blotter to see if it had some carryover marks or indentations from a letter or note Bender might have written, but nothing appeared that was relevant.

He squatted in front of the safe. It was a combination lock. He found Anne Bender sitting in the front room and asked if she knew the combination. She didn't. He also asked her if she had been absent from the house at any time since her husband's death.

'Yes, I had to go into town a few times. A friend took me.' She teared up. 'And I had to go to the funeral home and bring the clothes for Cedric to be buried in.'

'Did you lock everything up before you left?'

'No, folks around here don't lock their doors, Mr. Archer. It's very safe, never had any trouble.'

Until now, thought Archer.

'The key you gave me to open your husband's office. Where do you keep it?'

'Cedric kept it on a hook in the kitchen pantry.'

'Did you notice anything unusual when you came back from town those times, or when you got back from the funeral home?'

'Unusual? No.'

Archer had already seen that there were no other homes close by, so it was doubtful anyone would have seen someone go into her house.

'Did you go to the funeral home at night?'

'Yes, it was dark when they called and asked me to come in. Funny, though.'

'What?' said Archer sharply.

'Well, when I got there no one knew I was coming. Whoever had called I guess had gone home for the day.'

'Right, I'm sure.' *Okay, so that's how and when they did it.* 'One more thing — did your husband ever mention working for a Mallory Green?'

She shook her head. 'But he never mentioned any of his clients, Mr. Archer. He was a real stickler on —'

'— confidentiality, yes, thanks. Last question: Did your husband keep a calendar?'

'Oh, yes, it should be on his desk.'

So someone did take the calendar. He wondered what else they had taken besides all the files on Mallory Green.

He went back to the office and looked around some more. The safe only had a few inches of separation between its back and the wall. He tried to lift it.

222

The thing was bolted to the floor.

He noted scratches on the wall and something occurred to Archer. He quickly felt behind the safe, and his hand brushed against something hard. It was the back of the safe. As he touched it again, it fell against the wall. Someone had managed to shear off the metal backing. He slid his hand into the narrow opening and felt around. Nothing. He did more probing and all he touched was the felt liner inside the safe. They probably had cleaned the damn thing out from the breached rear opening.

He found a flashlight in a desk drawer and used it to take a closer look behind the gap. He saw an edge of something white wedged between the sheared off back plate and the safe at the very bottom edge.

He went and got a coat hanger, bent it into a precise angle, and used it to snag what turned out to be a piece of paper. He pulled it free and read through the document. It was a copy of an invoice for aviation fuel at an outfit operating at LA International. And the bill was addressed to Green and Ransome at the office in Beverly Hills. He scanned the invoice for any other useful information. The plane in question was a Beechcraft Model 18, and the aircraft was owned by BMG, Inc. Archer figured the initials might stand for Bart and Mallory Green.

Our plane, our pilot.

He folded the invoice and put it in his pocket. It would make sense that Bender would be interested in Green's plane, since he could be using it to fly mistresses out of the city and to safer climes for a little party and sack time. In the files that had been taken Bender might have had itineraries for the plane, lists of passengers and the like. And the calendar would show

223

meetings Bender would have had and with whom. Someone had obviously not wanted that information to remain in his hands. But there was a key question: Was infidelity a motivation for murder? Green had cheated before. His wife didn't want a divorce because that would give her ex a clear field to run amok while doing her professional damage. So why would Bart Green care if the truth about his affairs came out?

A knock on the door preceded Anne Bender's poking her head in. 'We should go. Did you find anything helpful?'

'Yes, Mrs. Bender,' said Archer. 'I think I did.'

She moved into the room. 'Will you do one thing for me, Mr. Archer?'

'Certainly, anything.'

The mask of grief and solemnity vanished for an instant and the woman's features flashed with the anger and fierceness of the prematurely bereaved.

'Will you find the son of a bitch that did this to my husband?'

39

The funeral service was sparsely attended, and Archer kept watch out for anyone whom Bender didn't recognize. He knew that sometimes people responsible for the deaths of others came to the funeral looking for things helpful to their cause. But Mrs. Bender reported no strangers.

After seeing the body in the coffin, Archer noted that the mortician had done a good job covering up the wound that had killed the man. However, Cedric Bender looked deflated, as though his life's ending had sent much of himself elsewhere.

Later, at the gravesite, a minister said all the religious words required during such an occasion and then the coffin was dropped into the hole and everyone left, as everyone always did after a funeral, except for the deceased.

Archer drove Mrs. Bender back home and left her there with a hundred extra dollars of his own money in her pocket, funds he said had been collected through a group of PIs who had known and respected her husband.

He backed out of the driveway as she stood at the screen door contemplating the rest of her years living alone amid the stench of the fruit and nut groves. A gun fired and a life totally transformed.

Find the son of a bitch that did this to my husband.

Yes, ma'am.

He drove back to LA, and, using a fake name, checked into a cheap motel in Silver Lake, north of downtown Los Angeles. Just like many things in this area, its name was a fantasy. There was no lake. There was a reservoir named for the politician who helped in its creation. Archer left his bag there and drove straight to the airport.

He asked enough people to finally find where he needed to go. And from what he was told, he might just be in luck.

He walked over to a small, low-slung building with fuel pumps out front. There he found a man in his forties dressed in overalls and a greasy snap brim hat, who looked over the invoice Archer showed him.

'Oh, yeah, sure. The Greens' Beechcraft. Real nice machine. Seats six, plus two pilots, but they only got the one. You know Mr. Green?'

'I know his wife.'

'Do you now, feller? Well, I'm sorry to hear that.'

'I take it you don't care for Mallory Green?'

He rubbed his bristly mustache. 'Let's just say I like the quiet lady types who do what they're told and who respect the rule of order in a household with the man at the head. That sure as hell ain't her.'

'She said I could fly to Las Vegas in the plane, but maybe it's already there or coming back this way with Mr. Green?'

'No, it's here.' He pointed to a distant building and said, 'That's where they keep it. Pilot's name is Steve Everett. Good man. Loves that plane. Dotes on it, you could say.'

Archer thanked him and headed on to the distant building. He found Everett under the Beechcraft's fuselage with a wrench tugging on a bolt. He was a small, lean man in his midthirties, with pomaded jet-black hair and an unlit cigarette dangling from his lips. He wiped his palms off on a rag and shook Archer's hand.

'Nice plane,' said Archer, looking over the twin engine Beechcraft with the dual tails.

Everett smiled and patted the plane's skin. 'Flew one as a trainer during the war. Army Air Force called it the C45.'

'I was infantry but we flew some. Can't say I loved it.'

Everett grinned and lit his smoke. 'Best place for me is up there in the clouds. No problems, no nothing except you, your ride, and God.'

'So, Bart Green is a nice guy to work for?'

'Sure, sure. And it's a sweetheart job. He flies mostly to Vegas. Easy-peasy.'

'He's in Vegas now?'

Now Everett's expression became more guarded. 'Who wants to know?'

'Mrs. Green wanted me to fly up there to talk to him about one of his writers who's gone missing.'

'What writer?'

'Eleanor Lamb.'

'Black hair, little, skinny number with glasses?'

'Yep. You know her?'

'She's flown to Vegas with us before.'

'Really? Is she a gambler?'

'Don't know. I just fly 'em there. I don't party with them. I go to a bar, have a few beers, pull a few slot machine levers, check out the show gals.'

'So is Green still in Vegas?'

'He is. Was going to come back today, but I got a call pushing it back.'

'So what about flying me up there? Can you do that?'

'I'd have to get permission. This baby costs money to fly.'

'Why don't you call Mrs. Green? Her husband doesn't know me from Adam.'

'Okay, just sit tight and I'll see. It's a nice day to fly so I wouldn't mind getting up there.'

He was gone a few minutes and when he came back he said, 'Be ready to go in about an hour. Mrs. Green gave the okay on you.'

'Does she use the plane much?'

'Oh, yeah. But they never fly together. As I said, Mr. Green usually goes to Vegas and I don't think Mrs. Green cares for the town much.'

'He have a regular place he stays out there?'

'Used to be the Desert Inn, then the Sahara, that opened about three months ago. But as of two weeks ago the Sands is his new favorite. Just opened in December. They got the Copa Room there. That's where he's staying now. Mr. Green likes all the new-new, if you get my meaning.'

'Does he gamble?'

'Oh, yeah, big roller. I hear he loses a lot more than he wins, but the guy is printing money in this town, so who cares?'

I do, thought Archer.

40

As they rose off the tarmac Archer gripped the armrest of his seat. He was directly behind Everett and could see out the front windscreen. The Beechcraft was surprisingly spacious, especially with only two people on board. The seats were comfortable and there was a small credenza which Everett had told him contained tumblers and a bottle of Bart Green's favorite scotch.

As they climbed toward their cruising altitude he looked out the side window. There wasn't a cloud in the sky. The last time Archer had been on a plane was during the war. It was a troop transport. The flight was fairly short, around two hours, and there were fifty other fully geared-out grunts on board with him. As the plane was descending to land, they had taken unexpected enemy fire from a couple of German fighter planes. Archer had watched as rounds had pierced the fuselage and killed four of his comrades, including one man sitting beside him. The plane had crash-landed short of the runway, killing more men. And then Archer and the other survivors had dutifully marched off and gone straight back to fighting a war.

He hadn't liked riding in planes much after that, but this was a breeze. Even when they hit some rough air and downdrafts and the Beechcraft bumped, swayed, and jostled some, Archer just kept looking out the window thinking of other things. He eyed the thermometer set in the ceiling of the plane and saw that they were already well into frostbite territory. When the plane reached its cruising altitude of nine thousand feet and leveled out, Everett said, 'You want to sit up here? Nice ride and views at a hundred seventy knots.'

Archer changed seats and looked at the instrument panel. 'Never could figure out how all this mumbo-jumbo works.'

Everett laughed. 'The most important things in this plane are me and this here yoke. Either one of those gets screwed up none of that stuff will save your ass.'

'So, when was the last time Lamb flew up here with Bart Green?'

'Not exactly sure, but it'll be in the passenger log. It's in that compartment over there.'

Archer opened it and pulled out a leather-bound book. He flipped through the pages to the most recent flights and worked backward from there.

'A month ago tomorrow,' he said. 'It was her, Green, and a guy named Tony Gleason.'

'Yeah, Little Tony. He's Mr. Green's bodyguard.'

'So exactly how *little* is Tony?'

'About four inches taller than you with about a hundred extra pounds and none of it fat that I ever saw, so of course he's called *Little* Tony.'

'Why does Green need a bodyguard?'

'Man's rich. Makes you a target.'

'Ever have any problems?'

'None that I heard of, but I wouldn't necessarily.'

'You ever talk to Lamb?' asked Archer.

'Just to say hello. She didn't strike me as a chatty Cathy.'

'Green talk to her while you guys were up here?'

'When the boss is on board I just do my job as the flying chauffeur and try not to listen. And he mostly reads scripts and drinks his scotch.'

'Anything between Lamb and Green?' asked Archer.

Everett laughed. 'Don't think they're either one's type, if you know what I mean.'

'He take anybody else up on the plane? A Cecily Ransome from his office?'

'Nope, never met her.' Everett looked at him slyly. 'But he'd have some other gals. Gals a man, married or not, would love to hang out with for a good time.'

So was that why Bender was interested in the plane? Because Green was ferrying his honeys to Vegas on it?

He leafed through the pages of the flight log while Everett concentrated on his flying.

He was about to put the book back when he saw a name he recognized.

Simon Jacoby? He thought back. *Alice Jacoby's husband. He finances films, so it makes sense he's pals with Bart Green.*

'Simon Jacoby flew with Green?'

'Oh yeah. They're good friends.'

'His wife ever fly with him?'

'No. But I have flown Mrs. Jacoby and Mrs. Mars with Mrs. Green to Lake Tahoe.'

'Just to confirm — Gloria Mars? Married to the director Danny Mars?'

'That's right. Bart Green and Danny Mars are best pals.'

Archer had a hard time envisioning Gloria the warrior and Alice the dreamer getting along, but maybe the older and cynical Mallory Green was the glue that held them all together.

'What's in Lake Tahoe? I've driven past it, but that's all.'

'A lot of water surrounded by mountains. Part of it's in California and part in Nevada. From the sky

231

the lake sort of looks like a heart shape. It was pretty empty a few years ago, but it's really getting built up, especially on the California side.'

'But why do you fly up there, is what I mean.'

'Oh, the Greens got a big house right on the water. It's like what you call a chalet or something.'

'Does Simon Jacoby gamble, too?'

'Oh, yeah. I heard him and Mr. Green talking about what they were going to do this time.'

'Wait a minute. Jacoby flew here with Green on this trip?'

'Yeah. He's staying at the Sands, too.' He eyed Archer, who was scanning the last filled-in page of the logbook. 'He comes up with Mr. Green so often I just started putting his shorthand name in the logbook as *SJ*. That's probably why you didn't spot it.'

'What's he look like?'

'About your height, early forties, brown hair, graying at the temples. Running to fat. Why your interest?'

'It's a bad habit of mine. How about Danny Mars? He flies up, too?'

'Oh, yeah, all the time. He and Mr. Green are as thick as thieves.'

'I bet they are. Gambling, boozing, the ladies?'

'Yeah on the gambling, at least for both of them. The booze and the ladies are more Mars, at least what I've seen. Mr. Green isn't really into that. Never seen the man gassed. But I've watched Jacoby and Mars get lit up like a pair of firecrackers.'

'Did Mars come up on this trip?'

'Nah, understand he's shooting some movie.'

Archer put the logbook back and stared out the windscreen.

As they started their descent into Vegas a bit later,

Everett pointed to his left. 'About seventy miles north of Vegas they have the Nevada Proving Grounds.'

'Who's trying to prove what?' asked Archer.

'You know atomic bombs?'

'Not personally, no.'

'Well, they drop 'em over there from a plane or else explode them underground. You can see the mushroom cloud all the way to Vegas. People come out for a look. It's pretty neat.'

'Yeah, but is it safe?'

'Government says not to look directly at the detonation, but that's about it. I was coming in for a landing once when it blew. Really surprised me. That mushroom cloud is something. But I really had to hold on to the stick because the Beechcraft was bucking all over the place with the wind coming out of that sucker. First time I was ever scared up here. Good thing I didn't have any passengers on board. They would have been puking and screaming. Felt like I was back in the war with the Nazis in a dogfight.'

'I bet,' said Archer, looking around at the interior of the plane and hoping it would not suddenly disintegrate if a mushroom cloud appeared on the horizon.

As they landed smoothly and taxied to the terminal Everett said, 'Short flight.'

'Beats driving,' said Archer. 'And you've sort of restored my faith in air travel.'

'Anytime. Hey, you need a ride back later? The plane is equipped for night flying.'

'Not sure. Is there a number where I can contact you?'

Everett wrote on the back of a card and handed it to Archer. 'Just leave word at the terminal. I can't

233

hang here overnight, though. I'm flying Mrs. Green to Lake Tahoe tomorrow.'

Archer walked to the terminal, hailed a cab, and headed to the Sands.

41

Archer had been to Vegas before to work on cases. The town was only skin deep in looks, but very serious about how it made a living. The mob had its felonious fingers in casinos, bars, lounges, prostitution rings, numbers rackets, and every other criminal and legal enterprise that made a buck off people's weaknesses.

Archer knew that everyone from the Teamsters Union to nearby Mormon bankers had jumped aboard the Vegas train and had loaned money to put up more gambling dens. The Desert Inn, the Sahara, and the Sands had just been the latest wave, and it had forced existing casinos to up their game. Since coming here, Archer had seen the Last Frontier become the Silver Slipper, and the Eldorado transform into Binion's Horseshoe Casino.

From the cab, he looked out at the forty-foot-tall cowboy neon sign that sat atop the Pioneer Club. Nicknamed Vegas Vic, the cowpoke could wink, light a cigarette with its dexterous mechanical hands, and blow smoke rings skyward with the same engineering. It also used to call out, 'Howdy, pardner,' every fifteen minutes until enough people complained about the noise and the creepiness that Vic was now, thankfully, mute.

Once it was dark, doses of preening neon, like high-kicking stockinged legs seducing all comers, would flash on. The sign for the Sands was up on a lattice-style structure that also added the phrase, 'A Place in the Sun.' *Well, that's what you get when building in a desert*, thought Archer. And, perhaps symbolizing that, right across the street was just a pile of dirt.

In the spacious lobby, Bart Green's photo and a ten spot paid over to a bellhop scored Archer the information that Bart Green was staying at the hotel.

Archer checked in, went to his room, took off his jacket, and rolled up his sleeves. On the spur of the moment, he called Dash long-distance and told him where he was and what he was planning to do.

'Okay, Archer, but Vegas can be a very dangerous place in unforeseen ways. Watch your back and your front.'

'Got it, Willie. Thanks.'

Archer found Bart Green at a poolside seating area ensconced with two ladies and a young man in a seersucker suit, the latter in deep conversation with the tubby Green. There was no one matching Simon Jacoby's description. Bender's reports that Green never went public with the ladies didn't seem to apply here.

A man who could only be Little Tony was hovering near his boss. He was dressed in beige lightweight linen slacks and a brown-and-green-checked jacket. A hand-painted tie fronted his white shirt. His gaze swiveled as he kept his eyes on Green and everyone near him.

Archer sat at a poolside table, ordered a club soda, and smoked a cigarette while pretending to read a newspaper someone had left behind. The sun was starting to go down and, as the daytime temps had only reached the low sixties, Archer could sense that the evening temperatures were going to dip dramatically. The number of people around the pool was limited because of the cooler weather, and there were only two hardy souls in the water.

Green wore a Panama hat with a black band and had on a dark T-shirt under his crisp, monogrammed white shirt. His brown slacks were pleated and cuffed, and his shoes were shiny. He had a protruding belly that he seemed either proud or sick of because he kept rubbing it. He wore aviator reflector sunglasses, which was in keeping with a guy with his own plane. He had given up on the reedy mustache Archer had seen in the photo Mallory Green had provided him, and was now clean-shaven. A tall, cool drink sat next to him on a table.

The ladies were in their early twenties and dressed in matching two-piece bright blue swimsuits with open terrycloth robes that stopped right below their bottoms. One was blond, the other brunette. They were tanned and toned, and they sipped on drinks with umbrellas and looked vastly contented with their young lives so far. A bottle of suntan powder was on the table between them.

The seersucker man had a notepad and was writing things down as Green dictated. Next to him on a low table was a movie script open about halfway. Archer couldn't hear Green's words, but the young man was apparently taking them as seriously as Moses had with God.

The young man finally closed his notepad, picked up the script, rose, gave a comical salute to his boss, and walked away. Green said something to one of the girls and she laughed right on cue. Little Tony didn't even crack a smile. He was staring at Archer as a potential threat, because Archer had risen and was walking directly over to them.

Little Tony barred his way while Green looked

237

intrigued. The two girls studied Archer, giving each other a revealing look and then giggling.

'Keep moving, buddy, this is private real estate,' said Little Tony, whose voice was, counter-intuitively, high-pitched and reedy. Maybe that was why he looked so pissed, thought Archer. He proba-bly preferred going through life with his mouth shut and letting his impressive size do the talking for him.

Archer held up his license and said loudly enough for Green to hear. 'Name's Archer. I'm working with the LA County cops on a missing person's case and a homicide.' He peered around Little Tony to eye Green. 'The missing person works for you, Mr. Green. Eleanor Lamb?'

Green looked at him and said in a baritone voice that would have seemed more in keeping with the giant Tony, 'Have a seat, Mr. Archer. Pick which fruit of the loin you wish to sit next to. Be careful, they both bite.'

The girls tittered on cue and began to look cute and batty-eyed.

Little Tony moved aside reluctantly.

Archer chose the brunette who let her robe fall fully open and curled her long brown legs up under her nice blue-clad bottom, where a sliver of enticing white skin peeked at him. She smiled while tugging provocatively on her straw with lips the color of cher-ries. She had gone overboard on the eyeliner and her eyelashes were long enough to catch flies. She looked a few seconds from jumping Archer.

'Hi,' she said. 'I'm Mitzi.'

'Archer, nice to meet you.'

'And I'm Gayle,' said the other. 'We're sisters.'

'Well, isn't that convenient,' said Archer.

They both tittered over this until Green told them to take a hike back to their rooms and get fluffed up and decked out for dinner.

They reluctantly left, each still batting her eyes at Archer, while Little Tony just scowled.

'Little Tony, you can move a few feet away. I doubt Archer has anything dangerous planned.'

Little Tony moved exactly four feet away, Archer noted. He said to Green, 'How's Vegas? Casino treating you all right?'

'What casino treats any gambler all right?'

'I hear they tear up Sinatra's chits so long as he keeps singing and bringing his buddies along.'

Green half lowered his sunglasses to reveal a pair of deep-set blue eyes. 'They do. But I can't sing like Sinatra.'

'I see you were working on a script.'

'Might as well. I'm writing this whole trip off to the business.' He took a long drink from his long glass. He wiped his lips with a paper napkin with the Sands logo on it and said, 'Mind telling me how you knew I was here?'

'Confidential sources, but they turned out to be good ones.' Archer wasn't about to tell him that he had used the man's plane to get here. That might earn him a headlock and attempted drowning in the pool by Little Tony. 'Lamb told me someone was trying to kill her. Then she vanished. I've been hired by your partner to find Lamb.'

'Cecily? Really?' Green didn't seem to believe this. 'So you've spoken to her?'

'I've spoken to a lot of people.'

'You mentioned a *homicide*?'

'Guy found at Lamb's house. Somebody put a

bullet in his brain. PI from Anaheim named Cedric Bender.'

Archer waited for a reaction to this. He didn't expect the man to do what his wife had, but he was hoping for something. But he didn't get it.

'If Ellie already had a PI why did she want to hire you?'

'I don't think Bender was working for her.'

'Who then?'

'You've got no ideas on that?'

'Why should I? Sure, Ellie works for me. But we aren't close friends.'

'So you'd have no idea why someone would want to kill her?'

Green took off his glasses and rubbed his eyes. 'She did her work — she's a good writer — but that was it. No intrigue as far as I knew.'

'I understand she flew with you here sometimes.'

Green took another drink and set the glass down. 'For someone who doesn't know me, you sure know a lot about me. Why don't I like that, Archer? Tell me.'

'I wouldn't like it, either. But that's what I was hired to do. Did she stiff the casinos on some debt? She tell Meyer Lansky to get out of her face?' added Archer, referring to one of the leading mob bosses in Vegas.

'Lansky would have no reason to even know who Ellie Lamb is.'

'So no reason why anyone here would want to see her dead, then?'

'I'm a film producer, Archer, not the mafia. You'll have to snoop somewhere else.'

'I'm sure you want Lamb back safe and sound. She's working on a lot of scripts for you.'

'There are a lot of writers in LA. Ross Chandler,

240

the eager beaver kid in the seersucker you just saw? He could step into Lamb's shoes if need be. He costs a few dollars more but so what? They're a dime a dozen.'

'He's a lot younger than Lamb. Why is he more expensive?'

Green gave him a 'come on' look. 'Lamb is a skirt, Chandler wears pants. *Comprende?*'

'Does that rule include Cecily Ransome?'

Green fidgeted. 'No, I'm not including her. She's got what most Hollywood hacks don't.'

'What's that?'

He glanced sharply up at Archer. 'Depth. Now, is there anything else?'

'I saw Bernadette Bonham yesterday. You do business with her husband, Peter?'

'I do?'

'That's what she said.'

'What does a wife know about what her husband does, Archer, I mean, really?'

'You speaking from experience?'

'No, actually, I'm not. My wife is the unfortunate exception to what otherwise is a good rule.' He paused for a moment and seemed to look right through Archer. 'Why don't you have drinks with us tonight? Nine o'clock. Right here at the Copa Room. I'll put your name on my reservation. They put on a good show. Now, I've got business to attend to. Little Tony!'

The big man came over and escorted Archer away. When he turned to look back, Bart Green only had blue eyes for Archer.

241

42

In his room later, Archer called the number Steve Everett had given him and left a message that he would not be flying back that night. He showered and put his clothes back on after sending them out to be pressed. He looked out the window and saw that Vegas had turned on its best neon for the night's entertainment. Greens and purples and oranges and reds in various shapes and sizes loomed up in the darkness like electrified ghouls looking for victims. And, in a very real way, they were, only the blood they sucked out of their prey was all green.

He took the stairs down to the bar, had a scotch and soda and a bite of dinner. He watched the gambling crowd get greased up for their nighttime ambitions of throwing their hard-earned money right into the flusher. And they all did it with impressive smiles if not downright glee, he noted. Curious animals, human beings.

At nine on the dot he entered the Copa Room. It was large and grand, with a stage at one end. Archer had heard it was a replica of the Copacabana in New York. The ceilings were high and painted a garish greenish blue except for a strip of orange by the stage. The light fixtures were gold-plated with multiple bulbs set in a circle. The tablecloths were white and the chairs were upholstered in red. There were about five hundred people in the room, he calculated, and they were dressed to the nines, with white dinner jackets the most popular cover for the men. That made it look like all the waiters had gone on strike for the night and were having cocktails and watching the show with the paying customers.

On stage were the Copa Girls, as one of the valets had told him they were called. Their outfits were the same shade of red as the seats, but the ladies looked far nicer wearing them than the chairs did. They danced and sang to the accompaniment of an orchestra, and it looked like everyone was having a swell time.

He was escorted to Green's table, which was close enough to the stage to see the performance easily enough but far enough away to carry on a conversation. At the table were Green, the young screenwriter, Ross Chandler, and the two giggling sisters, who were now outfitted in flimsy pale blue dresses that looked closer to lingerie. Chandler wore a white tux jacket, while Green was dressed far more informally in a dark blue rayon jacket, slacks, and an open-collared shirt. He held a cigarillo in one puffy hand.

Archer greeted everyone and then looked for Little Tony. He spotted him on the periphery staring at Archer like he had personally killed the man's entire family. Archer sat down and ordered a whiskey and soda, then pulled out his pack of Luckys and lit up. His drink arrived less than a minute later.

'Nice, efficient place,' he said to Green, who was staring at him with serpent eyes.

'Yeah, it is,' answered Chandler, who had his eye on Mitzi, who had her eye on Archer. Gayle just stared into her drink like she could see her reflection and was checking her lipstick.

When Gayle looked up at him, he could see her pupils were swollen like a full moon, and he wondered what barbiturate she was on.

'So, I hear you're a writer for Mr. Green?' said Archer, pulling his gaze from Gayle and depositing it on Chandler.

'That's right. I got my degree from Columbia and jumped on a train west. Where else should a writer want to be these days? Writing in LA for the pictures is where it's at.'

'Hemingway's in Cuba,' noted Green, taking a sip of some weird-colored concoction. 'And Faulkner's back in Mississippi after trying his hand at screen-writing and not liking it one bit. CBS just broadcast a documentary on him last month about his life in Oxford. And he did win the Nobel Prize. And Hemingway probably will, too.'

Chandler seemed worried for a moment until Green smiled. Relieved, he said, 'Hey, they're serious novelists. I'm just writing for the movies.' He glanced at Archer. 'I mean, you know?'

'No, I don't know. But do you like it?' asked Archer.

'I like it.' Chandler glanced at the buxom Mitzi. 'A lot.'

'You know Eleanor Lamb?' asked Archer.

'Sure.'

'Archer,' said Green. 'Not now. If you want to interrogate the boy, do it on your own time. And, Ross, get up and let Archer have your seat. I want him closer to me.'

Chandler immediately stood and seemed surprised that Archer took his time, stubbing out his smoke and taking a sip of his drink before rising.

He sat next to Green, while Chandler immediately struck up a conversation with Mitzi.

Archer pointed to Green's glass. 'What's that stuff?'

'A specialty liquor that I'm fond of. Would you like

to try one?'

'No, I'm good with what I have.'

'I made some inquiries about you after you left.'

'And?'

'And you have a good reputation.'

Archer glanced at the stage as one of the Copa Girls, with a slit right up the front of her skirt, commenced a solo. She had good pipes and nice legs, which in Vegas could make you a star. 'Nice to know. But I could've told you that.'

'You also met with my wife.'

'I could've told you that, too.'

'So why didn't you?' Green said sharply enough for Chandler, Mitzi, and even sky-high Gayle to look over at them.

Archer scooped up a handful of nuts from a bowl and put one in his mouth. 'You never asked, and I never volunteer information if I don't have to.'

'And would that include flying up here in *my* plane?'

Archer studied the man for a moment. *So it* was *his plane*. 'Your wife gave the okay, which I was told she could. It was the fastest way here so I could talk to you and cross you off my list.'

'What list?'

Archer ate another nut and sat back. 'Were you in LA on New Year's Eve?'

'What's it to you?'

'A man died and Lamb went missing then.'

'Why would I kill a guy I didn't know or make a writer of mine disappear?'

'I'm listening.'

'Okay, I think we're done here. Finish your drink and be on your way.'

'You like the Jade Lion in Chinatown?'

'Never heard of it.'

'Lamb apparently liked it. And the guy who manages it, Darren Paley? I hear he has Vegas mob connections.'

'I see you have some of your drink left. I think I asked you to finish it.'

Chandler leaned over and said, 'You better do what he says, buddy.'

Archer didn't take his eyes off Green. 'For starters, my name's not *buddy*. The Jade's got a drink that'll sear your insides. Regulars there swill it like it's nothing. Amazing what people can work up to if they really want something, and I'm not just talking about booze.'

Green looked at Little Tony and gave him the high sign. The giant began lumbering over.

'You're handling this all wrong, Archer. You know that, don't you?' said Green.

'Maybe I am,' conceded Archer. 'But then maybe so are you.'

Green wagged his head. 'You don't even know what you don't even know.'

'Ever heard the story of the frog and the scorpion?'

'It's probably the basis for a quarter of the movies ever filmed.'

'Well, the way I see it, maybe you're the frog. You built something good, you're chugging along, just want to get to the other side. And here comes Paley. He's a free rider. He sees something good, too. He makes himself indispensable to you. But on the flip side, at a certain point, that doesn't make *you* indispensable to *him*.' As Little Tony was arriving at the table Archer leaned over and said, 'And where did gorilla boy come from? Courtesy of the mob and Darren Paley? If so, what do you do about it?'

That got a reaction from Green all right.

Archer turned, smiled at Little Tony, and said, 'Hey, what a coincidence, *Little* Tony, I was just leaving. 'Night, ladies.'

Mitzi wouldn't look at him now. She gazed fearfully at her lap. And Gayle was too far gone into the drug abyss to do much of anything except look pouty and dazed.

As Archer left, he turned and saw Green whispering something to Tony.

That was good, he thought. *And that was also bad.*

And that was the PI business in a nutshell.

43

Archer sat on a stool and stared into the mirror behind the bar to watch for Little Tony trying to sneak up on him. He knew he had taken an aggressive posture in the Copa Room, and made perhaps some unjustifiable leaps of logic. But the fact was, the odds of Lamb's turning up alive were decreasing by the minute. And he was tired of walking in circles. And a good man was dead and his widow wanted someone held accountable.

And so do I.

He had no idea if Bart Green was connected to whatever Darren Paley was doing at the Jade. That was why he'd voiced that possibility to Green with the frog-and-scorpion fable. A scorpion needs to get across a river but can't swim. So it enlists the aid of a frog. At first the frog is reluctant, afraid that the scorpion will sting it. The scorpion tells the frog that it wouldn't sting the frog because then they would both die. So the frog lets the scorpion hitch a ride. Halfway across the scorpion indeed stings the frog, who is astonished. When the frog tells the scorpion that now they will both die, the venomous creature simply confesses that it couldn't help itself. It's just its nature.

So Paley was the scorpion for sure, and Green maybe the frog, which made his surname spot on. But then again, maybe Archer was totally off base and hunting in the wrong direction. There was a point in every case he'd worked on where he'd had enormous self-doubt about what direction to go in, or whether

248

he would ever solve it. He was at that point right now, which was why he was sitting here drinking his way to viable answers.

He was surprised when Ross Chandler entered the bar and came to sit next to him.

'Wow, that was some powwow you two had back there,' he began.

'You should see me when I really get worked up.' Archer lit a Lucky and took a swallow of his martini. 'Tell me about Eleanor Lamb.'

'What do you want to know?'

'Everything and anything you got.'

'She's a good writer, one of the best.'

'You have much interaction with her?'

'Not too much. I did help her on a rewrite of a script for Paramount. Ellie does female roles really well. And Cecily helped on that one, too. All I did was play messenger boy, really.'

'Ransome and Lamb, they get along okay?'

'They seem pretty tight, actually. Going out to lunch and dinners. Working late. Cecily would run out to Malibu a lot to work over the weekends with Ellie.'

Archer tapped ash into a glass ashtray and stared at his drink.

Chandler said excitedly, 'It must be fun and danger-ous doing your job.'

'Yeah it is, but never at the same time. When was the last time you saw Lamb?'

Chandler ordered a whiskey and thought about the question until it came. 'She was in the office the day before New Year's Eve.'

'She ever talk about having a friend she was recon-necting with out in Malibu?'

'Not that I recall.'

'You ever heard the name Bernadette Bonham?'

'No, who is she?'

'Just a gal. What's the story on the sisters? Why are they here with Green? Are they his little playthings?'

'No way! They're his nieces.'

Archer side-eyed him. 'Come on, for real?'

'I thought the same thing, but they're his younger sister's kids. She died a while back and he takes care of them. Gives them money, flies them here.'

Then he might want to start taking care of Gayle's pill problem, thought Archer. 'Okay. Tell your boss if he wants to continue our conversation I'm staying here tonight.'

'He's going to be gambling tonight.'

'Hell, pal, we all gamble every minute of every day.'

Chandler left. Archer ordered another drink and carried it to the real reason they built the Sands.

The casino.

44

Archer made the rounds, from the one-armed bandits, to the roulette wheels, to craps and poker, and every other game of chance the place offered. Along the way he greased the palms of employees who looked like they might know things of value. After several dry runs he was directed to a medium-height, wiry fellow with a brown handlebar mustache and matching eyebrows. The man was standing guard in a hallway reserved for what he called the 'out-of-town big rollers.'

'Half of Boston and most of New York is in there,' he muttered to Archer, after money passed hands.

'What about LA?'

'They got their own room.'

'What about a man named Bart Green?'

'He may as well have his own room.'

'That bad, huh?'

'Not for the casino. I worked all over, friend. And I been watching Bart Green lose for years now at some of the biggest joints on the Strip. They love him.'

'How much are we talking about here?'

The man eyed his empty hand.

Archer filled it with a sawbuck, and he watched Alexander Hamilton disappear into the man's pockets, as his eyes roamed the floor. 'Shouldn't be telling you this stuff.'

'What stuff?'

A tiny smile lifted the mustache. 'He's laid down markers all over town. If I were to add them up, I bet

251

we're talking over two million bucks just in the time I've seen him around.'

Archer let out a low whistle because he couldn't help it. 'And he made good on it?'

'What do you mean made good on it? He's still breathing, right? Do you know who owns this town? Not people who let you walk away from your debts, that's for damn sure. You can enjoy all the perks. But when you bet and lose, you gotta pay. That's all ten commandments rolled into one, least for the sons of bitches who run these places.'

'Where'd he get that kind of dough?'

'He's a big film guy. Didn't you know that?'

'He's a film *producer*. I didn't think they made that much scratch. And that's on top of all his other bills. And he's got a big place in Beverly Hills. *And* his own plane.'

'What can I tell you, buddy? He pays what he owes. Else he ain't producing no more movies, or no more nothing.'

'The casinos don't forgive any of it?'

'You really are a choir boy. *Forgive?* What, you think God lives here or something?' He tacked on a snort.

'What's his game?'

'Blackjack and poker, and he sucks at both. But he's addicted. It's an illness.'

'Where does he play?' asked Archer.

'Upstairs. Private room. Just a handful of big rollers.'

'Any chance of me getting in there?'

The eyebrows lifted. 'You got a twenty-five-thousand-dollar stake? 'Cause that's what it takes to play in that room. Either cash or certified bank check. Or else it's a no-go, Kemosabe.'

252

'I've never even *seen* twenty-five grand all at one time.'

'You and me both, brother.'

'Does he play with a guy named Simon Jacoby?' asked Archer.

'No. Not in that room.' He pointed to one of the poker tables. 'That's Jacoby over there. On the far left. Poor, pathetic slob that he is.'

Archer eyed the man in a brown suit with broad shoulders and a thickening girth.

'Does he lose big, too?'

'Hey, it's not like I keep a scoreboard on every Tom, Dick, and Harry that comes here.'

Archer passed him another sawbuck and got a flick from the brown mustache.

'But the big winners and losers attract my attention. So I can tell you Jacoby used to play in the private rooms all over town, but he got busted back down to the main floor with all the other riffraff.'

'So a big loser?'

'Who came real close a couple times to getting visits from the knee-and-back-breaker squads. But he found the money somewhere.'

'And he's still here losing more.'

'The more you lose, the more you have to play so you win back what you lose. That way of thinking is the holy grail of the gambling business, and every casino counts on it. From the twenty-five-grand rollers to the nickel-slot suckers. But he's not losing what he used to. He's on a leash. A short one.'

'How about another friend of Green's? Danny Mars?'

The man rubbed his fingers together again and Archer fed the machine once more.

'Danny Mars is like poor old Simon. Banished to the kiddie pool.'

'I hear his wife is loaded,' said Archer.

'She is. And I have it on good authority that the casino has knocked on her door to make good on some of his markers.'

'I bet she didn't care for that,' noted Archer.

'Who would? Mars is a sap who loves to be with the big boys but doesn't have the engine power and never will. Green keeps him around for laughs, I heard. And Mars is one fun-loving guy, if you catch my drift. Actually, he'd take the gals over gambling any day.'

'Did Mrs. Mars pay her husband's markers?' The image of a female warrior thrusting her sword into Danny Mars's chest flickered into Archer's head.

'She and the hubby are still alive, right?'

Archer thought that might be the prime reason the Marses' marriage was on the rocks. Just like men, women could get sex anywhere, particularly a woman like Gloria Mars. Money was another matter. Even for a lady with an oil well of cash from J. P. Morgan and U.S. Trust.

'Okay, what do you know about the muscle with Bart Green? Little Tony?'

The man grimaced. 'He used to work here in Vegas.'

'Doing what?'

'His job was to make sure people paid their markers. If they didn't, then Little Tony taught them a lesson, a tough one.'

'Why would Green have a guy like that hovering over his shoulder?' Something dawned on Archer, something close to what he had intimated to Green earlier, but hadn't really thought through. 'Wait a minute, is it so Little Tony won't have to go far to

254

break *Green's* knees?'

The man gazed up at Archer. 'You're *not* a choir-boy, are you?'

'So Little Tony is less guardian and more guard? For the casinos?'

'You didn't hear that from me,' said the man as he nodded.

'Is Little Tony the one who almost had to break Simon Jacoby's knees?'

The man rubbed his fingers over his palm, and Archer planted a fin there. At this rate he was going to run out of Lincolns *and* Hamiltons.

'Little Tony busted his nose and was about to do the same to his back in the alley behind the Flamingo.'

'What happened?' asked Archer.

'The money came through at the last minute.'

'How?'

The man shrugged. 'I don't wear the green visor, son. But the money did come, or else Jacoby would be in a wheelchair, sipping through a straw, guaranteed.'

Archer had one final question. 'What do you know about a guy named Darren Paley?'

The man's features tensed. 'You don't want nothing to do with that man. I was a Marine. Fought at Iwo Jima and Guadalcanal. And I seen all the tough guys in this town. He's one of the few who really scares me. He's got a couple screws loose and he's meaner than a rattler.'

'I might not have a choice. So, what do you have on him?'

'He worked here in town. Deep with the mob. He ran enforcement for them. Little Tony was one of his foot soldiers, in fact.'

255

'But he's in LA now.'

'Right. Heard he left the mob and was running a place down in LA's Chinatown.'

'He is. The Jade Lion. What do you know about it?'

'I don't know nothing about it. But I *do* know Paley. He's a mob man through and through.'

'So maybe what he's doing down in Chinatown involves still working for the mob.'

'You said it, not me.'

Archer left the man and walked over to watch Jacoby play and lose at poker.

Jacoby was an old-looking early forties. His hair was rapidly graying, and his face was long, loose, and pouchy, and the color wasn't healthy. He had three half-empty drinks in front of him as he studied his cards with an unfocused air. His big belly was kissing the table. His ankles were crossed under his seat like a bobby-soxer waiting to be asked to dance for the first time. His trousers were ill fitting and rode up on the man. The few chips in front of him told Archer all he needed to know about the man's abilities and prospects at five-card stud.

Archer thought of Jacoby's elegant wife in her perfectly orchestrated attire in her perfectly designed mansion. He wondered how the dreamer Alice Jacoby handled this little weakness of her hubby's. He thought the same about the flinty, give-no-quarter Mallory Green. Bart Green's addiction could sink her as well as her husband. But perhaps neither woman knew the extent of it. And maybe their husbands were getting their bills paid in a way that wasn't legal. And maybe the source of those funds had something to do with Darren Paley and the Jade. But right now, Archer had no idea how they might be connected.

He was so intent on Jacoby and his own thoughts that he only noticed Little Tony standing next to him when he felt the gun muzzle saying hello to his right kidney.

'Let's walk, Archer. And just so you know, I *will* shoot you right here out in public and I'll have five guys say it was self-defense, and the cops won't hassle me one little bit.'

'Why do I believe you?' said Archer as they headed off.

45

With a gun wedged against his spine, Archer could smell the stink of his own fear, along with the heavyweight cologne Little Tony had smeared all over himself. They traversed a long, dark hallway, and passed through a door, which Little Tony closed behind them.

There were two other people in the room. One was the young Chinese woman from the Jade who had directed Archer to the bar using the same words: 'That way, honey.'

The woman was dressed in canary yellow. All she needed was a set of wings and she could simply fly away from all this trouble, thought Archer.

The other person was the one Archer instinctively kept his eye on.

Under the weak light the scars on Darren Paley's face seemed electrified. He was dressed in a dark suit and tie. His white shirt seemed heated and shiny in the light. A white pocket square was set just so. A new-looking fedora lay on the table beside him. Archer could see the hump of a gun under his jacket. Up close he indeed looked to Archer like a rattler: lean, curled, and deadly serious, with eyes that never forgot anything they saw. And the man's warning rattle was echoing in Archer's ears like cannon fire.

He was smoking a cigarette and tapping a finger on the table he was seated at, with the woman beside him. He hadn't once looked at Archer.

'Him?' asked Paley. 'This the guy?'

At first Archer didn't know who he was speaking to.

Then the woman nodded. 'Yes. He is the one that night.'

'You're real sure?'

'Yes. I'm sure.'

'Thanks. Beat it.'

The woman quickly rose, passed Archer and Little Tony, and left the room. She never once looked at Archer. He figured she was the kind who didn't like being around dead people.

That way, honey.

As soon as the door shut, Paley motioned to Little Tony, who pushed Archer forward and forced him into the chair facing Paley.

The man methodically smoked his cigarette down while Archer watched. He had known men like this before. Nothing ever hurried them. They took everything they did seriously; it required that level of thought and attention because if they made a mistake they would no longer be alive. And every single one of those men Archer knew had been either a soldier or a crook.

Paley crushed the butt of his smoke into the ashtray and finally looked up at Archer. 'You know why I had the skirt here?'

'To identify me.'

'Yes and no. Yes on the ID. I had other people I could have used, but she saw you up close. I like to be sure because I like to be fair. I'm not doing nothing to nobody that they don't deserve because I don't want nobody doing that to me. I take my lumps *if* I earned them.'

'The guy outside the Jade saw me.'

'And he also let you get away. So he couldn't ID

259

you. That's why I brought the skirt here.'

'Then he's dead?'

Paley gave Archer a look like he thought that was quite obvious.

'What was the *no* part?' asked Archer.

'That dame and her kind don't mix good with the white folks, but I need them to do the work that needs to be done. Now, you got to earn the respect of the Chinese, or else scare the shit out of them so they don't try and cross you. I prefer the scare route myself. So if I prove my seriousness to her, then she gets the word out to the guys who are maybe thinking of taking what don't belong to them. Then those guys stop thinking that way because they don't want nothing bad to happen to them.' He paused and gave Archer a look that did nothing to bolster his confidence about leaving here alive. 'Just like I'm sure you don't.'

'That's right.'

Paley moved his head from side to side. 'Kraut tried to break my neck during the war. Gutted him with his own knife. Gets sore when the weather changes. Desert air seems to help.'

'Yeah, I got some of that, too.'

'You're a PI. You're trying to find a broad who's gone missing, *and* you're trying to find out who plugged a PI named Bender and dumped his body at the broad's house. Am I missing something or is my line pretty straight?'

'You're doing okay, actually.'

'Thanks. I came from nothing and never went to no fancy schools, and here I am surrounded by all these rich, educated people. It can intimidate a man.'

'I would think it would be the reverse.'

Paley gave him a knowing look. 'You *would* think

that, wouldn't you? Now, I *can* intimidate people. When the stakes are really high. That's when I'm in my element, so to speak. I don't care how much they got in the bank, or how famous they are, because I mean what I say and I have the facts on my side.'

'I can understand that.'

'I could tell you stories of grown men you see in the movies all the time playing these big, tough guys, who have sat in rooms like this *weeping* because they were afraid of what I was going to do to them. It's a very heady experience for a guy like me. I mean, I look up to these men. I consider them heroes. But when they're not in front of the camera they're nothing but scared little fuckers because they did wrong. And they have to be held to account for that, and they know I'm the guy to do it. Do you see what I'm saying?'

'I see what you're saying.'

'Now, you came to my place of business and caused me a lot of problems and cost me one of my guys. Your bill is very long and it's come due.' He tapped the wood. 'Now.'

'But it's not just me. The LA County cops are investigating all of this, too.'

Paley put up a hand. 'Let's leave the cops out of this. They'll do what they have to do, but not more than that. We both know that, right?'

'And I thought everybody was cleaning up their act.'

'They are. Hell, most of the mob left LA and came here. Easier pickings and even that element don't like to slam their head against a brick wall. Now, they'll go down there and horn in on some of the crummy card club action or the ponies, but that's not really over the money. The money is right here. But they do it so the

261

boys in LA don't get too comfy. You know the name Sammy Rummel?'

'Mickey Cohen's lawyer. Got knocked off in Laurel Canyon a few years ago.'

'As an example of what I'm talking about.' Paley adjusted his cuffs. 'Now, as far as *my* business goes, I'm sensing the presence of some third party that ain't supposed to be there. You know anything about that?'

'Third party?'

'Yeah. Let me explain. If I expected to get a hundred packages of something and I only get seventy-five, that's a problem for me. But then the next week the difference gets made up and then maybe I get more than I thought I'd get. The next week, the same shit happens.'

'So what's the problem if it evens out in the end?'

Paley shook his head. 'If they could only get me less than x one week and then get me more than y the next week, something fishy is going on. It makes me feel like they could get me z anytime they wanted, but maybe they don't because they're feeding another hungry mouth. And I'm losing money because of it. And I do not like to lose money. It's an obsession with me.'

'So that's where the third party comes in?'

'Now you're catching on. But you obviously know nothing about it.'

'I wish I did.'

Paley gave him another knowing look. 'Yeah, I bet you do. Now I just need to find out where along the supply chain somebody else might be at the trough drinking my stuff.'

'Does Bernadette Bonham know anything about it? I saw you two talking outside of the Jade.'

As soon as he said this, Archer regretted it.

The scars started to twitch. 'So she let you follow her to my place?'

'She didn't *let* me do anything. I'm good at my job. She stonewalled me on everything, so I decided to see where she was going.'

Paley lit another cigarette and sat back. 'Good, Archer, good. You told me something I didn't know. That's valuable to me.'

'So, do I just get to walk out of here?'

'No, Archer, that's not what I'm saying. You knew that as soon as Little Tony got the drop on you, didn't you?'

'I guess I did.'

'But you bought yourself some time. Not much, but some while I check out what you told me. And then maybe you get to walk out of here.'

'Are you serious?'

'No, Archer, I'm lying to your fucking face. Why? It's just my nature.'

Archer wasn't fast enough.

The butt of the gun came down on his head, near where he'd been sapped before. It didn't hurt any less the second time around. He slumped forward, hit his chin on the desk, and fell sideways to the floor.

★ ★ ★

When Archer came to, all he could see was black. And he thought he was dead. And that he was in hell because heaven was not supposed to be dark and he could hear no angels playing their harps. When he reached out, he found he was encased in some sort of scratchy material, like burlap. It was close to his face

263

and it was difficult to breathe. He had the sensation of movement, and, coupled with the sound of a motor, he knew he was in a car, probably in the trunk. He pushed against the material but it was so close to him he couldn't get any leverage.

Then the sensation of movement stopped. The engine died. Doors opened and closed, and footsteps headed his way. There was another sound as the darkness became just a shade less black. The trunk had been opened. Archer's adrenaline kicked into a higher gear and his breaths started coming more rapidly, as he sensed the end of his life drawing near.

Hands grabbed around parts of him and he was lifted out and placed on the ground.

A voice said, 'Shoot him in the head and do it quick. We got to dig the hole deep. Critters around here.'

Archer instinctively started to kick and beat against whatever was holding him. He heard a laugh. 'Hey, look who woke up.'

Then the laughter died and shouts took their place. Archer flinched when he heard the shot. Then he heard several others. There was a grunt, followed by a flow of expletives. More shots. Then a car started and he could hear the wheels grinding into the dirt. A few seconds later all became quiet.

Something seized him and he fought against it once more.

'Just hold on, Archer. We got you.'

Archer immediately relaxed at the words because he recognized the voice.

A knife bit carefully into the fabric around him, cutting an opening near his head. A light was shone in his eyes and then the beam was reversed and he was looking at a familiar face.

Willie Dash said, 'How many times am I going to have to save your ass, son?'

But then Dash smiled, and Archer could see the sense of relief on the man's features.

Still, it didn't come close to the one on Archer's.

46

'Paley will have a dozen witnesses swear he was never in Vegas tonight,' Dash said to Archer. 'So that's a dead end. And word is he's wired tight to Lansky and some other big boys, so the cops will be more hindrance than help. The mob pays way better than the government.'

They were on a United Airlines night flight back to LA from Vegas. Archer glanced out the window as the prop plane wended its way over mountain ranges and valleys and back to Southern California. He still felt the suffocation of being in that burlap sack. He had barely been able to get on the plane, because he sensed the fuselage walls reaching out to crush him.

The stewardess had brought him some ice, which he'd applied to his head and his chin.

One more hard knock to the head, and I might just be done.

When Dash and two other men had cut him out of his burial cloth, he'd asked Dash how he'd come to even be there. Dash had told him that as soon as he'd learned Archer was in Vegas, he'd gotten the next flight out. Before he left, Dash alerted two veteran PIs who covered Vegas and had worked with Dash before. They had picked up Archer's trail at the Sands, seen him disappear with Little Tony, and then had been quick enough to spot two men loading Archer into a sack and placing him into the trunk of a Plymouth. They had followed, and when the men had stopped and were about to finish off Archer, they'd stepped in

266

with guns firing. Dash figured he winged one of the guys, but they had both gotten away.

'What about Little Tony?' asked Archer.

'Guys like him don't do the grave digging. He'll claim he doesn't know what you're talking about. He works security for the casino, you looked suspicious. He took you aside and talked to you and then let you go on your way. Anything happened after that, he knows nothing about and he'll have witnesses to back that up.'

'They could have killed me *inside* the casino,' Archer had pointed out.

Dash shook his head. 'No way Paley would do that. Shots fired, blood spilled, evidence all over? Even the cops couldn't look the other way on that. And Paley isn't gonna disrespect the likes of Meyer Lansky and Moe Dalitz and their kind by using a brand-new property like the Sands for a personal execution site; that costs the mob money. Sure, Paley is a sadistic prick. But mobsters like Lansky have a hundred Paleys on the payroll. It would be a slaughter and Paley knows it. So they get the drop on you at the casino, then knock you out and do the deed in the middle of nowhere. They just didn't know the middle of nowhere would be so populated.'

'Paley seems to believe there's another party getting some of his dope.'

'That's interesting. What else?'

Archer filled Dash in on this and also all he had learned about Green, Jacoby, and Mars.

'So the three guys are gambling addicts and Mars also likes the ladies and the booze.'

Archer nodded. 'And they've all been able to cover their debts. But Green seemed to have fared better than the other two. He still gets to play at the adult table.'

'And Mars? How'd he cover his markers?'

'I forgot to tell you that part. The casinos put the touch on Gloria Mars.'

'And Simon Jacoby?'

'His wife said his business was going gangbusters, so maybe that's how he covered his. And he inherited their big house and maybe some cash along with it.'

'Now, I know Bart Green is a big-time producer, but two million bucks of gambling losses? No way that's all coming from the man's business pocket.'

'I agree. And the Bonhams are involved with Paley somehow. At least the wife is.'

'With a guy like Paley, you never know *who* he owns.'

'So, do we go to the cops?'

'With what?' exclaimed Dash.

'Let me play out a theory for you, Willie.'

'Fire away.'

'A guy is at Lamb's house when I call. He answers the phone. I go out there, see Bender's car, stumble over Bender's body, and somebody blackjacks my skull. I wake up, find a Wheeldex card in Lamb's house with the Jade Lion mentioned on it and a name, Jonathan Brewster, which is code for scarface Darren Paley. I call the cops. I head west so I won't run into them and hit the beach. On the sand I trip into smugglers carrying crates up from a boat. On the very day that Bender is killed! I tussle with a guy and get away. In Lamb's office at Green and Ransome I find Jade Lion matchbooks. Alice Jacoby swears she's never been there when I show one of the matchbooks to her, but I have a witness who swears she's seen Jacoby there. You follow so far?'

'You're doing fine, Archer. Keep going.'

'I go to the Jade. I stumble over crates with sand all over them. I find a vial with heroin under a bed there. Then I roust Bernadette Bonham at the airport and she immediately flies to Paley. I get fingered by the gal at the Jade as being the guy running around the place that night. Then Paley gets Little Tony to snatch me, and Paley asks me if I know why his shipments are getting shortchanged. I don't, and then he tries to kill me.' He stopped and looked at his partner. 'Okay?'

'Okay what? I have no doubt Paley is selling dope. But we can show absolutely no ties between Paley and what you saw on the beach that night. And we have no proof it's even dope running that they're doing down there.'

'I think the crates I saw at the Jade were full of —'

'There are a lot of sandy crates *and* heroin in LA. And a DA could give a shit what you *think*. You're up against some big muscle, Archer, and you can't bring a slingshot to a war. The mob can afford the best lawyers in the business. By the time they finish with you, your ass will be in jail for dope running.'

'But Bernadette Bonham knows Darren Paley. For me that ties what happened on the Malibu beach to the Jade. And it's not a big leap from there to Bender's murder in the canyon. And Lamb disappearing. She was scared because maybe she knew something. Maybe she knew about the dope running.'

'And maybe I'm the Queen of England, only I can't prove it. And Bonham knowing Paley is not a crime.'

Archer sat back and closed his eyes. He knew Dash was right. He had no connection between what he'd seen on the beach that tied into either Bender's murder or the Jade Lion and Darren Paley. He opened his eyes. 'Okay. Let's go back to square one. Why would Alice Jacoby lie about the Jade?'

'Maybe you need to ask her.'

'Maybe I do. But what about Paley? Do I have to go around with eyes in the back of my head?'

'He's going to lie low for a bit. He's got to after what happened tonight.'

'So his boys will tell him about messing up tonight?'

'Are you kidding, Archer? Those *boys* are probably halfway to Mexico by now. They were just a couple of punks hired at the last minute to do the deed. They won't even know Paley was calling the shots. That way no stink floats back to him. But Paley will know they screwed up, and if he can catch them he'll put them in the same hole they were supposed to dig for you. But he'll have heard the bad news by now. And he'll have to step back and think about his next move. Which means we got some breathing room.'

'Sounds like a checkers game.'

'Chess, Archer. You play checkers for fun. You play chess for keeps.' Dash handed him a slip of paper. 'Liberty's new address and phone number.'

'Thanks.'

Dash waved to the stewardess and ordered them two bourbons on the rocks.

Archer drained his in nearly one gulp.

'Rough night.'

Archer glanced at Dash, who had a funny look in his eyes. 'I know it was a close shave, Willie, too close.'

'It's not like you did anything too wrong, Archer. Sure, you shouldn't have let Tony get the jump on you. But in our line of work, you can do things perfect ninety-nine percent of the time, and that last percent puts you in an early grave.'

'Like Cedric Bender?'

'Yeah, like him. So, you still in?'

'You're kidding, right?'

'Let me tell you something. When I was with the Bureau we did a raid on one of Capone's booze operations. This was during Prohibition, you understand. And it was Chicago, so we were playing on Big Al's home field. The raid went sideways because we got some bad information from a stool pigeon. And then I let one of Capone's goons get the drop on me. He was one second from drilling a bullet right here.' Dash pointed to the spot between his eyes. 'Then my boss, a guy named Melvin Purvis, who was a crack shot, nailed him. That night I was even closer than you were to being dead. After that, Purvis, who was a hell of an agent and taught me a lot, pulled me aside and asked me if I wanted to keep going. Sure, the possibility of getting killed is part of being a federal cop, but a man is still a man and when you get right to the edge, it can change you. And Purvis knew that.'

'Change you how?'

'Make you indecisive, unsure of yourself, hesitate when hesitation just can't happen. And Purvis wasn't asking because he was worried about me. He was asking because he was worried about his team. A chain is only as strong as its weakest link, Archer. And if I couldn't carry my weight anymore, that could lead to other agents being killed. That's what Purvis was getting at.'

'And what did you tell him?'

'I told him thanks for saving my bacon, and I'd be glad to do the same for him.'

The men looked at each other for a significant moment.

'Thanks for saving *my* bacon, Willie. And I'll be glad to return the favor if I need to.'

Dash grinned, cuffed Archer on the shoulder, drained his bourbon, put his seat back, and slept the rest of the short flight.

47

When they landed in LA, Dash and Archer drove to Silver Lake in Archer's rental car, which he'd left at the airport. Dash got a room at the same motel and went to bed. Archer went to his room and dialed the number; a moment later Callahan picked up.

'Hey, Liberty.'

'Hey, Archer.'

'Sorry, I know it's really late.'

'You know I never go to bed early.'

'You all settled in?' he asked.

'Sure, sure.'

'And you're keeping a lookout and all?'

'Just like you said,' she told him.

'Look, I know you didn't need all this to drop in your lap. I'm sorry.'

'Ellie Lamb is my friend. You took the case to help her. So how's it going? You find any clues?'

'Yeah. A few.'

'You didn't get hit in the head again, did you?' she asked.

Archer rubbed the spot where Little Tony had sapped him. 'No, nothing like that. It was a pretty normal day.'

'Normal is nice.'

'Yeah,' said Archer quietly. 'Well, I hope you have a good sleep. And I . . .'

'And you what?'

'I just wanted to hear your voice.'

'Don't go all soft on me, Archer. You'll lose your

tough-guy rep. Good night.'

Archer put the phone down and looked around the confines of the cheap room that looked like no one had touched it since the 1920s. He had stayed in many cheap rooms over the last three years. Maybe too many. He had also gotten close to dying at times, but not as close as tonight. If Dash had not been there and done what he had? If on the spur of the moment Archer hadn't called Dash and told him that he was in Vegas and what he was planning to do? Dash would not have been there.

And I'd be lying under six feet of desert. I wouldn't even get a lousy funeral service like Bender. And Liberty would spend some time wondering what became of me. And then she'd get on with her life. Because we all have to.

That last thought made a part of his heart he maybe didn't fully understand lurch sideways. *She'd miss me, at least. That's something.*

He took out his flask and added a whiskey chaser to the airline's bourbon. It burned all the way down, and Archer needed to feel that.

You're alive, not dead. And you get another shot at taking down the folks who wanted to end things for you. Play that game as hard as you can, Archer. But play it smart from now on.

It was not a simple matter of revenge or payback or getting even. Archer wasn't sure what it was. Justice was a simple word with a mountain range's worth of complexities behind it. Good versus evil was the same sort of equation. But with guys like Paley, it wasn't a close call. He was scum and didn't deserve to breathe air.

So next time you get him in your sights, Archer, make sure he's not breathing after it's over. Because he'll try

274

to do the same to you. And it won't bother him nearly as much as it will bother you. That's the difference. That's the whole beeswax, really.

★ ★ ★

He woke the next morning, took a shower, changed into fresh clothes, and had breakfast with Dash at a greasy-spoon diner near the motel.

'Got some news, Archer. They found Bender's car.'

'Where?'

'In the ocean off Malibu Pier.'

'Anyone in it? Like Eleanor Lamb?'

'Nope. It was a nice little oyster without a shiny pearl inside.'

'Oldham find it?'

'Off a tip, yeah. But get this — word is he's not working the case too hard.'

Archer took a sip of his coffee. 'Yeah, I thought his big speech to me about not being on the take was a load of horseshit.'

'I don't think he's on the take. Don't get me wrong, some county cops are. Only they don't need a guy like Oldham.'

'Then why is he pulling back?'

'Look at it this way, Archer. LA runs on lots of things. But the primary thing it runs on is the Hollywood fantasy. You got millions of tourists coming here for that very reason and hundreds of thousands of new people wanting to call this place home every year so they can try and jump on that train. All that adds up to a mountain of money for everybody, good and bad. And my thinking is that somebody knows about the little private film business at the Jade that

275

you found out about. And maybe they know a bunch of stars are ensnared in it. That comes out, all of a sudden the little fantasy that creates tons of jobs and sells magazines and keeps butts in seats in front of TVs and at theaters all over the country gets blown into a million little pieces.'

'Jake pretty much said the same thing. But how can the cops know Bender's death is tied to what's going on at the Jade?'

'If I knew the answer to that, Archer, I'd know everything. And the rank and file like Oldham don't have to know. All I'm saying is, money talks but shit still stinks.'

'Then are you saying Paley gets a pass?'

'I'm saying some folks might think it's worth it to give him a pass. So, what's your next move?'

'First up, talk to Alice Jacoby. Then I'm going to track down the Bonhams. I'll start in Malibu. I want to know how she knows Paley. And I might have slipped up and told Paley too much about Bernadette. I don't want her getting fished out of the water off Malibu Pier.'

'Okay.'

'What will you be doing?' asked Archer.

'Going to see Jake. We got a few things percolating. And I won't have your back today, so you watch it real, real good.'

'But you said Paley would be lying low,' noted Archer.

'But Paley ain't the only killer out there, is he?'

48

Alice Jacoby was in her design studio at Warner Brothers. After his call requesting a meeting, she had put Archer on the visitor's log. He had found street parking, cleared the front gate, and arrived at her office minutes later. She was dressed in high-waisted dark green slacks, a white blouse, and a navy blue jacket with a double row of brass buttons, giving her a military appearance. Her hair was done up in a ponytail. She looked younger and carefree away from her inherited mansion, like a fresh-faced woman about to set out on life.

But she might end up not being so carefree after he said what he was here to say.

Her office had shelves of books and files, and elaborate drawings tacked on corkboard. There were framed movie posters and autographed photos grouped on one wall and also set on low tables. A large armoire that looked like it was built in the previous century took up one corner. On a large waist-high table in the middle of the room was a mockup of a lavish bedroom, a large library, and an old English-style conservatory.

Jacoby sat at her drafting table, which was filled with drawings on loose paper, and notes taped to its wooden surface. Archer sat in a chair and used his hat to point at the mockup.

'Working hard, I see.'

'A Ginger Rogers picture. I've worked on at least a dozen of them since I came to town, many during the war years. She's not the big draw she used to be,

277

but she was in a movie with Cary Grant and Marilyn Monroe last year called *Monkey Business*. It did very well. So now we have another Ginger Rogers picture. Oh, we had such fun during the war.' She added wistfully, 'I know that time was bad for so many, but I felt like we were doing something important. Cheering up people, giving them a reason to hope. You know?'

Archer had no inclination to chitchat, and he also didn't think much of her statements. It was like everybody in this town thought the movies had won the war instead of the blood of real soldiers.

'I've got some questions to ask you and they may not be pleasant to hear,' he said bluntly.

She looked shocked, thought Archer. He supposed she might as well get used to it, because he only had forward gears this morning. Almost ending up in a grave still lingered with him. He figured it would until he ended up in a grave for real. And he was sure the woman had lied to him. Even though most people lied to PIs, including their own clients, the practice had never set well with Archer.

'All right. What are your questions?'

'You told me you had never heard of the Jade Lion, and never went to Chinatown?'

'That's right.'

'Only I have a witness who saw you at the Jade on multiple occasions.'

'What witness?'

'I'd rather not say. But I can tell you the person is very reliable.'

'Well, this person must be mistaken in my case.'

'You're sure you don't want to tell me something?'

'There's nothing to tell. I have never been to Chinatown, period.'

278

'You said your husband's business was going gang-busters?'

'That's right.'

'Well, he was seen in Vegas last night playing at the kiddie poker table, because he didn't have the financial horsepower anymore to play with the big boys.'

'Who saw him?' she said sharply. 'Another of your *reliable* witnesses?'

'Even better. *I* saw him there. He's lost a lot of money gambling, Mrs. Jacoby. A whole lot. And he also got his nose busted and he came real close to getting his knees and his back broken for nonpayment of what he owed. But then the cash came in, and somebody put him on a short leash in Vegas. Was that somebody *you*? On both counts?'

The whole time Archer was talking Jacoby seemed to be shrinking down to a size that could fit into one of her mock rooms. He briefly imagined her in front of the little fireplace holding a little drink and wondering what the hell had happened to her fabulous life.

She rose and walked over to the armoire and opened the doors, revealing a bar set up inside. There was a line of pint and half-pint bottles that probably formed the dividing boundary between sobriety and drunkenness for the woman. For some reason he couldn't quite fathom, Archer was not surprised by a bar in the armoire. But then he *could* fathom it. This was a lady who liked to hide all vices under grand veneers.

'Would you like something stronger than coffee?'

He checked his watch and hiked his eyebrows. He knew everybody in LA drank too much, but this was a little ridiculous. 'I like to wait until I've at least digested my eggs and toast.'

'Well, it's never too early for me these days, I'm afraid. If you don't mind.'

'I don't get between anybody and their booze.'

She mixed a whiskey sour over ice and drank it down like it was a Coke.

She pressed the glass to her forehead before setting it down. 'Have you ever been married, Mr. Archer?'

'No.'

'Don't. It's not worth it. Well, I say that from the wife's perspective. It is very different from the man's side. They can do whatever the hell they want.'

'You're not alone on that score. There's a lot of unhappiness out there. Keeps me gainfully employed, for better or worse.'

'My children make me happy. My work makes me happy. My marriage does not.'

'Has he tried to get help? They do have people who specialize in that stuff.'

'I tried to get Simon help many times. But one cannot do the work for him.'

'I understand he flies up to Vegas with Bart Green and Danny Mars on a regular basis?'

'*Too* regular a basis. Do you know what they call themselves?' she added shrilly.

'I'll take a wild guess: the Three Musketeers.'

'How on earth did you know that?'

'I'm a guy. We think shallow and all manly when it comes to stuff like that. So, how does his firm view his gambling?'

'Simon's partners are teetotalers and deacons in their churches. They see gambling as a sin.'

'So not good then?'

'To put it mildly. To put it realistically, they might kick him out of the business.' The phone rang and

Jacoby answered it. She listened for a few moments and then said, 'I'll be right there.' She put the receiver down. 'I have to deal with something. It won't take long. Can you wait?'

'Yes, I can.'

While she was gone Archer walked around the room and looked at the framed movie posters on the wall and pictures autographed by nearly two decades' worth of Hollywood royalty. He stopped at one framed photo separate from the rest. It was a duplicate of the one at Jacoby's home. The Wellesley crew. He eyed Jacoby and Lamb straight away and then let his gaze wander up and down the rows. Until . . .

Damn.

A nearly two-decades-younger Gloria Mars was staring back at him from the second row, far left. There was no mistaking those eyes nor the haughty manner that the lady still carried around like an old fur. *So why hadn't Jacoby ever mentioned that college connection?*

He kept looking until he came to another set of framed photos perched on a table. And Archer's jaw dropped once more.

In the photo a much younger Mallory Green was dressed up in an eighteenth-century period costume and standing next to a fresh-faced, early-twenties Alice Jacoby. The picture was signed to Alice from Green, and was dated eighteen years ago. That was when Jacoby had started out in the film business as a set designer, Archer recalled. So that was probably how they'd become friends, then.

Green had been both far lovelier and heavier back in the day. The shrinkage in her weight over the years had done her no favors, diminishing her natural

281

beauty into a hard, mean little shell, like someone had lit a piece of paper on fire and let it burn down to ash. He was initially surprised that the woman had once been an actress. But she definitely had the steel in her spine to do just about anything, he figured.

He heard footsteps coming and retreated to his seat before Jacoby walked back in. She looked a bit frazzled, and a few strands of her hair had worked free from their binding.

'Sorry. There's always drama on the set, and I'm not talking about the actors.'

'I understand. So, you know Gloria Mars?'

She looked surprised by this but said, 'Yes, from Wellesley. Why?'

'Just curious. And did Eleanor Lamb know Mars, too?'

'Yes. Wellesley's not that big. We were in the same graduating class.'

Archer pointed to the photo. 'And Mallory Green. She was an actress?'

Jacoby smiled. 'That was taken right at the end of her acting career — her last picture, in fact. I worked on the sets. It was my first assignment. She'll tell you she was not a great thespian. But she's a wonderful documentary filmmaker. She's won two Oscars.'

'So she mentioned. Is that how she met her husband?'

'Yes. Bart was producing a film she was in. This was many years before that picture was taken, of course. They fell in love and got married. Raised four children. Well, Mallory did. Bart was always working.'

'Okay, now do you want to take one more whack at the Jade Lion?'

She bristled. 'I have already told you the truth, Mr.

Archer. And if you provide me with the name of the person claiming I was there, I'll sue them for slander.'

'That's why I won't. If you really haven't been to the Jade, I wouldn't bother going. The liquor is undrinkable for people like you and me. And the rest of their offerings are nothing to write home about.'

'Thank you, but I have no intention of going there.'

'And you haven't heard from Lamb?' asked Archer.

'No.'

'I understand you fly around with Mallory Green in their plane?'

Jacoby looked down. 'Sometimes. It's nice to get away.'

'I'm sure.' *Like from your husband.* 'They have a place up at Lake Tahoe.'

'That's right.'

'When is your husband coming back?' asked Archer.

'I'm not sure. Simon's gotten to where he doesn't tell me.'

'I'm sorry.'

'I made my bed, now I have to sleep in it. Alone.'

Archer put on his hat and left.

He walked all the way out of Warner Brothers wondering why Jacoby kept lying to him.

49

Archer made the long drive out to Malibu. It wasn't nearly as pleasant in the squat Buick. Even the Pacific didn't look as magnificent from the dumpy car's window. It was sunny on the mainland, but dark clouds were gathering offshore. The temperature had dropped, and though Archer wasn't worried about snow in Southern California even in January, he wasn't juiced about a ton of rain coming his way, either.

He drove up Las Flores and arrived at the cluster of three houses. The silver coupe was still parked at Lamb's house. He pulled to the curb and got out. He tried the passenger door of Lamb's car, and it opened right up. Oldham's locksmith had apparently done his job. There couldn't have been a body inside, or Archer would have heard. He did a quick search, but found nothing helpful. He shut the door and headed to the Bonhams'.

This time his knock was answered by a tall, broad-shouldered man in his early fifties with fine salt-and-pepper hair, and a chiseled and tanned face that held two slightly discolored patches of skin on the jaw and cheek. He had on a gray double-breasted suit with a yellow polka-dotted tie and a matching pocket square. He looked like he could take care of himself and often had to.

'Yes?' he said.

'Peter Bonham?'

'Yes?'

284

Archer pulled his license. 'I'm working the Eleanor Lamb case.'

'What case?'

'She's missing. A man's body was found at her place. I spoke to your wife about it.'

'Bernadette *did* mention that. But I've been out of the country and rather busy.'

'Can I come in? I have a few questions for you. And your wife, if she's here.'

Bonham took so long to consider this, Archer thought the man might slam the door in his face. But then he stepped aside and motioned Archer in.

Archer felt like he had entered a castle in some far-off land. The walls and floor were stone, the ceiling vaulted, the walls festooned with paintings and murals depicting starkly medieval scenes. There was even a full-size suit of dull armor silently standing guard, but not appearing too excited about it.

Bonham led him down the hall and into a large study that held much the same decorative vestiges as what he'd already seen. Dark beamed and paneled, with luxurious Oriental rugs over walnut floor planks, the place instantly made Archer feel like he was in some ancient feudal keep awaiting an audience with the resident lord. Twin axes formed an X on the wall above a sandstone fireplace and there were swords galore hung on the walls. If one were going to duel here, one wouldn't lack for choice of weapons. A desk, a couch, and comfortable upholstered chairs were strewn around as though an afterthought to the historical renderings.

Archer thought the only things missing were the stuffed heads of vanquished beasts. And perhaps a human head or two thrown in to keep everybody honest and afraid.

He settled in a chair while Bonham took up residence behind his desk. 'Not your typical Malibu beach house.'

'I don't live on the beach, Mr. Archer. This is very much a canyon house, at least to my mind and sensibilities.'

'I take it you travel a lot?'

'Why do you say that?'

'All the things I'm seeing here. And you just said you were out of the country.'

'Right. Though I was born in America, my ancestors were French. I much prefer that world and those tastes to my native country's. Now, you mentioned some questions?' He made a show of looking at his watch.

'I understand that you knew Lamb.'

'Who do you understand that from?'

'She was at a party you had here.'

'I have a number of parties.'

'You were seen speaking to Lamb, and it didn't seem the discussion was pleasant.'

Bonham thought about this for a moment and then said, 'Yes, I remember now, it was a property dispute. The woman felt she had more land than she did. She insisted on encroaching on my property, and I just as strongly insisted that she could not.'

'Did you know your wife and Lamb went to school together back east?'

Bonham hiked his eyebrows and fiddled with a pen on his desk. 'I think I recall her mentioning it, but I couldn't swear to it.'

'Do you know the Jade Lion in Chinatown?'

Again, Bonham fidgeted. 'No, I don't. What is it?'

286

'A bar and maybe some other things.'

'Why do you want to know about it?'

'It seems that Lamb had some ties to it,' replied Archer.

'So what? It's a free country.'

'You and your wife returned separately from France?'

Bonham leaned back in his chair and studied Archer. 'Yes, we did. Again, so what?'

'It seems that Lamb disappeared on New Year's Eve, and the body was in her house around that same time. Did you see anything unusual that night? Because I know you were back in town by then.'

Bonham took his time answering. 'I wasn't here on New Year's Eve.'

'Do you mind telling me where you were?'

'Yes, I do mind.'

'Is your wife here now?' asked Archer.

Bonham glanced toward the door. 'No.'

'Do you know a man named Darren Paley?' asked Archer.

'Never heard of him.'

'Does your wife?'

Bonham drew a long breath. 'No idea. She has friends whom I don't know. And vice versa.'

'A very European arrangement.'

'If you say so,' replied Bonham. 'Are we just about done?'

'Just about. What car do you drive?'

'I don't know why it matters, but it's a black-and-silver Bentley.' Bonham picked up the phone. 'Now, if you'll excuse me, I have work to do.'

'What sort of work would that be?'

'Good day, Mr. Archer.'

Archer rose and left. As he was walking down the hall, he saw more than a dozen photos on a side table. He looked around to see if anyone was watching and then snagged a small one from the back, moving the others next to where it had been to close the gap. He put the framed photo in his side pocket, opened the front door, and left.

As he headed down the sidewalk he looked back to see Bonham watching him from the window. He tipped his hat and kept going.

Well, that was productive, thought Archer.

But it had nothing to do with the questions and unhelpful answers he'd received.

The man had been wearing makeup to cover the bruises on his face.

Because he's the guy I tussled with on the beach that night and clocked with my head and fist.

And Archer had recognized something else about the man. His voice.

He's also the guy who picked up the phone at Lamb's house the night I called.

50

Archer got back into his car but he didn't go far. Out of sight of the Bonham house, he did a U-turn and parked behind two other cars on the opposite side of the road. He slid down in the seat and waited. A few cars passed him, and then an old pickup truck with MALIBU LANDSCAPING stenciled on the door panel glided past. Ten minutes later a black-and-silver Bentley with Peter Bonham at the wheel passed by him heading down the canyon road.

Archer had to make a decision: Follow the man, which would be tough to do on a narrow canyon road in broad daylight without being spotted. Or take advantage of his absence and see what he could find on the property. Archer decided on the second option and drove back to the Bonhams' house. The old pickup truck he'd seen was parked at the curb.

He parked behind it and made his way quickly to the Bonhams' rear yard. He saw a short and stocky man in his fifties pushing a wheelbarrow with gloved hands. He had on a broad-brimmed straw hat, faded dungarees, and a dark blue work shirt. When Archer drew closer he saw the man looked to be of Japanese descent.

In the wheelbarrow were a shovel and a bush with long green leaves. Along both sides of the rear yard were thick hedges that formed a boundary line. To the left was a line of fruit trees with dark green oranges dangling from the limbs. Raised flower beds and terraced shrubbery sat in well-designed configurations.

The rugged, dry canyon walls soared behind all of this manmade horticultural pleasantry. To Archer, it was simultaneously lovely and tragic looking.

The man stopped the wheelbarrow next to a spot where a bush had clearly been. A mound of shoveled dirt lay next to the hole.

'Hey, pal,' Archer said.

The man looked at him from behind thick-lensed, round spectacles. 'Hello.'

'Are the Bonhams in? They were expecting me, but no one answered the door.'

'I do not know. I just work here in yard.'

'Right, planting that bush. What happened to the other one?'

'It died. Something killed it.'

'Well, that happens. To plants and people. What kind is it?'

'Coffeeberry.'

'Coffeeberry?'

'The seeds, they look like coffee beans.' He lifted his hands high over his head. 'It grows to fifteen feet. Birds love coffeeberry fruit. And it is quite good against fire. It grows good just about everywhere. It is very, very pretty.'

Archer looked around the lush grounds. 'You did a real good job back here.'

'Thank you.' The man lifted his shovel out of the wheelbarrow and set it next to the hole where the bush would be going in.

Archer knelt and looked at the ground around the bush, where there were traces of something white. 'What's that, some sort of plant food? Or maybe a fungus? Maybe that killed the bush.'

'I do not know what that is. It was on ground, I guess.'

Archer straightened. 'You got moles?'

'What?'

'Over there where the lawn is lumpy.' It was the patch that Archer had seen previously.

The man shook his head. 'There are no moles here. That is Mr. Bonham's bomb room.'

'*Bomb* room?'

'He is very afraid of them dropping bombs here. Big bombs. You know. Like they do on islands out there.' He pointed toward the Pacific, his expression turning somber. 'They can kill many, so many.'

'So he has a bomb shelter over there? Can you show me?'

The man led him over to the spot. Archer knelt and saw a clasp in the lawn with a large padlock on it. He touched the grass around it and saw that it was fake. That was why it was lumpy. It was covering a metal plate — the entrance to the shelter.

'Who has the key to the lock?'

'Mr. Bonham.'

'You ever been down there?'

The man shook his head. 'No. I like sky and sun. Not dark places.'

'How do you know it's a bomb shelter, then?'

'I ask Mr. Bonham when I try to cut the grass there, and it all go bad. It is not real grass, see. Then he tells me to not worry about this part of the grass. See?'

Archer stood. 'Yeah, I see. Hey, you need some help getting the bush in the ground?'

'Sure, mister, sure. Thank you.'

Archer helped him lift the bush and its root ball out of the wheelbarrow and they got it situated level in the hole. While the man was fetching his shovel, Archer used his handkerchief to scoop up some of the

291

dirt laced with the white powder, and thrust it into his side pocket.

'You leaving now?' asked the man, turning to him.

'I'm leaving now.'

'Hey, mister, you got bomb room where you live?'

'No, but in light of things, I might seriously think about getting one.'

51

Archer sat in his car and looked at the white powder. He couldn't be certain what it was without getting a lab to test it. But from the look of it and the smell he thought it might be heroin. And maybe that was what killed the coffeeberry. The question was, how did heroin get in Bonham's backyard? He had some ideas about that. Maybe the connection he was looking for between Paley and Bonham was starting to solidify.

He parked in front of Danforth's house, got out, and knocked on the door. He heard the pitter-patter of her little feet and the door opened. She had on a creamy white day dress and slippers. Her fake hair was in a bun and she had reading glasses on and a *Life* magazine in her hand. Two cats trailed her.

'Mr. Archer, you're back.'

'I am. Can I come in and ask a few more questions?'

'Certainly, certainly. Would you like something to drink? I have lemonade, coffee.'

What, no scotch? 'Lemonade will be fine, thanks.'

She brought it to him in the same room they had sat in before.

He sipped on the drink for a moment as she perched in a chair across from him. Her cats formed a protective circle around her, though one did jump up next to Archer to make inquiries with a paw lightly tapping his arm. He responded by scratching its ears.

'I met Mr. and Mrs. Bonham.'

She took off her specs and stared at him dumbly.

'You did? Did you go all the way to France? And you're already back?'

'No. *They're* back. You didn't know that?'

'No.'

'He just drove off a few minutes ago in his Bentley. He actually got back into town on December thirtieth. The missus came in a few days later.'

'Why would they come back separately? And why come back at all? They're usually gone much longer than that.'

'Well, I wouldn't know that and they didn't say. But maybe they're worried about something. They do have a bomb shelter in their backyard.'

'A what?'

'A bomb shelter. You know, if the Soviets decide to bomb us they can go and hide in a little metal box underground.'

'I never heard of such a thing.'

'Yeah, I'm not sure how much protection something like that would be with an atom bomb dropped on your head.'

She let out a sigh. 'Mankind has gotten so very sick. Sometimes I'm glad that I'm very near the end of my days on earth.'

'Don't say that. What would your cats do without you?'

She smiled. 'That is very kind of you to say. And for your information I've made suitable arrangements for each of them when I die.'

'That's good of you. Look, it turns out that Peter Bonham *was* married before. At least that's what his wife told me.'

'Really. To whom?'

'I don't know. Why did you think he hadn't been?'

'Well, he never spoke about another wife. I've been to their house several times. There were no pictures of his first wife or children from a first marriage or anything. And Bernadette never mentioned anything like that.'

'Well, he might not want pics of his first wife around for his second wife to see. You also told me they drove their car to the airport and left it there. Turns out they didn't do that, either.'

'But I saw them drive off when they left. I waved to them. So where was the car?'

'Could have been kept any number of places. Look, I know you said you go to bed early, but late at night, do you ever hear noises?'

'What sort of noises?'

'Like a car or a truck coming up or down the road.'

'I don't believe so. My room is at the back of the house.'

'Okay.'

'But it's funny you asked that. I had a young friend of my granddaughter's stay here with me during the summer last year. She was trying to break into pictures, like so many of them do and none of them succeed.'

'Right, so what about her?'

'She complained a couple of nights about hearing someone driving on the road, oh, around three or four in the morning. Her hearing is better than mine, and her room was nearer the front of the house.'

'Did she ever go out and see what it was?'

'She looked out the window. She said it was a truck of some sort.'

'Did she see where it went?'

'No, at least she didn't tell me if she did.'

'Where is this girl now?'

'Back in Connecticut. She decided to become a secretary instead.'

'In the long run the money will be better and she'll live longer.'

Archer took his leave and drove toward the ocean. He hit the coast road and turned left to head back to town.

Less than an hour later he was on Santa Monica Boulevard after having just passed Cahuenga. He drove by Hollywood Memorial Park, where the likes of Douglas Fairbanks and Rudolph Valentino were interred. Backing up to the cemetery on its southern edge was Paramount Studios.

And that was when Archer saw it. A movie theater where a film called *On the Run* was playing. The marquee said it was an MGM production and it starred a man Archer had never heard of. But he wasn't interested in the man. He pulled to the curb and got out. He hustled over to the movie poster for *On the Run*, which was on the wall next to the ticket window.

The female star was Samantha Lourdes. On the poster, she was wrapped around the male star and they were looking deeply into each other's eyes. Archer also didn't care about that. What he cared about was that Samantha Lourdes had been the movie actress he had seen and spoken to at the Jade Lion.

52

Archer headed west to Culver City, where the MGM studios were located.

He had learned from Callahan and his own work in Hollywood that MGM had been late to the game on talking films, but had quickly come to dominate the movie business in the 1930s with films such as *Gone with the Wind* and *The Wizard of Oz*. They had also pretty much invented the studio system whereby stars were basically owned by their studios but could be loaned out to other studios by mutual agreement with cash or other benefits exchanged.

It was ironic, he had thought, that arguably the greatest studio in Hollywood had never been in Hollywood, but seven miles to the southwest in Culver City, closer to Marina Del Rey than Tinseltown. Archer also didn't really care about that right now. He was interested only in Samantha Lourdes, MGM's big star.

He pulled in front of the enormous edifice that occupied a chunk of Washington Boulevard's frontage. The classical colonnade setup was barely a few feet deep, which was the most perfect representation of the town Archer had ever seen. There was literally nothing behind it except back lots with more facades and no depth, other than the actors acting, and even that was all over the place.

He wrote a note on a slip of paper and handed it and a five spot to the guard at the gate. The guard was tall and thin and old and looked beaten down, barely able to carry the weight of his cap and uniform or his holstered Colt .45. He looked at Archer warily when he told the man whom he wanted the note delivered to and that he was a friend of hers.

'You know how many of these I get a day for that gal?' he barked. 'You know her like I know Dwight D. Eisenhower, fella. And for the record, I've never met the man.'

'Lourdes owns a silver Rolls-Royce and her driver is an old guy named Alan. She knows me, pal. Bet on it. And that note will bring a smile to her face. Who knows, you might even get a little kiss out of it.'

This new information seemed to clinch the deal. 'Okay, buddy, she *is* here today. But they're filming.'

'They have to turn off the cameras sometime. And what do you have to lose?'

The man called another guard over to work the gate and stalked off while Archer waited.

And waited. An hour, two smoked cigarettes, and vigorous fedora twirling later, the man came back. He seemed amazed beyond all reckoning.

'Damn, you were telling the truth, fella.'

'I try to at least once a day, Pops.'

The man gummed his lips in his astonishment. 'Miss Lourdes said she'll meet you at the Formosa at seven o'clock tonight. You know it?'

'Yeah, it's on Santa Monica across from Sam Goldwyn Studio.'

'She said to wait for her in the trolley car and order her a Gibson with three pearl onions. Trolley car? Do you know what that means, because I sure as heck don't.'

'I do. Thanks.'

298

Archer checked his watch and contemplated what to do until then.

He dipped into a drugstore and called Dash's room at the motel where they were staying. There was no answer, so he called Connie Morrison long-distance and told her everything he had learned both in town and out in Malibu from Peter Bonham and Sylvia Danforth.

'Fill him in when you can. If I see him, I'll do the same. He mentioned going to see Jake.'

'This case is getting curiouser and curiouser,' commented Morrison.

'Just what I needed today, a little Alice in Wonderland,' replied Archer, which made him think of Alice Jacoby and all her lies.

He drove to West Hollywood and then north to Sunset. He had a late lunch at Greenblatt's Deli and took his time over a sandwich, fries, and coffee.

He knew F. Scott Fitzgerald had walked into Greenblatt's in 1940, bought a Hershey bar, carried it back around the corner to the apartment where he was staying, and dropped dead of a coronary next to the fireplace mantel. He wondered if the man had any inkling his end was coming.

Archer took a bite of a fry and contemplated his own sense of doom.

I almost died in the lousy desert. Maybe I'm not good enough to make it in this racket. Maybe my end is coming faster than I would like it to.

He paid his bill and made a call to the Ambassador Hotel from a phone booth. The maid answered and relayed Archer's request to Gloria Mars. The maid came back on the phone and told Archer that Mars would see him now.

299

He cut a diagonal across midtown to Wilshire, wondering what sort of reception he'd get from the woman.

Maybe the warrior will run me through with her lance.

53

He took the automatic elevator up and walked down to the penthouse suite. One of the double doors was open, and there stood Gloria Mars. Her dress was red and tight and slitted, the heels were high and the fishnet stockings midnight black, lending a remarkable contrast with the sunset burn of the dress. Her auburn hair was piled on top of her head except for a few curlicue dangles around her cheeks. She looked him up and down like he was an object of purchase at the Farmer's Market.

Archer was afraid that something had gotten seriously lost in translation with the maid.

'Archer, I was wondering when you were going to make your way back to me.'

'Well, here I am.'

She slipped her arm through his. 'Yes you are. Let's have a drink.'

She led him into the penthouse.

'Your husband around?'

'I'm not really sure where he is.'

'How about Vegas with the other Musketeers?'

She glanced at him, sharp as a tack. 'How do you know about that?'

'Just heard it on the street.'

'Some street. So he's in Vegas?'

The lady did not appear to be happy about that, thought Archer. 'My best guess,' he replied.

She mixed them martinis and she placed Archer on a blue chesterfield while she perched close to him.

'What other helpful information do you have for me?'

'You went to Wellesley. You were in the same class as Eleanor Lamb and Alice Jacoby.'

Mars sipped her drink. 'I already knew that,' she said, not looking pleased.

'You never mentioned that when I was talking to you about Lamb.'

'What was there to mention? I didn't even know her.'

That doesn't match what Jacoby told me. 'But you know Alice Jacoby?'

'Yes. She was Alice Buckner back then. From West Virginia, if you can believe it.'

'We're all from somewhere.'

'I understand that Lamb is missing.'

'How do you understand that?'

'That same street you walk on, big fella.' A young maid passed by them, her gaze averted. Mars added, 'But let's find a place a little more private than this.' She rose and pulled him up.

Before Archer realized it, they had passed through a door and into a bedroom that was about twice the size of his entire apartment back in Bay Town, and very feminine in its décor.

In answer to his look, she said, 'Danny and I maintain separate bedrooms. I like my own space. His bedroom looks like a combo hunting lodge and bar. Give me a minute, Archer.'

She disappeared into an adjacent bathroom and closed the door.

While she was gone Archer looked around. There was a large armoire about the size of the one in Jacoby's office. He eyed the bathroom door and then tried to open the armoire. It was locked. That intrigued him enough to use his knife to push the bolt back and look inside. There were just piles of books. But then he looked at some of the titles and came away surprised, knowing what he did about Mars.

He closed the armoire and moved over across from the bed, but keeping his distance from it.

About thirty seconds later Mars came out of the bathroom with her hair down around her shoulders and her lipstick freshly applied. She smelled of vanilla and honeysuckle.

'You look more relaxed,' she said.

'Do I? Not really feeling that way.'

'Let me see if I can help.' Mars glided across and kissed him on the mouth. She pulled slightly away and gave him a searching look. 'Well?'

'That helped,' he said.

'Well, let's keep working on it.'

Mars led him over to the bed and put her drink down. She reached behind her, slid her zipper from her shoulders to her bottom, and stepped out of the dress. Underneath she had on a lacey lavender bra, white, high-cut underpants, and a black garter belt holding up her stockings. She stepped out of her heels, which brought her three inches closer to the earth.

'I don't do this for just anybody.'

'Which makes me wonder why I'm so lucky.'

'Because you're young and tall and handsome, and I like all those things in a man.'

'Your husband is a lot taller than me.'

'But he's not young and he's not handsome and he's certainly not interested in *this* anymore.'

'Then maybe he should go see a doctor.'

'And you can sweet-talk, too. Even better.' She kissed him again, this time with her tongue, but didn't get the reaction she wanted. She stepped back and looked up at him. 'Is there something wrong?'

'I actually came here to ask you some questions, not jump into bed with you. I'm sorry if I let this get out of hand, but you threw me some curves I didn't quite know how to handle.'

'Can't you ask your questions while we do it? Interrogation while having intercourse, it might be kind of sexy.'

'You're married,' he said.

'It's 1953, for God's sake. And do you really think Danny isn't sleeping around?'

'I'm working what is now a murder investigation. In fact, I was almost murdered up in Vegas while I was checking on Lamb's disappearance. It makes a man think. It makes a man careful.' He eyed her up and down. 'All the time.'

She gave him a hard look right back. 'Are you sure you want to forgo this opportunity?' She fiddled with her bra strap, apparently still trying despite his earlier rejection. 'It might not come around again.'

He eyed her soft breasts. 'Trust me, it's a difficult decision. And a few years ago we'd already be in that bed over there. But it's not a few years ago. So put your dress back on and let's talk.'

She didn't look pleased by this, but she didn't slap him or order him to get out, either. What Mars did was step back into her dress, sit on the bed, and rub at one stockinged foot. 'You said a murder investigation? Lamb isn't dead, is she?'

By her tone, Archer didn't think she cared one way or another. Yet when he looked at the woman's tensed features, he thought he might be wrong about that.

'No, a PI from Anaheim named Cedric Bender is.'

'What's the connection to Lamb?'

'His body was found in her house.'

'Maybe she killed him,' said Mars.

'Maybe.'

'What questions do you have?' Mars asked.

'Did Alice Jacoby ever strike you as being addicted to drugs?'

'Alice? She's as straight a shooter as I've ever seen. I doubt she even takes aspirin.'

'Jacoby was friends with Lamb, so it seems odd that you didn't know Lamb, too. Jacoby seemed to think that you two *did* know each other.'

'What can I tell you? She was wrong. We all had our little cliques, Archer, and Lamb was not part of mine.'

'Lamb was a political science major. Which makes sense because her father was in the diplomatic corps. She traveled all over because of that. Speaks multiple languages.'

'How interesting,' said Mars, who looked bored and distracted. She walked over to a side table, plucked a cigarette out of a bowl, used a chrome lighter next to the bowl to light up, and resumed her seat on the bed, her legs drawn up under her. She said in a prompting manner, 'My attention span is waning, in case you hadn't noticed.'

'How much did the casinos tap you for Danny's gambling losses?'

She puffed on her smoke without taking her unblinking eyes off him, a remarkable feat, he had to concede. 'How do you know they did?'

'He's still alive. And so are you.'

'I'm just a bit thrown here, I have to admit. I was ready for a very different afternoon with you. No talking, no thinking. Just some time with me, right here,'

305

she said, patting the bed.

'So, the debts?'

'What possible business is it of yours?'

'If it makes you feel better, Mallory Green and Alice Jacoby have the same issues with their husbands. Bart Green's is just on a bigger scale.'

'Well, I'm sure Mallory will be able to handle it.'

'He's lost millions of dollars gambling, Gloria. Now, maybe you could pay that back with your J. P. Morgan and U.S. Trust inheritance. But Mallory doesn't have those kinds of assets.'

'Bart makes a lot of money.'

'Not *that* much,' he said.

'What can I tell you?'

'I was hoping more than you have. So, Green never came to you for money?'

'If she did, why should I tell you?'

'Maybe you just did. How about Alice? Did she put the ask on you for bailout money?'

'As I told you before, Archer, I never touch the principal.'

'But what about a little interest? You probably have a bit to share for an old friend.'

She dropped her gaze. 'If you must know, yes, I did help a little. But that was all.'

'Did you find some spare change for your husband, too?'

'Can you find your own way out, or do I have to call one of the servants to show you?'

He slowly walked over to the door.

'Oh, Archer?'

He turned to see her standing there all confidence and swagger, her hands on her hips.

'Just take a good long look at my bedroom, tall,

dark, and *stupid*. Because you'll never see it again.'

Yep, Archer thought, *the warrior just got me with her sword right in the gut.*

54

In the hotel lobby Archer phoned Mallory Green's house after getting the number from the directory. Green's personal assistant, Sally, answered and told him that Green had flown to Lake Tahoe.

'That's right, I remember now.' It was actually the pilot Steve Everett who had told him that. 'Do you have the phone number and address up there? She wanted me to fill her in on developments.'

She gave this information to him and Archer wrote it down in his notebook.

Later, he drove to the Formosa, where he walked into the red train car that the owner, Jimmy Bernstein, a former prizefighter from New York, had attached to the building to give him more space for customers to spend money and have a good time. Being across the street from the Goldwyn Studio, the Formosa saw its share of stars. Archer wasn't guessing about this. There were hundreds of autographed pictures on the walls, with everyone from William Powell to Joan Crawford represented.

He waited until seven on the dot and ordered a Gibson with the trio of onions. It was delivered to his table at just the moment a back-door entrance opened. Sidling into the train car was a woman wearing a long black coat, a broad-brimmed black hat, and sunglasses big enough to hide most of her face. She spotted Archer and headed over, depositing herself in the chair across from him with her back to the entrance.

She took her hat off, revealing the platinum-blond hair, but kept the glasses on. She smiled at Archer and set her plastic purse on the table, then took a sip of her Gibson and slowly put it back down. 'God, that tastes so damn good.'

'Must be the extra onions. They do it every time.'

She smiled. 'I don't even know your name. You signed the note, 'Sincerely, I'm cute.' Nice touch.'

'Name's Archer, Miss Lourdes.'

'Please, just call me Sam. And Samantha's not my real name. Pretty much every star out here has changed theirs. Many of them because they're Jewish. Heaven forbid. Right?'

'Right. What film are you working on?'

'Does it really matter? The next one before the next one. They're paying me so much money I could never spend it all.'

'But other people could, so be careful. Lots of stars end up with nothing. Don't be one of them, Sam.'

She took another drink, while he sipped on his scotch on the rocks. 'How's your hand?'

He flexed it. 'I'm a fast healer.'

'I didn't think I'd hear from you.'

'To confess, I didn't know your name until I saw it on a movie poster. No knock against you. I'm a nobody and you're a star, but I'm just not much of a movie guy.'

'It's actually refreshing. I almost didn't answer your note, but you seemed like, well, like a nice guy, not a swooner or a grifter, and I can usually spot them.' She set the drink down. 'So, it seems you had a close call at the Jade.'

'I also had a close call in Vegas with the guy who runs the Jade, Darren Paley. Almost ended up residing forever in the desert.'

She reacted to the name in a way that surprised Archer. 'I think he has lots of close calls like that with people. Only most of them don't get away like you did.'

'So you know who he is?' asked Archer curiously.

She made a face that Archer couldn't quite read. 'I know *what* he is. You got a cigarette?'

He shook out a Lucky and lit it for her. She blew the smoke to the wall and lifted the Gibson with her free hand. It was a pretty hand, Archer observed. But there were indications of old calluses on the palm and fingers, along with a certain strength. The lady had known hard manual work, he concluded.

She noted him looking, eyed her hand, and said, 'I grew up in Minnesota, like I told you. On a farm. Lot of hard work and heavy lifting. Riding mules and horses. I still like riding horses. Only now I do it for pleasure; back then it was just so we could eat or get from one place to another.'

'I can see that.'

She tapped her ash into the ashtray. 'Can you, Archer? Then you're in rare company in this town.'

'I didn't grow up on a farm. I grew up poor in a city where every day you could see all the things you would never have.'

'I think that might be as bad as living on a farm with nothing to see except how *little* you have.'

'They're both tough.'

'As soon as I turned fifteen I got out of there. Saved money, got on a bus, and left. And that trip? Let me tell you, I could write a book on it.'

'I bet.'

She blew smoke out and rested her chin on her

knuckles. 'But MGM doesn't want me to ever mention where I came from. It's apparently too *common*. And people don't like to lay down dough for movie tickets to watch common. So the studio invented a past for me, and I can tell you for a fact it's simply *marvelous*.'

She took off her glasses, dipping her gaze for a moment before swinging it up to him and giving him a look that froze him to his bones with its sultry, honest frankness. He didn't know if this was a perfected signature movie move of hers or not, but she did it with a lot of class, exhibiting both a fragility and a longing that made one ache, or at least it did him.

She smiled at his reaction, and the look vanished instantly. 'You should see me do that shtick with the right lighting. They say the difference between being a film star and a run-of-the-mill actress is how good your lighting guy is.'

'Okay.'

'You see, Archer, this is a fantasy town, and I'm now part of that fantasy.'

'You can choose not to be. Go back to Minnesota.'

'I think about that. A lot. Some days I almost work up the courage to do it.'

'Why can't you go all the way?'

Her wide eyes became sad and distant. 'Because working your fingers to the bone on a farm in the middle of nowhere for peanuts is not all that great, either. I busted my butt to escape it, in fact. That makes it hard to rush back to. At least here I can mostly call my own shots. And the money? I make more in one day than I'd make in a lifetime working that farm.'

'Money's not everything.'

'It is if you never had much of it.'

311

'You still have any family left?'

'My parents are dead. I have two sisters. They think I'm an evil hussy who has blackened the family name.'

'What was your real name?'

'I'll take that to the grave, thank you very much. So, why did Paley want to kill you?'

'Maybe I know more than I should know, at least about what he's doing.'

'And what do you know?'

'Some of what I saw that night.' He glanced at her pupils. They were normal. She noticed his scrutiny.

Lourdes said sharply, 'When I work, I don't play. And I worked today.'

'Okay. But you may get to the point where your body doesn't give you a choice.'

Furrows covered her lovely brow. 'Is that why you asked to meet with me? To lecture me? Because others have tried. And failed.'

'No, I said my piece the first night I saw you.'

'And I said my piece right back.'

'How well do you know Paley?'

'Pretty well, considering I was *married* to Darren for two years.'

Archer just sat there for a few moments. It had been a long time since he had been that stunned.

'Yeah, I didn't think you knew about that. I was only seventeen.'

'Seventeen?'

'Really young and even more stupid. We didn't meet out here. It was in Reno. I tried to make it as a dancer and singer there after escaping the farm. I met Darren. He was a lot older than me, an ex-con, all tough and smooth and dangerous and involved in some shady deals and with some seriously bad people, and he swept me right off my little naive farm girl feet. Then it became apparent we were not a good match and we got a quickie divorce; in that regard Reno was perfect. It was mutual, by the way. Darren had already moved on to another woman before we separated. And then the war started and he joined up. And I came out here and finally got the brass ring. When he got out of uniform I heard Darren went to Vegas and started working at the Flamingo.'

'Bugsy Siegel and those boys?'

She tapped her ash in the ashtray. 'Yeah. He was their enforcer. And he was really, really good at it. He did a bunch of stuff for them and for himself. And then he came here.'

'I think he was pulling double duty between Vegas and LA during that time.'

'How do you mean?'

'He was operating a gambling ring for the mob out of Chinatown about five years ago. Cost a friend of mine the use of his legs. He blew town after that and then he came back to run the Jade. Maybe with the mob's blessing and participation.'

'Nothing Darren did or will do would surprise me.'

'You said you were seventeen when you got married?'

'And nineteen when we got divorced. I'm thirty now. I've got maybe, *maybe* ten good years left for pictures. I've got to hoof it while the hoofing is good. And don't worry. I invest my money in blue chip stocks and government bonds and prime real estate, and I have ownership pieces in some of the best restaurants and nightclubs in LA. I'll be sitting pretty when I blow this joint and go wherever I go.'

'And when Darren got to town and found out you

313

were a big star, what did he want?'

She finished off her Gibson and raised her hand for another. After it was delivered she said, 'Why do you think I go to the Jade?'

'He's blackmailing you. What with?'

'Let's just say that while we were married I helped my husband with some of his business dealings and some people got hurt. I mean, really hurt. I knew nothing about any of it, of course. I was just a kid, but Darren doesn't care. He could make my life miserable and my career would flame out just like that.' She snapped her fingers. 'And if you repeat that to anybody I'll sue your ass off and take everything you have.'

'I don't repeat things and I don't have much to take. But if he spills, he brings himself down.'

'I've got a lot more to lose than he does, Archer. And Darren always lands on his feet. Always. He's the cat of all cats.'

'They're filming you at the Jade.'

'I know they are. But only from the ceiling angle. They sell it to the Japs and the Chinese and the South Americans, and maybe here, too, who the hell knows? They just see the top of my platinum-blond head . . . and then the rest of me. Nobody knows it's the *wonderful* Samantha Lourdes, of course. He makes money, and when Darren makes money he lays off me. And that makes it worth it.'

'And do you get others to go there, too? Your fellow stars?'

She looked down into her glass, her expression flexing to despondency. 'He wants me to. But I keep making excuses. I don't want anyone I care about to get mixed up with that man. He was bad in Reno.

Now he's far worse. Maybe it was the war, or maybe it was the stuff he did for Bugsy and that crowd. Whatever, he really scares me. But I'm running out of excuses with him. And I'm not the only *star* there, I can tell you that.'

'And he got you hooked on drugs?'

She sat up. 'No, in fairness, I can't blame Darren for that — it was all my doing. I dabbled when I was married to him; Darren won't touch the stuff. He doesn't even drink booze. He has to always be in control. Me, I kept dabbling. Now the studio feeds it to me so I'll keep working my cute little ass off for them. But I'm not hooked, not per se.'

'I don't think there's any *per se* when it comes to being an addict.'

'You might be surprised. I only take ten percent of the stuff they throw my way. Same at the Jade. It's starting to bore me, actually. I might just chuck it all one day and be dry as a bone with pupils that don't go *pop* anymore.' She shot him a curious glance. 'So, is Darren coming for you?'

'At some point he will. For now, he's lying low after his boys blew the hit on me. It was close. They were already digging the grave and about to drill a bullet into my skull when the cavalry arrived and saved my butt.'

She reached out and took his hand, her features now full of sincere concern. 'Archer, don't mess with that psycho. He won't miss again.'

'I'm not sure I have much choice in the matter.'

'You could hop a train or a plane and head east. Far, far east.'

'I can do a lot of things. But then Paley will still be here doing what he does to people. Like you. How

315

does that make the world a better place?'

She sat back and gazed at him in wonderment. 'What are you, a preacher or an idiot or both? Or is that just a line you throw out like I do my movie look?'

He pulled his license and showed her. 'None of the above. Like I told you before, I'm a private detective.'

She didn't look impressed. 'Darren eats cops for breakfast. PIs are just a hiccup to him.'

'He might have met his match this time. I'm not in the fight alone.'

Her expression quickly changed. 'You *really* think you can take him down?'

Archer knew exactly why she was asking. 'If you can help me, I might. I'm sure you can see the personal benefits.'

'Is that why you'd be doing it?'

'I could lie and say yes, but until you told me of your connection, I didn't know you had skin in the game. But I guess, in a way, I did. If the Jade goes down, you don't have to go there and play the bad girl anymore.'

'You're not a preacher. You're a Boy Scout.'

'People keep saying that, doesn't make it true. But do I want to make the world a better place? Yeah, because I live in the world, too. As do people I care about. Like you.'

Her face flushed beautifully when he said this, and she gave his fingers a squeeze before draining her Gibson. He finished his scotch and both seemed now to hunker down to business.

'How can I help you?' she said.

'Do you know where he gets his supply of dope?'

'No, but sometimes I've nosed around and seen the stuff coming in late at night. It's at least once a week.

Comes by truck.'

'Surprised he lets you roam the halls.'

'Darren doesn't think I'm a threat, you see, because he has dirt on me. They put the empty crates behind that room divider in the entranceway. When the next shipment comes, the truck takes the empty crates away.'

'I also saw some smuggling going on in Malibu early on New Year's Day. A boat with crates coming in to shore. I almost bought it then, too, on the beach. And I saw some of those sandy crates in the Jade behind that room divider, with what looked like heroin dust inside one. And I found a glass vial in one of the rooms with what I think is heroin, too. What I need to know, are his shipments coming from what I saw happening on that beach?'

'They could be, but I don't know for sure.'

He pulled out the photo he had snagged from the Bonhams' house. 'Have you ever seen these people at the Jade?'

She looked at the picture and then smiled at Archer. 'What?'

'The woman Darren moved on to before he divorced me?'

'Yeah?'

She pressed her thumb against Bernadette Bonham's elegant face. 'That's the bitch.'

55

'So, Bernadette Bonham and Darren Paley were a couple?' asked Dash.

He and Archer were in the latter's motel room discussing things over cigarettes and drinks and sometimes muddled thought. Archer had given Dash the white powder traces he had taken from the dirt at the Bonhams'. Dash had dropped them off at a private lab in LA he had used before.

'That's what Samantha said.'

Dash cracked a grin. 'Samantha Lourdes — who would have thought?'

'You've seen her pictures?'

Dash now snorted. 'Hell, Archer, you seem to be the only one who hasn't.'

'And she was married to Paley for two years.'

'I think she can count her lucky stars she's still alive after living with that psycho.'

'She's not free of him yet,' Archer pointed out.

'And you want to be the white knight swooping in to save the damsel in distress?'

'I'm not a knight of any color, and she didn't strike me as the damsel-in-distress type.' He paused. 'Bernadette would have entered the picture around the time Lourdes and Paley got divorced. That would've been around 1941. Bernadette told me her family moved to Canada to avoid Hitler when the Nazis took over France, and they were there until the war was over. France surrendered to Germany in June of 1940, so Bernadette and her family were in Canada

318

before then. But she must have left Canada and gone to Reno probably sometime in 1941. And she met Paley there. Then Paley joined up and was in the war for years. I don't know if he and Bernadette got together again after that. But they seem tight now.'

'How long has she been married to Peter Bonham?'

'I don't know exactly. She told me they met after the war and were married in Nice. Then they came here. He already had the place in Malibu.'

'So, at most, they've been married maybe six years, give or take?'

'Right. But Bernadette could have rekindled things with Paley even if she was married. The French look at these things differently.'

'Hell, Archer, Americans do, too.'

'And she said that Bonham had been married before, but that his first wife was dead. Now, their neighbor Mrs. Danforth didn't think he'd been married before, but she had no way of knowing that for certain.'

Dash picked a bit of tobacco off his tongue and took a swallow of bourbon. 'Okay, let's get down to basics, Archer. Namely, to nail Paley we have to figure out what he's doing. Now, he's a guy with connections to the mob and Vegas. So if he is selling dope out of Chinatown, I'm sure he keeps some for the LA locals, but the excess probably goes out to the rest of the country through dope rings. And those dope rings, I have no doubt, have ties to the Vegas mob. It's a big money maker for them. Maybe even more than the casinos. But you said Paley thinks someone is horning in on his business?'

'That's right. Jake have any insights on that?'

'No, but that doesn't mean *we* can't find out.'

'And I told you Peter Bonham is the man I fought with on the beach that night. Now I know he was there waiting on the dope shipment. I remember seeing a truck parked on the beach. You think Bonham is supplying Paley? Because at some point we have to make that connection, or not.'

'Could be. And you say Bonham's the same guy who spoke to you on the phone that night when you called Lamb's house?'

'Yes. And that means he had something to do with Bender's death, because I'm pretty sure the man's body was there while Bonham was talking to me.'

'If Bender was killed by Bonham, he must have had a good reason. Dead bodies make things complicated.'

'Mallory Green hired Bender to track down who Bart was fooling around with. So how does Bender end up in Lamb's house?'

'We know he was shot elsewhere. Maybe Bonham killed him and dumped him there.'

'Why and why?' asked Archer.

'If Bernadette *was* cheating on Bonham with Bart Green and Bonham found out, he might have killed Bender to keep that under wraps.'

'It's hard for me to believe that the lovely French lady would have much interest in Bart Green, his status as a big Hollywood producer notwithstanding. I thought the babes he had in Vegas were his mistresses, but turns out they were his nieces. And I got it from a reliable source that of the Three Musketeers, Simon, Bart, and Danny, only Danny is the skirt chaser.'

'I get that. But if Bart Green and Bernadette Bonham *did* have a fling, most cuckolded guys don't like their shame to be broadcast publicly. And you said Bernadette saw her husband arguing with Lamb?'

320

'That's right.'

'Lamb worked for Green. So maybe she found out about the affair and was threatening to tell the world if Bonham didn't pay up.'

'But why kill Bender?' asked Archer.

'Bonham could have killed Bender and dropped the body at Lamb's place to get her off his back.'

'That actually fits together. Lamb told me she'd been getting strange phone calls and someone broke into her house and left a bloody knife in the sink. And maybe Bonham's plan worked, because if she's not dead, she *has* vanished. So you might be right, Willie. Bonham could have been behind all of that to deep-six Lamb and her blackmail hooks.'

'And I also might be way off the mark, too. Only time will tell.'

Dash put down his drink, looked at Archer, and checked his watch. 'We'll head out to Malibu in about an hour. If I recall correctly, Danforth said the trucks were heard in the middle of the night?'

'That's right. And Lourdes said the shipments to the Jade come in at least once a week, late at night.'

'Okay, let's talk about the smuggling piece some more. Paley is selling dope. He knows Bernadette Bonham and possibly her husband, too. You tussled with Peter Bonham on the beach, and there was a truck there. So, yeah, a *possible* connection between the Malibu beach smugglers, the Bonhams, and Paley is definitely established. And even though we don't know for sure what was in the crates being brought in off that boat, dope is certainly the most probable answer.'

'It all fits,' agreed Archer.

'But the Bonhams also go to France for months at

a time. Who covers for him while he's gone?'

'He must have a partner. Paley?'

'No, can't be. Bonham is too smart to let Paley know the source of the dope. That way Paley could cut him out of the loop.'

'Right. And if Paley were overseeing the incoming shipments he'd know who was drinking from his trough,' added Archer.

'So, the trucks the girl heard were the shipments coming up from the beach, probably to Bonham's house. You were down on the beach around five in the morning?'

'Yeah, and those guys were rushing like crazy because they were probably late. At that hour you might get some early beachcombers or people heading out to their jobs.'

Dash rose. 'Okay, see you in a bit, Archer. And don't forget your gun.'

Dash left, and Archer immediately called Callahan's number.

'Archer, it's good to hear your voice. I miss you.'

'Same here. Willie is down here helping me.'

'Well, that definitely makes me feel better.'

'Hey, what can you tell me about Samantha Lourdes?'

'Samantha Lourdes? Why?'

'She was the actress I saw at the Jade. I finally made the connection. But you can't tell anybody. She's a good egg.'

'I won't tell anybody because I respect her as an actress and she's also got a great head for business. I heard that Lourdes is close to getting out of her MGM contract and starting her own production company. She's sort of her generation's Carole Lombard. It kills me that she's mixed up in crap like that.'

'Well, she came by it in a weird way.' He told her about Lourdes being married to Paley when she was seventeen.

'God, she's lucky to be alive.'

'And I want to keep her that way,' said Archer.

'Wait a minute — have you seen her again since the Jade?'

'Yeah, we had a drink at the Formosa earlier tonight.'

'I can't believe this is happening. What was she like?' asked Callahan.

'Down-to-earth, smart, hardworking. She grew up on a farm in Minnesota.'

'I've been dying to meet her and you run right into her.'

'Hell, Liberty, when I met her I was *running* for my life at the Jade Lion! But I can tell her about you the next time I see her.'

'You're going to see her again!' exclaimed Callahan.

'Well, we sort of left it open. But if I can get Paley out of her hair, I think I'd have a fan for life.'

Callahan didn't say anything to this.

'Hey, you still there?'

'Yeah, I'm still there. Look, don't mention me to her, Archer. I'd hate for her to think I'm trying to use you to further my own lousy career.'

'But everybody in this town does that. You know that's true.'

'Well, I'm not, not this time, anyway. But . . . I'm happy for you, Archer.'

'Happy for me? Look, Liberty, I'm not marrying the woman. I'm just trying to help her out of a jam, same as she's doing for me.'

'Okay, sure, if you say so. I got an early set call

tomorrow. Good night.'

Before he could say anything else, he heard the receiver click back into place. He slowly put the phone down and wondered what the hell all that was about.

56

'Something bothering you, Archer?'

He and Dash were walking to the car.

'No, it's fine.'

'It's obviously not fine, so let's hear it.'

'Okay, I called Liberty and it didn't go well.'

'Why, what did you tell her?'

'About meeting Samantha Lourdes.' Archer went on to tell him the details of the call.

Dash listened and said, 'You just hobnobbed with one of the most famous skirts in Hollywood and you told Liberty how swell Lourdes was. And how grateful she'll be to you if you get her out of this crap with Paley.'

'So you're saying Liberty's jealous?'

'I'm saying she's human.'

The sky was rapidly growing cloudy as a storm system headed in. Archer observed this and said, 'You think they'll chance bringing a boat in tonight with this bad weather rolling in?'

'Dope smugglers can't necessarily wait for fair winds and following seas, Archer. And even if the boat doesn't come, they might be moving the dope from Bonham's to the Jade via truck.'

'So they probably don't take it directly to the Jade as soon as it comes in on the beach?'

'I don't think the timing works for that. They need to check the stuff. Make sure it's all square. That takes time. And since Bonham might have other customers he's servicing besides Paley, my thinking is he's stashing it somewhere and *then* taking it to the Jade and the other places later.'

'Makes sense.'

'You got your camera?'

'Yeah.'

They climbed into the Buick and headed off with Archer driving.

They made it to Malibu, drove up Las Flores, and parked around a curve from the Bonhams' place and behind a massive Chrysler station wagon. Archer settled back in his seat and took a drink from his flask. He passed it over to Dash, who declined.

Dash looked around and said, 'Nice neighborhood.'

'Yeah, except for all the dope smuggling and dead bodies,' quipped Archer.

The rain started to fall about a half hour later. Archer drew his dark slicker around him as the cold crept into the car. He felt his eyes growing heavy several times, but he would yawn and stretch to keep himself awake. Every time he looked over at Dash, the man was fully alert and staring out the window.

At close to midnight they both looked behind them as the pair of headlights came into view. Both men slunk down in their seats. The truck passed by them, rounded the bend, and disappeared from view.

'Give it another minute, Archer,' said Dash.

Sixty seconds passed and the men got out of the car and hustled down the street, rounded the curve, and then squatted down as they saw the truck parked in the Bonhams' drive.

They watched as several men climbed out of the truck and disappeared into the back grounds.

'Okay, Archer, hit it.'

326

Archer ran forward, reached the truck, and squatted down. Then he used the light to locate the rear axle, took from his pocket what he had brought with him, and affixed it to the metal axle.

He rounded the far side of the house and joined Dash, who had taken up a surveillance position there.

The group of men from the truck had gathered around the site of the bomb shelter, while a tall man in the middle, clothed in a long black trench coat, bent down and unlocked the entrance. He lifted up the metal hatch and motioned the men inside. They headed down what seemed to be a set of steps. A few minutes later they reappeared with wooden crates. And something else.

People wearing white hoods and whose hands were bound behind them. They swayed and stumbled along as though drunk or drugged.

Archer heard Dash say, 'Son of a bitch.'

Archer shot multiple pictures with his Kodak, capturing clear images of Peter Bonham — who was the tall man in the trench coat — the crates, and the hooded prisoners. It was a montage of malevolence, with mood lighting provided by nature and preservation of evidence by Kodak, hopefully for future felony prosecution.

Bonham shut the entrance and replaced the padlock.

Dash whispered, 'Let's get back to the car.'

Five minutes later the truck appeared on the street and passed them heading down Las Flores.

Archer waited until the truck was out of sight, then he started the Buick and followed.

When the truck came back into view, Dash smiled. 'Bingo.'

.The thing Archer had put on the rear axle was a reflective strip that fluoresced in the dark. They could see it.

'Stay back. Dollars to donuts they're going to the Jade.'

Archer nodded and sat back as he lowered the car's speed. 'The crates I figured. The people in hoods I didn't.'

'Looks like the scum are into selling dope *and* human beings.'

'You figure they're coming up from Mexico?'

'The dope, yeah. The people, maybe from China, considering where they're probably going.'

'What will they use them for?'

'The usual crap. Domestics, hard labor, farming, prostitution. Same old same old.' Dash gave him the eye. 'This and bringing dope in over the border gets us to federal crime territory, Archer. Now, wake me when we get to Chinatown.'

Only the truck didn't end up going to Chinatown.

57

The first surprise was the turn the truck made before it reached Pacific Palisades.

'They're heading north,' said Archer. He thought for a moment. 'Will Rogers State Park is in that direction. Could they be going there for some reason?'

They kept following the truck, and, later, Archer cut the Buick's lights as the truck turned down a single-lane road surrounded by woods.

'What do we do now?' he asked Dash.

'We can't risk being seen or getting stuck heading down that road. The rain's stopped, so make your way down on foot and see what you see. I'll pull the car around and out of sight. I'm figuring they have to come out of there at some point.'

Archer climbed out. Dash slid into the driver's seat and wheeled the car around and behind a slab of bushes. He cut the lights and engine and waited.

Meanwhile, Archer picked his way through the wet ground as water from the rain-laden tree canopies splashed down on him. He turned up his slicker's collar and kept going, a flashlight his only source of illumination. His path paralleled the road leading in. He finally reached a clearing and peered around the trunk of a burly oak.

There was another truck back here, and a transfer was being made. The hooded figures were being led off the one truck and loaded onto the other. Two of the guards then closed the overhead door of the truck and secured it. One of them patted the back of the door and the truck started up.

Archer made his way back to Dash. He climbed into the Buick just as the truck with the prisoners emerged from the wood line. In a few hurried words he told Dash what he had seen.

As the truck passed by their hiding place, Dash said. 'We got a choice to make. Follow that truck with the people or the other one with the crates. I opt for the crates. We got the reflective tape on that truck. It'd be too easy to lose the other.'

'Agreed.'

The second truck appeared a minute later and headed back down the way it had come. Archer and Dash followed at a discreet distance.

They got back on the main road, made the curve around Santa Monica Bay, but instead of cutting east to LA and Chinatown, the truck kept going south.

'What the hell!' exclaimed Dash. 'This is really getting screwy.'

They kept following in light traffic. They passed the Venice Pier when Dash said, 'Maybe they're heading to El Segundo or Manhattan Beach, something like that.'

'Now they're heading east,' said Archer a minute later.

The truck had indeed changed directions again and was moving inland.

Then it dawned on Archer. 'They're going to LA International.'

Sure enough, the truck did enter the airport, which even at this late hour was busy.

Archer looked around at the activity. Tugs pulled baggage cars, and multi-engine propeller planes taxied to or away from the runways now that the storm had passed. Cargo trucks zipped hither and thither to make sure the air commerce on the West Coast held up its end of the bargain.

As they drove along well back of the truck, it approached a gate and stopped. The guard spoke with the driver, there was a flash of paper, and then the guard waved him on.

'We're not getting past that gate,' observed Dash. 'And the guard didn't even check what was in the back of the truck. I'm thinking some money has changed hands there.'

'Hold on, this is looking familiar.'

Archer parked the car and pulled out his binoculars. He hopped out and went over to a remote part of the field and peered through the fencing. The truck had stopped next to a plane. He continued to watch as the crates were off-loaded, weighed on a portable scale, and then loaded into the plane's cargo hold. He saw the man in the truck hand another man some papers, then he and the other men climbed back into the truck.

And Archer had recognized the man who had received the papers and the cargo.

He returned to the car and climbed in. 'Okay, the plane they just loaded the crates into is Bart Green's Beechcraft.'

'You're sure?'

'Yeah, I'm sure. I flew in it. And the guy who accepted the cargo just now is Green's pilot, Steve Everett. He's the one who flew me to Vegas.'

They watched as the truck passed through the gate and headed on into the darkness.

'Should we follow the truck?' asked Archer.

'I'd like to know where that plane is flying tonight.'

'I'm not sure how we'd find that out. It's not a scheduled commercial flight. It's private. We probably could find out, given time and a few palms greased.'

'Okay, we can do that later. Let's follow the truck.'

However, the driver had now parked the truck and gone into the terminal while the other men waited in the front seat. He came out a few minutes later with some paper cups of coffee in hand, climbed back in, and set off.

As they left the airport, following the shiny stripe on the truck's rear axle, Archer looked up and thought he could see the Beechcraft pass overhead with its shipment of dope to points unknown. But that might just have been his imagination.

They followed the truck at a steady pace.

'Maybe we're finally going to Chinatown,' said Dash as they passed in a northeasterly direction through South Central LA, past downtown, and hooked around Union Station.

It did indeed look like they were finally venturing into Chinatown.

However, when they rounded a corner, the truck was no longer in sight.

'He must have turned down that alley,' said Dash, pointing to his left.

At that same instant, three men stepped out from that alley. And they were pointing something at the Buick.

'Hit it, Archer, it's an ambush,' barked Dash.

Archer gunned the engine, cut the wheel, and slammed down on the gas even as the men opened fire, shattering the side and back glass of the Buick. Archer felt the crack of rounds whizzing past him; some lodged in the upholstery, others clanged off the

332

metal inside the car. It was like he and Dash were stuck in a pinball machine and ricochets were everywhere trying to kill the two men. He piloted the Buick around a corner and kept the pedal to the floor. The car's engine wound up high, screaming like a woman in distress.

Archer exhaled a relieved breath as he slowed down. 'Damn, that was close.'

He turned to look at Dash and his lungs seized.

An unconscious Willie Dash was lying sideways in his seat with blood pouring from his back.

58

Archer hung up the pay phone for the third time at the hospital where he had driven the badly wounded Dash. He had first called Connie Morrison to tell her what had happened. She was on her way to LA. He had next called Jake Nichols and woken him up.

His response had been terse. 'Come and see me in the morning, once they're sure Willie's in the clear. If things turn bad, call me anytime no matter how late.'

He had finally phoned Callahan and told her what had happened. He could hear the woman quietly sobbing, and part of him knew that she was also thinking about what if it had been him who was shot and lying near death. He had put down the phone with her still weeping because he was afraid he would start crying as well.

The doctor on duty had called the police, as was required by law. While Dash was in emergency surgery Archer had met with two uniformed officers and a plainclothes detective from the LAPD. They seemed to be honest and forthright and eager to do their job. And yet he left out everything except that they had been riding in a car minding their own business when the shots had rung out. He had no desire to get into a lengthy explanation about everything until he knew what they were really up against.

The plainclothes, in his forties with a calm face and low voice, said, 'You might've just been in the wrong place at the wrong time. We're cleaning this town up, but it's not all scrubbed yet.'

'Could be gangs,' said one of the uniforms, who looked too baby-faced to be a cop, and whose speech had a southern strum to it. 'Puerto Ricans or Chicanos most likely. Or the coloreds. They don't care who they kill.'

They had examined the Buick, and the surgeon promised to deliver the slug that was still in Dash to the police. Archer had left his answering service number with them, and they promised to be in touch with regard to their investigation.

Connie Morrison arrived just as her boss and former husband was wheeled out of surgery. Archer had never seen her look so pale and flustered in the three years he had known the woman.

They met with the surgeon, who told them Dash had come through the procedure well, but his recovery would take some time. And he would be unconscious for a while.

'I think he's out of the woods,' said the doctor, a short, thin man with a face as pale as his lab coat, but who possessed a reassuringly calm demeanor. He cleaned his specs with his coat sleeve and said, 'He's strong, certainly, for his age. But he was also lucky. The bullet missed a major artery by about two centimeters, and didn't hit any bone along the way, either. While he lost a lot of blood, I feel he'll make a full recovery. Somebody was looking out for him tonight.'

Archer looked guiltily at his shoes. *Only it wasn't me.*

They thanked him, and Morrison went to sit next to Dash in his private room. Archer knew she would be there every second of every day until her ex got up and walked out of the place under his own power.

Archer stood behind her and looked down at the man who had become like a second father to him. Dash was alternately pale and gray, and his limbs twitched spasmodically in his induced slumber. The perimeter of a large gauzy bandage poked up from under the gown near his neck. He looked old and beaten and . . . nothing good. But it *was* good, Archer had to remind himself, because Dash was alive when he could so easily have been dead.

Morrison turned to stare resolutely at him. 'I'll take care of the bills and all the paperwork, Archer. You just do what you need to do to find the ones who shot Willie.'

He squeezed her shoulder and turned to leave.

'Archer?'

He looked back to see her staring dead at him.

'Do not get killed.'

He gave her a quick grin that died on his lips, because there was nothing funny about what she had said, meant, and felt. He nodded, lifted his hat an inch, turned, and left.

He drove to the motel in Silver Lake, grabbed a few hours' sleep, rose, showered, shaved, dressed in clean clothes, and had some coffee. He turned in the Buick at a local franchise of the company he had rented it from in Bay Town. He had to pay a substantial penalty, since the company was not fond of having their cars shot up. They would also not lease him another one for the very same reason.

So Archer walked two blocks to an Avis office and drove out a half hour later in a gray 1952 Oldsmobile two-door sedan.

He headed straight to Jake Nichols's bar. The man was waiting for him inside. He was sitting at a table in his wheelchair staring at the door like the worst news in the world was about to march in and crush what little life he had left.

Archer took off his hat and said, 'He's going to be okay. But it's going to take a while.'

Nichols wheeled himself over to a cabinet, took two glasses out along with a bottle of whiskey, wheeled back over, and poured himself and Archer shots.

'To brave men and lucky ones,' said Nichols with his glass raised. Archer mimicked this movement, and each downed his drink in one swallow. Archer then told Nichols in greater detail what had happened during the night.

Nichols quickly absorbed all of this and said, 'You got made. Guy goes into the terminal to get a cup of joe, but also makes a phone call. The trap is set and he runs you right into it.'

Archer nodded, looking deeply chagrined. 'That's the way I figured it, too.'

'So selling people *and* dope.'

Archer said, 'I don't know where the people went. But the dope didn't go to the Jade, at least not all of it. Some went on Bart Green's plane. Which convinces me that Bonham and Green are working this together, and Green is the one drinking out of Darren Paley's trough, to use the man's own words.'

'Then they're taking a big risk. You don't cross a guy like Paley unless you have a death wish.'

'Bart Green's motive is clear. He has big gambling bills to pay. And if he doesn't he's dead anyway.'

'Okay, but how do you think Paley and Bonham hooked up?'

'His wife knew Paley years before she was married to Bonham. They met in Reno.'

'And how did Peter Bonham get into the dope and slavery business?'

Archer lit a cigarette and sucked on it. 'His elderly neighbor told me he once worked overseas, all hush-hush. She joked that he was a spy.'

'Maybe he got his drug connections when he was out of the country. Anybody check into his business, where he gets his money, at least on the surface?'

Archer shook his head. 'No, I haven't. But I guess maybe we should.'

'Let me deal with that. We know the guy's a smuggler, but he has to clean the money off his doping somehow.'

Nichols poured another swig of whiskey into his glass. He held up the bottle, but Archer shook his head. Nichols looked at the liquid in the glass for the longest time, but didn't drink it. 'It's not your fault, you know. Willie never saw it coming, so how could you?'

'I've been working this case solo for days. Willie really got on it just yesterday. I should have had his back. I should have suspected something. But I didn't.'

'You can blame yourself, but it's not helpful. You can see that, right?'

'Yeah, I can, even if I don't want to right now.'

'He's a tough guy and the doc says he's going to make it. If Willie was dead, we'd maybe be having a different and more difficult conversation. But right now you need to keep focused on what's important. Paley will be thinking of nothing else other than this. You need to at least match the man on that.'

Archer straightened and looked around the empty bar. 'You ever regret any of it? Doing what you did? Your life? Your choices?'

338

'Since I'm human, the answer is 'all the time.' You can spend half your life second-guessing what you did and didn't do and in the end it doesn't amount to a hill of beans. So you can either live your life or pretend to have another one where you never made a mistake.'

'That may be the hardest thing in the world to do, Jake.'

'The *easiest* thing in the world to do is die. It takes almost no effort or time. You're here and then you're in a grave. It's the stuff beyond dying that's hard.'

'What's that exactly?'

Nichols now drained his glass. 'Living.'

59

Archer drove out to Malibu. The sky was clear, the sun warm but not too warm, the humidity nonexistent. And still Archer was sweating. The investigation was close to getting out of control and he had just lost for the time being the one man who had given him a decent shot to bring this case home.

He stopped at a gas station and phoned the county cops. Two pass-throughs later and Phil Oldham came on the line.

'Heard on the wire about Willie and Chinatown. How's he doing?'

'He's going to make it, but it was close. Too close.'

'You were there?'

'I was. How's the Bender case coming? Got the killer yet?'

'Why should I spill to you?' Oldham said brusquely.

'No reason that I know of other than we're both trying to get to the same spot.'

'We've made some progress. We fished his car out of the ocean.'

'I heard. You know a guy named Darren Paley, manages the Jade Lion in Chinatown?'

'Is that why you two were there?'

'Do you know him?'

'I know *of* him. Is he involved in what happened to Bender?'

'I don't know. Maybe. And you might want to patrol the western half of the Malibu beaches, say around one to four in the morning.'

340

'For what?'

'What do you think?'

'Smuggling? What?'

'The usual,' replied Archer.

'You seen this action?'

'Maybe I have. And it's not just dope.'

'What else?' asked Oldham.

'Try people on for size.'

This seemed to get Oldham excited. 'I want you to come in and make a statement and tell us what you know.'

'Why? I heard you boys weren't working extra hard to get Bender's killer.'

Oldham didn't answer right away. 'Who'd you hear that from?'

'Is it true?'

Again, Oldham didn't answer right away. 'Where are you?'

'Seventy-six station in Malibu.'

'I'll be there in fifteen minutes.'

Eighteen minutes later the old Plymouth lurched into the parking lot of the gas station and Phil Old-ham rolled himself out.

'Let's walk,' he told Archer.

They headed to the beach. It seemed to be a popular spot for confidential talk, thought Archer.

The tide was coming in, so they kept to high ground as the breakers covered their discussions and the seagulls fought against the wind in making their dives for mealtime.

Oldham looked even pastier than before, his clothes grungier, but his eyes were bright and alert, and the man looked pissed.

'Your source was right,' he said as they walked along.

341

Oldham's hands were shoved deep into his pants pockets and the remains of a stogie rolled around in his mouth. 'Soon as we pulled the car from the water I got assigned to another case.'

'You can't just sweep a corpse under the rug.'

Oldham shot him a glance. 'Can't you, Archer?'

'I thought you county cops were immune from the LAPD disease.'

'Says you.'

'No, says *you*.'

'Then maybe I was wrong.' Oldham turned and hurled the stogie toward the water.

'I promised Bender's widow I'd find out what happened.'

'I checked into Bender. He was a good guy, but he had a lot of unpaid bills. They were threatening to take the house.'

Archer stopped walking and looked at him. 'Seriously?'

'Yeah. I guess he'd borrowed big against it when his business wasn't doing too good. He couldn't make the mortgage payments. They were foreclosing on it.'

'But his widow still has the house.'

'That's because the debt got paid off. I didn't dig deep enough to find out how. I didn't have the chance.'

'But this sort of changes things.'

'How?'

Archer looked off for a few moments and studied the breakers coming in. 'Even good guys can make bad choices when things get desperate.'

'How do you mean?'

Archer continued to stare out at the rising ocean. And in that moment certain things seemed to come together with startling clarity. 'How much was the mortgage on Bender's house?'

'What? Oh, about five grand, something like that.'

'No private dick is going to make that running down regular cases in a couple of weeks.'

'What are you getting at, Archer?'

'Like I said, good guys make bad choices when they get pushed.'

'You talking about Bender?'

'I'm talking about all of us.'

60

Archer drove back into town and dropped the film off from the previous night with the same guy, and asked for another rush job. Then he checked with the private lab where Dash had taken the powder samples for analysis.

A stern-looking man in a white lab coat confirmed to Archer that they were indeed heroin.

Archer took the certified lab report with him and headed across town to Green and Ransome. Both name partners were in today, so he took Cecily Ransome first.

She was dressed in navy blue slacks and an oversize dark green sweater that covered her narrow hips. She had on a black beret and an uncomfortable look as she sat at her desk with a pen in hand and a film script set in front of her. She laid her pen aside. 'So, what do you have to report?'

'I brought a partner up here to work with me.'

'Okay.'

'He got shot last night in Chinatown. I almost did, too.'

Ransome jerked forward. 'What! Is he going to be okay?'

'Yes, but not for lack of trying by the guys doing the shooting.'

'Does this have to do with Ellie?'

'I think it does, yes.'

'Tell me what you know.'

'Strange things going on in Malibu. Trucks come

and trucks go. And dope crates and people in hoods go with them.'

Ransome flushed so deeply Archer thought she might collapse. 'P-people in h-hoods?'

'Smugglers, Miss Ransome. A slavery ring. It's a business. Just a really nasty one.'

'Do you think Ellie found out about this and that's why she's gone missing?'

'Could be, yes.'

'Do you know who's involved?'

'Chinatown is involved, that's for sure.'

'The Jade Lion you mentioned?'

'I believe so, yes.'

Ransome looked down at the document in front of her, with her brow furrowed. 'Then you may want to look at this.'

'What is it?'

She spun it around. 'Ellie left this script for me about two weeks ago. She wasn't paid to write it, she did it on her own.'

He read over a couple pages. 'Just give me the short-hand of what the story's about.'

Ransome's voice trembled. 'Chinatown, the mob, dope dealers, and . . . other things. Like . . . a slavery ring. It . . . it must be a coincidence.'

'I don't believe in coincidences. Tell me more.'

'It's dark and violent. Very different from what I normally see from Ellie. Right on the edge, and it has a remarkable feeling of authenticity. Like she knows that world intimately. And it has a terrific female lead. I mean, this might have Oscar written all over it.'

'Why would she give the script to you?'

'Because she wants me to direct the film. And I think I might want to.'

'So the question becomes: How does she know that world intimately?'

'You said you found Jade Lion matchbooks in her desk. She might have gone there, for research.'

Archer looked dubiously at her. 'I don't see that happening. The guy who runs the place doesn't really like folks snooping around. I can personally attest to that.' But something else occurred to him. 'Does she have a star in mind for the film?'

'Yes. She left a note about casting.' Ransome rummaged around and picked up a piece of paper. Before she could say anything, Archer spoke.

'Is the lead actress, by chance, Samantha Lourdes?'

Fear flitted through Ransome's features as she looked down at the paper she held. 'Yes. What is going on, Archer?'

'A little piece of the puzzle just fell into place, but there's a lot more to go.'

61

Bart Green sat at his large desk with a fat cigar crammed into his small mouth and a glass of what might be water next to him, but it also might be something stronger, too. He was dressed in a white shirt and a pinstripe vest with a red tie and gold collar bar. In the background Archer could hear the soft purring of phones, and the harsher clacks of typewriters spinning tales to make money for Tinseltown and this man right here.

'You look a lot spiffier than in Vegas,' said Archer as he sat down across from the man.

'I like to dress up for the office. Vegas is to play.'

'Speaking of Vegas, I had a nice chat with Darren Paley.'

'I don't believe he's capable of nice chats,' replied Green snidely.

'So you've had those chats with him?'

'I go to Vegas a lot, and he's there sometimes.'

'Did you ever talk to him about your gambling debts?' asked Archer.

'Why would I?'

'Before he moved here to run the Jade Lion in Chinatown, Paley ran the enforcement squad for the mob in Vegas. It's what your Little Tony used to do, and maybe still does.'

'So?'

'So Tony isn't your guardian. He's your executioner if your debts pile up again.'

Green drank from his glass and patted his mouth

347

dry with the back of his hand. 'Let's get something straight right now. You know nothing about nothing.'

'On the contrary, I can count to two million.'

Green gave a little belch and Archer thought he could smell vermouth across the span of the desk. 'I don't know what you mean by that.'

'It's what you've lost in the casinos.'

'I pay what I owe. End of story. And I don't *always* lose.'

'Yes, you do. And I know you pay your debts because you're still living. I almost wasn't. It nearly ended for me in the desert right after I left you at the Copa Room.'

'Then let that be a warning to you to keep your nose out of places it doesn't belong.'

'I'd have to change professions.'

'Then do.'

'Is that a threat?'

Green leaned forward and started speaking in a low voice. 'Look, Archer, as hard as it may be for you to believe, I actually like you. I don't know why, but I do. No, I do know why — you're brash and willing to take risks and you don't take no for an answer. In other words, you remind me of me when I was your age.' He paused and drained his glass. 'Darren Paley and his kind are not to be messed with. I know you're looking for Ellie Lamb and all, and trying to find who killed that other PI. But is it worth your life?'

'Again, sort of goes with the territory. Speaking of Cedric Bender, you sure you never heard of him before?'

'*No*. Why would I have?'

Archer thought the man was actually speaking the truth, and that was troubling. 'You said you know the Bonhams?'

'I know them like I *know* most people. I've been to a party at their house. They're acquaintances. I don't really *know* them.'

'So you've never done business with him?'

'Archer, I don't even know what business the man is in. But I'd like to.'

'Why's that?'

'No one I've ever talked to seems to know where all his dough comes from.'

'Lamb moved out to Malibu because she and Bernadette Bonham went to school together back in Washington, D.C.'

'I recall Ellie mentioning that her father worked in the government back east.'

'She paid over seventy-two thousand dollars in cash for her home and renovations.'

'Bullshit. Where would she have gotten that kind of money?'

'Not from you?'

'Hell, I could hire a half dozen writers for that.'

Archer rubbed his jaw while Green said, 'Look, maybe her family had money. Why don't you check with them?'

'You know, that's a great idea.'

'Now, are we done here?'

'Sure. Is your wife out of town?'

'Yes. She's at our place in Lake Tahoe.'

'I hear it's fabulous.'

'It should be, for what she spends on the place,' he groused.

'You never go there?'

'What is there to do at Lake Tahoe except stare at the water, or the snow in winter? And most of the lake is in California. But could she pick a spot closer on it

349

to LA? No, she has to go way up on the Nevada side. Bitch to get to in the winter. It gets snowy up there this time of year. Whole place can shut down.'

'Would you have a number for Lamb's parents?'

'Audrey, the receptionist, has information like that for the people who work here, next of kin in case of emergencies, that sort of thing. And I suppose *someone* should tell Lamb's family that she's missing.'

'Thanks. And *Audrey* and I have met.'

Archer stopped at Audrey's desk and asked for that information. As the woman searched her files, Archer leaned over the counter and glanced at the switchboard located there. Above each number and switching port were initials. He saw CRR over one of them.

'Is that for Cecily Ransome?' he asked.

Audrey glanced where he was pointing. 'Yes. Her middle name is Rachel. We have enough people working here with similar initials that we had to start using their middle initials to distinguish them so I don't make an error transferring calls.'

Archer looked at another number. 'And EDL?'

Audrey smiled. 'Eleanor Dorothy Lamb. I know them by heart now, you see.'

'I *do* see.' Archer glanced at another set of initials — BMG — that he recognized from the aviation fuel invoice for the Beechcraft. He had thought BMG, Inc., the company that owned the plane, originated from a combination of Bart and Mallory Green's initials. But this phone line label threw a wrench in that theory.

'And BMG is Bart Green. Right? What's his middle name then, Michael or something?'

'No, that's *Mrs.* Green's private line, not her husband's.'

350

This took Archer by surprise. 'But those aren't her initials. She's *Mallory* Green. Why is there a B then?'

'Because her full name is *Belinda* Mallory Green. She goes by Mallory because she prefers that to Belinda.' She pulled a piece of paper from the file, wrote something down on a blank sheet, and handed it to Archer. 'This is the name and number that Ellie left us.'

Archer glanced down at the information. *Margaret Lamb*. There was a D.C. area code and phone number.

But Archer was still reeling from the initials. 'Does Mrs. Green own the Beechcraft?'

'I don't know anything about that. I've never even seen it. Why, does it matter if she does?'

It sure as hell might, thought Archer.

62

He stopped at a pay phone and called the hospital to check on Dash. After being patched through, he finally spoke with Morrison and found that Dash's vitals were improving and there was no indication of any problems. She also told Archer that the slug taken from him was a .38.

He next made a long-distance phone call to the number in Washington, D.C. A woman answered and told him that Margaret Lamb was not in. Archer left the number for his answering service and told the woman it was very important that Lamb contact him, as it had to do with her daughter, Eleanor. The woman promised to deliver the message promptly when Margaret returned.

He made one more call to a PI firm in Reno that he and Dash had used before. A woman answered the phone and he asked for Jim Swinson. A man came on the line, and Archer told him what had happened to Dash.

The only question Swinson asked was 'How can I help, Archer?'

Archer gave him a short sketch of the case and provided Mallory Green's address in Lake Tahoe. He asked Swinson to get someone out there to keep the place — and Green, if possible — under surveillance.

'Some really bad guys are involved in this, so everybody needs to watch their backs. I'll have money sent up by Western Union to cover your fees.'

'Don't worry about that, Archer, consider this one

on the house. For Willie.'

He got back into his Olds and drove off, Chinatown his destination. He found the alley where the shooting had taken place. The cops had obviously come and gone, because the place was deserted. Archer got out and, one hand on the butt of his gun, walked down the alleyway. It was full of doors and windows and passageways, lots of means of getting in and out. When he cleared the alley, there was the Jade, right across the street. The truck must have done a quick turn into this alley, passed the shooters, and kept going while they came out from hiding to fire on Archer and Dash.

In the daylight the Jade didn't look overly menacing; it just looked cheap and gaudy. Inside was not a den of iniquities but a place where people did awful things to each other, exploiting weaknesses all humans had to varying degrees, wrapped around a bar serving one type of drink that, if it didn't kill you, might, ironically, make you swear off booze for life.

He closed his eyes for a moment and imagined a scantily clad Samantha Lourdes bound to a bedpost so men halfway around the world could get their jollies. And then his mind pulled a dirty trick on him and transposed Liberty Callahan's face over Lourdes's. He opened his eyes and thought he really might be sick.

You need to focus, Archer, like Jake told you to. You think you're taking down Darren Paley acting like this? Right now you couldn't take down a sixteen-year-old punk running numbers for a buck a bag.

He retreated to his car, climbed in, and drove off.

He got back to Wilshire and became immediately bogged down in traffic. In the distance he thought he

353

could hear a PA system in use and some sort of message echoing across all of LA.

In frustration, he finally parked his car and started to walk, making much faster progress on foot. He finally discovered that the PA system was attached to the roof of a station wagon. A sign was plastered on the sides of the car, which was crawling at a turtle's pace.

REDS ARE EVERYWHERE. BE VIGILANT. BE ALERT. AND INFORM ON TRAITORS.

And that was what the man holding a mike in the car was reciting over and over again through the PA system.

Archer spotted a traffic cop at the next intersection and pigeonholed him.

'What's up with that?' he asked.

The man in blue grinned. 'Uncle Joe's in town.'

'Uncle Joe?'

'Senator Joe McCarthy. He's speaking at the Ambassador tonight.' He lowered his voice and said with a sour face, 'This town is full of reds, buddy.'

'Is that right?'

'Half the movie people would line up to kiss Stalin's ass.'

'*Joe* Stalin. He and McCarthy have the same first name. That's kind of funny.'

The cop looked shocked. 'What, are you drunk?'

'Smell my breath, nothing on it.'

'McCarthy is trying to save this country and he should start right here. Commies all over.'

'Then why are you here?'

'Hell, the union takes real good care of us.'

'Right. Unions. You might want to take that up with Karl Marx.'

'Who?'

Archer just had a sudden, jolting thought. 'What time tonight is 'Uncle Joe' speaking?'

'Seven.'

'Thanks.'

'You going?'

'Maybe. But I might get my hair cut instead. You have to have priorities these days.'

Archer strolled back to his car, got in, and turned around.

He was heading to the Ambassador. But not to get a seat to hear *Uncle* Joe.

He had just had an improbable thought. It probably wouldn't pan out. But if it did, today would be a helluva lot better than yesterday. Not that any day wouldn't be.

He had a phone call to make first. And a question to ask. He could do that at the hotel. And then he'd take the automatic elevator all the way *up* again.

Right to Hell.

And all this time, I thought it was the other direction.

63

Archer knocked on the door of the penthouse, and a few moments later the same young maid answered. She eyed him cautiously.

'Hi, I'm Archer. I was here yesterday.'

'Yes, sir,' said the woman, who did not open the door any farther.

'I'm here to see Mrs. Mars again. Can you let her know I'm here?'

'She is not seeing anyone today.'

'So she *is* here?'

The woman looked uncomfortable. 'She does not want to see *you*.'

Archer took out his notebook and a pen and wrote two words on the sheet of paper. He ripped it out, folded it over, and said, 'Show this to her. But don't peek.'

'No, sir, I won't. Please wait.'

'Oh, I will.'

A few minutes passed before the door was flung open with such force that it slammed into the wall. Gloria Mars stood there outfitted in a light blue dressing gown with a sheer lacy robe over it. Her hair was down and her hackles were up. She had a drink in one hand and Archer's note in the other.

She flapped the note in his face. 'What the hell is *this*?'

'Can I come in, or do you want everybody to hear?'

She stood there silently for so long that Archer wasn't sure what her answer would be. Then he wondered if she had a gun hidden in the lace.

She finally stepped back and waved him in.

'Nice day clothes,' he noted, glimpsing her exposed cleavage before she pulled her robe tighter.

'I was fighting a headache and I was almost there and then you and your damn note showed up.'

'Where do you want to talk?'

She led him into a small room off the dining room that didn't have a bed or liquor cabinet in sight. Mars settled herself primly in one chair while he sat in another. She held up the slip of paper.

'Explain this,' she ordered, and it was clearly a command.

'Karl Marx. He was a German political writer.'

'That's like saying Michelangelo was a house painter.' She balled the paper up and threw it at him. 'What did you *mean* by it?'

'You have Marx's collected works, three books about Lenin, and one by Trotsky.'

'They were in a *locked* armoire, you fink!'

'You know what we PIs are like. Just can't trust us.'

Mars let out a soft groan and drained her drink. 'I was afraid that might come back to haunt me.'

'Not from me it won't.'

She shot him a glance. 'Okay. Then why are you here if not to blackmail me?'

'I'm not the blackmailing type, Gloria. I'm here to tell you that Joe McCarthy is speaking at the Ambassador Hotel tonight at seven.'

She looked at him blankly. 'You must be joking.'

'Nope. There's a sign in the lobby and a helpful cop told me this town is full of reds. And that made me think about what you told me about Joe McCarthy when I met you the first time. You said the

SOB's time was running out, something to that effect. You're clearly not a fan.'

'I don't like wannabe authoritarians who lie in order to destroy people who disagree with them. In that regard, I despise Stalin, too. Are *you* a fan of McCarthy's? Or are you not political? So many people aren't in this town. They apparently don't have the guts.'

'I don't like stuffed shirts who wave little lists around without ever showing what's on them. And I thought this country was about letting people say, think, and believe what they wanted. If not, then how are we different from Stalin's world?'

She glanced at him with a fresh look. 'Did I misjudge you?'

'We'll leave that for another time. And what I'm about to ask you might decide it one way or another.'

'Oh, great. Fire away,' she added wearily, rubbing her temple.

'Were you a member of the Communist Party at Wellesley?'

She looked shaken by the question. 'I need another drink.' She started to rise.

He said, 'Just so you know, I don't give a damn one way or another.'

She sat back down. 'Then why did you ask me?'

'I asked you because I need to know if someone *was* blackmailing you because you were a communist.'

She stared at him with a resigned expression. 'When did you figure that one out?'

He tapped his head. 'It's been percolating up here for a while. But I didn't assemble enough pieces until about ten minutes ago. And then you said you thought I was here to blackmail you over the very same thing.' He paused. 'Seventy-two thousand, five hundred bucks sound about right?'

She stiffened and then slowly nodded. 'Yes, exactly.'

'When did Eleanor Lamb put the squeeze on you?'

'You're smarter than I thought, Archer.'

'You mentioned that Lamb might have come into some money before. Only you *knew* she had. Yours.'

'She came to me when she decided to move to Malibu and needed the dough.'

'And you had all those trust funds handy and all.'

'That was one reason I started looking at alternative political theories in college, Archer. I didn't lift a finger for all that money. I was just lucky enough to be born into the right family.'

'You could give it away.'

'I give what I can. But my grandfather tied up what I can do with it pretty tightly. I think he might have guessed how I was going to turn out. No trust-fund preening capitalist am I.'

Archer looked around. 'Okay, but you don't have to live like this, either.'

'You're right, I don't. Which shows that I'm much weaker than I think. And the draw of all that money is far stronger.'

'You still a card-carrying member?'

'It doesn't matter if I am or not. If my history came out I'd be ruined. They'd probably find a way to take all my money away. And Danny's career would be ruined, of course. They'd assume he was a communist and he'd be blackballed. So many already have been.'

'I didn't think you cared all that much about his career.'

'Talk is cheap and I'm the queen of it. Sure I spoke ill of Danny with you. But it wasn't because of his work, really. Okay, he's no Frank Capra or Howard Hawks, but then who is? He *did* bust his ass to get out of poverty, something I never had to do. And then he had to bust his ass to make it in this town. Again, something I never had to do. I just came here and bought the penthouse. I actually admire my husband's work ethic. His hustle. What I *don't* admire is his cheating on me with every big-breasted skirt that comes within range of his pecker. Do you blame me?'

'Can't say that I do. And his gambling?'

'Yes, I had to take care of that, and I did. And he's now got a limit and the casinos know anything over that limit is *his* problem, not mine. And Danny knows it, too, so he's a good boy. He wants to make films and chase women, not end up in the ocean with fish for friends.'

'How did Lamb get her hooks into you?'

She drew a cigarette from a bowl on a table and let Archer light it for her.

'Ellie was always smart, cunning, observant. I lied to you before. We *did* know each other. See, I was a political science major, too, and our friendship deepened in the Agora Society. She made me believe that she thought as I did. That she cared about the things I cared about. We . . . were very close. I liked her . . . very much.'

She stopped speaking and her eyes suddenly filled with tears.

Watching her closely, Archer said, 'Were you more than just . . . friends? I'm just asking because when we talked before you seemed worried that she might have been killed.'

She fiercely brushed the tears away. 'Ellie didn't love me, if that's what you want to know. She was using

360

me, biding her time. She broke my heart because it turned out she fell in love with a *man*.'

'Do you know the man's name?'

'No.'

'Then what happened?'

'The years passed. I didn't even know she was in LA when I got here. But she obviously found out I was here. Because one morning I got a special delivery letter.'

'What was in it?'

'Copies of certain documents with my signature on them. Pictures of me at events and with people who . . . are on certain government lists now. And a letter addressed to me.'

'When did you know it was Lamb?'

'Oh, she made no attempt to hide her identity, Archer. The letter told me to meet at a certain place and time. And there she was. I don't know where she got all the stuff, but she had the goods on me, all right. She hadn't really changed, other than her hair was black and straight. She was naturally blond and curly in college.'

'So she made the blackmail pitch and you bit on it.'

'What else could I do? I had plenty of money.'

'And you weren't afraid she'd come back for more?'

'That was the thing with Ellie — with all her faults, when she told you she was going to do something, she did it. The reverse was also true. She told me that would be the only touch. And she never came back for more. And she returned all the original documents and the negatives of the photos.'

'And the times you dropped by her place in Malibu that you mentioned, other than the dinner with the Greens? It wasn't to take script notes, was it?'

Mars closed her eyes again, and Archer watched as her jaw trembled, but in a way that was probably jarring to her soul, the difference between feeling an earthquake tremor a hundred miles away and being at the epicenter of an entire undulating city. She didn't look like a warrior now, he thought. She just looked human, like everybody else.

She put a hand to her face as if that would force the earthquake to stop. Eyes still closed she said quietly, 'I know it sounds crazy. I mean, the woman did blackmail me. But . . . I . . . I hoped we might see each other again. She wasn't seeing anyone, or so I thought . . .'

'But that was a no-go?'

'There . . . is apparently somebody else in her life now.'

'Do you know who?'

'No.'

Archer thought he knew who that person was, but he wasn't going to tell Mars. The woman was hurting enough as it was. 'I heard she bought the house in Malibu because she had a friend there.'

'Who told you that?'

'Your husband, right here on New Year's Eve.'

She regained her composure and blew out smoke. 'I don't know anything about that. And I don't know why Danny would know.'

'Have you ever met Peter or Bernadette Bonham?'

'Never heard of them.'

'Okay. Where do you think Lamb is?'

'I don't know.' She looked at a wall and seemingly beyond it. 'I hope she's okay. I've never wished her ill.'

'Most people would not wish their blackmailers well.'

'I'd like to think I can rise above such things. And I

362

have a lot that I didn't deserve.'

'Despite your wealth, you didn't *deserve* to be black-mailed. So stop beating yourself up over it. Did you know Mallory Green owns a plane?'

'No, I believe *Bart* owns it.'

'I don't think so.'

'Does it matter?'

'Everything matters, Gloria.' He rose. 'And thank you for your frankness. I know it was hard, but you've helped me a lot.'

'Do you think you can find Ellie?'

'I think I'm going to have to.'

She walked him to the door.

'I take it you won't be attending the McCarthy event tonight,' he said.

'On the contrary, I'll be right there in the front row, with the biggest, fattest tomatoes I can find. And I have a helluvan arm.'

'Remember to take pictures.'

She reached up on tiptoe and kissed him on the cheek. 'Thank you, Archer.'

'For what?'

'For being a nice guy. They're a lot rarer than you might think, as every woman out there can tell you.'

As Archer walked out he again envisioned Mars as a warrior, only this time armed with tomatoes instead of a sword, to do battle against the forces of evil.

He thought Uncle Joe might truly meet his match tonight.

64

Today, under the sun, Bel Air was just as pretty as the less affluent parts of LA, Archer thought.

At least on the outside. The inner core was a whole other sordid tale.

He stopped in front of the Jacoby estate. The tall, skinny palm trees waved to him in the wind like flitting fingers.

He knocked on the door, and the hinged-butler statue answered after a bit of a wait.

'I'd like to see Mrs. Jacoby. I was here before. The studio said she was at home today when I phoned earlier.'

'Who in the hell are you?'

Simon Jacoby was looking over the butler's aged shoulder. He had on dark tweed pants and a salmon-colored shirt under a white cotton sleeveless golf sweater. He seemed well hydrated and had a tumbler of what looked to be scotch in hand. Archer had another marker to test that hunch: The man reeked of it.

He squinted at Archer. 'Don't I know you, fella? You look familiar, and not in a good way.'

'Name's Archer.' He showed the man his official ID. He thought maybe Jacoby had seen him at the casino, while he'd been losing at kiddie poker.

Jacoby's face flushed as his anger hit another level. 'A private investigator? What the devil are you doing showing up at my —'

'I'll take care of it, Simon,' said a voice. A moment

later Alice Jacoby appeared. Her hair was down and she had on a colorful bandana. She wore a pair of jeans with a green sweater and low heels. Her cheeks were flushed, and she looked like she might have been crying. When she turned to the side, Archer saw a yellowish bruise on her cheek and a blackened mark around her eye. He glanced at her husband and felt his hand curl to a fist.

'Who is *he*?' demanded Simon. 'What is he doing here? By God, if —'

She put a calming hand on his arm. 'He's trying to find Ellie Lamb. She's gone missing. I told you, dear. I spoke to him before. It's all right. It has nothing to do with . . . us.'

'D-damn right, it d-doesn't,' he sputtered, glaring at Archer and finishing his drink.

'Mr. Archer, this way, please.'

Simon Jacoby shouted after Archer, 'And a wife can't testify against her husband. You remember that, Mr. PI.'

She led him quickly down the hall. Archer looked back once to see Simon Jacoby staring at the floor like he wasn't sure what he was actually standing on.

She led him into a small study and closed the door, then turned and faced him.

Archer eyed the room. It looked insubstantial, profoundly wanting after the grand space he had been in previously here. And Alice Jacoby looked smaller, too, less significant, as though she had gone from the lead role to a bit player, diminishing the woman in every meaningful way.

'Did he do that?' asked Archer, pointing at her injured face.

She subconsciously worried at it with her long

fingers. 'It was a misunderstanding.'

'No, it was a *beating*.'

She shot him a dull-eyed glance, although it still carried gravitas. '*That's* how most men handle misunderstanding.' Then she pulled at her wedding band like it was a tumor she wanted to excise.

'Is that what he meant when he said you couldn't testify against him? He's wrong. You can if you're the victim. If you're in danger.'

'Which I'm not. Not really. He'll be fine after he . . . after the drinks . . .' Archer didn't believe this and she didn't seem to, either.

Archer took off his hat and twirled it between his fingers. 'He sticking to his Vegas betting limit?'

'He has to, doesn't he?' she said resignedly.

'Nice to hear. Gloria Mars is a good friend of yours, but friends have their limits, and she has her own *misunderstanding* to deal with at home.'

'Yes, I know. There's an awful lot of misunderstanding in this town.' She motioned to one of the two chairs in the room. 'Please, sit.'

He did so, while she remained standing.

'Do you need a drink?' he asked, staring at her.

Jacoby wouldn't meet his eye. 'I would very much love one, which is why I'm not going to have one.' She glanced in the direction of the hall, where her drunken husband was probably still standing and wondering where he was.

'A good friend of mine was shot last night, nearly killed.'

Her face flushed as she looked down at him. 'What?'

'A block over from the Jade. The truck with a dope shipment was heading there. They'd already dropped off the people they sell.' He stopped twirling his hat.

366

'Is that selling-people bit in Eleanor Lamb's script? And how do you design a set for something like that, I wonder. Do you just describe the interior of the truck, or the shithole where they keep those poor souls before they get delivered straight to hell?'

He had decided on the way over how he was going to play this. Just blast it out like water from a fire hose. But it was actually a subtler move than it looked to be.

She first turned white, and then crimson, and then gray in her own little version of a bastardized rainbow.

Now she sat. It seemed her legs could no longer support her full-figured body. She took out a pink Kleenex from her jeans pocket and dabbed at her eyes.

Archer watched her. 'Cecily Ransome was really bowled over by Lamb's script. I think she wants to direct it, so your wish of working with her might come true. By the way, how did you and Lamb get inside the Jade to do the research? Or did you just feed her what she needed? Because my witness was right — you have been to the Jade, multiple times. Which means you lied to me.'

Jacoby rubbed her thighs, her hands moving in jerky motions as though she had partially lost control of them.

'See, my friend who almost died would like to know. And so would I. Because this is all tied to the Jade. And now, so are you.'

'D-does this have to be a p-police thing?' asked Jacoby hopelessly.

'I don't know. Does it?'

She lifted her gaze to his, her eyes promising depth, but there was really nothing in them that Archer could see. Except stark fear. He could certainly understand that one.

'Do you know where Lamb is?'

She shook her head, the eyelids fluttering, like they had come loose from her face and were desperately trying to hang on.

'Do you know why she disappeared?'

Another shake of the head; the hands were now kneading the thighs with more vigor than was probably required, but Archer didn't stop her. He didn't care really what she was doing to herself. Willie Dash's almost dying had changed pretty much everything for him.

'Your friend is a blackmailer, you know. She got her claws into Gloria Mars for all the money she needed to buy and fix up the Malibu place. Did you know about that?'

Jacoby managed to say something, but her voice was too low.

'I'm sorry, I didn't hear your answer.'

'I knew,' she said more boldly.

'What makes no sense to me is how somebody like you goes into a place like that and just, what, looks around? Darren Paley doesn't like people just looking around. But he is a guy who will do pretty much anything for money. So did you pay him? Did you tell him you just wanted to experience *Chinatown*? I don't see why, since there's nothing really Chinese about it. Hell, you could have designed it on one of your little mockup boards. But then again, he really doesn't strike me as a guy who would buy into that bullshit no matter how much dough you flung at him.' As Archer had been talking, his gaze had been wandering.

Until it reached a large tapestry hanging on the

wall. He rose and walked over to it, studied the design, knowing that he had seen it before.

On a bed at the Jade.

He turned to her. 'What does that symbolize?'

Jacoby looked up at where he was pointing with the rim of his hat. She slowly rose and joined him. 'It's the Chinese symbol for fire.'

'They have that in their damn *baijiu*, that's for sure.'

'Fire. Which, in the Chinese culture, can mean strength, persistence, vitality.'

'Just that?'

'No, it can also mean . . . destructive behavior. As in fire burns everything to ash.'

He looked at her, his face flushing because he could feel the waves of revulsion slamming over him. 'Well, that fits the old Jade, doesn't it?' He pointed accusingly at the tapestry. 'You didn't pay Paley so you could go to the Jade and snoop around. He paid *you, Miss Set Designer*, to decorate all the rooms there, didn't he?'

She turned and dropped back into her chair like all the blood had flowed right out of her, leaving empty veins and a useless heart.

Archer said, 'They were all the same because they were designed by somebody who knows little about the actual subject, but put together something that looks authentic on the *surface.*'

Still no answer. She was kneading her thighs again. Part of Archer wanted to stop her, twist her arm, hear the woman cry out in pain. But he didn't. That would make him like her husband. And that was a line he would not cross.

Tears slid down her face, making trenches in her makeup and causing her bruises to glisten.

369

'I mean, with this big house, big gambling bills, three adorable kids, and a drunk of a hubby who's probably going to lose his job and slap you around even more, you probably needed the commission.'

Jacoby gripped the arms of her chair, having apparently reached her limit with Archer's taunts. She rose and exclaimed, 'You have no idea how hard I've worked. How much I've had to sacrifice. What I've had to do to get where I am. To escape where I came from.' The voice, tone, and posture were all different now. It was like someone had heated a rock to such a stark temperature that all sorts of things were oozing out of it. And she wasn't yet finished oozing. 'How dare you come here and insult me like this. Nothing was given to me. You know nothing about me and what I've had to do to make it here.'

Archer did not retreat an inch. 'Sure I do. I hear it from everybody every day in this goddamn town. Everybody has their sob story. 'I was born on a stinking farm,' or 'in a shack' — or, in your case, 'a *holler.*' With nothing. Well, most people are born with pretty much nothing and they never get to where you got to. They never live in a place like this. But they don't complain. They just live their lives. And my friend who almost died? He's got no sob story. He owns his mistakes. He doesn't make excuses. He taught me to do the same. And it comes in handy because I tend to make mistakes. But not with you, I don't think. And you won't own up to them, lady, because you don't have the damn guts. Only in your mind is your life perfect. And you can't see it any other way.'

'I want you to leave. Right now.'

'And I want my friend to not be in the hospital with a bullet wound that nearly killed him. But sometimes we just can't have what we want. And one more thing. You obviously figured out what Paley was doing at the Jade with the dope and the slaves and fed it to Lamb, because it's in her script. So why do I think you never told Paley that this was also about you getting to set-design a movie that was simpatico with Cecily Ransome's sensibilities? Because I'm not sure he'd be all that happy about it. And when that man gets unhappy, *everybody* gets unhappy, trust me on that one. That thought ever cross that little, self-absorbed mind of yours?'

'Please leave!'

'Did you find out what goes on in those pretty little rooms you decorated? Did you maybe have people there to spy for you, take dirty little pictures, do written reports for you? Like the little 'that way, honey' gal with the leg tattoo they got there? She snoop around for you? Feed you stuff? If so, she'll be fish food if Paley ever finds out. But maybe you don't care. It's just one little Chinese gal, after all, they got lots more of them. But you *should* care, because Paley has a way of making people spill their guts before he kills them with a knife or a gun. And then he'll be coming to Bel Air. And you won't like it one little bit. And neither will your drunk punk of a husband. Or your three innocent kids. Why don't you think about them instead of just yourself for a change?'

She looked up at him with a miserable expression. 'You don't understand anything.'

'I *understand* you and Lamb want Samantha Lourdes to play the lead in your movie. I wonder why? Could it be you saw her there doing something she'd rather keep secret? Did you take pictures? Did you get parts of some of the filming they do in there? Could it be

371

you and Lamb wanted to blackmail her into doing the role to give it star power?'

'You have no idea what —'

'I have every idea, lady. But let me tell you something. You have just as much of a chance of corralling Lourdes to be in your crummy movie as I do of marrying her. Which means zero. She's got way too much class and brains to get mixed up with pathetic amateurs like you and Lamb.'

'What in the hell do you *want* from me?'

Archer put on his hat. 'I have to think about it. And then I'll call you. And then you're going to do exactly what I tell you to. Or else, yeah, this becomes a police *thing*.'

He walked out of the room and down the hall. Not surprisingly, Simon Jacoby was still there looking at the floor. He glanced up at Archer. 'What the hell are you still doing here?'

'I'm leaving.'

'Not fast enough, bub.'

Jacoby swung a fist, but Archer easily caught it and twisted it behind the man's back. Then he jacked the doughy man face-first against the wall, causing a framed painting of a stately horse in front of a stately manor to fall and crack.

And if that wasn't poetic justice filled with a pound of irony.

Archer drove the man's elbow so far up Jacoby's back the man cried out in pain and belched up some of his scotch onto the fine wallpaper.

Into his ear, Archer breathed, 'Just give me a reason, pal. And you lay another hand on your wife, they won't find all the pieces to put you back together again. Scout's honor.'

He pushed a weepy Jacoby to the floor, stepped over him, and walked out the front door into the daylight. And he still felt like he was in the grip of hell.

But it was just Bel Air.

On a good day.

65

Archer called Anne Bender from a pay phone and made arrangements to meet with her. He filled up the Oldsmobile's gas tank and drove straight to Anaheim. Bender looked the same as before, only older and sadder, as the reality of her husband's death no doubt weighed more heavily on the woman with each passing day.

He had asked her on the phone about their bank records, but she said they had been in the safe. When he got to the house he took a moment to check her husband's Wheeldex again. He had had an idea of what to look for and he found the card. Just to be sure, he phoned the number on the card long-distance. When someone picked up the call, Archer had his answer and set the phone down.

Yep, good people make bad decisions when things get tough. And Cedric Bender had, because I just found out who had hired him. And it wasn't Mallory Green.

He drove Bender to her local bank and arrived there just before it closed. She signed what she needed to sign and they made copies of the bank statements for her. Out of her earshot Archer asked the branch manager about the foreclosure proceedings on the Benders' home. The man volunteered that Bender had paid the debt off in full. His widow owned the house free and clear. This had been about a month ago, he told Archer.

'Where did the money come from?'

'Mr. Bender told me that he had gotten some

lucrative work and the payments were more than sufficient to pay off the mortgage.' He looked slyly at Archer. 'And I have it on good authority that the company that owns the orange grove next to their house wants to expand. His widow will be sitting pretty if she sells.'

'Well, thank God for orange juice. And what would be a good price for the house and land, do you think?'

The man cleared his throat and fiddled with his tie knot. 'Mrs. Bender has some decent acreage. If it were me I wouldn't take a dime less than ten grand.'

'Thanks. By the way, does the company that owns the orange grove bank with you?'

The man paled. 'I can't divulge that information.'

Archer leaned in with a smile. 'You just did, pal.'

Back in the car, Bender handed the file over to Archer. 'Are you making progress?' she asked.

'I am. And you might have more in your account than you probably think.'

'Why do you say that?'

'Just a hunch. I'll confirm it or not later. But if you do, maybe you can move away from the oranges. Bet you can get a pretty penny for your house and land.'

'You do? How much?'

'If anybody approaches you, don't take a dime less than sixty grand.'

'Sixty thousand! We only paid twelve hundred for all of it.'

'Chalk it up to appreciation and living next to an orange grove. Not a penny less, okay?'

'All right.' Bender gazed out the window. 'I never thought I would want to leave here, oranges or not. But now that Cedric's gone . . .' She said nothing else. She didn't have to.

He dropped her off and returned to LA. He'd forgotten that he hadn't eaten today until his stomach started protesting in earnest. He ate at the Idle Hour on Vineland in North Hollywood. The place was in the shape of an enormous keg. So what else could Archer have with his meal other than a pint of their finest steam beer?

He went over the bank statements and found that several large deposits had been made from checks drawn under the account of a company named PID. He looked at the copies of the checks the bank had kept. The signatures were so sloppy he couldn't make them out. But coupled with the corresponding index card for PID he'd found in Bender's Wheeldex, he had a pretty good idea of who had signed them. He put the file away and slipped into a phone booth to check his answering service.

Earlier, Margaret Lamb had called back and said she would be in tonight. He checked his watch. It was well into the evening back in Washington now. He got change for a five from a waiter, slung in the quarters, and connected to the East Coast number with the help of the long-distance operator.

'Hello?' said a woman's voice.

'Mrs. Lamb?'

'Yes.'

'This is Archer. I left the message for you. I'm in Los Angeles.'

'Yes, Mr. Archer. Please tell me what is going on. Is Eleanor in some sort of trouble? I'm very worried. I've called her house but there's been no answer.'

Archer took a couple of minutes to fill in the woman. He didn't tell her about the dead body, only that Lamb had not been seen since New Year's Eve.

'So there's been no word from her? After all this time?'

'No. But the police know about it and they are looking for her.'

I just don't know how hard.

'This is all very distressing. She's my only child.'

'I can understand that. Look, can you tell me about your daughter? Anything that might help me locate her. I know she went to Wellesley.'

'Yes, yes, she was a very good student. She graduated from there and came back and worked in Washington. My late husband, Charles, was in the diplomatic corps. Eleanor had lived all over, as we moved for Charles's assignments. It was quite an adventure. He died of a heart attack five years ago.'

'I'm sorry to hear that.'

She said sharply, 'I hope this has nothing to do with that no-good husband of hers. I thought he was long out of the picture.'

'Her *husband*? I didn't know your daughter was married.'

'Tall and debonair and so cosmopolitan. Ironically enough, it was my husband who introduced them. You see, they were in the same profession, diplomacy. There were a lot of nice young men in the State Department, only he turned out to be not nice at all. A scoundrel, in fact!'

'She got married in D.C.?'

'No, they went to France for that. He insisted for some reason. Luckily, this was all before the war, so we were able to go.'

'What was her husband's name?'

'Nathaniel Sommers.'

'Can you describe him, please?'

She did so. Archer asked her for more physical details and his age, and she provided them. He added on the intervening years and got a very clear picture of the man. So clear it was like a photograph.

'Why do you call him a scoundrel? What went wrong?'

'He was transferred to South America shortly after they were married. They had no children yet and none on the way — which I guess was a good thing, seeing as how it turned out.'

'What happened?'

'He traveled there alone to set up their household, start his assignment, and get things ready. Then he just vanished. Never called, never wrote. Charles made inquiries through the State Department. South America was not the safest place back then. The armies down there seemed to keep overthrowing governments and shooting people. The State Department could find nothing out and then washed their hands of it, if you can believe that. The official word was to not muddy the waters, to keep international relations smooth. Poppycock, I said, but Mr. Lamb's loyalties were with his precious department. Eleanor never gave up hope, though, and finally traveled down there about a year later. She was convinced that something had happened to him. But nothing had. He had just walked out on her.'

'What did she do?'

'She came back home and had a nervous breakdown is what she did, Mr. Archer. Then she pulled herself together. She headed west and got work in LA as a writer.'

A thought occurred to him, a critical one. 'But are you saying they never divorced?'

'I told her she should, but Eleanor refused. Maybe she thought he was going to come back to her, as if he ever would. He was a thorough scoundrel. I could see that from the first.'

'And she never had him declared dead?'

'Oh, I forgot that part. He left her a letter at his lodgings in Brazil. They kept the letter all that time and gave it to her when she arrived. I guess Nathaniel paid them to do it. He told her of his plans to vanish and start anew. So she had no grounds to declare him dead, because he wasn't. Makes my blood boil to this day.'

'Did he give a reason for wanting out?'

'If he did, she never shared it with me. I imagine he believed the grass would be greener somewhere else. Maybe he found some young senorita to tango with. As I said, over a decade older than Eleanor. He probably needed young women around him to boost his ego. A scoundrel through and through.'

'When was the last time you heard from your daughter?'

'She sent me a Christmas card and a check.'

'A check?'

'Yes. She sends me a check every month. And the amounts have gone dramatically up over the last eighteen months or so. She explained that she had gotten a huge raise. I suppose writers in Hollywood make a great deal of money. And it is certainly very welcome to me. Mr. Lamb served his country honorably, but he never made much money.'

'Would you mind telling me how much she sends you each month now?'

'I suppose it doesn't matter. A thousand dollars, just like clockwork.'

'So twelve thousand a year?'

'Yes, as I said, she's done very well out there.'

'Yes, she has. Better than most, in fact. When was the last time you spoke with her on the phone?'

'Oh, about two weeks ago.'

'She seemed okay?'

'Oh, yes, fine. Now, will you please tell me what's going on out there?'

'I would if I knew. But I promise as soon as I find out anything I will let you know.'

'Have I told you anything helpful?'

'You can't even begin to imagine how helpful you've been.'

Archer hung up the phone and leaned back against the wall. He took the picture out of his pocket and looked down at it. An older Nathaniel Sommers stared back at him.

So, Eleanor Lamb and Peter Bonham were married. And apparently still are.

66

Archer next called Jake Nichols and filled him in on all recent developments with Bender, his widow, and what he had learned from Alice Jacoby about the Jade. Nichols also had some information for him.

'Peter Bonham is in the import business. On the surface it's antiquities from South America and Mexico and Guatemala, places like that.'

'And underneath the surface, dope,' added Archer.

Nichols said, 'His company is private, so there're no dollar amounts I could find, but he has no deadbeat debts hanging out there, and his home alone is worth a small fortune and has no mortgage. He has accounts at about a dozen different banks. He's also got interests in a string of hotels and restaurants around LA. And he has his fingers in local card clubs and even has a small stake in Hollywood Park Racetrack. So that's how he cleans his dirty dope money. The business address listed is his home in Malibu, where I guess he maintains an office. He also has a big warehouse near the airport, probably where his legit business is run out of.'

'But you didn't look in his backyard. He has a bomb shelter. That's where he keeps the dope, and the people he's selling.'

'A bomb shelter, huh? Okay, first time for everything. Funny thing was I couldn't dig up anything on the guy past ten years ago.'

'Yeah, I think I know why.' Archer filled him in on what Margaret Lamb had told him about

Bonham's past.

'So, Lamb and Bonham sitting in a tree all those years ago?'

'He was the 'friend' she moved to Malibu to be closer to. I thought it was Bernadette, but it was Peter Bonham. Bernadette and Lamb also knew each other back east. My hunch is Bonham might have met Bernadette back then, too, while he was courting Lamb. Bernadette told me her father and Lamb's father were both diplomats, the families were friends, and that she and Lamb went to school together as young girls. But they met up again in Washington, after college. Bonham married Lamb in France and years later he did the same with Bernadette. He ditched Lamb, changed his name, and put together a new identity.'

'You think Lamb was blackmailing him? I mean, she's got the goods. He's a bigamist. You can go to jail for that. Not to mention being quite the bad surprise for his current wife.'

Archer said, 'That actually makes sense. Bernadette knew he was married before, but she said the first wife died, at least that's what Bonham probably told her. And then Bernadette might have introduced Peter to her old flame Paley. And with Peter's overseas connections and Paley's mob ties in this country, a match was made in hell for selling people and dope.'

'But then Bart Green and Peter Bonham start playing footsie and cutting Paley out of some of his shipment and transporting it in Green's Beechcraft. How do you figure that happened?' asked Nichols.

'I don't know, but it did. Bonham really had to walk a fine line there. I mean, if his wife was chummy with Paley, he had to keep her in the dark about all of this, or else she'd run to Paley and spill the beans.'

'And then Peter Bonham gets dumped in the Pacific,' said Nichols.

'And I'm betting Lamb stumbled onto this arrangement some time before she moved to Malibu. Her mother told me Lamb started sending her a grand a month about eighteen months ago, so that timeline fits.'

Nichols let out a sharp whistle. 'Twelve grand a year to her mother? Makes you wonder what Eleanor Lamb is pulling in from Bonham to keep her mouth shut.'

'And that would explain what they were arguing about at that party. She was probably demanding more money. And then Bonham gets tired of paying, a body ends up in Lamb's house, and she goes on the run.' Archer stared off for a moment. 'Although, I did find something down in Anaheim that points a finger in *another* direction.'

'What was that?'

'Bender had no files on his work for Mallory Green.'

'Maybe someone stole them. You said the safe had been broken into.'

'Yeah, but why would they take that stuff? And there was no Wheeldex card for Green, either. And Mallory had already volunteered to me that she had hired him previously. So why would someone want to try and hide a fact that the lady freely admits is true? And his calendar was taken, too. Why?'

'You're right. Something doesn't add up. You have a theory?'

'I don't think there was ever a Wheeldex card or a file on Mallory Green because Bender never worked for her. I think she was lying about the whole thing.'

'Come again?'

'I think Green staged the 'robbery' at Bender's to make it look like someone had cleaned out any record of her having hired Bender. But there wasn't any record because she *didn't* hire him to investigate her husband's allegedly adulterous behavior, not before and not now. So if I went there and found no record of that, I'd come back to her with a lot of questions. So she had to take action. The robbery was how she covered her tracks.'

'But, Archer, what possible reason would she have to lie about hiring a PI?'

'It could be she's covering for her husband. If he's mixed up in smuggling dope with Bonham, she may be trying to protect him. See, that money is the only thing keeping Bart Green safe from the mob. And while it's clear Mallory Green does not love her husband anymore, she told me that she needs old Bart around, or her career goes kaput. So they might be working this thing together.'

'So if she didn't hire Bender, who did? Because Bender was clearly investigating something that ended up getting him killed.'

'I found a Wheeldex with a curious name on it, a company called PID. And I discovered from looking at his bank records that Bender had gotten several large payments from PID. Large enough for him to pay off his mortgage of five grand.'

'PID? Did that ring a bell with you?'

'Maybe, but I needed confirmation. So I phoned the number on the Wheeldex card. Can you guess whose number it is?'

'Tell me.'

'The Jade Lion.'

'The Jade! But where does PID come in?'

'What's Paley's middle name? Do you know?'

'I know everything about the guy. It's Isaac.'

'So his initials are DIP. Now flip that around.'

'Damn. DIP becomes PID. So *he* hired Bender. But why?'

'Bender must've known Paley was bad news, but he was hard up for money. So he was a good guy who made a deal with the devil. And Paley paid way above the going rate. So Bender's widow is going to be okay.'

'But what did Paley hire him to do, Archer?'

'Bender was hired by Paley to find out who was drinking out of his dope trough. And Bender found out it was Bonham selling to Green.'

'Okay, I see where this is going, all right,' said Nichols.

Archer continued, 'If Bonham learned that Bender was investigating him and might finger him to Paley, it would be a motive for Bonham to kill the guy. Bender was beaten up pretty badly. They probably worked him over to make him talk. And then Bonham kills him and dumps the body in Lamb's house, not only to throw suspicion off him, but also to scare the black-mailing Lamb into going on the run and getting off his back.'

'Rings true to me, Archer. Nice bit of deduction.'

'Yeah, only now I just have to prove it.'

67

Archer left the Idle Hour and drove to the hospital to check on Morrison and Willie. The former was sitting like a statue in the same chair, her hand gripping one of Willie's. The latter was still unconscious, but now looking far more alive than dead.

Archer called Callahan from the hospital and made arrangements to drive over and pick her up from the studio in Burbank, and take her to where she was staying.

She was waiting outside of Warners wearing a brown overcoat and clutching her purse with both hands.

Archer had been to so many studios lately he figured they should give him a SAG card.

He opened the passenger door of the rental and motioned her in.

'This isn't the Delahaye,' she remarked.

'Hell, what is?'

Callahan told him she was staying at an apartment in Brentwood rented by a friend of hers who had just gone away to shoot a movie in Mexico for Paramount. It was in a pink stucco building and nicely laid out with Spanish tile floors the color of sunset; grainy, darkened wooden beams; plaster walls; and ceiling fans in every room, and a balcony with wrought iron railing overlooking a courtyard garden with a trickling fountain in the center.

They had picked up some dinner from a nearby deli and brought it to the apartment. Archer had driven a circuitous route and backtracked twice to make sure no one was following them.

Callahan changed into white linen slacks and a light green long-sleeved blouse and put her hair up with a clip. She poured out some white wine, and they sat on the balcony and ate and listened to the strengthening wind and the fountain.

'So, Willie is really doing okay?' she asked.

'I talked to the doctors. He's out of danger. He's going to make it.'

'Thank God.'

'Thank the doc and Willie being too stubborn to die. Got a question,' he said, taking a sip of the wine. 'I found out from a banker guy that women can't get a loan for a house without a man signing, too.'

Callahan set her wine down and glanced at him. 'That's right.'

'So how did you manage it?'

She took a bite of food. 'Somebody at Universal helped me. The studios, well, they understand the problem. Single actresses make enough money to buy a home but can't get a loan. So they have men who will guarantee the loan.'

'Guarantee the loan? What do they get in return? You mean you have to pay them?'

She glanced at him. 'Yes. They get a monthly fee. It's an added cost women have to pay.'

Archer looked down. 'I'm sorry, Liberty.'

'For what?'

'That you have to go through crap like that. You make way more than me, but I don't need you to cosign a house loan.'

'It's just the way things are, Archer.'

'And that doesn't make them right.'

'Forget it. I'm doing fine.'

'How's the new film coming?' he asked after a few moments of silence.

'I play a frustrated housewife married to an American scientist secretly working for the Soviets. My part has some real meat to it. She turns out to be very heroic.'

'That's great. What about that other film you were looking at doing, *Dial M for Murder*? You thought you had a shot at the lead?'

She took a drink of wine and shook her head. 'I did a screen test, and I thought it went okay. But the thing is I'm not a big star, Archer, and Hitchcock only works with the best. I heard they want Grace Kelly for the lead. She's all over town right now. Hell, she'll probably get the lead in *Rear Window*, too. But there are other roles in both films I can try for.'

'Hey, it's still *Hitchcock*, right?'

She mustered a smile. 'Yes, it is. So, how is the case coming?'

'It's coming maybe faster than before.'

'And Darren Paley?'

'We're zeroing in on him, Liberty, have no fear.'

She said sharply, 'But I *do* have fear, Archer, for *you*.'

He put an arm around her shoulders and squeezed. 'I know this one has been close.'

"Close' doesn't come *close* to describing it.'

'After what happened to Willie, I can't walk away from it, Liberty. You know that.'

She finished her wine and poured them some more. 'I know it so well I can't sleep.'

He dipped his head. 'I'm sorry.'

'It's not your problem. It's mine.'

'That doesn't seem fair.'

'Since when is life that? Sometimes you make your own bed and sometimes you make somebody else's and have to sleep in it.' She looked around and her expression lightened. 'Sherry, the gal that rents this place, was really keen to meet you, Archer.'

'Why was that?' he said, looking surprised.

'I showed her your picture. I can't imagine what she saw in it,' she added in an impish tone.

'Don't mess with my ego, Liberty, it's right where I like it.'

She smiled. 'Sherry knows Ellie, too. She was working on a picture with her before Ellie disappeared. I told her what happened. She's really upset about it, too.'

'Is that right?'

'Yes.' She glanced at him with a mischievous look. 'I also told Sherry about our date at Chasen's. She joked that she was going to crash it so she could meet, as she said, the world's most handsome gumshoe.'

This had a remarkable effect on Archer. He sat up straight and his expression was tight and focused. 'You told your friend Sherry that I was a private detective and that we were having dinner at Chasen's on New Year's Eve?'

'Yeah, why?'

'Do you think she could have told *Lamb* that?'

'Ellie? I don't see why. But so what if she did?'

'Lamb told us she was there that night for dinner, but her date didn't show up.'

'Right, so?'

'I know guys stand gals up, but on New Year's Eve? Where's he going to get another date? And she didn't seem all that upset, either. That always seemed off to me.'

'Yeah, you're right.' She lightly punched him in the arm. 'I would have been steamed if you'd stiffed me, Archer.'

'But there would be no reason for her to be upset if there was never any guy.'

'But then why would Ellie have been there?'

'To meet me.'

Callahan laughed. 'Okay, I know Sherry said you were handsome and all, but don't let your ego —' She stopped and looked at him, understanding alighting on her features. 'You don't mean that. You mean it was because you're a *detective*?'

Archer nodded. 'She was probably waiting for you or me to mention my profession and if neither one of us did, she'd figure a way to work it in somehow. And then she lays her whole story out for me. Says she wants to hire me. And I go out there and trip over a dead body.'

'But she couldn't possibly have known you'd go out there that night.'

'She didn't have to. It was enough that she told me she feared for her life. That would explain why she disappeared. And I'd run around making inquiries after she didn't show for our meeting, to give her vanishing legitimacy.' He looked at her. 'I would be the reason people would think she was missing because someone had done something to her. Otherwise they'd think she'd just run off on her own. And people would look for a reason why she would do that. And that would not be good for her.'

'But she had no idea then that a dead body would show up in her house.'

'Bender had been dead since around two that afternoon.'

'Wait a minute. Are you saying she came to Chasen's to meet you *knowing* that there was a dead body in her house?'

'That's exactly what I'm saying.'

'Do you think she killed him?'

'I don't know. I do know if she did she couldn't have moved him from where he was killed to where he was found, not by herself.'

'But why put somebody you killed in your own house? Why not dump him in the ocean?'

'It might not have gone down that way. I have another theory, but that's all it is.'

'So *was* someone trying to kill Ellie or was that all just a lie, too?'

'I haven't figured that part out.'

'What the hell is going on, Archer?'

'I don't know all the pieces, just some. But the more pieces I find, the more the picture comes alive. And by the way, Lamb is married.'

Callahan's jaw slumped. 'What?'

He explained about Lamb and Peter Bonham. And also that Lamb had blackmailed Gloria Mars. And that the woman had also worked with Alice Jacoby in infiltrating the Jade for research on a script that they wanted Samantha Lourdes to star in and Ransome to direct.

'They knew about the dope and maybe the other stuff and they never told the cops. And I can bet you that Lamb would have blackmailed Lourdes into starring in it. She'd threaten to expose her dirty little secret at the Jade if she didn't go along.'

Callahan looked gobsmacked. 'You think you know somebody. What a thorough bitch.'

'Nobody in this town really knows anybody else.

I know that and I don't even live here. I just trespass from time to time.'

'I guess you're right,' she said glumly. 'Do you think they'll ever get the movie made?'

He looked upset by the query. 'Who cares? I only care about the *real* part of this whole thing, Liberty. I'm not into fantasies.'

'I can see that now, Archer. I really can.' She said this in a voice so despondent and her expression was so forlorn that he took her hand and held it. And they listened to the wind and the fountain until it grew quite dark and Archer had to take his leave.

It was time to go back to Malibu.

68

Archer sat in the Oldsmobile and stared at the Bonhams' place. It was midnight and there was a light on. Danforth's house was dark, the same for Lamb's. But the light on at the Bonhams' was like a heat lamp for Archer. It might lead him where he needed to go. The wind picked up, and a quilt of clouds covered up the dull glow of moonlight.

Earlier he had retrieved the developed photos he'd taken at the Bonhams' house. The glossies were clear and looked good and were probably enough evidence to send the man away for life. He put them back in their folder and kept surveying the house.

Archer stiffened as he saw movement in the breezeway. Then a light came on in the garage. Next, he saw the garage door being lifted up. There was Bernadette Bonham doing the honors. Outlined in the glow, she looked like she was on a movie set getting ready for her big number under a hot spotlight. Then a car started up. She moved out of the way as the Bentley backed out. She turned off the light and closed the garage door. She got into the car and it pulled off down the road. As it passed by Archer, he couldn't see who was driving, but he had a pretty good idea.

He waited until the car was out of sight, then he headed across the street and into the backyard. He reached the entrance to the bomb shelter and pulled out two items from his trench coat. Bolt cutters and a flashlight. He snipped the padlock with the cutters, tossed it away, and lifted the hatch. He grabbed his flashlight, looked around, and started his descent.

The steps were metal, and the entrance hatch was the most elevated part of the shelter. When he reached the bottom step he figured the shelter was about six feet underground with the dirt and grass covering it.

He didn't think that would save you from an H-bomb blast, but he wasn't a scientist, just a shamus. He shone his light around just about the time the stench hit him. It was so overpowering he almost gagged. He covered his nose and mouth with the fabric of his coat and stood there looking where the light was shining. Cheap sleeping bags were on the floor that was covered with trash and filthy clothes. There was a bucket used as a toilet. Half-eaten food and empty cigarette packs were lying around everywhere. There was a glass jug of dirty water. Benches were built into the walls and there were grimy blankets and sheets piled there.

He figured it would get pretty damn cold down here. There must be air vents and filtration somewhere so people wouldn't suffocate, but he knew it wouldn't be easy to breathe the foul atmosphere down here even with those devices.

He walked around and shone his light on the metal walls. He stopped when he saw the words that people had etched into the painted metal, maybe with fingernails, maybe with something else.

Ayúdame. Peligro. Muerte.

Archer knew enough Spanish to translate those words into 'Help Me. Danger. Death.'

And then there were other things marked into the walls, but they were from another alphabet. Maybe Chinese or Japanese, he thought. Despite the language difference, he believed these messages said pretty much the same thing.

Help me. But no one had. And the Bonhams had a nice big house and drove a Bentley.

Sometimes Archer just wanted to shoot life right in the face.

He had been standing right above here with the gardener. Why hadn't he heard anyone? Why hadn't they cried out? Or pounded on the door above?

Then he saw the pile of chains under one bench and the large bolts inserted into the walls where those chains would go through. And he discovered a large bottle marked *chloroform*, along with a canvas bag filled with cloths formed into gags for the mouth.

That was why the folks down here had remained silent. And also why they had been stumbling the night Archer had seen them emerging from here. They must have been drugged during the day. At night there would be no one close enough to hear them.

He kept moving around until he reached the very back of the shelter. A bundle of blankets was on one of the benches. He moved closer and shone his light over it. He grabbed an edge of one blanket and pulled it away. And he did the same with another layer. Then he drew back.

Revealed was a pale hand, the veins underlying the skin waxy and still.

He knelt down and pulled away more coverings until a face was revealed. It was a mask of white and, like the hand, very much dead.

Well, somebody else had been driving the Bentley.

Because Peter Bonham was right here, in his own little chamber of horrors.

Archer pulled more of the blankets off him until the man's fully clothed body was revealed. He had on a nice suit, the tie was blue, the shirt was white. And red.

Where the knife blade had gone in. Right into the heart, was Archer's estimation. The hand wielding the blade knew just where to strike. Bonham's death would have been pretty much immediate. A stopped heart halted everything else. Fast.

And Bernadette had gone off with her husband's killer, Archer assumed. Of her own free will. Hell, she'd even gotten the garage door for the man. And it was a man, Archer knew. The knife wound was in the front. Bonham was a big, strong guy. Archer knew this; he'd fought the man on the beach. His wife hadn't taken him like this. Archer knew one guy who could have.

And he had the scars to prove it.

He made his way out and over to the door into the house off the breezeway. He turned the knob and found it unlocked. He made a quick search and found that Bernadette's closet had been largely emptied, as was a jewel case he found in a drawer.

He knew she had a valid passport because of the trip to France. Were they making for LA International right now?

He used the phone to call the LA County Sheriff's Department and asked for Phil Oldham. Fortunately, he was on duty tonight. When he got on the phone Archer told him about finding the body.

'Jesus' was how Oldham broke the silence.

'Jesus isn't going to help Peter Bonham. And I don't care if you got pulled from the Bender case. You need to put out an all-points for the airport, train station, and bus depots, shipping ports, and all the highways. It's Bernadette Bonham and Darren Paley you're looking for.' He gave Oldham a description of them,

396

the Bentley and the license plate. 'I found out that they knew each other back in Reno. My take is that Paley hired Bender to find out if Bonham was cheating him on the dope supply spigot. Bender apparently did his job, only Bonham found out what he was up to and killed him. Paley then took his revenge on Bonham. Bonham's wife showed her loyalties lay with Paley and not her dead hubby. Now they're on the run together.'

'Okay, I'll take care of all that, to hell with my pension.'

'You know Jake Nichols?'

'Yeah. He was a damn good PI. Real bad what happened to him.'

'He's the reason Willie got on board this case. Jake and Willie are tight. And that SOB Darren Paley is really the guy who put Jake in that wheelchair.'

'*That* I didn't know.'

'And Paley was the reason Willie almost died. So I want the guy real bad, Phil, real bad.'

'Okay, Archer, I hear you loud and clear. I can be there in about thirty minutes. You sit tight.'

'No, Phil. I can't. I've got something else to check.'

'Archer, if you —'

'Now listen closely. On Bonham's desk in his study I'm leaving a folder with pictures showing Bonham with the crates of dope and the hooded prisoners. Along with that is a lab report that analyzed some white powder I found in Bonham's backyard. Turns out it was heroin. They probably dropped some of the stuff when they were bringing it in from the beach. Situated in the middle of the rear lawn is the bomb shelter. I left the hatch up so you can't miss it. You'll find more evidence down there along with Bonham's

397

body. And another thing — you need to do a raid on the Jade Lion in Chinatown.'

'That's not my jurisdiction, Archer.'

'Which is why you need to get on the horn to LAPD, somebody you trust in narcotics and vice, and work with them. If the LA cops want some good ink in the dailies, this will do wonders. That truck was heading to the Jade. They sell dope out of there along with a lot of other rotten stuff that you boys in blue need to stop.'

'I can't organize a raid tonight.'

'Then do it tomorrow night, but just do it. You'll get a promotion and you can buy a new car and take the wife to Chasen's all by yourself.'

He hung up before the detective could fire off another response.

Archer was in the Olds and down the canyon road in under three minutes.

He knew if he passed any prowlers they'd be looking for his Delahaye, not the dumpy Oldsmobile. Oldham would have assuredly told them that.

Sure enough, ten minutes later two county radio squad cars shot past him without even a look at the Olds as they headed to Las Flores.

Archer drove straight to the airport in LA, and was lucky enough to get a plane reservation that would deposit him in Reno around five in the morning. He made a call from an airport pay phone to Jake Nichols, who was fully awake, and told him about the latest developments. Then he filled the man in on exactly where he was going and why. He next called and woke up PI Jim Swinson in Reno and told him the same, and that he had booked a flight.

'Can you meet me at the airport?'

'I'll be there,' said Swinson.

'What's the word from your guy on the ground?'

'There's activity, Archer. I'll fill you in when you get here.'

Archer made one more call to a number that a certain someone had given him.

That certain someone answered in a sleepy voice, 'Hello?'

'Sam?'

'Who is this?' asked Samantha Lourdes.

'Archer.'

'Archer! Do you have any idea what time it is?'

He could envision her sitting up in bed, in a lacy, sheer negligee maybe, and being all indignant. For some reason that made him smile. And he needed to smile right now or else he might pull his .38 and start shooting people. 'Yeah, actually, I do. I'm feeling every minute of it.'

'What do you want?'

'Don't go back to the Jade.'

'Did you really call to lecture me in the middle of the night about *that*?' she snapped at him. 'Of all the crazy things —'

'I'm not generalizing, Sam. I'm being real specific. The cops are going to raid the Jade probably tomorrow night, just in case you were thinking of going. I wanted to warn you to stay away.'

She didn't say anything for a few moments. 'I actually was going tomorrow night.'

'Then you can stay home and read a detective novel instead of getting booked by LAPD for real.'

'What's happened, Archer? Tell me.'

'That gal you pointed out in the photo?'

'The one who hooked up with Darren while we

were married?'

'Yeah. She and Paley just murdered her husband in Malibu, and are right now legging it out of here.'

'Oh my *God*.'

'Yeah, I hear his name a lot lately, only he doesn't seem to be showing up to do his job anymore. So don't go back to the Jade, *ever*, okay? Paley has too much going on to worry about you anymore. You are off his gravy train, Sam.'

'All right, I promise, I won't. And . . . thank you for the heads-up. What are you going to do now?'

'What I always try and do. Catch the bad people.'

'Why is that so important to you, Archer?' she said breathlessly. It made his skin tingle all the way across the ether. He imagined her giving him the Samantha Lourdes classic movie look. That image actually calmed him.

'I guess it's just my nature.'

69

The flight took off into a cloudy sky, but when they broke through the heavy cover, there was the moon looking bold and bright. But Archer wasn't impressed with the moon even a little. He spent the flight staring out the window at a sea of clouds below and a sky that had no defined horizon, much like his thoughts. The clouds looked like ocean breakers frozen in midarc, which was unnatural and thus unnerving. The sky looked unfamiliar and unsettling, but he could not look away. Their final approach into Reno was extremely turbulent because of low-level crosswinds, but Archer barely noticed, even as a baby wailed, and the young woman sitting next to him threw up into a little paper bag helpfully provided by the airline with its logo on it.

They landed and Archer was the first one off the plane. In the small terminal Jim Swinson waved at him.

Swinson was in his late forties, about five-eleven, lean and tightly built with a swell of brown hair frosted at the sides, and a trim mustache of a similar color combination. He had on a dark suit, no tie, and a snap-brim hat with a checkered band held in one hand, along with a poker face.

'You got a gun?' Archer asked.

'I got a pocket, I got a gun.'

'Good, because right now we can't have too many guns.'

They walked out to Swinson's car. It was a Ford, as

401

trim and lean as its owner.

Dawn was still far from breaking, but the darkness was a shade lighter than the one Archer had left back in LA.

'So, Paley is on the run with Bonham's wife and her hubby's dead?'

'Yeah. The county cops are on it, but Paley is an old hand at this. He could slip through easily enough. The guy's a planner and he must have planned for this eventuality.'

'But once he offed his supplier, what did he think he was going to do?'

'Who knows? But there are possibilities. Maybe he was cutting out the middleman. Then he could deal direct with the suppliers.'

'But he has a dead body to contend with.'

'But he probably figured no one would find the body in the bomb shelter for a long time, if ever. And if the cops figured out Bonham was selling dope, the murder could be blamed on any number of people, most likely in Mexico. Bonham stiffed them on a payment, that sort of thing. You play dirty, you end up dirty. And dead.'

'And Mrs. Bonham? Wouldn't the cops have wondered what happened to her when they found her husband's body?'

'*That's* Mrs. Bonham's problem.' Archer lit up a Lucky because he really needed to. He let the stiff breeze carry the spent match away. 'And she may not know it, but she's a French princess who just turned back into a frog, and a scorpion just hitched a ride on her slimy back.'

Swinson narrowed his already narrow eyes. 'What frog?'

402

'So did I. But now I think I was wrong. He's not smart enough to pull this off, and his balls aren't big enough. I just wonder why she left the house when she did. And no one was with her when she came back?'

'Nope. Not that I could see,' replied Reid.

'You got a spare walkie-talkie?'

Swinson got one and set it to the right frequency. 'What are you going to do?'

'You guys sit tight. I'm going to pay Mrs. Green an early-morning visit.'

70

Archer always liked to approach a problem from the rear. He had learned in the war that frontal assaults made generals look heroic, but made their soldiers simply dead.

About halfway to his destination he halted and took in the lay of the land. The snow-capped Sierra Nevadas were marshaled on the shore across the breadth of the wide lake. They stared back at him like a vastly arrayed army just waiting for the order to charge the waters.

He continued on, finally broke free of the tree line, and came out on the beach, and immediately felt the wind gusts pummel him through his overcoat. Sand propelled by the wind nipped at him, and he turned away from the stinging grit. A long, wooden deck stretched from the house out to the water. There was a weather-beaten dock at the end of it with a wooden boat on a lift, its top covered for the winter season, with only a bit of its varnished underbelly exposed.

He eyed the rear deck set in stone pavers, where some covered outdoor patio furniture sat. Cut into one wing of the house was an arched stone tunnel that led to the front of the house. That was an unusual feature, thought Archer. But it did give access to the beach and water without going through the house.

He ducked inside the tunnel and spied a yellow pre-war Packard convertible with whitewalls and a top in the up position parked there. It was in superb condition and must have cost a mint new, thought Archer.

And this had to be the car that had been seen coming and going from the house. He opened the passenger door and peered inside. The interior smelled of old, cracked leather and cigar smoke. He looked at the registration tag on the steering post: *Mallory Green*.

That was who Reid had seen driving it.

He closed the door softly and crept to the rear. He lifted the trunk hatch expecting to find a spare tire and some tools.

He stood there for a few moments gazing down at it.

The *it* had once been a person.

He reached down and touched the man's jaw. It was cold. He lifted one of his arms. It was not difficult to bend. By the look of the body, the man had already passed through rigor mortis. That meant he'd been dead a while, thought Archer, maybe since Green had driven back that day.

Steve Everett, the now *former* pilot, was dressed in clothes similar to those he'd been wearing when he'd flown Archer to Vegas. Archer looked for the wound that had ended the man's life, and finally found it under the right arm. A small bullet entry hole in the side of the chest wall. And the bullet was still in there, because Archer could not find any place where the slug had come out.

The wound was so insignificant that on the surface it seemed doubtful it could have ended a life. But small things often could: a tiny tumor grown large, a minuscule virus expanding out of control in one's lungs. Or possibly a .32-caliber aimed just right. He thought about possible killers and motivations. They seemed relatively straightforward. The only unknowable right now was *how* the body had gotten here.

He said goodbye to Everett and closed the trunk.

Archer noted a door halfway down the tunnel and tried to turn the handle. Of course it was locked. Instead of his knife, because the lock looked substantial, he took out his felonious tool kit. A minute later the door was no longer an obstacle. He slipped through and closed it behind him. He found himself in a hallway with a set of steps heading up at the far end. The floor tiles were blue and white and designed such that they gave the impression of one walking on water.

'Jesus,' he said, with more than a hint of irony.

He walked across the watery tiles and up the steps to dry land. He checked his watch. It was not yet seven. He should have been exhausted, yet he had never felt more awake in his life.

If I survive this, I swear to God I'm sleeping for a week.

The place was cavernous and chilly, like a real cave would be. The hall he was on was long and as straight as a knife blade. His ears hummed as he listened for any sound, and he was rewarded, and also disappointed, when he heard none.

He left the hall and entered a soaring two-story great room with a vaulted ceiling filled with beams and tongue-in-groove woodwork. The rear-facing windows were nearly as tall as the room and gave breathtaking views of the lake. Another wall held a stone fireplace; its metal doors were open and a fire, probably from last night, was doing its last bit of dying out. Archer could still feel the warmth from the embers, which sharply contrasted with the frigid snow-capped peaks that filled the windows.

The furniture was large and looked handmade. Not a stick of middle-income department store furniture in this place, thought Archer.

He made a quick search of the rooms down here, which wasn't easy because the interior was a labyrinth. The kitchen was large and modern and laid out with elegance and functionality; a set of windows looked out onto the lake from a small breakfast nook with built-in banquette seating upholstered in cobalt blue. Every room was optimally furnished, not too much, not too little. And Green had classic taste, which meant that most of what Archer was seeing would stand the test of time. He had been expecting this by virtue of having already seen their main house back in California, and thus none of it really made an impression on him. Not that it could, with what he now knew.

He reached one door, which intrigued him, because locked doors always did. He forced the matter with his pick tools. The space wasn't large and it only had one item in it, but it was a significant one item. Archer knelt down in front of the leather-bound trunk and tried to open it, but it wouldn't budge. He inserted his tool once more and did the requisite manipulations, with which he had grown quite adept over the years. The lock gave way and Archer slowly lifted the top. Inside were neat stacks of carefully folded wax paper packets taped down. He picked one up and undid the tape. Inside was white powder. He sniffed it. The stuff sure as hell wasn't flour. They had held back part of the shipment for some reason.

He put the packet back and closed the trunk.

He had a dead man in a car trunk, and a large shipment of heroin in a house on a lake.

Now he needed to find something else. *Someone* else.

He headed up the stairs, which had polished wooden handrails and twisted wrought iron pickets; the stairs were carpeted with a colorful runner, which was secured to each riser with brass piping.

He made it to the upstairs landing and was confronted with two halls leading in opposite directions. These must be the bedrooms, he figured.

It would take precious time to search them all. Archer decided to opt for a shortcut.

There was a large shelving unit on the landing. It showcased dozens of colorful ceramic plates. He picked one up, moved back out of the sight lines of both halls, and tossed the ceramic plate across the width of the space. It shattered on the tile floor with an unholy clatter.

Archer waited and waited.

And then the third door on the hall to his left was flung open, and Mallory Green came rushing out holding a baseball bat. She was dressed in a white negligee, and her hair was done in a French braid that followed her out the door like the tail on a racoon. She reached the top of the staircase, glanced at the shattered plate, and looked around for the source of the disturbance.

And that was when Archer stepped out, gun in hand.

Green froze when she saw him. Then she raised the bat but he raised his gun, and that battle was quickly over.

'What the hell are you doing here, Archer? You broke into my house. I'm going to call the police.'

'Don't bother. *I'm* going to call them. Then you can explain what your dead pilot is doing in the trunk of your Packard.'

Green had her back to the broad windows and Archer took a moment to glance over her shoulder.

That was when he saw something that hadn't been there before. A boat was tied up to the dock. And it wasn't the boat he'd seen earlier.

A voice barked, 'Drop the piece, Archer, and both of you get down here. Now.'

Archer and Green looked toward the stairs.

Darren Paley and Little Tony were halfway up them. With guns pointed and expressions radiating serious business.

71

Archer and Green were forced to sit side by side on a lovely couch, the beauty and costliness of which Archer ignored since twin guns were pointed at his head.

Bernadette Bonham was perched on the arm of an upholstered chair. She was wearing the same clothes Archer had seen her in the previous night. She looked haggard and scared, but also a bit triumphant as she gazed at Archer, as though he had never amounted to much of a challenge.

Paley sat across from them; Little Tony stood to the man's left.

Archer said to Bonham, 'So, is this where you tell me 'c'est la vie'?'

In answer she took out a Gaulois Bleu cigarette and lit it with a chromium-plated lighter with the initial *B* on it. She followed this with a tiny smile. 'Say what you want. What will it matter? I will tell you. Nothing. It matters nothing. And you will, I think, tell no one anything ever again.'

He noted the initial on the lighter and said, 'You know, you're not really Mrs. Bonham.'

'She's his *widow*,' interjected Paley.

'No,' said Archer. 'She's not.'

'And why not?' demanded Bonham.

'Because he was already married and never got divorced. That makes him a bigamist and your marriage illegal and nonbinding. A sham. But hell, 'c'est la vie.''

412

'You have no idea of what you are talking about,' she retorted.

'I have every idea. Your husband's real name was Nathaniel Sommers. He married Eleanor Lamb a long time ago.'

'Ellie! This is insane what you say!' exclaimed Bonham.

'You really didn't know he had married your little school friend?'

'This is a lie.'

'No, this is all true. You knew he was married before, only he lied to you about his first wife dying. He courted and married Lamb. He worked for the State Department. He got transferred to South America. He went there to set up house for himself and the missus. Only he did a runner instead. They never divorced, so *she's* the widow, not you, in case you were thinking of inheriting everything — which I wouldn't advise.'

Bonham glanced nervously at Paley, who only had eyes for Archer. She spat, 'Peter would never marry someone like her. She is ugly.'

'Well, he did. He married her in France, same as he did you. Maybe there are multiple other women out there he walked down the aisle with. Of course it didn't last long with Lamb.'

'I do not believe any of this.'

'Lamb was blackmailing him with the fact of their marriage. *That's* why they were arguing at your party. It had nothing to do with property lines, but you already knew that, because you told me you didn't believe it, either.'

Bonham shot Paley another glance.

Archer continued. 'But *you* had your old pal Paley

waiting in the wings, so maybe you didn't care what was going on with your 'hubby' and Lamb. Or maybe he'd been cheating on you with other ladies and this was payback time.' Archer turned to look at Green. 'And here *you* are, partners with Bonham in the dope business. Drinking at Paley's trough, to use his words. Gee, Bernadette, here Paley was trying to figure out who Peter was screwing him over for, and you couldn't even find out that it was Mallory Green. It's a wonder Paley didn't slit your throat for gross negligence.'

Bonham shot Paley another, far more nervous glance.

'That wasn't her job and dames don't know business,' Paley said. 'She introduced me to her husband, but business is strictly between the men. I never mentioned what was going on to Bernadette because my rule is simple: If you don't have to know, then you won't know. And I didn't even know where, when, or how the stuff was coming in. Bonham was no dummy, he saw to that, and I knew he told Bernadette nothing, either. And Bernadette just likes the nice things the dope business can bring, right, honey?'

'This is true,' she said, but Archer noted the lady didn't look nearly as confident now. 'And I think Peter would slip sleeping pills into my drink on certain nights. I would wake up in the morning and there he would be next to me, smiling and so attentive. But it made me think: What is he doing during the night that he does not want me to know?'

'Well, now you do know,' said Archer.

'I know nothing about any dope business,' said Green.

Archer looked at her incredulously. 'Then there's a

trunk here full of heroin that'll knock your socks off, lady.'

Paley eyed Green. 'Even this stupid PI's got your number.'

'Yeah, Paley, so stupid I found Bonham's body where you left it. The cops got an All Points out. It's over.' He glanced at Tony. 'You hitched your ride to the wrong pony, *Little* Tony. You should've stuck with the mob.'

'None of that matters, Archer,' said Paley, plucking a cigarette from his pocket and lighting it up with his free hand, while holding his gun on Archer. 'So what if she's not married to the guy? And cops will do what cops do. We won't be around to catch.'

'All Points is tough to beat. Feds will be involved, too, because of the dope. And the slave operation,' added Archer. This wasn't true, yet, but Paley didn't have to know that.

He shook his head. 'I don't know nothing about no slaves.'

'Sure you do — half your staff at the Jade probably came that way. Profits go way up when you don't have to pay your 'employees.''

'Again, it doesn't matter. We'll be out of here in a few hours.'

'How is that?' asked Archer. 'The road's being watched, though I know you have a boat. But boats are slow, and when the lake ends the boat has to stop.'

Paley looked at Green. 'We're leaving in the lady's plane. It's parked at a private airstrip near here.'

'The pilot's dead,' Archer pointed out.

Paley said, 'I was in the Army Air Forces. Got my private pilot's license. I can fly anything.'

Archer sucked in a breath because he *did* know that.

415

Jake Nichols had told him.

Paley turned to Green again. 'And you'll be going with us.'

'Why?' she said with an alarmed expression.

'Because I want to drop your body over the ocean in the middle of the night on the way to South America.'

Green stiffened and looked like she might be sick.

'Oh, don't worry, I'm going to shoot you first. You'll never know it when you hit the water. I got *some* compassion.'

'I think we might be able to work something out,' she said hoarsely.

'You horned in on my business to pay your prick husband's gambling markers. And now you have to pay for that. And I never forgive a debt. Archer here knows that, right?'

Archer said, 'You hired Bender to find out about who was horning in?'

'Paid him damn good money and he came through in the end.' He glanced at Green. 'He had pictures of this bitch and Peter Bonham with the truck and on the beach where the dope came in. Then he ran down who she was. Never would have figured a dame for being in this business. I admit that one threw me, all right. And Bart Green's lady on top of it.' He eyed Green again. 'If I had any inkling your hubby was involved in this, I'd kill him, too. But in his report Bender said it was all you. Don't matter. Without the dope money to pay his gambling losses, Bart's history. The boys in Vegas will see to that.'

Archer said, 'But when I saw you in Vegas you had no clue who was taking some of your dope.'

'That's 'cause I just got Bender's report. He must've mailed it before he got whacked. It told me everything.

416

That's why I'm here. To take care of this lady. I just got you as a nice, little bonus.'

'So who killed Bender, then? My take is Peter Bonham.'

'I'm thinking the same. He must've found out Bender was on to him. He kills him and dumps the problem in another house.'

'Yeah, but not a *random* house. You didn't know about Eleanor Lamb's involvement in blackmailing Peter Bonham over his bigamy?'

Paley shook his head and eyed Green. 'All I know is this bitch screwed me.'

'And *she* wouldn't have killed Bender and dumped his body at Lamb's house because that could have messed up her dope business.' Archer glanced at Bonham. 'And that's probably why your bigamist hubby came back early from France. He got wind of Bender and decided to take care of him. I wonder how that happened.'

She shrugged. 'I say nothing.'

Archer was about to say something but then stopped. A thought had just occurred to him and he wondered why it hadn't before. It had been staring him right in the face all this time. He just hadn't put the pieces together. He hoped he had a chance to see it all through. From the looks of things, he was going to carry this latest deduction to the grave.

Then another thought hit him. They had taken his gun, but not something else. While everyone was looking at Bonham, he lowered one hand next to his side and felt the object in the side pocket of his coat. He moved his finger around slowly until he felt it. Then he pushed against it and held down the talk button on the walkie-talkie.

Archer next looked at Green and said loudly, 'Only you pretended *you* were the one to hire Bender. You're a much better actress than you give yourself credit for. You had me fooled with your little seizure act when I told you Bender was dead. Then you hired some goon to break into Bender's office in case I went down there to check. That way I would think someone had taken his case files on you and whatever else he had showing you had hired him. Of course there never were any files. But your goon missed an invoice for plane fuel that led me right to you and Bart, only I didn't know all the curves it would throw me along the way. And I don't know if Bender had made copies of his report and photos for Paley. Probably not, because he knew the guy was scum and Bender didn't want a reminder of what he'd done for the money.'

Green said wearily, 'I suppose I should have hired a better goon.'

'But I had figured it was screwy as soon as I went down there to look at his office. The reports you gave me, supposedly from Bender? They were all typed.'

'So?'

'First, your husband wasn't having affairs. Your pilot mentioned beautiful ladies flying around with Bart, but those were his nieces. And what I found out in Vegas showed he was no ladies' man. So the reports you gave me were wrong. And Bender didn't have a typewriter or a secretary. All his other reports were handwritten. That's because *you* typed those reports, which was one reason they were so vague. You were just making it up.'

'I think you chose the right career, Archer,' she said bitterly.

'Short though it might be,' interjected Paley with a

malicious look.

She looked at him and said, 'Mr. Paley, you can have it all. Every shipment. I'm done.'

'I know you're done because I say you're done. And I have other plans, in another country. I got my stash. I can live like a king.' He looked at Little Tony. 'Chit-chat's over.'

Paley rose and pointed his gun at Archer. 'You first.'

Archer thought back to what Samantha Lourdes had told him about Paley: He wouldn't miss the second time.

Goodbye, Willie and Connie. Goodbye, Liberty. I'm sorry, real sorry.

The ensuing gunshot flung him right back into the grit of reality.

72

At first, it seemed that Little Tony didn't know he'd been shot. A second later, it became all too apparent. To him. The bullet had gone into his chest and stayed there, about two inches to the right of the heart. Blood spurted out and sprayed across Green's fine negligee and sofa like someone had let go of a fire hose filled with plasma. She screamed and jumped back, toppling over the sofa, as Little Tony fell sideways to the floor. By the startled, fixed state of his eyes, he would not be getting back up.

With a shriek, Bonham dropped her Gaulois Bleu and took cover behind the chair.

Paley calmly fired up the stairs at where the shot had come from. He fired twice more, and that was all the time Archer needed to grab the dead Tony's weapon, aim, and pull the trigger.

Paley had a different idea, though, and he had flipped over a thick, wooden-topped table and took cover behind it. Archer's slugs lodged in the wood. Archer glanced up the stairs to see who was up there. Had Swinson or Reid somehow gotten into the house and upstairs after hearing everything over the walkie-talkie? He couldn't imagine how they would have managed that so fast.

He ducked down as the cracks of bullets fired by Paley whizzed by overhead.

'Oh, God, help me.'

He looked over to see Green clutching her bloody arm. Her skin and sleepwear were stained with red from the blood seeping from her wound.

Archer looked back as a window shattered.

He saw that Paley had thrown the table through one of the huge windows and was climbing into the opening and pulling Bonham along with him. Archer pointed the gun, but the only thing he would hit was Bonham in the back. And despite everything, he couldn't bring himself to do that. His finger slid away from the trigger, even as a bullet smacked near his head. He looked up and saw the muzzle of a pistol resting on the handrail. He fired until his gun banged empty. The muzzle disappeared. He heard the sounds of running feet.

'Help me!' cried out Green.

He knelt beside her, looked at her wound, and said brusquely, 'That won't kill you. Wrap your robe belt just above the wound as a tourniquet. Now, shut up and sit tight.'

Archer searched Little Tony's pockets and found his gun, which they had taken.

He took the steps two at a time and reached the second-floor landing. He looked back at the window and saw Paley and Bonham reach the boat they had come in. He was torn between going after them or seeing who had just tried to kill him. The latter won out.

Archer took the hall to the right when he heard a door slam down that way.

He kicked open three doors in a row and then peered inside. The fourth door he kicked open answered him with two shots. They ended up in the wall behind him because he had ducked out of the way. He was getting a little annoyed with all the gunplay. He fired two well-placed shots into the gap between the door and doorjamb. He heard a scream, and something fell.

Archer pivoted into the open doorway, his gun swiveling in front of him.

She was lying on the floor, the gun next to her.

Eleanor Lamb was dressed in striped pajamas. She was clutching her hand, and the gun was a foot away from her. She had gone back to being a curly blonde.

Archer raced over and kicked the pistol out of the way as she lunged for it.

'I've been shot,' she said, gripping her hand. 'You shot me. My finger is bleeding.' He looked at the minor wound there.

'That's always a possibility when *you* shoot at someone.'

'I'm a guest here. And I was defending myself.'

He picked up her gun. 'You're not a guest, Lamb. You're an inmate in waiting.'

'I've done nothing.'

'You're a blackmailer, a dope dealer, a killer, and a thoroughly rotten piece of work. I want to throw up just looking at you.'

Feet pounded up the stairs, and Archer ran to the doorway with two guns in hand. He pointed them both, ready to fire, but lowered them when he saw it was Swinson and Reid.

'We heard everything over the walkie-talkie, Archer, and came running,' explained Swinson. 'What the hell is going on? There's a dead guy and a lady bleeding downstairs.'

'Call the cops and an ambulance,' he told them. 'And watch the bleeding lady. And especially this one,' he added, pointing at Lamb.

'Where are you going?' said a breathless Swinson.

'I got a couple more to round up.'

'You can't keep me prisoner here, Archer,' said Lamb. 'I've done nothing wrong.'

'Lady, your arrest sheet will be so long the cops are going to need a really fast typist.'

He and Swinson ran down the stairs just as Green staggered to her feet.

Archer barked at her, 'You need to do two things: Give me the keys to the Packard and tell me how to get to wherever you keep your plane.'

She looked up at him in defiance. 'Why should I help you?'

'Because it might be the difference between you living or dying. And in Nevada they let you pick, firing squad or hanging.'

Thirty seconds later Archer was running flat-out for the prewar Packard, dead body in the trunk and all.

73

Archer wound up the old Packard and hit the road heading south toward the California state line. Paley had a head start, but he figured he could make up time in a car versus a boat. Four miles and then turn left, that was what Green had told him. And if she had lied to him, he would go back and probably shoot her in a spot far worse than she already had been.

But he should have known there was a landing strip up here. Steve Everett had described what the lake looked like from the sky, which meant he had flown directly here.

The road curved and Archer was now running parallel to the lake. It was long and majestic, and there was only one boat on it. And it was the boat he was chasing right now; it was ahead of him. But not *that* far ahead of him.

However, the boat was moving like a rocket, and Archer could just make out the man at the wheel. Paley was a daredevil, for sure. He had that boat moving at its absolute limit of speed. The lake surface wasn't all that smooth, because the wind was creating some chop. The boat's bow was a battering ram, lifting into the air and coming down hard. Paley seemed unfazed.

Archer felt a grudging admiration for the man and he could understand how so many Nazi pilots had fallen victim to his skill and fearlessness. But that was where the admiration ended. He was the reason Willie Dash had almost died. He had put Jake

Nichols in a wheelchair. Archer was not going to let him get away a third time.

He pushed the Packard even harder, but its horsepower just couldn't match that of modern vehicles.

If only I had the Delahaye.

When he looked back over at the lake he could no longer see the boat. But Archer knew where Paley was going. He just had to get there in time.

He reached the turnoff and took it on maybe two wheels, he wasn't entirely sure. What he was certain about was that when that part of the Packard slammed back to earth, the rear axle cracked.

'Son of a bitch!'

He leaped out of the car and took off at a dead sprint, but feeling he had lost the battle.

No. No excuses, Archer. You finish this right now.

He redoubled his efforts, running faster than he had since the war. After a half mile he saw his destination up ahead. A private airstrip that Green and some other Lake Tahoe wealthy families had probably put in so they wouldn't have to make the long journey from LA by car, or fly into Reno with the plebeians. It had one small wooden shack, a set of fuel pumps, but no employees that he could see. It was basically just a long strip of asphalt; that was his Mecca right now.

When he reached the runway, he was sucking in cold air so hard his lungs couldn't process it, and his head started to pound and he felt nauseous.

Then he saw the plane was on the tarmac and the props were already spinning at a high velocity. Despite running flat-out, he had arrived perhaps too late.

Archer looked frantically around and saw which way the windsock was blowing.

Thank you, God. Because you gotta come straight at me, Paley.

He took up position in the middle of the runway strip about halfway down, a gun in each hand as the big Beechcraft pivoted, made its turn, and lined up squarely in the middle of the tarmac as it prepared to take off into the wind gusts coming in behind Archer. He eyed the right prop and then the left. Man versus machine, David versus Goliath.

The plane rocketed down the runway toward him, its engines shrieking with rising thrust. Through the cockpit windscreen, Archer could see Paley, but there was no sign of Bonham.

Paley only had one chance — to lift off before he came within range of Archer's weapons.

Archer knew this, and so he started sprinting right toward the aircraft. He couldn't see Paley's expression at this tactic, but he didn't imagine it would be a happy one.

He was within two hundred feet of the plane. He was aiming for two things with each weapon: the tires and the props. He opened fire with the .32 he'd taken from Lamb. When he tried to fire it again, it banged empty. He tossed it down and aimed his .38. As he ran ever closer and fired again, one of his shots hit a blade on the right propeller. It sheared off, and destroyed the exact synchronicity that propeller engines required. The plane started to zigzag wildly as Paley struggled to control the aircraft. Another chunk of the damaged prop soared across the runway. Luckily, Archer ducked and it passed over him.

Archer knelt, took careful aim, and shot out the left front tire of the gyrating plane. The rubber ripped apart and sprayed across the tarmac. Archer wasn't lucky or fast enough this time, and a piece of the rubber whipsawed into his left calf. He fell flat to the asphalt, groaning in pain.

This was actually a good thing, because the Beechcraft came back around like a lame-winged duck, and hopped over him at that point. It soared a bare twenty feet into the air before coming back down far too hard on the runway. The struts on the landing gear collapsed, and the plane pitched to the right. The right-side wing struck the tarmac and cracked in half. The engines died and the props stopped spinning. Fuel started leaking onto the tarmac, creating an ever-growing pool of highly flammable liquid.

The Beechcraft was officially no longer airworthy.

Hobbled by the strike from the tire remnant, Archer limped slowly over and approached the plane on the pilot's side. He pointed his gun at the glass.

Paley straightened, and looked at him through the side window.

'Out, now,' Archer ordered. 'Before that fuel ignites.'

The man slowly opened the door and stepped out, holding his right arm stiffly against his body. His left shoulder was set at an odd angle and there was blood on his shirt. There were also twin gashes in his head and the blood was trickling down his face. Lacquered in this crimson, his scars seemed to pulsate with hate.

'Where's Bernadette?' Archer asked.

Paley chuckled. 'In the lake.'

Archer glanced in the direction of one of the deepest lakes in the world, where the current temperature would kill a person in a few minutes.

Bernadette Bonham was no more. He looked back at the still-grinning Paley.

Archer didn't even bother to ask him why he'd done it. He knew the answer.

It was just in the man's nature.

74

Archer sat in a chair and stared across at the two women. More than a week had passed where everyone involved had grabbed a collective breath, and the rest of the world had managed to run smoothly along on its axis, despite the little hiccups in LA and Tahoe.

Mallory Green sat stiffly with her surgically repaired arm in a sling. She stared at the concrete floor with seemingly abject fascination. Eleanor Lamb's hand was wrapped with gauze, her eyes opaque. Her blond tresses burned auburn in the garish light from overhead. Police stations seemed to have no other kind of illumination, Archer thought. They were designed to drain most of the life and fight right out of you, while the barred doors sopped up the rest.

The LAPD, with an assist from the county cops led by Phil Oldham, had raided the Jade Lion. They had come away with crates of heroin, a dozen enslaved workers, and an assortment of Hollywood's landed gentry of both sexes who were in various stages of undress, as well as bondage. And drugged up.

Archer had spoken with Alice Jacoby and told the woman that her only chance to stay out of jail was to spill everything she knew about Paley, the Jade, and Lamb. And she had sung like nobody's business. But he had learned that when her role in all this had come to Warners' attention, they had fired her. Maybe she should go back to West Virginia, thought Archer. Compared to Hollywood, the hollers might make for a decent change. In any event, Alice had gone down her last rabbit hole.

They had recovered Bonham's body from the lake. The Frenchwoman looked startled in death, as though she had never seen it coming with Paley next to her.

Now the epiphany Archer had had back at Green's chalet was going to be tested, in the form of Eleanor Lamb.

Green looked at him defiantly. 'I'm not sorry. I did what I had to do in order to survive.'

'Well, you may not *survive* this.'

This seemed to surprise her. 'I have an excellent lawyer.'

'You're going to need it. And what about the people they were smuggling?'

Green shook her head. 'We knew nothing about that. I would never be engaged in *that*.'

'Good to know you have a speed bump on your moral boundary line.' He looked at Lamb. 'Up until the showdown with Paley, I thought your role was limited to blackmailing Peter Bonham over the little matter of bigamy. But then how would Mallory know about the drug dealing going on at the Jade? But Alice Jacoby found out lots of things about the Jade so you could write the script. And then you took advantage of that for personal gain.

'So, how'd you get hooked up with Lamb? Just because she worked for you?'

Lamb answered. 'We're kindred spirits. We're men trapped in women's bodies in a man's world.' The little, edgy face sharpened even more. 'And if we were actually men, we wouldn't be here. Men lie, cheat, and steal all the time and get away with it.'

'I think Darren Paley and Peter Bonham would beg to differ. So, how did Alice Jacoby get hired to redo the Jade?'

Green said, 'Bart owed money from an old gambling debt that Paley covered for him. Paley wanted to spiff the place up. Bart recommended her for the job. Alice gave him a good price, and he cut Bart some slack. It was the only time he ever did.'

'But did you really understand what you were getting into?' he asked Green.

'Yes. But to make amends I can use some of the money I made for charitable purposes.'

Archer's jaw dropped on that line. 'Amends? People have been *killed*.'

'I didn't kill Cedric Bender or Peter Bonham.'

'What about Steve Everett, your pilot?'

'Oh, that,' she said, as though Archer was merely referring to an odd smell in the room.

'He found out and wanted money.' This came from Lamb.

'How'd he find out?'

Green said, 'Apparently on his last flight here the cargo broke free and shifted while he was trying to take off. He had to go back there and reorient it. One of the crates had cracked open.'

Archer said, 'And there it all was for him to see — his little pot of gold.'

'It was *our* pot of gold, not his,' said Lamb.

'So you shot him,' said Archer.

'I didn't say that.'

'No, *I* did. You fired a total of four times in the house with your six-shooter. But there were *five* cylinders empty in the wheel. I fired one round from it before there were no bullets left. The slug they dug out of Everett matched your gun.'

Lamb apparently had nothing to say to this, so she

431

kept silent.

'How did it go down and what were you going to do with the body?'

Green said, 'I met him at the little airstrip. Ellie hid in the floorboard and then did what needed to be done. We were later going to dump his body in the lake.'

He turned to Lamb. 'You must have been delighted when you found your missing husband on the other end of a dope pipeline.'

Lamb's eyes seemed to electrify with the memory. 'I knew even before then. Mallory and Bart had been to a dinner party at their place in Malibu. They'd taken photos. Mallory later showed me the pictures. And there was Nathaniel. He'd barely changed. Still handsome, still insufferably arrogant.'

'So how did you figure him to be in the dope business? When you went out to Malibu?'

'No, years before, when I went to South America to look for him. I discovered some 'business associates' of his down there. They were, how shall I say, not of the lawful mind. So when I learned he had this new wife and big house in Malibu, I started spying on him. That's when I found out what he was doing. I wasn't surprised. Then I moved out to Malibu, right next door to him. I threatened to tell his wife and the cops.'

'This was *after* you blackmailed Gloria Mars for the purchase price of the house.'

'She has more money than she knows what to do with.'

'She also has a heart. That you broke.'

'What are hearts for?' said Lamb pointedly. 'Except to break?'

Archer looked at Green. 'And Lamb told you about her *opportunity*?'

'Bart's gambling losses were bleeding me dry. I saw we needed a way to transport the drugs in a way that absolutely wouldn't be detected. We had the Tahoe place as a base, so I borrowed money from Gloria Mars for a down payment on the plane.'

'Yeah, she alluded to her helping you out.'

'I put it in my name for, as I told Bart, *tax* purposes. He knew nothing about things like that. We flew the shipments there and then they went onward by truck. With my documentary work, I had met people in both high and low places. Those contacts proved invaluable.'

'And then it was off to the races, I guess.'

She nodded, looking a little startled by it all. 'Within six months I had paid Gloria back and bought the plane outright. I finished the Tahoe chalet and took care of Bart's debts. I started socking money away in my own secret accounts. Within another year or two I was going to pull a vanishing act and leave my husband holding the proverbial bag.'

He glanced at Lamb. 'And Cedric Bender?'

'I found him dead in my house after I came back from running an errand.'

'And then you found out I was having dinner with Liberty and you showed up with your bag of lies to build a plausible reason for your upcoming disappearance.'

Lamb nodded. 'It was the best I could do given the timing.'

'It was actually pretty good. But why didn't you just get rid of the body?' asked Archer.

'He was too heavy to move. Even with Mallory's

help. And we didn't want to be seen carrying a body somewhere.'

'Did you take his wallet and ID?'

'Yes. I also checked the Ford outside. That matched the name in the wallet. We found out he was a PI. That's when Mallory concocted the plan about hiring Bender to check into Bart's affairs. She'd have time to do that because it would take the cops a while to identify the body. I was planning to lie low for a while and then come back with a plausible story.'

'You brought all this on yourself, I'm thinking.'

'What do you mean by that?' exclaimed Lamb.

'I'm betting before all this happened *you* contacted Bonham in France and said there was a guy snooping around. So Bonham did some digging too, and finds out Bender was a PI. He naturally thinks the guy is snooping around *him*, not you. And he was right. So he comes back early from France, kills the guy, and then comes up with the idea to double-cross *you*. Then he takes the Ford and sends it off Malibu Pier. I thought he might have hidden the Ford in his garage. But it was *his* Bentley that leaked the oil I found. Which showed he'd come back early from France.'

'You're right. I did contact him over there. I should have known I could never trust him.'

'Bonham goes off to France for months at a time. Who looked over the business then?'

Green said, 'He had associates, but I also meticulously documented every shipment and oversaw the entire operation. I did it better than he did, actually.'

'Congratulations on being such a wonderful criminal.' Archer lit up a smoke. 'By the way, Lamb, I went to your house on New Year's Eve.'

She looked startled. 'Why?'

434

'Believe it or not, I was worried about you. I called your house. A guy answered. I didn't know then, but now I know it was Peter Bonham. I said I was your brother. He told me you didn't have a brother, which should have clued me in that, whoever it was, he knew you well. Later, I went down to the beach and stumbled into a dope shipment coming ashore. I got in a tussle with a guy who, once more, turned out to be Bonham. It was only later I realized it was connected.'

'Why would Nathaniel have been at my house that night?'

'Probably to see if you had found the body and done a runner. Or maybe he was hoping you'd be there so he could kill you, too. Then he was probably going to exit stage left.'

'Well, he was very good at vanishing. I'm glad he's dead.'

'Well, you two committed murder. That won't end well for you, either.'

Lamb said, 'Don't worry, they won't execute us or anything.'

Archer looked blankly at her. 'Oh yeah? Why's that?'

'Because we're women. I mean, the men can't have it *all* their own way, can they?'

On that, Archer rose and left.

He needed to get away from these ladies, particularly Eleanor Lamb.

And Archer needed to drink an entire bar in the worst possible way.

75

'You did good, Archer. Better than good actually.'

Willie Dash stood outside the hospital dressed in a new three-piece double-breasted suit Morrison had brought him because he'd lost weight in the hospital. She was waiting in the car for him. He was mostly healed and on his way back to Bay Town. 'And Jake sends his thanks for nailing Paley. And I want to add my thanks on top of that.'

'Couldn't have done it without you.'

'Sure you could. And you *did*. You coming back to Bay Town today?'

'No, not yet.'

Dash eyed him keenly, understanding dawning on his features. 'You ever coming back?'

Archer couldn't answer that, so he said nothing.

Dash smiled knowingly. 'Every baby bird has to find his own way eventually. Can't stay in the mother's nest forever.'

'So I'm a baby bird, then?'

'You were when you hit town over three years ago, Archer. You're not anymore.' He ran his gaze over him. 'Your wings look pretty strong from where I'm standing.' He gripped Archer's hand. 'But you ever need an old gumshoe to work something through, I'm your man.'

'Thanks, Willie. Thanks for everything.'

He watched them drive off and he headed to his Delahaye, which he'd retrieved from Bay Town.

He reached Beverly Hills and pulled to a stop in

436

front of the building housing Green and Ransome Productions. He took the elevator up and entered the office.

The stories about Mallory Green and Eleanor Lamb and the Jade Lion and Darren Paley were in every proper paper and rag in town. The stories had even hit the national wire. But the story of finding movie stars in compromising situations didn't see the light of day. Archer wondered how much that had cost the studios. And with that payoff, the rags would be throwing parties all over town, with bonuses to follow.

Audrey, the receptionist, looked woefully up at Archer. 'Ms. Ransome is on set at Warners. It was a last-minute thing. We tried your answering service but they couldn't reach you in time. You're on the list with the guard.'

'I can head out there now.'

Her sad look deepened. 'It really is so terrible what happened. Mr. Green is so upset.'

'I bet he is. He lost his private wings and he can't piss money away in Vegas anymore. But I'm not sure who's more depressed, him or the mob for the loss of revenue.'

He climbed into the Delahaye, headed northeast, and drove the dozen or so miles to Warner Brothers.

Cecily was sitting all alone in a huge soundstage on the backlot.

When Archer walked in and looked around at the cavernous space she said simply, 'Everyone's on lunch break. I wasn't hungry.'

He sat in a director's chair across from her. 'I've been calling you for two weeks.'

'I'm sorry. It's been difficult to process everything.'

'You got my report?' he asked.

437

She was dressed in a black skirt with bare, unshaven legs, a man's black suit vest over a white tuxedo shirt, and black flats.

Bohemian to her soul, he thought.

'I read your report word for word. Quite a story.'

Archer said, 'Feel free to film it. Just invite me to the premiere. That way I can finally see a damn movie. Just make sure you cast some nice-looking guy in my role who doesn't mind getting sapped or shot at.'

'I'm actually leaving Bart's place and starting my own company.'

Archer eyed her with respect. 'Good for you.'

'It's a little scary, but I feel it's the right thing to do and the right time to do it.'

'Always go with your gut. Overthinking things has ruined more good dreams than I don't know what.'

She looked to Archer like a woman batting around the idea of either spilling her guts or never speaking again. 'How was Ellie when you saw her?'

'Not particularly happy, but then who would be in her situation?'

'What will happen to her?'

Archer leaned forward. 'You love your granduncle? And respect him?'

'I told you I did.'

'Well the loved and respected Sam Malloy told me that he had never trusted Eleanor Lamb and didn't think I should, either. And guess what? He was right. And on top of that she's a curly blonde again. See, she was using you, Cecily. Just like she used everybody her whole life. No, I take that back. Her husband used her and she's been paying him and the rest of the world back for his original sin. I'm not saying he didn't deserve it, because he did. But nobody else she

438

hurt did. Including *you*.'

'Everything you say makes perfect sense.'

'But?'

'But it's not that easy.'

'Of course it's not. These things never are. But in six months' time, with all you have going on, you won't even remember her.'

'I can't believe that.'

'Call me in six months and tell me what you believe,' he said sharply because that was just the way he felt.

'You don't know anything,' she retorted.

'I know this much. You're not the only one to get hit with something like this. Only in your case you got lucky as hell. Because at some point Eleanor Lamb would've fired one right between your eyes. Trust me. She tried to do it to me.'

Ransome looked shaken by his harsh words.

'Good,' said Archer in response to her expression. 'You're a gal who likes to explore the gritty and troubling instead of the flowers and sunshine. Well, guess what? That crap *really* exists. Guys like me roll in it all day. So take your broken heart, channel all the hell you're feeling right now, make a film, and go win that little statuette everybody in Hollywood is so keen on. It'll be loads better than the best therapy money can buy.'

He rose, tipped his hat, and left.

76

Archer had gone maybe ten paces out of the sound-stage when someone called out to him. He looked over at an alleyway. There was Samantha Lourdes, dressed in eighteenth-century garb and shiny baubles, with hair as fake as the jewels piled high on her head, motioning to him.

He walked over to her. 'Who are you supposed to be, Marie Antoinette?'

'Who told you?'

His jaw fell. 'No, really?'

'Yes, really.'

He looked up. 'How do you get through your dressing room door with that hair?'

'It's all fake, comes off in one piece. Just like this town.'

'Funny meeting you here.'

'There's no funny about it. Cecily told me you were coming by.'

'You know her?'

'She and I have been in talks. Cecily's starting her own company.'

'Yeah, so I heard. I also heard your deal was coming to an end with MGM. And what are you doing over here at Warners, anyway?'

'They loaned me out. It's complicated. But did you know that employment contracts in California can't last longer than seven years?'

'No, because I never had a contract. I live hand-to-mouth with the occasional gunplay and sapping thrown in for no extra charge.'

'Anyway, my contract came up. MGM was keen to re-sign me but I told them it was a no-go.'

'Yeah, my friend told me the grapevine had you starting your own production company and charting your own path.'

'And one of my first projects will be with Cecily. Not the Jade script. I wouldn't give Eleanor Lamb the satisfaction. But another story that might actually force me to act.'

'My money's on you.'

'Wait a minute — what *friend* are you talking about?'

'Liberty Callahan. She's an actress, too. Not at your level, not yet anyway. But she's a big admirer of yours. She was here shooting some atomic secrets picture a while back.'

'Wait — tall, blond, sultry voice, moves like no one I've ever seen, and all the guys swoon over her?'

'That's the lady. Although you could be talking about yourself.'

'She might be someone I need to know.'

Archer took out a card, wrote Callahan's name and number on the back, and handed it to her. 'She's over off Melrose near the country club. You two remind me a lot of each other.'

'Thanks, Archer. Look, I read all the stuff in the papers about what happened. It was horrible. You were almost killed.'

'That was just the stuff in the papers. There's a lot more that nobody needs to know.'

'You must've been very brave to do what you did.'

'I didn't have time to be brave, Sam. I just had time to *duck*.'

'Will Darren ever be getting out of prison?'

441

'*Darren* is going to San Quentin for an appointment with the gas chamber. And good riddance.'

'I suppose so.'

He looked at her with a large dose of incredulity. 'Don't tell me you harbor any feelings for him? It makes every guy trying to do the right thing feel like a dope, including me.'

'I harbor nothing for Darren, Archer. In fact I'm deeply indebted to you for getting him out of my life. For good.'

'Now that's what I like to hear.'

'You really were clever to figure all this out, you know.'

'Hell, I'm *so* clever I could've become a doctor. But I had no idea what I'd do with all that money, so I became a detective instead.'

Smiling, she edged closer. 'I think the two of us need to get to know each other better.'

'Really?'

She started to give him the look that Archer knew would wrap him up in unbreakable knots.

'Don't, Sam.'

She looked surprised. 'What?'

'You're a fabulous gal and your only flaw is falling for the wrong guy. You got the world by the throat, so you need to aim a lot higher than yours truly.'

She rubbed his arm. 'Which is exactly why I like you. I have to work for it with you, Archer. It makes a girl think.'

'It makes a guy think, too, at least this one.'

She took a step back, her gaze searching his features. 'Wait a minute. Are you in love with someone?' She paused. 'With this Liberty, maybe?'

'Don't hold it against me and please don't hold it

442

against her.'

'Does she know?'

'I maybe didn't know until two seconds ago.'

Lourdes gave Archer a hug that he felt to his soul and soles. 'Then I think you should go and tell her. A woman always wants to know.'

'She's been through a lot with me. And I would do anything for her. So . . .'

'Sounds about as right as these things get.'

He twirled his hat. 'No hard feelings, then?'

'Hell, Archer, you've single-handedly renewed my faith in men.'

She kissed him on the cheek and he went on his way, still twirling his hat.

And smiling to a degree like maybe he never had before.

77

Archer had on his best suit, his shoes were polished to a high sheen, his hair was freshly cut, his jaw freshly mowed, and he'd even bought a new hat.

He knocked on the door and held the flowers in front of him as he eyed the Volkswagen in Callahan's driveway.

Callahan opened the door and smiled at him. But he noted she made no move to hug him or give him a kiss, as was usual after they had been apart for a while.

She had on a black-and-white sleeveless number with white gloves, black fishnet stockings, and black pumps. An elegant diamond necklace he'd never seen before encircled her long neck. And her hair was done up in some intricate manner that looked like it had taken both time and talent.

'Archer, I didn't know you were coming over tonight.'

'I thought I'd surprise you. It's been a long time.'

'Yes, um, yes it has.'

He saw a sable wrap on a table next to the door. That was new, too. 'Damn, you're going out. That's why you're all dressed up.'

'I am, I'm sorry.' She looked over his shoulder. 'But please come in. I've been meaning to talk to you.'

He passed through the door and handed her the flowers. For some reason, all the things he had thought to say to her at this moment were lost somewhere in his head. He went back in his mind, sentence by sen-

444

tence, idea by idea, and then, before he got to where he needed to go, they dropped off into nothing, like Cedric Bender's Ford off Malibu Pier. He heard the splash, and then all his carefully crafted remarks proceeded to drown in the Pacific.

'These are lovely, Archer, thank you. Let me put them in water.'

While she was gone he took a moment to look around. He had been so busy with wrapping up the case and Callahan had been on location in Arizona shooting a film that they hadn't seen each other in person for well over a month. He noted a cigarette lighter he didn't recognize lying on a table. He picked it up and ran his nail along the initial *S*.

When Callahan came back into the room with the flowers in a vase he said, 'Somebody leave this behind?'

She glanced at it, put the vase down on a table, and said, 'Please, sit.'

Archer sat and studied her as she settled not next to him, but across the width of a coffee table. The stark symbolism in that caused his chest to tighten.

'You look beautiful,' he said cautiously.

'Thanks.'

'Hey, did you land that part in the Hitchcock film? What was it again?'

'*Dial M for Murder.* And no, I didn't. But I did have a good part in a film that'll be out this summer, *Gentlemen Prefer Blondes.* I actually filmed it last year. I don't believe I mentioned it to you. I play a song-and-dance girl. Had a few lines.'

'Well, *this* gentleman prefers blondes,' said Archer, still trying to break the ice floe he sensed all around him.

445

'Marilyn Monroe is in it. She's really terrific. She croons 'Diamonds Are a Girl's Best Friend' like nobody's business. And she's got two other pictures coming out this year. She's going to be a star.' She paused. 'And she's four years younger than me.'

'So what, Liberty? Everybody has a different schedule in life.'

They fell silent, with all the Hollywood chitchat exhausted.

Archer could feel it coming, just like he had before every battle he'd fought in during the war. You could sense the doom creeping closer and your hand flicked to your dog tags and you prayed that when you died they would still be there, so the Army would know where to send the telegram about your death. And your remains.

She finally said in a tremulous tone, 'I read the papers while I was away. My God, everything you've been through. It was a *miracle* you survived.'

He didn't like the way she said the word *miracle*, not at all.

'Everything turned out okay,' he said. 'No bullet holes in me or anything.'

As soon as he said it, Archer regretted it.

Callahan had turned deathly pale and put a hand to her mouth.

'Liberty, I'm okay. I'm fine, really.'

'I . . . talked to Connie.'

'What about?' he said quickly.

'She told me about . . . Vegas, the desert. Darren Paley . . . You.'

Archer started to twirl his new hat faster and faster. It felt funny in a bad way. Not lucky at all. The nerves didn't recede, they fireballed. 'I didn't know that.'

'*You* didn't tell me.'

'I'm not going to bore you with every little thing —'

She stood, her features tortured and savage. 'Little! You coming two seconds from being murdered. You call that little!'

Archer didn't know how to respond to this, so he said nothing. He just eyed her, looking for some opening to bring this thing back to a level he could handle. But he wasn't finding it.

'If Willie hadn't been there . . .' Her voice trailed off and her skin turned from white to near gray. She fell rather than sat back down.

'But he *was* there, Liberty. That's the whole point.'

'But he won't always be. *That* is the point!'

'What do you want me to say?' he asked, a touch of anger creeping into his voice.

'You don't have to say anything, Archer. Things are pretty clear. My dream of stardom is starting to fade, and yours . . .'

'Mine what?' he said a bit more harshly than he probably intended.

'Has turned into a nightmare. At least for me.'

There was a knock on the door.

'You expecting someone?' asked Archer curiously.

'Yes, I am.'

Callahan composed herself, rose, smoothed down her dress, primped her hair, and went to the door.

78

The man standing there was around forty-five, close to Callahan's height in bare feet, thinly built with a mustache and a wickedly sharp widow's peak that had little hair behind it, like a low tide with no high tide left to come. He was dressed in an expensive blue wool suit with a yellow carnation in his lapel. He held a snazzy hat in his hand. Callahan gave him a kiss on the cheek and took his arm. He was holding a bouquet of flowers much larger than the one Archer had brought.

'What beautiful flowers, Harold, thank you.'

Archer rose and looked at him and then at Callahan, who took a moment to lay the flowers aside.

'Harold Stevens, this is my friend, Archer. Harold and I met while I was away filming on location in Arizona, Archer. He's producing the film I'm working on for Warners.'

Stevens came forward with his hand out for Archer to shake. 'Liberty likes to build me up more than I deserve. I'm really a humble CPA who got a production credit on this film as a thank-you from Jack Warner for some work I did for him, that I guess he considered above and beyond. I've got a good business, though, employ a lot of people, and live pretty well. But the best thing that came out of this producing thing was me meeting Liberty.'

'And accounting is nice steady work, and he takes weekends off, right, Harold?'

'Absolutely, babe.' He slipped his arm casually

448

around Callahan's waist.

This innocuous move ripped at Archer more than even the Paley-piloted Beechcraft coming for him had.

Stevens touched her necklace. 'I knew that would look fabulous on you when I saw it in the jewelry shop in Beverly Hills.'

'It was a lovely gift,' she said, glancing at Archer. 'We're going to a studio function tonight. Dinner and then dancing.'

'Sounds like fun,' said Archer in a voice so low *he* could barely hear it. He glanced at the sable wrap. That had probably been a gift from the man, too.

Stevens said, 'Wow, that is one swell ride out there. Are those your wheels, Archer?'

'Yeah, it's a Delahaye. I won it gambling in Reno, if you can believe it — right, Liberty?'

'It was a little more involved than that, Archer.'

Stevens looked pensive. 'Archer, Archer, I know that name for some reason. Weren't you in the papers recently about something?'

Archer looked at Callahan before saying, 'I think that was another Archer.'

'So, what do you do for a living?' asked Stevens.

'Little bit of this and that. I'm in between gigs right now.'

Stevens laughed. 'I know just what you mean. I used to be like that. Then I thought, what's certain in life, death and taxes, right? And because of that people will always need good accountants. So, voilà. I've been lucky for sure.' He eyed Callahan. 'Still am.'

'Well, I don't want to keep you. Oh, I think this is yours.'

He handed Stevens the lighter.

449

The man chuckled. 'I must have left this the last time I was here.' He grinned at Callahan while Archer ran his gaze over her. She was staring trancelike into space.

'I'll see you out, Archer. Harold, fix yourself a drink. You know where everything is.'

'Right, babe. Nice to meet you, Archer. Hope you get another gig real soon. Anything I can do to help, just let me know. A friend of Liberty's is a friend of mine.'

'Yeah, thanks. Nice to meet you, too.'

Callahan led him outside and over to the Delahaye. Parked behind it was a 1952 baby blue Cadillac Eldorado convertible with whitewalls, tail fins, and a full mouth of chrome teeth on the front end.

'This Harold's car?'

'Yes.'

'Sweet ride.' It dwarfed the Delahaye size-wise and had all the latest bells and whistles. Compared to his car, the Eldorado seemed to symbolize one thing: Out with the old and in with the new.

She ran her hand over the Delahaye's car door.

'Yeah, but this is still one of a kind,' Callahan said. She looked at Archer, who was just staring at her. 'Okay, I know that you're confused and hurt and . . . lots of other things.'

'Look, if you love the guy it doesn't matter what's going on in my head.'

'He's a nice enough man, but I haven't known him long enough to know whether I love him or not, Archer.'

'It usually happens pretty fast when it's the real deal.'

She leaned against the Delahaye, frowning at him.

450

'And what would you know about that?'

'Maybe more than you think. And him giving you that necklace shows *he* thinks this is something important.'

She crossed her arms over her chest. 'Why did you come over here tonight?'

'I don't think it matters, not now anyway.'

She looked back at the house. Back at . . . Harold. 'He treats me really well, and he's . . . he's . . .'

'*Safe*, I think is the word you're looking for. I guess the worst that can happen to him is that he'll get a paper cut from all the money he has to count.'

She lifted her eyebrows along with her eyes. 'That's exactly the point.'

'Yeah, I can see that now.'

She clasped her hands as though girding herself for what she had to say. To Archer, she looked like she was about to deliver the most important role of her life. And maybe, in a way, she was.

'I can't live your way anymore, Archer. I can't go to sleep every night wondering if you're going to see the sun come up or not. One time *I* might not wake up. It's killing me.'

He looked down. 'I guess I didn't understand how much it was affecting you.'

'Then you must be blind,' she said sharply.

'Maybe I am,' he conceded.

Her tone became lighter and she managed to smile, if just a bit. 'And we don't even live in the same town. So . . .'

There was no fight left in Archer. He knew it and so did she — which was why, he realized, she was no longer coming at him with both barrels. The woman didn't have to. The battle, if you could even call it

451

that, was over.

'Look, I hope everything works out. If not with him, then with some other guy.'

'When are you going back to Bay Town?'

'I'm not sure that I am.'

'What?' she said in a startled voice.

'You don't want to keep him waiting. Have a good time tonight.'

Callahan's mask of lighthearted indifference collapsed, and she stepped forward and wrapped her long arms around him. She cried quietly into his broad shoulder as he absently patted her back and said some words he forgot as soon as he uttered them.

She kissed him on the lips, gave him a searching look, and said, 'Goodbye, Archer.'

He watched her hurry back up to the bungalow, wiping at her eyes. When she opened the door to go inside he heard the radio playing, a tune maybe about loss, he couldn't tell for sure. But maybe every damn song ever written was about loss, in some way.

He put his new hat on, fixed it just so, and climbed into his old, bullet-marked Delahaye.

'Goodbye, Liberty,' he said before putting the car in gear and driving away.

79

'Thanks, Jake,' said Archer. 'This means a lot.'

Archer had always known that Jake Nichols owned the bar on the ground floor of a three-story building. What Archer hadn't known was that Nichols owned the rest of the building, too.

They were in the corridor on the top floor right outside of a two-room office. On the pebbled glass was fresh black lettering announcing the space as being occupied by one Aloysius Archer, Private Investigator, duly licensed, bonded, and insured by the State of California.

'Been trying to lease this crummy space for a year now.'

'Bet you didn't offer anybody else a buck a year in rent. I think you would've had some takers.'

Nichols spun around in his wheelchair. 'But they wouldn't have brought down the guy who put me in this glorified baby carriage. A buck a year is more than fair. To me.'

Archer looked at his name on the glass. 'It wasn't an easy decision. I really like Willie and Connie. And Bay Town isn't bad.'

'But LA is its own creature. And something tells me you and Willie will still be working lots of cases together.'

'Probably so. I'll need the help.'

'Hey, let me give you this before I forget it.' He handed Archer a white envelope.

'What is it?'

'Old geezer dropped it off earlier today. How'd he know your new office was here?'

'I put an ad in the paper and made some calls and told a few people. I guess word gets around.'

'He said he was a retired LAPD dick.'

'Wait a minute — was his name Sam Malloy?'

'Yeah, I think that's right. You know him?'

'We met. Nice guy.'

'Well, he made me promise to give you that. And he told me to tell you good luck and thanks for what you did for someone he cared about a lot. I think those were his exact words. You know what he's talking about?'

'Yeah, I do.'

'You want to come down to the bar for a celebratory drink? You know, starting a new phase of life and all. On the house.'

'Sure, but give me a little bit of time to soak this all in.'

Nichols looked at him steadily. 'Archer, you made the right decision. It was time. I talked to Willie about this. He thinks the same.'

'It's actually time for a lot of changes in my life.'

'Meaning what, exactly? Hey, didn't you have some gal? Willie mentioned that. What does she think of you hanging out your shingle?'

Archer touched the lettering on the door. 'She doesn't need to know.'

'Why not? Wait a minute, are you two not together anymore?'

'On second thought, I'll take a rain check on the drink, Jake. Maybe tomorrow?'

'Okay, Archer. Suit yourself.' Nichols spun around and headed for the elevator.

Archer unlocked the door to his new office and stepped through, closing the door behind him.

It was nothing to write home about. The tiny reception area had nothing in it, because Archer didn't have a receptionist right now and probably would never have one. But with a couple of chairs, a coffee table, and a few moldy magazines, it could be a waiting room for prospective clients. They could sit here and wait until he was ready to see them, or so his dream went.

His office was twelve by twelve, with plaster walls and lackluster paint on them. A dirty ceiling with a lazy fan frowned down on him. The space held a desk and one chair for him and a pair for clients. There were two file cabinets with nothing in them. There was a little scuffed credenza on which he intended to set up a small bar, so he could have a drink when he wanted, and offer one to clients in case they needed it, which they probably would. One window behind his desk looked out onto a window of another building, where maybe some other poor sap was trying to make an honest buck.

He sat behind his desk, took out his hip flask, poured some rye whiskey into a glass pulled from his desk drawer, and took a sip. It felt good going down, like a kiss on the cheek or a kind word at just the time you needed it.

He opened the envelope and found two things inside. The first was a check made out to him from Cecily Ransome. The sum written in was more than he would have charged if he had worked the case for a month, and that was on top of the $500 retainer. The second item was a handwritten note on Warner Brothers stationery.

Thanks for the advice, Archer. I plan on taking it.
And know that you will always have a friend in me.
Cecily.

Ordinarily, Archer would never accept more than he had dutifully earned, other than a small bonus for a job especially well done. He didn't like feeling that he owed other people. But this one he would take, because it would all be going to Willie Dash. Hospitals and surgeries to dig out bullets weren't cheap, and the man had more than earned the extra dough.

He folded up the check and note and put them in his jacket pocket.

Then he sat back in his chair and stared at the pebbled glass door with his name on it.

From now on his path in life would be pointed steadily forward, right at the fresh waves coming for him, rather than the choppy ones that had just passed underneath and battered him.

Hell, they can only hit you once.

It was all about what was coming up. And whether you could handle it. And even if you couldn't handle it, it was about how you *tried* to handle it.

Being alive and living were also two distinct things, he had come to realize. The former was strictly biological; the latter was everything else.

Yeah, safety was one thing, an important thing. But actually living was something else. He had decided to pick the something else. And it had cost him plenty, maybe more than even he realized right this minute. Yet he had a pretty good idea.

It cost me everything else.

And so Aloysius Archer settled back in his seat and

456

waited for somebody, anybody, to walk through that door.

Acknowledgements

To Michelle, thanks for always being there for me, and handling everything else so I can sit and spin stories!

To Michael Pietsch, Ben Sevier, Elizabeth Kulhanek, Jonathan Valuckas, Matthew Ballast, Beth de Guzman, Anthony Goff, Rena Kornbluh, Karen Kosztolnyik, Brian McLendon, Albert Tang, Andy Dodds, Ivy Cheng, Joseph Benincase, Alexis Gilbert, Andrew Duncan, Morgan Martinez, Bob Castillo, Kristen Lemire, Briana Loewen, Mark Steven Long, Thomas Louie, Marie Mundaca, Rachael Kelly, Kirsiah McNamara, Lisa Cahn, John Colucci, Megan Fitzpatrick, Nita Basu, Alison Lazarus, Barry Broadhead, Martha Bucci, Ali Cutrone, Raylan Davis, Tracy Dowd, Melanie Freedman, Elizabeth Blue Guess, Linda Jamison, John Leary, John Lefler, Rachel Hairston, Tishana Knight, Jennifer Kosek, Suzanne Marx, Derek Meehan, Christopher Murphy, Donna Nopper, Rob Philpott, Barbara Slavin, Karen Torres, Rich Tullis, Mary Urban, Tracy Williams, Julie Hernandez, Laura Shepherd, Maritza Lumpris, Jeff Shay, Carla Stockalper, Ky'ron Fitzgerald, and everyone at Grand Central Publishing, for always exceeding expectations.

To Aaron and Arleen Priest, Lucy Childs, Lisa Erbach Vance, Frances Jalet-Miller, and Kristen Pini, for getting better all the time.

To Mitch Hoffman, for continuing to make me dig deep with every book.

To Anthony Forbes Watson, Jeremy Trevathan, Lucy Hale, Trisha Jackson, Alex Saunders, Sara Lloyd, Claire Evans, Laura Sherlock, Stuart Dwyer, Jonathan Atkins, Christine Jones, Leanne Williams, Andy Joannou, Charlotte Williams, Rebecca Kellaway, Charlotte Cross, Lucy Grainger, Lucy Jones, and Neil Lang at Pan Macmillan, for continuing to send me to new heights.

To Praveen Naidoo and the crackerjack team at Pan Macmillan in Australia. Number one after number one. You're the best!

To Caspian Dennis and Sandy Violette, for always being so supportive.

And to Kristen White and Michelle Butler, none of this happens without you two!